PRAISE
THE TROUBLE WITH LEXIE

"There isn't a human alive who can resist the charm of Jessica Anya Blau's novels! In her latest, Blau once again weaves incisive social commentary with deft, laugh-out-loud comedy. A coming-of-age tale for the new millennium, *The Trouble with Lexie* is one of the most deeply enjoyable—and deeply satisfying—novels I've read in ages. I couldn't put it down!"

—Joanna Rakoff, author of *My Salinger Year*

"I swear *The Trouble with Lexie* must be the first full-bodied and deeply defined novel written at one of those tricked-out standing desks, equipped with its own purring treadmill. Jessica Anya Blau writes with all-in velocity, vim and vigor, a ripping high-performance performance. She runs rings around the boarding-school coming-of-age novel, making her separate peaces in spades. A delightfully wry catcher of the intense staging of the classic classy classroom class, Blau out-garps Garp, owning this rich and panting world all on her own."

—Michael Martone, author of *Michael Martone* and *Winesburg, Indiana*

"*The Trouble with Lexie* is the book you will want to read this summer! Lexie will make you laugh, make you scream, make you grimace—but mostly she will make you fall in love with her."

—Ann Hood

"When reading *The Trouble with Lexie*, everything else seems less important. Sleep? Nourishment? Caring about the escaped convict who's loose in your neighborhood? Meh. Far better to soak in Jessica Anya Blau's hilarious and fascinating tale of illicit sex, ill-advised break-ins, and stolen vibrators. But I am sorry about growling at that guy at the airport."

—Greg Bardsley, author of *The Bob Watson* and *Cash Out*

"Jessica Anya Blau is one of the funniest writers—*ever*. No one captures the oddities, joys—and yes—the pain of modern life with such frankness, humor, and sly-witted style."

—ZZ Packer, author of *Drinking Coffee Elsewhere*

"Jessica Anya Blau's Lexie gets into some serious trouble, and you'll laugh and cringe as you turn page after page to find out what she'll do next. Wicked, sexy, and sly, this is a wildly entertaining novel."   —Robert Lopez, author of *Good People*

"School counselor Lexie's raunchy erotic affair with the father of one of her students is liable to blow apart the normal life she has carefully constructed from the ruins of a neglected childhood. Is she really that naïve or is she deliberately trying to destroy a life she doesn't believe she deserves? Only Jessica Anya Blau could make such an exasperating woman so funny. And only Blau could combine such guilty pleasures with real-world pain."

—Helen Simonson, author of *The Summer before the War*

THE TROUBLE WITH
Lexie

ALSO BY JESSICA ANYA BLAU

The Wonder Bread Summer

Drinking Closer to Home

The Summer of Naked Swim Parties

THE TROUBLE WITH

Lexie

A Novel

JESSICA ANYA BLAU

HARPER PERENNIAL

NEW YORK • LONDON • TORONTO • SYDNEY • NEW DELHI • AUCKLAND

HARPER PERENNIAL

P.S.™ is a trademark of HarperCollins Publishers.

HarperCollins books may be purchased for educational, business, or sales promotional use. For information please e-mail the Special Markets Department at SPsales@harpercollins.com.

FIRST EDITION

Designed by Jamie Lynn Kerner

Library of Congress Cataloging-in-Publication Data has been applied for.

ISBN 978-0-06-241645-2 (pbk.)

16 17 18 19 20   OV/RRD   10 9 8 7 6 5 4 3 2 1

For my daughters, Madeline Tavis
and Ella Grossbach

Love is like a fever, which comes and goes quite independently of the will.

—*Stendhal*

Prologue

THE PROBLEM WASN'T SO MUCH THAT LEXIE HAD TAKEN THE KLO-nopin. And it wasn't even that she had stolen them. At thirty ge-neric pills for ten dollars, the theft of a handful (one down the gullet, the rest down her bra) had to be less than . . . seven bucks? The problem, as Lexie saw it, was that she had fallen asleep in the bed of the owner of the Klonopin. And the owner of the Klonopin was the wife of her lover.

"Miss James?" Jen Waite said. Her dyed hair was blonder than Lexie's and her pale face looked prettier than Lexie remembered from their single meeting at Parents' Weekend—brow furrowed now, head tilted with concern.

Lexie looked down at herself. Her fitted red dress was scrunched up to her hips and she wasn't wearing underwear. A shadow of hair trailed from crotch to midthigh. Lexie tried to yank the dress down but her brain-hand-body coordination was off and she couldn't manage the required butt-lift.

"Miss James, do you know where you are?" Jen Waite said.

Lexie managed to sit up. Her eyes were wide open. She looked straight down at the tightly made bed (at thirty-three, she had yet to figure out how to make a bed this perfectly, this hotel- or military-like) and thought about the pill bottle. Yes, she remembered, she had put it back exactly where she had found it. Prescription label facing out, as it had been when she'd first spotted the drugs in the medicine cabinet.

"Miss James, are you okay?" Dear god, Daniel was in the room. And he was calling her *Miss*, as if they hadn't spent an entire week together in this very house only last month. As if they hadn't spent two nights together every week for the past eight months. As if he had never whispered *I love you* into her ear, her neck, and the usually hairless and opalescent insides of her thighs.

No. Daniel was calling her *Miss* as if their only relationship were through Ethan, the beloved Waite son, who earlier in the year had been one of Lexie's student patients at The Ruxton Academy. Ethan's condition had been nothing serious, nothing even half-serious: college-application-related stress, an exceedingly ho-hum and common ailment at the elite boarding school.

"Ambien!" Lexie finally said. She had read stories of people taking the sleeping pill and then eating all the dairy out of their refrigerator or driving to their ex-wife's house and trying on her underwear.

"You need an Ambien?" Daniel was staring at her with a hard, distant look. There was no glint of recognition, no slyness of shared secrets, mixed fluids, merged scents. "You're missing a shoe." He pointed at Lexie's bare right foot. On her left foot was the strappy high-heeled sandal she had originally bought for her planned wedding. Of course, she had intended to wear both shoes to the blessed event.

"I haven't been sleeping lately and I took an Ambien tonight and I must have driven over here on it—*wow*!" Lexie tried to act as stunned as one might be if this had actually happened. "*Wow*. Can you believe it?!" She got off the bed and pulled down her dress. She brushed her hand across the bedspread as if fleas or crumbs had fallen off her. "Wow."

"Wow," Jen said. "That's crazy! Was the door unlocked?" Jen looked at Daniel as if to accuse him of once again forgetting to lock the front door.

"I guess it was unlocked. I don't even remember coming in!"

"Don't you live on campus?" Jen was openmouthed and wild-eyed. This would be a story for her next dinner party. Lexie hoped it would be the only story Jen told involving Lexie. Until earlier in the night, Lexie hadn't understood that she was *that woman*. The one who may have broken up a twenty-year marriage by ruthlessly being the easy one in a man's life: never asking him to stop at the drugstore and pick up vitamin C, never demanding that he not chew his cereal so loudly, never insisting that he refrain from making sexist jokes in front of company. Always interested in sex.

"I do live on campus, but I have a friend who lives nearby on Scarborough Road, so I'm familiar with the area ..." Lexie pointed toward the window as if Scarborough Road were right there, although she wasn't even sure if it was within thirty minutes of the Waite house. She had passed a street sign for Scarborough Road during the drive over and remembered only because when she had read the sign, Simon and Garfunkel had started singing "Scarborough Fair" in some far away, echoey nook in her head.

"Oh, who do you know on Scarborough?" Jen smiled. She seemed happy to know they might have a mutual friend.

"What a lucky coincidence that of all the houses around here, yours was the one where I landed!" Lexie rolled right over the question. The muck in her brain couldn't coalesce enough to come up with a name.

"I guess that is lucky," Jen said.

"Well, I better get outta here." Lexie looked back at the bed as if she had forgotten something.

"No! You have to stay tonight," Jen said. "It's not safe to drive with that stuff in your system, and we have plenty of bedrooms."

"Short half-life"—Lexie waved her hand—"I'll be fine." She knew she was far from reaching the half-life of anything.

"Oh, please stay. I'll blame myself if something happens to you on the road." Jen extended a hand and placed it on Lexie's forearm. How odd to be touched by the wife of your lover. It was such a gentle touch, so natural. And yet Lexie hated it—it stirred up a soupy guilt for acts that had, in the past, felt wonderfully liberating.

"She'll be fine." Daniel went to the bedroom door and stood there, stiffly, as if to escort Lexie out.

"I'm sorry," Jen said. She shot her eyes toward Daniel to scold him for his rudeness.

"Oh, no, I'm sorry." Lexie felt a sheen of shame growing on her flesh like a fish-skin coat.

"Should we look for your shoe?" Jen glanced around the room.

"My shoe?" Lexie looked down at her leather sack-like purse

that sat on the floor by the bed. The rubber edge of Jen's vibrator peeked out the top of Lexie's bag like a periscope. Lexie swooped down and hoisted the bag up onto her shoulder. She shook the bag a little, allowing the vibrator to burrow out of sight. "No, don't bother. I'm pretty sure I left it at my apartment." Lexie forced a smile and then shrugged her shoulders as if this were a comical, weekend mishap. Something that might happen in a sitcom or a romcom starring a sitcom star.

For a few seconds, Lexie, Jen, and Daniel all stood motionless as if they were in a play and had each forgotten their blocking.

"Well, walk her to the car, at least, Danny!" Jen said at last.

Danny? Lexie had never heard that one before. "Thank you, Mr. Waite," she said. The *Mr.* felt foreign now, like a tin coin in Lexie's mouth, the edges beveled and sharp.

Daniel once told Lexie that the instant he met her, he craved her body with the hunger of a starving man in a Turkish prison. Lexie had been meaning to look up Turkish prisons ever since, to see if they actually starved people in them. Her sense of Turkey was that it was a pretty cosmopolitan place as long as you stayed on the European side. But like so much else the past few months, looking up Turkey was something she'd never gotten around to.

Fall
SEMESTER

1

IT WAS THE LAST DAY OF PARENTS' WEEKEND AND LEXIE WAS thinking about sex. She didn't necessarily want to be thinking about sex, but the startlingly handsome father who was only one table away was staring at her in a way that rang a bell inside her that tolled *sex, sex, sex*. In the end, we're just a bunch of monkeys, Lexie thought as she noted, uncomfortably, how a simple gaze could set her off like this. Lexie looked away. Why encourage him? She was almost angry at the intrusion into her mindspace—mad that he was sending out pheromones that were clicking against her like hail on a copper roof.

Lexie wasn't sure whose father the handsome man was, as the seat to his right was currently empty. To his left was Nic Patel (who was a photocopy of his father beside him). On the other side of the empty seat was an elegant blond woman who appeared to be texting or emailing on her cell phone. Was this distracted woman his wife? Lexie focused on the space where the table met the man's torso— she was waiting for his left hand to emerge in order to spot the ring finger. Alas, no movement. The staring man stretched his right arm out, spanning it atop the vacant chair like a pin-striped wing. His shoulders were so broad it looked like he had a lacrosse stick stuck in his suit. There were flecks of gray in his black hair, but only around the temples. Lexie's guess was that he was fifty, an age Lexie, at seventeen years younger than that, thought of as *too old*, even when you looked as good as this guy did. She turned her face away again.

More than once, Lexie had been mistaken for a student. She didn't really look high-school-aged, but if you blurred your eyes a bit and took in only the loose, long, honey-blond hair and her slenderness, she might pass for nineteen. Lexie hoped this guy wasn't some perv who thought she was a student. Without meaning to do so, she looked back at him. He was still staring at her. She looked away and dropped her head so he couldn't see that she was flattered, smiling. *Don't look again*, Lexie told herself, and she forced her focus on the boy seated next to her, Bruno. With self-conscious deliberation, Lexie moved Bruno's water glass out of the way as if he were a two-year-old who might knock it over.

As the school counselor, Lexie was seated with a group of kids whose parents didn't, or couldn't, make it to Parents' Weekend. There were quite a few; plenty of people in Europe and Asia shipped their kids off to The Ruxton Academy in the hope that it would set them up—like a stone in a catapult—for admission into the Ivy League. Lexie looked around her table: Bruno Carrera, Xu Li, Grace Pak, Magnus Skaarsgard, Allison Delury, Piet Cowenberg, and Liam Walsh. With the exception of Magnus, who was pushing six-three, they all looked young, making Lexie easily identifiable as the adult. At least the staring father couldn't think she was a student.

Ruxton's headmaster, Don McClear, was speaking at a podium

while the first course—green salad—was being served. Don was saying something about character, community, the integration of these boarding school kids into the small Massachusetts town surrounding the school (where the average income was certainly less than a year's tuition at Ruxton). Lexie had heard it all before. Don was sincere in his passion for Habitat for Humanity and the Clean Woods Project. Every kid at Ruxton (grades nine through twelve) did forty hours of service a year. But Lexie couldn't summon any interest in all that. She was distracted, edgy, feeling a little vulnerable. If students and faculty weren't strictly forbidden from using their phones in the dining hall, she'd have had hers out thirty minutes ago with a game of Yahtzee going full swing. Firmly, Lexie kept her back to the black-haired, square-jawed man with the powerful shoulders.

Peter, Lexie's fiancé, had no shoulders of note. Yes, he was fit. Yes, he was attractive—a biker who managed to wear skintight spandex shorts and not look like a character out of a *Saturday Night Live* skit. Peter was a kind soul, a dreamer. He would never, even if he were single, be so bold as to visually eat up a stranger while spraying great gusts of hormones into the atmosphere.

Lexie had insinuated herself into Peter's mind after meeting him at a friend's wedding. Over the four hours of the reception, she kept one eye on him while trying to act cool, nonchalant, disinterested. In truth, she had felt an intensity toward him that gave her the tunnel vision of a drill. She had known from their mutual friend that Peter was an accomplished musician, a classical guitarist, who had trained as a luthier and had a workshop where he made guitars, violins, and other stringed instruments for world-class musicians, famous and unknown. Lexie had never met anyone who did anything like that. She was impressed.

Tonight, Lexie thought, Peter would be the beneficiary of the lust being propagated from the neighboring table. Not that her and Peter's sex life needed any help; they'd been together only a year and a half. In three months they would be married.

Lexie searched the room for her best friend, Amy Hagan, the school nurse. She found her near the front at one of the other orphan tables (as the teachers privately called them). Amy, who unlike Lexie could sit firm as a turtle through hours-long meetings, was actively listening to Don McClear, her head tilted to one side, her lips parted into a sweet, Southern smile. No matter how much Lexie thought-shouted her name—*Amy! Amy! Amy! Amy!*—Amy could not be deterred from obedience.

Lexie turned to the back of the room and caught the wickedly, sly eye of the first friend she'd made at Ruxton, the eighty-year-old English teacher, Dot Harrison. Dot, like Lexie, could barely contain herself in her skin through meetings, lectures, and speeches. In her advanced age, she had grown tired of formalities and intolerant of meaningless obligations. Dot liked to put on her tap shoes and dance at parties. She cursed so much among faculty that Lexie thought it had to be a mild case of Tourette's.

With her puckered eyes honed into Lexie's, Dot lifted her right hand, extended her middle *fuck-you* finger, and false-casually scratched the barely perceptible wisps of hair on her head. It was a gesture intended to make Lexie laugh, and it did. Silently. She looked away before Dot did something even more outrageous, and then caught the caustic glare of Janet Irwin seated at an Honor Society table. Janet had been at Ruxton for thirty-five years and might as well have been running the place. She lived on campus, had never married, didn't appear to date or leave the campus for any reason, and never spoke of anything that wasn't school-related. Janet gave the single, swift nod of her head that never failed to make Lexie feel small, ridiculous, and adolescent. Lexie smiled at her, the smile wasn't returned, and Lexie looked away.

Ethan Waite, a senior Lexie had been counseling every Wednesday afternoon, loped across the dining hall. Where had he been all this time? Lexie watched as Ethan took the empty seat beside the wolf-eyed man. So her pursuer was his father. Daniel Waite. Lexie had heard much about Daniel Waite during her three years at Ruxton; he was one of the school's biggest donors. But because she didn't deal with that stuff—the schmoozing, the check collecting—Lexie had never before seen this particular famous alumnus. Lexie assumed that the texting woman seated on the other side of Ethan was Mrs. Waite.

As far as she knew from her sessions with Ethan, his parents were married. *Married*. Something she would be, soon enough, if she could only work out the final details of the wedding. Lexie needed chairs. Seventeen elegant chairs for the seventeen musicians who were to play at her December 12 wedding. Lexie examined the old-fashioned wooden chairs beside her . . . nah, too schoolroom-looking.

Lexie flicked her eyes over to Mr. Waite and damn if he wasn't still staring straight at her. She startled a bit and he laughed and winked. She quiet-laughed, too. Was this flirting? Was she actually flirting with this probably-married man? Since the day she first met Peter, Lexie hadn't flirted with anyone. The romance had been so easy, so fun, that she had ceased to think about, or even notice, any of the other attractive people in the world. Lexie had been so convinced of the perfection of their pairing that she moved in with

Peter after only five weeks of dating. Sometimes Lexie stood in the center of his cottagey two-bedroom house (her house, once they were married), thought of Peter, and wondered how she was so lucky that she had ended up here.

When she was a kid living on the second floor of a rickety apartment building with open-air hallways in San Leandro, California, Lexie had never dreamed she'd have the life she had now. After school, she often sat on the living room couch, avoiding the tiny craters left by her father's fallen cigarettes, and flip through catalogues, imagining that the rooms she saw were rooms she lived in. That the people she saw were people she knew. That the life they appeared to be living was her life. It seemed impossible that anyone could exist in a world that tidy, organized, and lovely.

Don McClear's speech had come to an end. People clapped and shifted in their seats. Many of the parents pulled out their cell phones; chins and necks accordianed inward, shoulders slumped toward tiny screens. Lexie tried to ignore the married Mr. Waite. Why even make eyes at someone like that when what she had already was so beautifully ideal. Who wanted anything to do with a man who was sleazy enough to flirt while his wife sat right beside him? Lexie took the salad she hadn't eaten and slid it to Magnus who was known on campus as the Human Garbage Disposal. She refused to look at Mr. Waite again.

Until an hour and a half later when he stopped her on the great lawn. It was seconds after the sun had dipped below the horizon and everything was cast with a sumptuous orangey light.

"Miss James," he said. "Daniel Waite."

"Are you Ethan's dad?" Lexie asked disingenuously. She put out her hand to shake. Mr. Waite held on, forcing Lexie to pull away.

"Yes, Ethan pointed you out to me in the dining hall. You're the only person at this school my son finds worthy of a mention." Daniel Waite winked as if there were some hidden meaning Lexie should understand.

"Really? Why?" Ethan had loads of great teachers this semester. He was taking English from Dot who, on the first day of every class, promised to tap-dance to any poem written by a student in perfect iambic pentameter.

"I think he's honestly grateful for your help with the college application mess. I'm grateful, too." Daniel Waite put one hand on his heart as if Lexie had done more than simply counsel the boy.

"It's my job and he's a pleasure." Lexie thought it was mentally ill the way these students and their parents put so much effort and money into chasing college admission. Some of the kids ended up at UNH, UVM, or even Framingham, all fine schools, but they could have made it there without the SAT tutors, honors calculus, and college application coaches costing thousands. And the ones who went to MIT, Dartmouth, Harvard, and Yale, well, you could bet they'd have made it into those schools without the booster system set up by their overanxious parents. In Lexie's mind, it came down to this: Overachievers overachieved no matter how you backed them up. And no matter how hard you tried, you couldn't create an overachiever out of someone who'd rather snowboard than study for an exam. Even when you sent that child to Ruxton.

Mitzy, Lexie's mother, could never remember the name of the school where Lexie got her master's degree: Tufts. Toots, her mother called it once during Lexie's weekly phone call. They both laughed at the time and Lexie didn't bother to set her straight. Mitzy quickly moved on to a story about the other waitresses at

Heidi Pies, where Mitzy had worked for as long as Lexie was alive, and the fuss people were making over the new menu.

"Well, I appreciate it," Mr. Waite said. "And I have to admit I'm glad he's anxious enough to get an early start." He took a step closer to Lexie. His square face was the color of caramel in the dimming light.

"Yeah, it's always good to start early." Was this really what Mr. Waite wanted to talk about? He was staring like he wanted to eat her. And although Lexie felt the thrill of being desired, she couldn't help but think of Mrs. Waite somewhere on the lawn, probably looking for her husband. While Peter sat at home waiting for Lexie.

"Do you and Mr. James live on campus?"

"Mr. James?" Lexie thought of her father, the only Mr. James she'd ever known. Her friends had called him that the rare times he was home and awake when they were over. If anyone called her mother Mrs. James, Mitzy pointed out that she and Lexie's father had never married and her last name was Smith. The embarrassment of this dimmed each year as Lexie got older and more and more friends came from two-name families.

"Your husband."

"Oh!" Lexie laughed. "Mr. James is my father."

Mr. Waite laughed, too. "So you're not married?" His head dropped slightly, his blue eyes dialed into Lexie's.

"Engaged." Lexie held up her left hand with the antique silver scrollwork ring that had belonged to Peter's grandmother. It suddenly felt puny and cheap.

"Congratulations."

"Thank you." Lexie shifted her weight. "How long have you and Mrs. Waite been married?"

"Mrs. Waite and I are no longer married." Daniel Waite's ringed left hand flickered against his thigh like a cat's twitching tail.

"Ethan never mentioned you were divorced," Lexie said, carefully. The school made it their business to know the standard goings-on in each student's home. As far as Lexie knew, Ethan Waite's file contained no news of this sort.

"Separated. It's currently a little undercover. We're waiting until Ethan goes off to college before we let him in on everything."

"Oh, I see." Lexie tried to suppress the smile that instinct insisted was the correct response to someone who was smiling at her the way Mr. Waite was now.

"I have an apartment in Boston, near my office. And the house on the lake is bigger than is reasonable, so it's pretty easy for us to stay there together whenever Ethan makes it home."

"Well, that sounds like it's working out well." What else could she say? Lexie thought. And why was he telling her all this?

"I trust you won't bring it up with anyone. Ethan especially."

"No. Certainly not." How tediously overprotective. The Ethan Lexie knew was more mature than most boys his age and could easily handle an amicable separation.

"I want to tell him but his mother doesn't want him to know what's what until he's safely away at college." Mr. Waite spoke with what Lexie had grown to think of as a *California intimacy*—a casualness that made you feel as if you'd known the speaker for years. She often encountered people like this in California.

"Not a problem, Mr. Waite."

"Call me Daniel."

"Lexie."

17

"Can I call you, Lexie?"

"Yes. Everyone calls me Lexie. Except the students, of course."

"No. Can I call you. On the phone. Can I see you?"

Lexie's heart thrummed with an unidentifiable emotion—she wasn't sure if she was thrilled or repelled, flattered or insulted. It was like having an itch in the center of your palm—a sensation that can't be located precisely enough to be dealt with. Lexie's eyes darted around. She and Daniel Waite were on the lawn; clumps of people stood near them, murmuring like background actors on stage; Janet Irwin was looking past Don McClear's shoulder, eyeing them as if Lexie were guilty of some sin outlined in the school conduct policy, which Lexie had never read; Ethan and Mrs. Waite were walking toward them from a distance. "I told you already. I'm engaged," she said shortly. Again, she flapped up her left hand.

He shrugged. "No, I mean to talk about Ethan."

"Oh." Lexie hoped the dimming light hid her red cheeks. "His time with me is like his time with any therapist." She tried to sound professional. Accomplished. Not like someone who had confused an interested parent with someone who wanted to get naked with her. "I'm sworn to confidentiality."

"I get that." Daniel Waite touched Lexie's forearm as if to tell her to relax, chill out, back up a bit. "I just want you to know what's going on with me and my wife, and how Ethan's doing at home so that . . . well, because maybe that will help you help him."

"Okay." Lexie wished she could go back and erase the moment when she thought he was asking for a date. Wasn't she too old to be embarrassed like this? She looked down to avoid Daniel Waite's face. His white shirt was stiff enough to crack like glass. He wore cuff links. Who wore cuff links these days? People who didn't launder their own shirts, that's who. Someone like Daniel Waite wouldn't be thinking of romance with Lexie. She was the poorly paid school counselor. And he was a friendly guy—easygoing with that *California intimacy*—who wanted to discuss the fabulous and expansive future of his progeny.

"How about one day next week?" Mr. Waite asked gently.

"That sounds perfect." Lexie faked confidence. "I'm usually free during second and third periods."

"Monday? Nine?"

"First period ends at nine. So nine fifteen?"

"Great. I'll meet you at nine fifteen. How about that little café at the Inn on the Lake?"

"You don't want to meet in my office? I have a coffee machine." Lexie was starting to feel more in control.

"I'm sure it's a great coffee machine, but I can't step foot on this campus without that hunting dog Janet Irwin sniffing me out to serve on a board or fund some film the kid from Iceland wants to make about the suicide rate back home."

Lexie smiled. Axel Valsson had made a movie last year about suicide in Iceland. It was shot in black and white, had a deafening electric guitar sound track, and was melodramatic to the point of comedy. Dot and Lexie had had a few good laughs over it.

"You were the one who funded that thing?"

"Yup. And I had a forty-five-thousand-dollar visit to the men's room today when I bumped into Janet and she talked me into subsidizing the Russian exchange program." Daniel grinned and Lexie laughed. After three years at Ruxton, she had acclimated to a world where the asking of a check for forty-five thousand dollars involved as little and as much coercion as Lexie and her best friend,

Betsy Simms, had used at age ten selling Girl Scout cookies outside the entrance of Ralph's.

"Okay, I'll meet you at the Inn on the Lake." Lexie had been there only once. The place was so expensive it was as if the owners weren't aware they were in the middle of the woods where most people ordered their "good" clothes from the L.L. Bean catalogue.

Daniel Waite turned to watch his wife and son approach. Lexie watched with him. Mrs. Waite's face was open and warm. She looked like a woman who took care of her skin but wasn't freezing it, cutting it, or injecting it with liquefied rubber. She had to be around the same age as Lexie's mother, if not older, but looked many years younger than Mitzy. This wasn't the face of divorce or separation. It was the face of a comfortable, cozy, loving life. Maybe she was the one who had wanted to end the marriage. Maybe she was done being a wife.

"Hey, Miss James," Ethan said, and he dropped his head a little as if to make himself smaller. Ethan was over six feet tall, maybe an inch shorter than his dad.

"Hey, Ethan." Lexie directed her smile at Mrs. Waite.

"Jen Waite," Mrs. Waite said, and stuck out her hand.

"Lexie James," Lexie said, shaking it.

"Ethan said he loves talking to you during his sessions." Jen patted Lexie's hand.

"Mom." Ethan rolled his eyes. "I'll meet you guys in the gym. See you Wednesday, Miss James." Ethan jogged off. His mother watched him go. Lexie watched, too. She could imagine that if you created a human like that, actually grew it in your body and then pushed it out a ridiculously small hole; if you fed it and shuffled it around like a hockey puck you were keeping from the net for years and years, you'd feel pretty great watching it simply move like that. Precision, strength, fearlessness. Like his dad.

Lexie looked up. Daniel Waite was staring at her again. He must be a starer. Jen hooked her arm into Daniel's.

"It was so nice to meet you both." Lexie deliberately looked at Mrs. Waite when she spoke. "I have to run to my office and get some paperwork done. If you ever need anything, please call me."

They shook hands and Lexie hurried off. It wasn't until she was in her office, the thick oak door shut firmly, that she realized she was feeling shaky, her stomach like a shifting bubble of mercury. Lexie thought of how Mitzy used to smoke a joint at the kitchen table while staring at a lava lamp. Her mother had found the thing at a garage sale, a relic of the '70s, and bought it specifically for the purpose of getting high and staring at it.

"See, try this," she had told Lexie, as she pushed a bong into her daughter's hand. "And then you look at this thing and *wala,* it's like you're hypnotized or something." Lexie was twelve. She had watched the red bubble in the glass beaker but handed the bong back to her mother and held her breath as best she could each time Mitzy lit up.

Lexie dropped into the Windsor chair at her office desk. Her head felt fuzzy with static. It had been so long since she'd suffered panic attacks, she thought she was done with them. Had left them behind with red-pepper-flake acne and fingernails chewed into ragged little claws. "Accept, acknowledge, face, and float," she said firmly. Those were the four steps toward controlling anxiety and OCD that she'd learned at Tufts.

At the time, the attacks took her completely by surprise, like getting hit in the face with a frying pan. She'd managed so much so well on her own: college, summers in Los Angeles when she waitressed to pay the rent, getting herself into grad school fully funded by scholarships, grants, and barely any loan money. And then, six months into her master's program, Lexie felt like she was dying. Like she had previously been tethered to some mothership that had kept her bobbing in place and then one day, without notice, she'd been cut free. It was a terrifying aloneness. Lexie had suffered quietly, dreading each class, where she sat in fear of vomiting or passing out as she walked to a desk. Eventually she made it to the counseling center where she was prescribed the four steps, 0.5 milligrams of Klonopin, peanut butter, mega B vitamins, complex carbohydrates, yoga, and sleep.

After twice-a-week sessions and behavioral therapy (she went to every class even if she thought she might throw up in the middle of it), Lexie floated her way through graduate school and eventually eased herself off the Klonopin while keeping up with the other habits. Since then, she'd been carrying a bottle of the pills in her purse for episodes like this—though an episode like this hadn't popped up in over three years. Surely the prescription had expired, but Lexie didn't quite believe the pharmaceutical companies with their expiration dates. These were drugs. Chemicals. Didn't that stuff last forever? Linger in the drinking water? Change the sexual anatomy of sea life?

Lexie grabbed her sack-like purse and dug around until she found the bottle. The label was merely a gray-white smear. She popped off the top and swallowed one pill, then poured the others out into her hand and counted them. Twenty-five. If this was the start of a season of anxiety, she had twenty-five days to get over it. Assuming she took the recommended dose.

2

*L*EXIE STARED AT THE PAPERWORK ON HER DESK. SHE WAS FLOATY and formless from the Klonopin and couldn't properly focus; the Waites played on repeat in her brain. Lexie was never jealous of the Ruxton students, but she often reflected on how lucky most of them were. Ethan Waite was a perfect example: A kid whose biggest gripe with his mother might be that she complimented the school counselor in front of him. As for his father, what could Ethan Waite ever say to impugn Daniel Waite?

Lexie's father, Bert, had been a bartender at a cinder block pub called Swallow at the Hollow. It was a name that had confused Lexie for years; she had always seen the bird when she said those words, not the bobbing Adam's apple of a drinker in action. Bert usually didn't get home from Swallow at the Hollow until three in the morning. He'd walk into the apartment, turn the TV up loud, and lie on the couch and smoke cigarettes until he fell asleep. When she was little, Lexie would come out of her room at the sound of the TV and lie on the couch with her father, falling back to sleep to the smell of menthol Kools and booze, and the blaring, whiney sound of an old movie. As she got older, Lexie stopped going out to join her father, but she would listen to the TV, trying to see in her mind images that went with the sound. When she got up for school, the TV was still on and her father was always asleep, a cigarette butt either hanging from his open mouth like a giant white cold sore or sitting on the edge of the beer can he used for an ashtray. A small pile of ash often sat beside his fallen-cake-looking face, and at least six or seven other empty beers cans would be strewn across the flattened brown carpet (no more plush than a car's floor mat). Lexie always picked up the beer cans and put them in a paper bag that she left in front of the door of their neighbor, Mr. Gordon. Mr. Gordon cut the cans apart with a pair of thick, beak-tipped scissors. He used the aluminum to make mobiles of flying birds and beady-eyed bats that he sold at the flea market on Sundays. In Lexie's mind, the idea that the cans were used all over again, in a way that allowed Mr. Gordon to pay his rent, made up for the sheer number of them.

A few days after Lexie's fifteenth birthday, Bert went to work and never returned. When Lexie asked her mother where her father was, Mitzy answered, "Hell if I know and hell if I care." Mitzy had been only seventeen when she'd had Lexie. She and Bert rarely slept in the bedroom together, and although there were times when her parents made it unfortunately clear that they were about to have sex, Lexie had no recollection of ever seeing them kiss or hold hands.

Lexie and Betsy Simms rode their bikes to Swallow at the Hollow a couple nights after Bert's disappearance. Lexie was told by Randy, the owner, that her dad had quit and said he was leaving town. The rumor was that he had moved to Reno. That night, when Lexie reported this to her mother, Mitzy suggested Lexie take a bus up to Reno to live with Bert.

"But I don't even know if he's there," Lexie had said.

"Well, Ronnie's moving in tomorrow and there isn't room for the three of us." Mitzy produced a guilty, pinched smile and crushed out her cigarette on a dinner plate.

An hour later, when Lexie told this to Betsy, Betsy suggested that she move in with them. The Simmses had a two-story house with four bedrooms and only one kid. Mr. Simms called Lexie The Twin since she and Betsy did everything together and even looked alike with their blue eyes and charcoal eyebrows.

"You think your parents would mind?" Lexie had asked anxiously. Betsy had yelled in a muffled voice (hand cupped over the mouthpiece, maybe, but Lexie could hear), *Mom! Lexie's mom's moving a boyfriend into the apartment and her dad disappeared, can she come and live with us?* There was silence as Mrs. Simms must have made sure Betsy obscured their conversation. Betsy came back on the phone and said, "Yeah, she's putting sheets on the guest bed. She said you can stay until you go away to college, and if you go to Ohlone College you can stay until you graduate from there." Lexie's throat had throbbed with embarrassment and gratitude.

When Mitzy claimed she couldn't come to Lexie's wedding because she couldn't afford a plane ticket, the Simmses bought her one as a gift to Lexie. The only reason Lexie accepted this gift was to save herself the embarrassment of having to explain why her mother wasn't there. An absentee father was nothing to explain—it was something people naturally understood. An absentee mother, however, made as much sense to most people as cannibalism.

Lexie pushed aside her paperwork and googled Daniel Waite. As expected, he showed up at Museum of Fine Arts fund-raisers, a who's who list of Boston lawyers, and a few articles in the *Boston Globe.* There was also a profile in *Forbes,* and a cover interview with the *Harvard Law Review,* of which he had been editor when he was a student. In addition, there were countless mentions of him in newspapers from the *New York Times* to the *Globe and Mail* in Canada.

She was about to google Jen Waite when her office phone rang. It was Peter.

"I thought you were going to get out of there as soon as possible," he said.

"I was, but I stopped in my office and did some paperwork." Lexie squinted and gave herself a little slap on the forehead. She'd never had to lie to Peter before.

"I'm so glad I never have to do paperwork." Peter lived outside the world of paperwork. His father, an accountant, did his taxes. Peter never saved receipts or filed for anything, not even a rebate when he bought a new sander.

"Wait. I didn't do paperwork. I was going to but I ended up on the computer, googling one of the parents. I'm sorry I lied."

Peter laughed. "Well, that was a waste of a lie."

"Can we not count it since I confessed right away?" Lexie asked. "Can we say that we've still never lied to each other?"

"Yeah, that one definitely doesn't count. You think I haven't googled everyone I've sold a guitar to?"

"Okay, so we're holding strong!" Lexie felt buoyant, unburdened. "I'm going to leave right this second." She erased her history and shut down her computer while she spoke. "I'll pick up a surprise dinner on the way home."

"I thought you had dinner with the families. The orphan table."

"I did, but you didn't have dinner, did you?"

"No."

Lexie knew that would be his answer. Peter usually only ate if someone else reminded him to, or handed him something. When he cooked, it was because Lexie had asked him to. He knew how to use a Crock-Pot, and whether it was a humid summer day or they were snowed in like a couple adrift on an ice floe, every meal Peter made was in that one pot.

"Should we do a guitar lesson when you get home?" Peter had been teaching Lexie guitar for months. Lexie had no natural talent or inclination, but she went along with the lessons because she knew Peter would love it if one day they could play together.

"I'm kinda tired, babe. Can we do it tomorrow?"

"Whatever you want."

They hung up. Lexie picked up her purse and rushed out the door. She took the long way to her car, walking along the pond and avoiding the spired, Gothic castle of a dorm in which Ethan Waite lived. At the end of these events parents could always be found near the dorms, lingering as they said good-bye to their kids.

Lexie's seventeen-year-old brown Saab was parked alone. After three days of parents' weekend, most of the faculty who didn't live on campus had fled as soon as dinner had ended. Teaching kids in a boarding school was great—there was an intimacy about it that you didn't get in day schools. But doing it with the parents around was a whole other social skill. For some, it took the same kind of effort as, say, pretending to be in love, or sitting through a monotonous three-hour play. A silent, ruminating exhaustion.

Lexie threw her purse onto the passenger seat and turned the key. As had happened a couple days ago, the engine wheezed, sputtered, and coughed. Saabs, especially ones from the previous century, were expensive to repair. With Lexie and Peter's savings being spent on the upcoming wedding there wasn't a dime for car-care. Lexie waited a minute as if the car needed to come around to starting in its own time. She spaced out in that Klonopin-headed way and almost forgot what she was waiting for. And then, as if a hypnotist had snapped his fingers, she blinked back into alertness and turned the key again. The car started. Lexie pumped her fist and gave a little *woot*. Now that the anxiety had been quelled and the lie had been cleared, she was feeling nearly giddy. It was almost like she'd forgotten the panic had even happened.

THE PARKING LOT AT JAMBOREE RIBS WAS FULL. LEXIE DOUBLE-parked behind a pickup with the license plate EAT RIBS. She assumed the truck belonged to someone who worked there, if not the owner. No need to worry about blocking them in.

Smoking indoors was illegal in Massachusetts but they did it here anyway. Smoke sat in the carpeted room like a sweetened fog—barbecue mixed with tobacco. Patsy Cline's "Crazy" played out of fuzzy speakers, making even the music sound smoky. Lexie went to the cash register where a girl with bright blue eye shadow stood, staring and waiting. "Can I place an order to go?"

The girl slowly pulled out a greasy, laminated menu. "We got everything but the Billy Basket."

"What's the Billy Basket?" Scarcity bred desire in Lexie.

"A basket made of onion rings and filled with chili fries."

"Holy moly." Lexie laughed, relieved that it wasn't something she or Peter would want. Would the cuff link–wearing Daniel Waite ever eat something like a Billy Basket? Probably not. His stomach was as flat as his son's. His jaw was cut to the bone.

Lexie placed her order and waited near the register. She watched as groups of two or three moseyed up to pay their bill. No one moved too fast. Maybe the ribs were laced with some kind of hypnagogic.

When she finally had her bag of food, Lexie hurried out to the double-parked car. She put the bag on the floor of the passenger seat in case the grease soaked through, and then turned the key. The engine sputtered and died. Lexie waited and watched two tall men in cowboy boots amble to a truck and roar away. She turned the key again. Nothing.

Lexie picked up her iPhone and played Yahtzee. She had downloaded the game shortly after she had started working at Ruxton, where she found herself entrapped in twice-weekly meetings that had the same prickling effect as sitting in completely stopped city traffic. Try to remain undistracted through an hour-long discussion of the school library's computers' printing system. Try not to roll your eyes when the lacrosse coach talks about school spirit and the importance of faculty attending games—even, and especially, away games. Try to sit through a ninety-minute debate about school uniform policy and the ever-expanding definition of a white button-down. Is cream *white*? Is the palest yellow *white*? Lexie couldn't even force herself to care.

Since her engagement to Peter, Lexie had been playing the game more and more compulsively. Every task connected to the wedding demanded a certain amount of meeting/traffic-like waiting; Yahtzee was the plug that filled the gaping hole of each wait. Lexie had even started making decisions according to what she thought of as the Yahtzee Gods. The wedding cake she'd ordered (vanilla cream with a vanilla cream icing) had been decided by the Yahtzee Gods when a roll of five aces pushed Lexie's score over three hundred and into the space in which the chocolate cake was a clear and decisive loser. Lately, Lexie had been playing so voraciously that she'd devised a system that brought her repeatedly high scores, scores she insisted on showing Amy (who usually refused to divert her attention to Lexie) during meetings at Ruxton where Lexie concealed the phone under her notebook.

Lexie glanced up at the EAT RIBS license plate, then looked back down at the phone and worked her thumbs with the same half-paralyzed fervor as the old women she'd once seen lined up on stools in Las Vegas. (Those women had reminded her of giant mushrooms that had grown there—their eyes more lifeless than the spinning bars on the machine six inches from their faces.) When she ended on a low score, Lexie closed the game and dropped the phone onto the passenger seat. She tried the starter again. And again. Once more. And then a fourth and fifth time. Nothing happened.

Lexie called Peter. She wanted this problem to not be hers. Weren't nights like this half the reason to get married?

"I've got your dinner from Jamboree all hot and ready but my car won't start."

"Shit."

"Yeah. Maybe you can come down here and figure it out? Give it a jump?"

"If it's doing that whining thing again it's not the battery. At least I don't think it is."

Lexie turned the key again. "Yeah, it's doing that whining thing."

"Why don't I drive down, pick you up, we'll leave the car there and deal with it in the morning."

"I'm double-parked. We can't leave it." Lexie couldn't help but hone in on the picture in her head: Daniel and Jen Waite cruising down the highway in a sleek, six-month-old German car that would never, ever, not start while double-parked outside a rib joint.

"What'd you get me to eat?"

"Ribs. Biscuits. Cole slaw."

"Dang. Well, call Triple A and I'll drive down there, eat the ribs in the car, and keep you company while we wait for the tow."

Lexie's gut tightened. She didn't want to wait for a tow. She didn't want to be a person who owned a car that needed to be towed. The life of towed cars, and cars running out of gas on the center lane of a six-lane freeway, and dented-door cars with windows that were stuck open, and cars with the *check engine* light continually on, and cars with a rearview mirror hanging from a wire like a loose tooth, was exactly what she thought she'd left behind in childhood. Lexie knew it was entirely irrational, but she was starting to feel as if this whole bad car situation were entirely Peter's fault.

FIFTEEN MINUTES LATER, PETER PULLED UP IN HIS WHITE CARGO van. Lexie had always disliked the van, but tonight she hated it. She suddenly realized why: It brought to mind perverts and pedophiles. On the sexiness scale of vehicles, the van lingered in the boggy bottom with sled-back trucks (like what Bert had driven) and '80s era Ford Fiestas (like what Mitzy had—until she totaled it when Lexie was thirteen). She knew the van was necessary for Peter's business, useful in that it could haul materials, tools, and guitars. But the utility of it currently felt pointless. All Lexie could see was the fact that as soon as she was married, she would be an official co-owner of that van. *You can take the girl out of San Leandro, but you can't take San Leandro out of the girl.*

Lexie watched Peter walk across the lot. He was all sinew and gristle—a rib bone sucked of its fat. At thirty-five he didn't have a wrinkle on his face and his hair was a boyish mop of brown curls. She had always loved his youthfulness, his wiriness, his smooth face that only needed to be shaved every third day or so. But in the time she'd waited for him (her Yahtzee game going full force), Peter's youthfulness had lost its appeal. She was pissed off that they couldn't afford a better car, and angry that the reason this car was dead was that Peter hadn't taken it in for her to get things checked out. Lexie wanted Peter to grow up and be responsible. She wanted him to be the man.

"Hey." Peter picked up Lexie's purse and put it in the backseat so he could sit down.

"Hey." Lexie tossed her phone onto her purse. She met him halfway between the seats to exchange what she intended to be a quick, angry kiss. But Peter didn't let her pull away. He took his long, lean arm, wrapped it around Lexie's head, and guided her in closer for another, softer, kiss. When she tried to pull back from that, he kissed her again. Lexie's eyes shut and she felt herself exhaling some anger. "Hey," Lexie said again. She felt a little better about him. About being stuck with a piece of shit Saab and the sex-offender van.

"This for me?" Peter picked up the bag from the floor, opened it, and pulled out a rib. "What'd Triple A say?"

"It'll be at least an hour. I hope that truck won't be going any-

32

where until the place closes." Lexie pointed toward the license plate in front of them.

Peter held a rib in front of his mouth like it was a flute he was about to play. He read the license plate and smiled. "Owner?"

"No idea. But they've got to work here, right?"

"Definitely."

Lexie watched Peter eat and her head and heart softened further. It was against Lexie's nature to hold on to bad feelings—an inclination that had helped her coast through her emotionally cluttered childhood with unreasonable alacrity. She knew she was a shit for being irked with him about the cars. She knew he wasn't callow and irresponsible. For all of her adult life, Lexie believed that a guy like Peter was a dream come true—even if they were sitting in a dead Saab outside a rib joint in nowhere Massachusetts. But the problem with dreams, Lexie had found, was each time she caught up to one, it started to feel less significant, and suddenly she was aiming for more. Time to be grateful, Lexie thought. Who knew how long something this good could last?

"How were the parents today?"

"Fine." Lexie blushed and shook her head as if to expel the redness from her ears. "There was this one dad who I thought was flirting with me. I felt like I was reading his mind and his mind was very dirty."

"I'm sure there was more than one dad with a dirty mind." Peter put the gnawed-down, raggedy bone back in the bag and removed another rib.

"Well, I was wrong about him flirting with me. He only wants to have coffee so he can pick my brain about his kid."

"So you're having coffee with a Dirty Mind Dad?"

"Yeah. But I think I misread the dirty mind part."

"I wouldn't be so sure about that. Who's his kid?" Lexie often told Peter stories and news about the students. She never shared the confidential stuff, though most of that, she thought, wasn't pulpy enough to be a real secret.

"Ethan. My favorite."

"Ethan's your favorite? I thought that girl Hadley was your favorite."

"Hadley was last year's favorite. Ethan's my current favorite. Of all the kids I see, he's the most . . . I don't know, I don't feel like I'm talking with a kid when I'm with him. He's a more fully realized human than the others."

"You were probably like that as a kid." Peter pulled apart a biscuit, eating it layer by layer.

"You don't care that I'm meeting his dad, do you?"

"Why would I care?" Peter rummaged in the bag and took out another rib. "It's your job."

"I'm meeting him off campus. He wanted to have coffee at the Inn on the Lake."

"Rich people." Peter shrugged. "Gotta have the best even if it's just a cup of coffee."

"Maybe we'll be rich people one day." Lexie leaned in toward Peter and licked a smear of sauce from the corner of his mouth.

"We're already rich in love."

"Holy shit, my fiancé's a Hallmark card."

"Hell, yeah. If I could draw, I'd draw a kitten crawling out of a red bucket beside a wheelbarrow and I'd say, in calligraphy, *you are the wind beneath my wings, the wind in my sail, and the . . .*" Peter took another bite of rib.

Lexie was laughing. Her prior anger had disintegrated into flecks of floating thought she had no interest in following. "And the cold wind biting my face?"

"But you're not the cold wind biting my face. You're the warm wind caressing my—" Peter took another bite.

"Your silky thighs?"

"Sounds too much like a Nair commercial."

"Your balls?"

"Too porny." Peter sucked the rib bone.

Lexie winced. Sometimes she felt like a pervert compared to Peter. Maybe she should be the one driving the van! "Your cheeks?"

"Yeah, my cheeks." Peter leaned in and kissed Lexie on the cheek in a way that made her feel sleazy and oily for having thought of the wind on his balls.

LEXIE SAT IN THE PASSENGER SEAT OF THE VAN AND ADMIRED PETER'S die-cut silhouette as he drove. The radio was on, classical, and Peter was singing along, la de de de dum dah. Soon, Peter started making up words using an operatic voice. "*The car has been toooowed . . .*" His alto was so deep that his voice cracked and they both laughed.

"*It was towed, it was towed . . .*" Lexie did her best soprano.

"*But we are in the van . . .*" Peter continued.

"*The VAAAAAAAN . . .*" Lexie held the note until Peter laughed.

In this way, they narrated the night's adventure: Triple A assessing the car, finding that the starter was broken, hooking it up to the tow truck, and hauling it off to H and M Repair a half-mile away. There was a notice taped to H and M's door that said they were closed for the weekend because of a family wedding in New

Hampshire (*THEY'D FLED TO NOUVEAU HAMPSHIRE!* Peter boomed dramatically) and so the car had been left there, outside the garage doors, with a note on the windshield.

When they got home, Lexie went upstairs and ran a bath. She wanted to float in the tub and feel the relief of nothingness. When the mirror was fogged and the room was steamy-warm, Lexie undressed and lowered herself into the water. Everything felt satiny and smooth, like she and the water were a single fluid being. Lexie sank down so that her long hair swirled around her head like golden seaweed. Her knees jutted up, glowing red from the heat. She was almost in a trance, spacing out in the way she'd done since childhood, when Peter came in to brush his teeth.

Peter rubbed the mirror clear and stared at Lexie's reflection in the tub. Toothpaste foamed out of his mouth as if he had rabies. "I need a bath, too."

She popped up a little and slid forward to make room for him.

Peter dropped his clothes on top of Lexie's—a pile of shed fabric skins. He stepped in behind Lexie and pulled her in toward him like the coupling of train cars. Lexie's thoughts swirled—no edges, nothing clear or articulate, everything flowing until she remembered she hadn't put in birth control.

"Pull out," Lexie whispered, and dutifully, Peter did.

She didn't think of Daniel Waite until she and Peter were climbing out of the tub. And then she thought only how odd it was that she was thinking of him at all.

PETER SAT AT THE KITCHEN TABLE, EATING A BOWL OF OATMEAL Lexie had made for him and reading the *Boston Globe* on his iPad.

It was Monday; he could saunter into his studio whenever he damn well pleased. Lexie was beside him, on the phone with H and M, drinking coffee and eating a bowl of Cheerio's O by O so that Howie (the H in H and M?) couldn't hear her chew. She looked at the clock on the oven every few minutes, aware that she needed to hustle and get to Ruxton. When she finally hung up, she didn't hustle. She stared at Peter until he looked up.

"It's a lot more than the starter, and he's not even sure he'll be able to find the parts." There it was. That irrational anger over the car again.

"Take the van. I've got all the materials I need. If I have to go somewhere I'll bike."

"I hate the van." Lexie gave a strained smile. She was such an asshole. What was wrong with her that she couldn't appreciate that she had transportation and didn't have to take a bus—not that there were any buses this far in the mountains.

As a kid, Lexie took the bus everywhere—she had spent hours of her life sitting at bus stops waiting. Around the time she was fourteen she began pick-and-choose hitchhiking, sticking out her thumb only if someone safe-looking was driving by. A couple times she'd stepped into a car only to find it wasn't as safe as she'd thought. There was the guy with the bottle of whiskey tucked between his legs who offered her a drink by sliding the bottle between Lexie's legs. And there was the French couple who pulled out a packet of naked photos of the wife, handed them to Lexie, and asked her what she thought. Lexie had told them that she thought she should get out at the next stoplight.

"I could drop you off and pick you up if you hate the van so much." Peter wasn't insulted. He was wise enough to take nothing personally. Lexie thought it was one of his better traits.

"But I have to meet Ethan's dad at the Inn at the Lake for coffee." Lexie looked back at the clock on the oven. She had to leave within the next five minutes.

"Call him and tell him to pick you up." Peter went back to reading the iPad.

Lexie imagined herself in the passenger seat of Daniel Waite's car. It would be a leather seat, she knew. Warm. Supple. Like sitting on a lap.

"I'll drive the van. I'm ridiculous." Lexie reminded herself that she shouldn't be coveting expensive leather laps.

Peter shrugged.

LEXIE HURRIED OUT OF THE ROOM WHERE SHE TAUGHT HEALTH and Human Sexuality. The semester had only started, so they weren't into the good stuff yet. For now it was simply anatomy. It was amazing how these kids, who could take the SAT in ninth grade and score in the top third, didn't know the difference between a vagina and labia. Well, they'd know it by the end of the semester.

In her office, Lexie brushed her hair, put on lipstick, and checked her face in the wall mirror. She'd worn a black wrap dress that dipped down a little too low for teaching and so she'd pinned it shut in the morning to avoid flashing her students. Lexie took the pin and readjusted it one inch lower in an effort to feel a little less schoolmarmish and a little more Californian. She turned off her cell phone, dropped it into her purse, and hurried to the van.

Her stomach churned on the drive to Inn on the Lake. "It's only a cup of coffee," she said aloud.

Lexie parked the van in the far end of the lot where she hoped Daniel Waite wouldn't see her getting out. She circled the van, hand-locking all the doors. It was a pointless exercise in a town where nobody locked their car, and half of the residents didn't lock their houses. But even after three years in Ruxton, Lexie never left a car, her office, or the house without revving up her lifelong *Did I lock the door?* OCD. Once the van was secured, Lexie walked—head high, shoulders back —into the café.

Daniel Waite was already there, sitting at a corner table, reading the *Wall Street Journal*. He put down the paper and stood. Lexie's stomach tumbled. She often got a little nervous before talking to parents, but this was unusually forceful.

"It's great to see you again." Daniel Waite pulled out a chair for Lexie.

"Oh, yeah, thanks." Lexie's hands shook as she laid her napkin on her lap. Her fingers jumped—two leaping crickets—to the spot where she'd pinned her dress shut. Was it too low? Would Daniel Waite think a woman in a V-wrap dress wasn't professional enough to be counseling his son? This would be so much easier if she had taken a Klonopin.

"Did you pin that dress shut?" Daniel's mouth was open, a loose, toothy smile.

"What?" Lexie dropped her hands. She felt her face flash with color, like a peacock's suddenly fanned tail.

"I can see that little stick of silver, like you pinned it shut from the inside." He was pointing at her, his finger only inches from Lexie's chest.

"Well—"

"It's those boys, isn't it! Damn those horny little buggers staring at Miss James so much she has to track down a safety pin and secure her dress shut!" He was laughing.

Lexie laughed with relief. "I was trying to be proper."

"I know, I know. You got Don McClear walking around with a broomstick up his ass and Janet Irwin the sheriff's deputy—"

"I thought she was a hunting dog, sniffing you out." Lexie felt her body easing into this. Daniel Waite wasn't so hard after all.

"Hunting dog, Deputy Dog, Colonel Klink, Barney Rubble to Don's Fred Flintstone, Barney Fife to Don's Andy Taylor . . . wait, how old are you? Do you get any of my references?"

"I know who Barney Rubble is!"

"Do you know who Barney Fife is? Please don't tell me that you're closer to my son's age than mine. I'm having a real hard time with this old man stuff." Daniel scratched his fingers along his jaw as if he were rubbing a hoary beard.

"You don't look that old."

"I'm ancient. Methuselah."

"Well, how old are you?" Fifty, she said in her head.

"Fifty-three," Daniel said. "And you're . . . twenty-six?"

"Thirty-three."

"So you are closer to Ethan's age than mine."

"Well, but—"

"But I can catch you up on late sixties and early seventies cartoons and sitcoms so quickly, you'll soon feel as old as me."

Lexie had chatted with many Ruxton parents in her three years at the school and not one of them ever was relaxed enough to talk about nothing. About TV. About ageing. It was always *The Child*. What he or she had done or what he or she should be doing. Sometimes the parents' interest in their kids bordered on pathological—as if the child were being sent out in the world as their parents' do-over. And most of the parents were oblivious to the idea that although Lexie loved her job and felt great respect and affection for the students, there were few things less interesting to her than listening to a list of any particular kid's accomplishments. Certainly, Lexie's childhood was an unhealthy opposite of that. She was ignored mostly, and mocked for her achievements ("Now don't you get a swollen head over all that and start thinking you're too good for us," Mitzy had said, when eight-year-old Lexie's fawn haiku was chosen for inclusion in the elementary school newspaper).

Daniel Waite was a parent unlike any of the others. He was playful. Fun. Lexie didn't sense that he was as focused on the status markers as the other parents. If there was a Christmas letter being issued from the Waite house, would it even mention that Ethan was a senior at Ruxton or that he'd done an internship in Washington, DC, last summer? And Daniel was the first lawyer Lexie had ever met who didn't talk about his practice. At all.

". . . the best thing about daytime TV was the ads—" Daniel said.

"Oh, yeah. I used to crave Rice-A-Roni when I was home sick 'cause that ad came on every fifteen minutes."

"*The San Francisco Treat*," Daniel sang, perfectly on tune.

"Exactly! And San Francisco was so close to where I lived but seemed so, so, far away, it could have been another country."

"When the commercials for TDI, Truck Driver Institute, came

on I'd think that as soon as I graduated from Ruxton, I was going to book out to Arizona and get my trucking license."

TWO HOURS LATER LEXIE FELT LIKE HER HEAD WAS AN INFLATED helium balloon. She was bobbing with lightness. And everything around her looked different than when she'd walked in. There was a yellow flashbulb clarity that gave Lexie the feeling she was seeing through helium as well. They had finished the snack Daniel had ordered: Frito pie, essentially nachos made with Frito chips. Comfort food, Daniel had said. Happy food, Lexie had thought. She was supremely happy and miraculously unfettered by the blurriness of real life. Often, since she'd arrived at Ruxton, Lexie felt like she was two people at once: her childhood self, a member of her original family—a group that sat far outside the dimensions of anyone's ideal. And her current self, a person Lexie hoped would never suggest her origins. But with Daniel, for the last two hours, Lexie had been so open and true that it felt as if she was one complete person. Her past and her present were now perfectly lined up like a foggy-edged camera shot pulled into crystalline focus.

When Lexie said she had to get back to Ruxton for her eleven thirty appointment Daniel finally brought up Ethan.

"So, about my son . . ." Daniel lifted his hands, face up, as if to ask for an offering.

"Can we talk on the phone or something?" Lexie gathered up her purse, pulled the napkin off her lap, and stood.

"I'll call you." Daniel Waite stood, stuck out his hand and held hers more than shaking it, a move that Lexie didn't quite know how to read. She didn't mind, though. Daniel felt like a real friend.

3

ETHAN WAITE WAS DIFFERENT. HIS BODY—LONG AND LEAN, WIDE at the shoulders like his father—held a new kind of power now that Lexie could see its future. Its potential.

It was Wednesday, and they were in Lexie's office, the louvered shutters tilted up, giving the room the hazy, muted light of an early-morning bedroom. Lexie liked this light when she saw her student patients. It dimmed everything enough to relax them—no one was under a spotlight. And she kept the heat up, too—seventy-four degrees—so that the students would melt into the old, leather couch, while Lexie sat upright in the tapestry wing chair facing them. This womb-like climate allowed the students to open up and trust Lexie. She wasn't their friend, but they could tell her everything they told their friends. And she wasn't their mother; they could tell her everything they wouldn't tell their mothers. And unlike an essay turned in to an English teacher or a presentation on colonial Africa, nothing that went on in Lexie's office was public. Students could admit the stuff they'd never before dared say aloud.

Even so, it was rare to be surprised. Teenagers were remarkably alike in their anxieties and obsessions, and predictably aligned in their desires by gender. Even the gay and lesbian students—the few of them bold enough to come out in a school where the preppy athlete was regarded as the ideal—fell in line with the masses. The only people who ever surprised Lexie were the Asperger's kids with their obsessions (Lexie's favorite had been the kid who collected ants, froze them, and then arranged them on paper, glued into words and phrases he repeated over and over again: *crispy critters, crispy critters, crispy critters*). These kids were often the smartest, too, and Lexie would find herself taking notes of things to google and research once they had left her office.

What did surprise Lexie, however, was how disinterested many kids were in their own families, and their parents, in particular. Even James Blue, whose mother had recently been killed in a car crash, had little to say about this matter. Like acne, or herpes, or shingles after chicken pox, Lexie knew the horrors of his mother's death would eventually resurface—popping out when he least expected it. But for now all she could get out of him was how much he hated Tori Spector because she didn't love him the way he loved her, and had chosen not to lose her virginity with him. Instead, she lost it with the boyfriend who followed James, the loudmouth, Human Garbage Disposal, sex-obsessed (according to James) Swede, Magnus Skaarsgard.

Ethan Waite drifted above the others as if he were made of a different material—something more buoyant, flexible; something that sought the light rather than surfing with the weedy, tangled undercurrents of the crowd. Ethan seemed, simply, better than the rest of them.

"It's hot." Ethan loosened his tie and undid the collar button of his dress shirt. This was the required uniform: For the boys—blue blazer, white button-down and tie, khakis, and loafers or Sperry's or some other shoe that did not in any way resemble a tennis shoe or a sandal. For the girls it was the same, but without the tie and with khaki skirts if they preferred them over pants. Naturally, the girls shortened their skirts as high as they could, as if their life depended on getting oxygen to the flesh above their knees, light on their thighs, wind on the backs of their legs.

Ethan rolled up his sleeves. Lexie could see the grapefruit bulge of muscle pushing through the thin, cotton shirt.

"I'm wondering about the value of it all," Ethan said.

"The value of what?"

"Going to one of the schools my parents want me to go to. I'm thinking of hucking all the applications in the trash, telling them I didn't get in, and then secretly applying to the schools I really want to go to."

"Hmm." Lexie wrote down the word *hucking* so she could look up the exact definition once Ethan had left. "So you want to huck all the apps to the schools your parents picked and apply to the places where you really want to go. Where do you really want to go?"

"Berkeley, Stanford, or UCLA. But my parents say it's Ivies or nothing. I'm their only child."

Funny, Daniel hadn't acted like the kind of father who would demand Ivies or nothing. Maybe this was his soon-to-be-ex-wife's doing. "You're still applying to Middlebury, right?"

"It's my safety. It's where my mother went."

"I guess they're pretty confident in you." So confident, Lexie thought, there was no need to boast.

"They're confident in my dad's connections. It's not who you know and who you meet, but who you fuck and who you eat." Ethan grinned. The therapy session was the only place where Lexie would allow a student to use expletives. If they were going to fully be themselves during their session, she reasoned, she had to allow them to speak the way they did when there wasn't a teacher around.

Lexie smiled back at Ethan. "Where'd you hear that?"

"My dad."

A silver string darted up Lexie's spine as she connected the word *fuck* with the idea of Daniel Waite.

The remainder of the hour didn't feel like work. Ethan riffed about the comically bad pot-brownie trip he'd had with his two best pals. Ethan had thought he was going deaf—everything sounded like it was coming to him through bulletproof glass. Lexie gave him her standard talk on marijuana being stronger and longer lasting in edibles. She cautioned him against using it in any form and offered the list of contraindications, none of which were too serious. Still, Lexie herself had never tried pot. She'd seen too much of it at the kitchen table as a kid to think that anything worthwhile could ever come of it.

From the pot story, Ethan jumped to naked swimming in the pond at night. For that one, Lexie sat back in her chair and laughed. The truth was, she didn't believe Ethan was in crisis, that he even needed to see her professionally. As far as Lexie could tell, Ethan simply wanted the time to sit in her office and decompress.

THAT NIGHT, WHILE SHE AND PETER LOUNGED ON THE COUCH, LEXie's bare feet resting in his lap, her computer resting on her own lap, Lexie got a text from Daniel Waite. She stared at the gray-bubbled words on her cell phone screen.

Frito Pie Friday. It's official. Must have Frito pie.

Enjoy! Eat one for me, too, Lexie typed.

But you are the Lady President of the Frito Club, you must attend.

"Should we do a guitar lesson?" Peter stared at the TV as he spoke. He was watching a science show, something with dolphins and sonar and fishermen lost at sea.

"Uh . . . maybe later, okay?" Lexie typed, *Hahaha!*

"Who're you texting?" Peter clicked up the volume on the TV.

"It's that Ruxton dad I had coffee with the other day." *I'm free at three on Friday.* "Ethan's dad."

Meet you Friday at the Frito Club, 3pm sharp, Daniel replied before she even looked away from the screen.

"Look at the size of that dolphin compared to the diver. Freaky, huh?" Peter had one long, slim finger pointed at the TV set. Lexie looked, but she couldn't see anything but Daniel Waite.

"Did you find the chairs?" Peter asked when Lexie didn't respond.

"Yes." Lexie clicked back through her history, past the three pages of articles she had read about Daniel and Jen Waite, past the *How to Make Your Stomach Flatter in Three Days* article she had read, past the diagrams of *Yoga Facelift, Start Today!*, to the first place she had been when she had opened the computer that night: a chair rental place in Northampton. She had briefly looked at the posh, gold chairs that were carved to look like they were made of bamboo. They were too delicate for the wholesome country look she and Peter were going for. But they were good enough. And at this point, good enough was good enough.

"These." Lexie turned the screen to face Peter.

"How much?"

"Two eighty-five."

"A little more than we wanted to pay, but who cares? You only get married once." Peter pulled a Visa card from his pocket. He held the credit card out with one hand while aiming the remote, like a sword, toward the TV. The stations clicked by so quickly Lexie didn't believe Peter could even see what he was zooming past.

PETER SNORED THAT NIGHT. MAYBE IT WAS THE THREE BEERS HE'D had while watching TV; maybe it was fall allergies. But he snored. And it was intolerable. This wasn't the sweet purring of other snorey nights, when Lexie had wanted to roll into him and push against his back like a cat. It was a full-on snore. An old-man snore. A drill-in-her-head snore. A leaf-blower-in-the-bedroom snore. Lexie wanted to take the pillow from beneath her own head and Cuckoo's Nest the life out of Peter.

"What the fuck?" Lexie whispered. She had never had such violent thoughts about Peter before and they awoke her like the fizzing vibrations from a forgotten cell phone ringing in a deep back pocket. Soon, Lexie was hit with the familiar crashing of a panic attack.

It was a school night. There was no time to lie awake in bed and breathe through this with the thunderous Snore-Man beside her. No time for cognitive therapy. Lexie got out of bed and padded downstairs. She went to her purse on the kitchen counter, pulled out the bottle of expired Klonopin, tapped one out into her hand, and swallowed it dry.

Back in bed, with her heart roiling and her head crowded with what felt like an electrical fire, Lexie licked her first two fingers, then slipped her hand down her pajama bottoms. As long as Peter snored she knew she was free to move her fingers against herself as forcefully as she wanted. Like a ghost, Daniel Waite tore through the panic and into Lexie's thoughts, where he stayed until she had rubbed herself into a climax (or three, for that's how it worked for her). Immediately afterward, Lexie plunged into a deep and immovable sleep.

4

THE NEXT MORNING LEXIE FOUND HER FRIEND AMY ALONE IN THE
infirmary—a room so antiquated it reminded Lexie of children's
books she'd discovered in other people's houses when she used to
babysit: *Madeline,* or *The Little Princess.* Lexie lay back on a tightly
made green iron bed that had a crank to raise or lower the top half.
Similar beds were on either side of Lexie.

Amy sat in the anachronistically modern rolling chair at her
desk and crossed her legs. She had calves that bulged out like a
man's fist. Lexie stared from Amy's calves to her face: soft, doughy,
with wide-set brown eyes and hair that was so light brown it read
as blond. Amy had been white-haired as a child, she once told
Lexie. She had never colored her hair and probably never would. If
you took a strand and held it up to the light, you'd say brown. But
damn if you didn't look at Amy and see blond. And not only blond,
but a shade of blond Lexie had to buy at a salon an hour away in
Boston, where the cost of a cut and color made her gasp each time
(even when she knew ahead of time what she'd be paying).

"You don't think that's funny?" Lexie had just read last night's text exchange to Amy.

"No. I mean it's not *not* funny. But it's not what you think it is." Amy appeared to be barely interested. Or not excited about it the way Lexie was. Maybe it was because Amy carried on like this with strangers and near-strangers almost every day. She was fully involved in the world of texting and sexting and different phone apps that allowed her to meet people or not meet them.

Lexie looked down at the text and laughed again.

"You have a crush on him so everything he says seems bigger to you. Better."

"I don't have a crush on him," Lexie protested. But yes, she did.

"If you don't have a crush on him, cancel Frito Friday and have your regular lunch with me instead." Amy clucked her tongue. She knew she was right.

Amy had married her college boyfriend the year they graduated from 'Bama. Seven years later she'd had an affair with his business partner, a man who was married to someone who had become her friend. When they were caught, the shame was too much, Amy had said, and so she fled Alabama to a state where no one knew her, her family, her ex-husband's family, her former lover's family, or his wife's family. When the divorce was being finalized, she changed her married last name, Jackson, to one that had no ties to people or places in any of the Southern states, a name picked on a whim from a copy of *Architectural Digest* sitting beside her: Hagan.

Amy didn't realize at the time that *Hagan* was German and often Jewish. When she discovered this (from a Jewish Hagan on a dating site who wanted to make sure they weren't related), Amy laughed hysterically as she imagined her former in-laws finding out that she had a Jewish last name. She was already the devil to them and, being rural Southerners who had never met a Jew in their lives (that they knew of), they had primitive ideas of what a Jew was. Amy once told Lexie that there were many kids in junior high who thought Jews grew little lumps of horn on their heads.

Lexie had never done most of the things Amy had done. But she liked that Amy's life was big and full of mistakes. It made Lexie feel safe with Amy, like anything she did or said would only elicit a shrug and a tongue cluck.

"Okay," Lexie confessed. "I have a mad crush on him. But so what, right?"

"Exactly." Amy pushed her chair back, kicked off her pumps, and put her feet up on the desk. "Have fun. Flirt your ass off. And don't worry about it."

"But I've been having panic attacks lately. I've even had to pop a couple Klonopin from the old bottle I've been carrying since graduate school." Lexie stared at Amy's stockinged feet. The thick, flesh-colored nylon blurred out Amy's toes into one smooth lump that reminded Lexie of the crotch of a Barbie doll.

"You've been having panic attacks because of a crush?"

"I think so."

"You have two choices: Don't go to Frito Friday, stop talking to the guy, and you'll forget about him soon enough. Or, accept the crush and let it be."

"What if I let the Yahtzee God decide?" Lexie pulled her phone from her purse and started playing. "If I get over two hundred fifty, I'll go to Frito Friday. Less than two hundred fifty . . ." Lexie stopped talking so she could focus on the game. Amy rolled her eyes in mock exasperation. She was plenty used to the Yaht-zee God. Sometimes Lexie corralled Amy into playing against her, making Amy the Yahtzee God (or Yahtzee Devil, depending on who won).

"Ooooh," Lexie hummed, when she got a Yahtzee. Unless she blew it—going for a second Yahtzee instead of taking the small straight before her—she was sure to get at least 250.

"Well?" Amy nodded toward the phone that Lexie was shoving back into her purse. "What did Our Father who art in Yahtzee say?"

"Roll with the crush, go to Frito Friday."

"You are what my mama would call Hayseed. That's Southern for shit-all crazy."

"You know what's funny?" Lexie flipped to her side and pulled up her knees. She was in a dress and stockings, like Amy, only Lexie's stockings were sheer and black. Her dress was black, too. Amy's dress was mint green. Only a girl from Alabama would wear mint green with flesh-colored hose. "My parents, who were completely nutzo, never ever questioned anything they did on the grounds that it might be crazy."

"Well, usually it's too hard to see crazy when you're right in the middle of it."

"Wait. What if Daniel kisses me?" Lexie lifted her head, a half-sit-up.

"He'll only kiss you if you give him the signal to kiss you. Don't give the signal."

"What's the signal?" Lexie rested her head on her bent arm.

"I think I usually say something like *Did you bring any protection?* And then they know I'll sleep with them and so they kiss me."

"Well, there's no chance I'll say that, so I guess I don't have to worry." Lexie was often stunned by Amy's forwardness. It played so jarringly off her naturally blond (brown) hair, her sherbet-colored clothing, and her reinforced-toe panty hose. She looked like an Avon saleslady. Not someone who would blow you under an umbrella on a rainy night (last weekend, with another phone-app date who had yet to call back).

"You know Peter and I didn't have sex until our ninth date, right?"

"That's absurd. You're adults."

"There was no way I was going to sleep with him until he'd done an STD panel."

"Are you kidding? You made him go to a doctor, fill out insurance forms, pay some unreasonably high co-pay, and then sit mostly naked, in a blue paper gown, so that you could have sex with him?"

"Yes. And I made the other two guys I've had sex with do it, too."

"I can't believe you found three men in the world to agree to that."

"But I never have to worry about it again for the rest of my life, 'cause I'm gettin' married, y'all!" Lexie put on an Alabama accent. One night when they were out drinking, Amy taught Lexie the regular sayings that came up in conversation back home: *How's your mama?* And, *cute shoes.* And if you didn't like the person under discussion: *Well, bless her heart.*

"Well, bless your heart." Amy sorted through the papers on her desk. "Now quit talking about fucking Frito Friday so I can get my work done."

"It's not Fucking Frito Friday. There will be no fucking, I promise."

"Oh, I know there won't, 'cause there's no way you can get a doctor down there with a rapid-response STD kit." Amy appeared to be reading something on one of the forms. She clicked open a pen and started writing.

Lexie watched. After a couple minutes of silence she said, "It's so strange to think that I've kissed the last person I'll ever kiss in my life. And besides Peter, not another man on earth will ever see me totally naked . . . I'm gonna get fat now. And I'm gonna stop dyeing or washing my hair and let it get all flat and oily. Oh, and I'm going to grow out all that wiry black hair on my body, too. And maybe, if it's at all possible, I'll cultivate some big ol' nipple-sized moles in my armpits or on my face." Lexie was cracking herself up. She was going to keep going until Amy tuned in and responded. Finally, Amy put down her pen and looked up at Lexie.

"Honey, even if you had greasy hair, nipple moles, and a bush the size of a Jackson Five afro, men would fall for you."

"They would not."

"Yeah, they would. But I don't have time for this. I gotta finish all these health reports. So you be sweet and quit frettin' about this Daniel Waite." Amy turned back to her paperwork. Lexie said the words *quit frettin'* over and over again in her head.

5

AND THEN IT WAS FRIDAY. AMY WAS STUCK IN THE INFIRMARY WITH a vomiting freshman, so Lexie had lunch with other teachers in the dining hall. The meal was almost unbearable as Lexie had no appetite and couldn't focus on the conversation.

"Have you heard that before?" Jim Reiger asked. He was the lacrosse coach, square-jawed; he called women *gals* and girls *ladies*.

"Me?" Lexie pointed at herself with her thumb.

"Yeah, you." Jim scraped his chair back and spread his legs even wider than they already were.

"I was spacing out," Lexie confessed. Frito Friday was monopolizing the real estate of her head. She felt like she had a date with the president or a movie star.

"I was saying that you remind me of Melanie Birkin."

"Yeah, a couple people have told me that before. Who was she again?" Lexie asked, though she couldn't care less who she was.

"Isn't it considered poor taste to discuss someone who is not present?" Janet Irwin said. "Can't we elevate this conversation?"

"Shit no," Dot blurted in her balled-up-tin-foil voice. "She abandoned us without saying a word!"

"Wait, was she that young French teacher who disappeared the year before I got here?" Amy had told Lexie the story once. Melanie Birkin was the dorm parent in Robert Frost Hall, a horrendous 1960s blockade that was inconveniently located on the farthest edge of campus and didn't resemble any of the other buildings. Since unmarried teacher residents weren't allowed to entertain their lovers in their apartments, Melanie was frequently AWOL, leaving the dorm proctor (always a senior) in charge. Rumor was, she was so horny for her townie boyfriend (whom no one had ever met, as she was ashamed of him) that when she was confronted about her absences, she simply packed her belongings and left. No notice. No good-byes.

"She was hot," Jim said, and most the women and even the men at the table groaned.

Lexie stood and picked up her plate. "I've gotta go. I'll see everyone at Monday meeting."

"No dinner tonight?" Janet Irwin asked.

"I do Friday dinner every other week." Lexie wanted to spit at her.

"Yes, and last Friday wasn't your Friday, so this is your Friday." Janet spoke with absolute authority.

"It is?" How and why did Janet Irwin keep track of this stuff? Lexie herself could barely remember her own schedule.

"I've been excused from regular dinner duties on the grounds that I'm—" Dot started.

"Foulmouthed?" Jim said.

"No! Old! I'm fucking old! Can you believe how fucking old I am? It's a travesty!"

Janet ignored Dot and kept her head firmly pointed at Lexie, waiting for a response. Maybe, Lexie guessed, Janet recycled the same old quizzes and tests she'd been using in her physics class for the last three decades. This would free her up enough to involve herself in every aspect of the school. Janet's devotion to Ruxton, along with her strict adherence to the rules and her rumored vow of celibacy (Jim Reiger once joked about her being a lesbian, although it was a remark, Lexie believed, that revealed more about the limitations of Jim's imagination than anything real about Janet's sexuality) made Lexie think of Janet as a mother superior in a Catholic convent. But not a kind and nurturing mother superior, more along the lines of a putty-faced, pinpoint-eyed nun who crippled your knuckles with a ruler, a wrathful smile on her face.

"No, wait," Lexie said. "I *was* here last Friday, it was the parents' weekend kick-off dinner."

"But that doesn't count as your Friday," Janet said. "We all were here."

"Miserable pile of shit night that was," Dot mumbled, and they all (save Janet) laughed. Lexie knew that Dot particularly liked to use expletives when Janet was around. It was like each *shit* or *fuck* was a fistful of tacks thrown at Janet's face.

"Okay." Lexie gave up. "So I'll see you at dinner, Janet."

"No, I'm off tonight. You'll see Roy, Katrina, Annabelle—"

"I've gotta run, I'll see you all later!" Lexie winked at Dot, then rushed off before Janet had anything else to add. People like Janet Irwin and Jim Reiger made her wonder what she was doing with her life. If she had a month to live, she'd never spend a minute of it in conversation with Janet about Friday-night dinner duty, or a second of it discussing lacrosse, or former "hot" teachers, with

Jim. Usually Lexie looked back at her small life growing up in the apartment and felt immensely grateful that she'd gone so far away, done so much—more than her mother had courage enough to dream up. But there were times, like today, when she felt like she hadn't done much other than transfer her body from one small area (San Leandro, California) to another small area (Ruxton, Massachusetts). Europe? Asia? Africa? South America? Lexie hadn't been to any of those places. The farthest she'd gone was Montreal when she and Peter drove up there last July.

Even worse than not having traveled, Lexie thought, was that she hadn't started her nonprofit. She hadn't changed or saved lives. And certainly her counselor's salary combined with Peter's guitar-making income wouldn't provide the surplus to execute the ideas she'd had simmering in her head since high school: a mobile home with Internet-connected computers that would roam cities and allow the homeless to use the Internet to find jobs and pick up mail. Or a mobile home that would drive out to rural areas with a full medical staff to give checkups, vaccinations, and necessary medical care to people without cars or insurance.

When she was thirteen, one rare night when her parents were getting along (which meant they were drinking and smoking pot together, half-dressed, with flirty laughs that implied she should get out of the house and stay out for a few hours), Lexie got on a bus without any destination in mind. It was spring break and the Simmses were out of town, so Lexie rode the bus, studying the faces of the other passengers and looking out the window. When the bus stopped in front of the Alameda County Fairgrounds and most people got off, Lexie followed.

The fairgrounds were being used for an RV show—lit up like

a museum exhibition of giant, shiny, rectangles laid flat. There was a fee for admission and Lexie had no money, only her bus pass and house key tucked into the back pocket of her jeans, but when one large family (large in both number and size) shifted past the ticket taker, Lexie hid among them and slid inside.

For two hours, Lexie walked from one vinyl-smelling box to the next, all the while dreaming of a life inside their walls. The RVs were magical with their compact, cleverly organized spaces. She loved that they could take care of all her human needs within an efficient, clean, and sterile environment. These were spaces she could control, maintain, rule.

From that night on, even when she was old enough to understand the flimsiness, the absolute cheapness of the materials, Lexie's fantasy of rescuing either herself or others was usually centered around an RV.

AGAIN, LEXIE PARKED THE CARGO VAN AT THE END OF THE PARKING lot. She circled the vehicle once, checking every door lock. Lexie paused by a black Mercedes that appeared brand-new and was pasted with a Ruxton bumper sticker. It had to be Daniel's. She took a deep breath and reached into her skirt pocket for the Klonopin she had tucked in there before leaving her office. Touching it, knowing it was nearby, made her feel better.

Lexie entered the darkened restaurant. Like their last meeting, Daniel was already seated. The physical reaction Lexie felt surprised her. Instead of acclimating to the sight of Daniel Waite, he'd become a bell that rang up every nerve in her body. Daniel stood as Lexie approached, leaned in and kissed her on the cheek. Was that the kind of friendship they had? Had it already developed into the cheek kiss? Fine by her, as even that small brush of his lips left a pleasant echo of sensation.

"Is that your Mercedes with the Ruxton sticker?" Lexie asked.

"Yeah. I'm sentimental about that place."

"That's sweet." Lexie sat. "Am I late?"

"No. But I like being early. I enjoy watching you walk in." Daniel sat.

Lexie blushed. Like the kiss, this seemed beyond the edges of normal. But it was a not-normal she enjoyed.

"Not sure you can call what I just did *walking*." Lexie kicked out one foot and revealed her black knee-high boot. The heel was five inches. "More like a teeter with these things on."

"It was a very sexy teeter." Daniel looked from the boot to Lexie's face. She took a clipped, short breath and hid the boot under the table.

"My mother once told me I walk like a spaz—bumping into everything, knocking things over with my hips." Mitzy had said it every time Lexie stormed around the kitchen, furiously trying to scrub away the fuzzy, greased layer of grit that went unnoticed by her parents.

"A spaz? Nah. You walk lightly. Like a cat. You look like you'd purr if I stroked you the right way."

There was a held breath of stillness as Lexie's mind hovered over the word *stroke*. "OK. I'm a cat and Janet Irwin's a hunting dog."

"You're never gonna let me live that comment down, are you?" Daniel was smiling.

"I guess not." Lexie liked the intimacy of an inside joke. "So, what animal are you?"

"Hmmm . . ." Daniel leaned forward as if to make sure Lexie had clicked into his eyes before he spoke. "You'll have to tell me after you've gotten to know me very, very well."

"You think I'm going to get to know you very, very well?" She patted the Klonopin in her skirt pocket and looked away for one second as she thought of Amy. If Amy could have a conversation like this, could have feelings like this toward a stranger without being pummeled by anxiety, so could she. Lexie dared herself to look back.

"Yes. Absolutely." Daniel's barely blinked.

The waitress approached. When Daniel turned to give their order (Frito pie and Perrier) Lexie instantly missed the way it felt to have him looking at her. The waitress left, and Daniel turned back to Lexie and stared.

"What?" Lexie asked.

"Last night I lay awake for hours thinking about you."

"Why would you do that?" Lexie imagined herself telling Amy she had said that and Amy laughing at what a flirting failure Lexie was.

"Because there's something about you—something special pulling me toward you in this unstoppable way. The first time I saw you, I craved your body with the hunger of a starving man in a Turkish prison. It felt like you were . . . like you *are*—"

"A hamburger?" Lexie said, nervously, and Daniel laughed.

"No. You're not ground meat—"

"All wormy and bright with that pink dye." It was anxious prattle. Lexie couldn't stop and look at what he'd said for two reasons: First, it was somewhat corny, overblown, and odd. And second, she didn't want to know that his crush on her was as bad as hers on him.

Because then, maybe, one of them would have to do something about it.

"You aren't food. But you're feeding me something I didn't realize I needed until I met you," Daniel said.

"But you don't even *know* me. You don't know my middle name, or what my feet look like, or how much face cream I put on every night before bed, or if my pits smell at the end of the work-day." Lexie kept deodorant in her purse because she believed that her pits stunk at the end of the workday.

"You've got it all wrong," Daniel said, "I know that your pits smell great. You have the face of a woman with flowery pits."

Lexie laughed. Amy was right, she'd laugh at anything that came out of Daniel Waite's mouth. "What if I have ugly feet?" In fact, her feet were the only part of her body that Lexie openly ad-mitted were gorgeous.

"You're right, I have no idea what your feet look like or if you have a birthmark or whether or not you floss your teeth. But you have to admit there was an undeniable connection when we met. It was powerful, and surprising, and I didn't ask for it, it happened on its own. And I know you're engaged. I know this is going no-where. I'll never try to persuade you to be unfaithful. But I want to be around you as much as you'll allow because there's something magical about you. You make me feel great."

"Oh, well, OK." Lexie laughed nervously. Maybe she should take the Klonopin and normalize her behavior.

"Listen. I promise, I won't bring this up again. Especially not after you're married." Daniel reached across the table and put his sprawling hand on top of Lexie's. She looked down and thought of a starfish covering a rock. "You can trust me."

This matter-of-fact declaration, and his insistence that he wouldn't pursue her, made Daniel even more compelling. Lexie felt almost ill with desire.

THEY AGREED TO NOT TALK ABOUT THE ATTRACTION AGAIN. (LEXIE didn't confess to being attracted to Daniel, but it appeared to have been assumed.) Instead, the conversation was steered once again to their childhoods.

Lexie told Daniel about Swallow at the Hollow and Heidi Pies; the drinking, the cigarettes, and the pot; the burn holes in the couch; and her mother's current boyfriend who, Mitzy had told her, showed up on their first date riding a bike and carrying a half-full bottle of wine in a backpack.

"So, other than your father providing the seed and your mother giving birth to you, what did your parents do for you? I mean, did they buy you food and underwear at least?" Daniel was getting angry on Lexie's behalf. Like they had wronged *him* with their unparenting.

"Uh, well . . ." Lexie never had nice underwear growing up. And she wore bras by the year: Her eighth-grade bra. Her ninth-grade bra. Her tenth-grade bra, etc. By the time each school year was ending, the underwire half-moon had shifted out of its seam pocket. Why even call it a wire? It was far thicker than anything that could be called wire: a flat, metal prong that, when uncovered, would stab her in the side of the breast until she went into a bathroom, lifted up her shirt, and fed it back into place. Lexie did have more than one pair of underwear as a kid, but none of them were fresh-looking. Once, as Lexie was changing in the locker room after gym in eighth grade, Kim Carnesale looked at her and said, "Are those granny panties actually hand-me-downs from your grandmother?" Lexie had laughed, painfully, along with Kim and the other girls nearby—most of them from the drill team—the blond girls, the ones with thick-skinned tan legs that you thought were panty hose until you got close enough to see it was flesh. Lexie didn't own nice panties to replace the ones she'd been shamed about. And she had no money to buy new panties (her babysitting money was used to buy school lunches) so for the rest of the year Lexie sat on the bench when she changed. With her jeans draped across her lap, she'd shimmy out of her gym shorts, then slip on her pants before anyone could see what was what.

"I had raggedy, ridiculous underwear," Lexie said. "We were poor. Underwear wasn't a priority."

"I know it would be inappropriate, but I want to buy you a hundred pairs of beautiful underwear." Daniel said this with only the slightest hint of a smile. He appeared serious.

"But I have totally sexy underwear now. That's the great thing about being a grown-up—you're in charge of your own underwear." Lexie regretted telling Daniel about her bad underwear. It was something Peter didn't know and now there was an imbalance in intimacy. And yet she felt an irrepressible urge to reveal even more private details about herself. It occurred to her that she'd gone completely mad.

6

THE AGREEMENT WAS THIS: ONE KISS. ONE LAST KISS FROM ONE man before Lexie got married and never kissed another man besides Peter in her life. And now they were in an elegant room at the Inn on the Lake (Daniel had already secured the room, he told Lexie, as he didn't want to deal with rush-hour traffic into Boston where his condo was, and he didn't want to deal with his soon-to-be-ex-wife at the lake house) and Lexie was completely naked. How she got from one kiss to naked was both mystifying and understandable. It was like saying you were going to take only one spoonful of chocolate mousse when mousse is your favorite dessert and you think you need to diet.

Lexie knew she sounded like a middle schooler—the only words she'd uttered in the last forty-five minutes were *oh my god* and *oh my god*. Currently, Daniel's face was between Lexie's legs in what Amy called "the signature move of a man in his fifties." Amy, who had dated many men in their fifties, found that every single one of them was ready, willing, and skilled at oral sex. "Maybe it's a way to compensate for a dick that isn't as hard as it used to be," Amy had wondered aloud one day. But Lexie had felt what was going on down there with Daniel and it didn't feel much less solid than what she'd experienced with Peter.

"You know I won't have sex with you," Lexie said.

Daniel came up for air. His face was dewy and damp, even with the haze of whiskers. "Isn't that what we're doing?" He winked.

"I mean intercourse."

"Okay." Daniel spoke as if he had never intended to go that far. Lexie felt embarrassed.

"I mean, were you going to try that?"

"Try that?" Daniel remained poised between her legs. He stuck one finger on the essential spot and flicked a little as they spoke.

"Intercourse." Lexie could barely get the word out, as the finger continued the work the tongue had started.

"We're two adults here. I wasn't going to *try* anything. Whatever we do is up to us together." Daniel removed his hand and waited for Lexie to look at his face.

"Oh, right." Lexie laughed, embarrassed. "I've only been with three people."

"Including me? So only your fiancé and someone else?"

"Not including you. So you're the fourth man who has seen my open vagina."

Daniel leaned down like he was looking through a speculum. He brought his head up again. "Well, I feel very sorry for the billions of men and women on the planet who have never, and probably will never, get to see a sight as lovely as this."

Lexie laughed. "How many have you seen?"

"Vaginas?" Daniel scooted up and pulled Lexie's body into his, suctioning them together.

"Yeah, how many people have you been with?"

"I'm fifty-three and I've been married for twenty years."

"Uh-huh."

"I first had sex when I was sixteen. So, between sixteen and thirty-one when I met my wife . . . I don't know. Maybe thirty people?"

"Am I your first affair?"

"I've never had an affair. We're separated. But yes, yours is the first vagina I've seen since I laid eyes on my wife's."

"How's your wife's compared to mine?" Lexie wasn't feeling competitive. She wanted to know what to look forward to, or dread. Would her labia be a mess of flappy, sea-creature wings when she hit fifty?

"Hers is fine. The thing about vaginas is this: Unless there's a strange smell, or a strange sound, they're all wonderful."

"So that thing you said about feeling sorry for all the people who wouldn't meet mine—"

"Yours is especially wonderful." Daniel kissed her. His mouth smelled oatmeally and tasted a little tangy.

The kissing led to more sliding around and suddenly Daniel had sliced inside Lexie. She jerked back, unlocking their two parts.

"You okay?" Daniel turned Lexie's face toward his and stared into her eyes.

"What about STDs? We haven't done a panel!" Could she get something from that moment?

"I haven't been with anyone but my wife in more than two decades. And I can guarantee my wife hasn't been with anyone else."

"How do you know?"

"Jen is gorgeous and smart, but she has no interest in sex. She hit menopause two years ago and that was it for her."

"Well, what if she fooled around before?"

"Believe me. I know my wife."

"You think there is no way on earth she's had sex with anyone but you in twenty years?"

"Twenty-two years. I'd bet my son's life on it. And I know absolutely that I haven't had sex with anyone else in twenty-two years."

"So why are you so calm?" Was he lying? Lexie felt the shallow water of nausea stir in her stomach. Had she been completely bamboozled?

"Calm?"

"This isn't freaking you out? I mean, for twenty-two years, you've been having sex with the same woman, the same naked body, the same vagina, the same breasts, the same mouth, night after night after night. And now you're here with me. And you're not totally freaking out?"

"I don't freak out. I'm not a freak-out guy." Daniel pulled Lexie in tighter and hugged her until she softened. He kissed her, sweetly, on the lips. The eyes. The nose. The chin.

Lexie let herself breathe deeply. She looked over at her skirt on the chair. She could do this without the Klonopin in the skirt pocket. She could relax. "Well, even if you don't have an STD, we need birth control."

"I was snipped. Not a problem."

"Snipped?" This was the first time fifty-three seemed old.

How odd that Daniel was over and done with all the child-rearing stuff that hadn't even yet begun for Lexie.

"Clamped. One of those reversible ones. You know, in case." Daniel slid himself in between Lexie's legs and rubbed back and forth like he was playing the violin.

"They can do that?" Lexie was growing breathless.

"Yes. You okay if I go back in?"

"You swear you don't have an STD? I've never done it without doing a full panel beforehand." Whatever resistance she had was being methodically rubbed away.

"You are a beautiful nutball. Don't you trust me?"

"Mmm, I keep flipping back and forth with the trust." She could barely keep her eyes open.

"I trust you." Daniel kissed her.

"OK. I trust you, too." Lexie was whispering. "I don't know why. But I do."

THE SEX WAS INCREDIBLE. OTHERWORLDLY. TANTRIC. OKAY, NOT tantric. But maybe mystical. Lexie had never before known sex like this existed. She thought of case studies she'd read of crack addicts, how the first time they did the drug their brains lit up so intensely and in such a novel and spirit-altering way that all they wanted from then on was more crack. Now something deep inside of Lexie, a place she hadn't known existed, was lit with an addiction-like intensity. And this internal light was entirely connected to the idea and the physical being of Daniel Waite.

Guiltily, Lexie thought about Peter—dear, sweet, Peter. Sex with Peter was good, she wouldn't have agreed to marry him if that weren't the case. Peter was a man with skills. He was strong. He never made demands, asked for very little, and gave a lot. But their sex had never had the intensity of what had happened with Daniel. There had never been the tsunami of emotion that had almost drowned Lexie with sensation. And there had never been this postcoital dreaminess. It was a feeling Lexie couldn't help but equate with the immaculate contentedness one feels when slightly drunk, after a perfect meal, with the very best company.

Lexie and Daniel lay side by side holding hands. Lexie looked around the room. It was the most luxurious room she had ever been in. She didn't realize the people of Ruxton, Massachusetts, would know enough to put such thick, soft linens on a bed, or to place a massive bouquet of yellow flowers near the window on a table that appeared to have no other purpose than to hold flowers.

Lexie pulled the sheet up around herself while strategically letting one breast fall out to the side. She kicked out the opposite leg: symmetry, visual balance. Daniel rolled to his stomach and kissed the nipple of the exposed breast. He turned his face up toward hers and they kissed. Lexie's head exploded as if it were a first kiss, though they'd been at it for two and a half hours.

"We're both in transition," Lexie said, when Daniel pulled away from the kiss.

"How's that?" Daniel dropped his cheek onto the pillow and stared at her. No one had ever stared at Lexie the way he did. Certainly not her parents. And not even Peter, who usually fell fast asleep postorgasm, and who shut his eyes so continually during sex that Lexie imagined he was listening to a symphony in his head and he needed to eliminate one of his senses in order to properly hear it.

"I'm on my way into a marriage and you're on your way out of one," Lexie clarified.

"Your situation, however, is much better than mine. You, my dear, can cleanly extricate yourself. There are no children. I'm assuming whatever assets you have can be easily divided. Have you merged your bank accounts yet?"

"No." Lexie whispered as if Peter might overhear this conversation. Even after all these days thinking about Daniel, and thinking about sex with Daniel, Lexie had never once thought about leaving Peter. Until now. Until Daniel planted the idea as if it were a full-blown possibility.

"So, all you have to do is step aside and it's over," Daniel went on. "No blood on the carpet. No bodies strewn in the hall."

"Are you leaving behind blood and bodies?"

"Well, a twenty-year marriage certainly isn't bloodless. And a kid, even if he's about to go off to college, is still a body."

Lexie had almost forgotten about Ethan. The thing, person, human she and Daniel had intended to discuss the first time they met. The topic on the slate for today's Frito Friday meeting. "Why is it again, that you don't want to tell Ethan about the separation?"

"His mother doesn't want anything to distract him from his last year at Ruxton, applying to colleges, enjoying senior year. You know."

"That's very generous of you two." Lexie's own parents never suppressed their desires or altered their behavior because there was a child in the house. The day Lexie packed to move into Betsy Simms's house, Mitzy was having sex with her new boyfriend in the bedroom. With the door open.

"MOM!" Lexie had said, and she'd turned her head and pulled the door shut.

"For godsakes you've been watching R-rated movies since you were five!" Mitzy had shouted through the closed door.

"I think Jen's coddling him a little," Daniel said. "But I'm letting her decide how things roll with Ethan. Soon enough it will be official and, hopefully, he'll be able to handle it."

"Are you sad about it?"

"Sad?"

"Yeah. About the end of the family. The end of your relationship with your wife."

"If we'd done it quickly, like an amputation, I might have been sad. But this separation has been like a long, slow gnawing off of a limb. I'll be relieved when it's completely over."

"And all this time you've never seen anyone else?"

"Until I saw you, there was no one worth seeing." Daniel leaned in and kissed her once more. Lexie felt liquid and boneless.

Her phone buzzed.

Lexie scrambled off the bed, taking the sheet with her. She wasn't confident enough to do the naked walk across the room. The tail of the sheet caught on Lexie's foot and she started to stumble but turned the fall into what she hoped would be taken as a deliberate plummet into the quilted chair by the window. She reached into her purse, on the floor, and pulled out her cell phone. It was Peter.

Lexie picked up. "Hey babe." Blood rushed into her ears. The sound was magnified, as if she were underwater.

Naked Daniel watched Lexie, carefully, calmly. She tightened the sheet around herself. How was it that a man could be more than half a century old and still have a body as solid as wood, carved in all the right places, nothing dangling, folding, puckering, or crimping?

"Where are you? I thought you'd be home hours ago." Peter was chewing as he spoke. Lexie clamped the phone against her shoulder, lifted her butt, and pulled out her bra. She slipped the bra over her arms so that it hung, unhooked, against her chest.

"I forgot I have dinner duty tonight because last Friday didn't count." Lexie stared back at Daniel. She wanted to remain in his world, this bed, his arms. She didn't want to detach and climb into the cargo van, drive down the road for dinner with the students, followed by a drive across the nearly-empty Massachusetts freeway to the trail of wood shavings that usually started around the front door—dropped from the bottoms of Peter's boots—as if she and Peter were hamsters living in a cedar-bed cage.

"Oh, man! I was going to surprise you with a Crock-Pot dinner! I put all those old vegetables and some broth in there today around noon . . ." Each word was followed by a cracking chomp.

"That's so sweet." Lexie wasn't listening. She took inventory of her clothing: Her bra was loose across her breasts; she was sitting on her skirt; her blouse was in a heap at her feet. Where were her panties?

"Well, I guess it wasn't a true broth. I used boullion cubes. Have you ever tasted one of those things? If you swallowed one whole the salt would probably kill you. It would kill an infant, that's for sure . . ." Peter worked alone all day. Sometimes he didn't talk to anyone until Lexie got home. He claimed he didn't need much human interaction, but around dinnertime, he often burst

74

forth with a stream-of-consciousness narrative that always made Lexie think he was wrong about his needs.

Lexie looked at her watch. She was due at Ruxton in fifteen minutes. Daniel continued to stare at her. How would she manage to put on the rest of her clothes without bending her body in any way that might reveal a bulge of dimpled flesh, a fold in her belly, a glimpse of her ass from an unflattering wide angle?

". . . and I programmed a movie for us tonight, that French new wave thing that you'd said you wanted to watch—"

"What are you eating?" Lexie asked. Using her toes, she plucked the blouse off the floor, lifted it to her hand, and placed it in her lap.

"What am I eating?"

With the sheet doubled around her lower half, Lexie hooked her bra and then put on and buttoned the blouse, all while managing the phone. "You're chomping." Lexie scanned the floor for her panties.

"Carrots. I put some in the pot for you. I also put in . . ."

Daniel shimmied across the bed on his stomach. He flopped one long arm off the edge of the bed and reached for Lexie's foot. He grabbed her big toe and tugged. Like a diver pulling her up to the boat for air. Lexie sent him thought-pangs of love.

"Babe, it all sounds so good, but I've gotta go. I've gotta finish a bunch of work before I show up at the table. Can I call you on my drive home?" Aha! The panties! They were curled like a napping kitten on top of Daniel's suit pants.

"No problem. Love you," Peter said.

"You, too." Lexie clicked the phone shut and turned it completely off so that she wouldn't risk a pocket call while she was with Daniel. She dropped the phone into her purse. "Shit."

"You're okay," Daniel said soothingly. "It's all going to be okay."

"What am I going to do?" Lexie reached under herself, pulled out the skirt and slipped it on beneath the sheet.

"You don't need to do anything."

Lexie stood and let the sheet drop to the ground. "I cheated on my fiancé." Her voice quivered. She patted her skirt pocket and felt for the Klonopin. She would take it only if she thought she was going to pass out.

"Do you regret it?"

"No." Lexie looked at Daniel. "I want to do it again."

"Don't think about it. Go to school. Eat dinner. Go home and don't question your relationship."

"Don't question my relationship? Doesn't this whole thing put it into question?" Lexie scanned the room. She went to where her panties were and instead of slipping them on, she discreetly tucked them into Daniel's pants' pocket. How she could be seductive and playful while simultaneously guilty and panicked was a mystery to her. It was as if she existed in two consciousnesses at once. "I mean, this was huge for me. Wasn't it huge for you?"

"Yeah, it was." Daniel almost sounded hurt, or insulted that Lexie might think it wasn't a big deal for him. "You're the first woman I've been with since my wife. It's monumental. But you're engaged and I'm not going to get my hopes up."

"For a New England boy you sure have some California mellow in you." Lexie tucked in her blouse and then dropped to her knees and flipped up the bed skirt, looking for her boots. One of them was there. She sat on the ground, pulled out the knee-high stocking and put it on inside out before tugging on the boot. She got up and tottered around the room, lopsided, as she looked for the other boot.

"I'm rational. Panic never does any good for anyone." Daniel continued to watch Lexie.

"Then why does panic exist?" Lexie looked behind the chair, under Daniel's clothes. She opened the minibar as if her boot might be in there.

"Originally, to save you from the saber-toothed tiger. But in the modern world it eliminates the rational. It fucks with you." Daniel lifted his arm and bobbed his pointer finger up and down as he directed Lexie toward the threshold into the bathroom where the other boot lay.

"Panic fucks with me frequently." Lexie hobbled to the boot.

"The only thing that should be fucking you is me." Daniel flipped his hand so his thick, square-tipped finger was pointing at himself. Lexie slipped on her other stocking and boot. She went to the bed and kissed Daniel one last time. He smelled so good she wanted to gather the scent in her fist and carry it around with her.

LEXIE DROVE THE VAN WITH THE WINDOW ALL THE WAY DOWN AND the fall chill needling her face. Outside it looked like someone had turned down the lights, everything was a black-and-white photo. But inside the van, inside her body, Lexie felt as if she were radiating pink and red. Different scenes from the afternoon replayed in her head. Like jumping songs on a great album, the sequence in which she saw the scenes didn't matter. It was all good.

Once she was parked at school, Lexie brushed her hair, put on lipstick, and checked her face in the rearview mirror. Her pupils were the size of pencil erasers; she was smiling at herself. Lexie got out and circled the van to check the locks, and then she ran—

as fast as she could in the high-heeled boots—toward the dining hall. She got there as Don McClear approached the podium for evening prayer. Although Ruxton wasn't a Christian school, it had been founded over two hundred years ago and some traditions (a chapel on campus, prayer before dinner, a tie worn to classes, and a jacket worn in the dining hall) had never been dropped.

Lexie quietly wove through the tables to her assigned seat. There were seven students at her table, four girls and three boys. The students would eat together for three weeks before being broken apart and reassembled into a different group. The groups rotated tables every night.

One of the more entertaining students, Desi Moreno, was at Lexie's table. His family was from Colombia and Desi had once told Lexie that they had bodyguards, armed men at the gates of their compound, and a mirrored stick was passed under the family cars before anyone turned an ignition key. Lexie usually loved dinner conversation with Desi Moreno. But tonight, even with Desi at her table, Lexie couldn't shift into the head space required for conversation with seven teenagers.

"Amen," the collective voices said. Lexie had forgotten they were praying. She added her amen a second too late. The students seated on either side of the teachers, in Lexie's case Craydon Covington (one of many girls with an asexual name that Lexie assumed was her mother's maiden name, or a family name that had been passed down for five hundred years) and Steffi Levine, rose to gather the serving platters. While waiting for the food to arrive, the other kids chatted about the usual: sports, boys, girls, teachers, classes, homework, and whatever dumb-ass behavior someone did that cracked them up.

Craydon and Steffi returned quickly with a platter of sliced turkey and a pan of eggplant Parmesan. They went back to the serving station and returned again with a bowl of peas, a bowl of mashed potatoes, a basket of rolls, and a green salad. Lunch at Ruxton was buffet, but dinner was served family-style, using painted china, real silver, and cloth napkins, with nothing indicating that the pan of eggplant was one of many, or that the mashed potatoes had been made in an industrial mixer big enough to stir up a Portuguese water dog.

"I had a meeting off-campus," Lexie said, once everyone had served themselves. There was a pitcher of water and a pitcher of milk on the table. Craydon and Steffi were filling glasses as requested.

"Anything exciting we should know about?" Desi asked.

"No. But I came directly here from the meeting so I didn't consult the topic directory. Does anyone know what's on the list for tonight?" Many teachers told their students in the last-period class what that evening's dinner topic would be.

"I only remember the stuff we've discussed already," Steffi said. "Is Violence Necessary? What Does It Mean to Know Thyself? . . ."

The students rattled off everything they'd covered. Lexie wondered how Don McClear came up with these lists. She imagined him spending insomniac summer nights reading Plato, Descartes, Berkeley, and Locke with a notebook and pen in hand, writing down ideas until he'd come up with enough to cover dinner every single night during the school year (except Saturday when there was no formal dinner and the kids were invited to go to the dining hall anytime within a two-hour window and serve themselves from what was laid out on the buffet).

"We could ask someone at another table," Desi pointed out.

"Nah," Lexie said. "That would be too easy."

"We could sit here silently, listen to the other tables and try to guess what the topic is," Emily Fleming said.

"That would be fun," Lexie said, although she worried that if they were to sit there in silence with little to distract them, the students would read the micro-emotions on her face and quickly realize she'd had the most mind-blowing sex of her life. Sex that she was worried might leak out of her and leave a spot on her skirt. Lexie crossed her legs tightly.

"We could make up our own topic," Desi said.

"Let's do that," Lexie said. "But you can't tell anyone, this has to be our secret."

"Do we vote on one? Or . . ." Ellie Goodrich asked.

"Everyone say your ideas and we'll all agree on the best one. But do this: Pick a subject that reaches beyond what's usually on that list. Go deeper or wider. Be imaginative." Lexie was buying time. She could barely hold herself in her seat, let alone eat peas and potatoes. She wanted to scream, rush back to the Inn on the Lake, rip off her clothes, and dive into bed with Daniel Waite.

While the students were throwing out ideas, Lexie scanned the room for Ethan. There he was, a few yards away, at Delton McGarry's table. Delton was the dean of academics, a poindexter with a beautiful, sexy wife. They were visually mismatched and this led Lexie to believe that they had a wild sex life, pulling in a third (or fourth!). Or maybe implementing complicated tools and appliances. It was hard to trust such a proper bow-tie-wearing exterior.

Ethan was sitting up straight while listening to Delton drone on. Lexie knew from the students that there was nothing worse than a teacher dominating the dinner conversation, treating the topic of the night as a lecture. And of those who did lecture at dinner, Delton McGarry was the most tedious, pedantic, and, usually, condescending.

Ethan's head dropped to one side. Lexie saw his eyes wander. He had the same beautiful angled jaw as his father. And the same coloring: black hair, blue eyes, white teeth trapped in a rectangle-on-side smile. Black Irish. Lexie wanted to text Daniel that very minute to find out if they were Irish. Unfortunately, she'd have to wait until she'd left the no-cell-phone zone of the dining hall.

The kids had chosen their topic: Is there a moral imperative for humans to mate for life? If so, why? If not, why not?

"That's a good one," Lexie said. "Who wants to start?"

Ellie raised her hand. Before she could speak, Craydon started talking. Lexie didn't stop her, but she should have. She should have saved Ellie from being pushed to the back of the conversation. But that simple act alone was currently too much for her. Lexie casually folded her hand across her nose and mouth; she was smelling him. Daniel. The musty scent of intimacy.

LEXIE TOOK THE SLIGHTLY LONGER ROUTE HOME SO SHE COULD stop—for one minute—at the Inn on the Lake.

Daniel's car wasn't in the lot. Lexie killed the engine and sat, parked in the space where his Mercedes had been this afternoon. He was probably out to dinner, Lexie decided. An eight o'clock reservation somewhere nice, or as nice as you could get within twenty-five minutes of Ruxton. People like Daniel didn't eat dinner before eight. They didn't finish work until at least seven thirty. They were in their own time zone.

Lexie's phone rang. She yanked it out of her purse, her heart thumping. When she saw it was Peter, she dropped the phone on the passenger seat, started the engine, and pulled back out on the road.

At home, Lexie parked on the long, uphill driveway. She footed down the parking brake. Eventually, Lexie opened the car door. She sat for a minute with her legs hanging off the seat toward the ground. Eventually, she stepped out and walked into the house. It wasn't until she had closed the front door behind herself that she realized she hadn't locked the van. It was as if she were a new person. Someone who didn't spend half her mental time in a movie theater wanting to run outside to double-check that she'd locked the car's doors. Someone who didn't return home, only seconds after leaving, to be sure the front door was locked. Someone who'd never need a Klonopin.

"Hey babe." Peter came right over to Lexie and kissed her on the mouth. She wondered if she tasted like Daniel.

"How was the Crock-Pot soup?"

"Awful. The vegetables were all bitter and dangly. I threw it away and ate the leftover spaghetti. But I made you dessert in the Crock-Pot." He leaned in for another kiss. Lexie ducked away.

"I've gotta take a shower."

"Take a quick one. You're going to love this dessert. I threw a bunch of blueberries, oatmeal, and brown sugar in there—it tastes great."

In the shower, Lexie thought about what had gone down in

the hotel room and quickly masturbated. Afterward, she washed herself inside and out, even opening her mouth toward the needle-fine spray and cleaning her throat, her teeth, the roof of her mouth. Lexie toweled off, wrapped her hair, and put on old blue flannel pajamas. She didn't want to look sexy. It had been five nights since she and Peter had had sex. That was about their limit, so she'd have to come up with a good excuse.

At the kitchen table, Lexie spooned the blueberry gunk in her mouth while smiling falsely at Peter. "Delicious."

Peter didn't hear. He was leaning over his bowl, scraping the last blueberry smears from the bottom and rapidly feeding himself. "Guitar lesson?" he asked.

"That'd be great." A guitar lesson was as appealing as a meeting led by Janet Irwin. Lexie looked at the spoon in her hand and saw she was shaking. "But no pick work, okay? Only chords."

7

AMY'S 'BAMA ACCENT WAS OUT IN FULL FORCE. "HONEY, YOU gotta be shittin' me!" She fell into her rolling chair.

Lexie had run to the infirmary straight from her morning class. She had wanted to call Amy all weekend, but there was never a second when Peter wasn't within five feet of her. And she didn't want to hide in the bathroom with the faucet running, or run to the front yard while Peter was in the shower. She knew the confession required a conversation she wasn't willing to have whispering in a corner.

Lexie hopped up onto one of the sickbeds. "Nope. I'm not shittin' you." Lexie was grinning. She felt great: like her hair had grown and thickened and her skin had smoothed out into glittering, waxy taffy. The physical manifestation of joy.

"So you did it without an STD panel?!"

"Yup. And I went to bed the last three nights without triple-checking to see if the front door was locked." Lexie could not stop smiling. She had smiled all through Health and Sexuality class as they talked about the endocrine system. So much so that Phillipa Graves had said, "Miss James, you totally love the endocrine system, don't you?"

"I hardly recognize you now." Amy looked up at Lexie. "You did use a condom, though, right?"

"Nope." Lexie threw her hair over her shoulder and lay on her stomach, facing Amy, her feet kicked up behind her. She was wearing the same high, sleek boots. They reminded her of Daniel. And they made her feel sexy.

"Are you kidding?"

"It's the new me!"

"Listen, Miss James—our revered Health and Sexuality teacher—I'm all for you getting over your door-locking and STD panel problems, but you've gotta hold on to a little fear of"—Amy opened the bottom drawer of her desk where she stored cases of condoms, pulled one out, and threw it at Lexie—"herpes, at least!"

Lexie ducked as the condom bounced off her head and landed on her back. "I'm the first woman he's been with in twenty-two years."

"He could still have crusty sores on his dick and you could still get pregnant." Amy crossed her arms as if to further make her point.

"He's fixed."

"So he says."

"I trust him. You would, too, if you met him." Lexie reached back and took the condom. She played with it, squishing it around inside the wrapper. It reminded her vaguely of sliding testicles around a ball sack.

"He told you this when you were naked or clothed?"

JESSICA ANYA BLAU

"Mmmm, naked I think."

"Honey, *I love you* and *bullshit* both have eight letters and there ain't a man on earth who doesn't confuse the two when he's talkin' to a nekked woman."

Lexie laughed. "Seriously, Amy. This guy is not a bullshitter."

"So you're telling me he's a brilliant, successful, good-looking man with a working dick, and you're his first affair?"

"It's not an affair. They're separated."

"Separated? That's not in Ethan's file."

"They haven't notified the school—they haven't told Ethan yet . . . I mean, he hasn't entirely moved out of the house—"

Amy threw her head back. "Then he's *not* separated! Jesus, Lexie!"

"I'm telling you, this guy *is it*. Daniel is . . . he has completely thrown me for a loop." Lexie felt a thrill in thinking about him— in saying his name.

"Well, before you call off that marriage and break a good man's heart, you better get to know this gentleman real good, so that you understand exactly what you're changing it up for."

"Did I say I was going to leave Peter?"

"You didn't, but you might as well have."

"Ach! Why did I have to meet Daniel at this time in my life?!" Lexie tossed the condom at Amy.

Amy caught it and returned it to the drawer. "Not to drop the subject, but I have to tell you that The Prince—who is more responsible than you, I must point out—stopped in for condoms."

"No way!" The Prince was Abioye Balewa, an African royal with impeccable manners, a mind beyond that of most of his teachers, and a sense of propriety that prevented him from removing his tie even in the library late at night when everyone else had abandoned the dress code. "Who's he having sex with?"

"Daisy. Can you believe it?"

"Daisy Whippet or Daisy Rhodes?"

"Whippet! You think Daisy Rhodes would have sex?"

"You can never tell. Who would have thought The Prince would be doing it? I mean, how's she going to get his tie off?"

"He probably wears it."

"Why didn't he come to me?" Lexie was jealous. The students, if they were willing to endure the required abstinence/STD/mutual consent talk, could obtain condoms from either Lexie or Amy.

"He couldn't come to you. It was Frito Friday, hon. Y'all were getting your freak on."

"How'd he respond to the talk?"

"It was almost hilarious. He sat up very straight on the bed you're on. He pulled out a notepad. And he took notes."

"Amazing."

"And at one point he said, 'Does it ever hurt for the boy the first time? Or does it only hurt for the girl?'"

"That's so great! What'd you say?"

Before Amy could answer, Lexie's phone buzzed. She jumped off the table and went to her purse on Amy's desk. As the phone continued to buzz, Lexie frantically unpacked her purse, laying wallet, lipstick, a compact, hand lotion, a hairbrush, and a small cosmetic bag on the desk. Amy rolled the chair back, crossed her legs and arms, and watched. Finally, Lexie pulled out the phone. She held it in front of herself and smiled. There were four texts from Daniel:

Miss you.

I'm fingering your panties in my pocket.

Going to carry them with me every day.

Until I see you again and you give me a new pair. Xxx

"Oh, this boy's got you knocked catawampus," Amy groaned. "What's he saying?"

"He misses me." Lexie held the phone high and thumbed out a quick text. *Miss you, too! With Amy. I'll text later. Xxxxxx!*

"Why are you texting with the phone up above your head like that?"

Amy's voice brought Lexie back to where she was. "Huh?"

"What the hell you doin'?" Amy held her hands up above her head and mimed texting.

"Oh, I read this face yoga article that said we're all going to get these ugly, wrinkly necks from having our heads pulled in and down when we text, so—" Lexie shrugged. Amy laughed.

"Were you texting like that all weekend?"

"No, I keep forgetting. But every so often I remember and I lift the phone."

"I meant were you texting with Daniel all weekend."

"Oh. Not in front of Peter. And only a couple times." Lexie had been lost in a thick fog all weekend. She was trapped in two existences, her mind and body never in the same place: life as oneself and one's ghost.

BEFORE STARTING UP THE VAN, LEXIE READ THROUGH DANIEL'S texts for the last time. Afterward, she brushed her thumb across Daniel's name and deleted everything.

The drive was lazy and lonely; it was nothing like driving in California. There, the freeway felt like a battlefield: Your fists sweated as you gripped the steering wheel, and your brain clicked through checkpoints like you were crossing a border into unknown terrain. And there were enemies all around you: the car changing lanes beside you, the car stopping short in front of you, the car pulled onto the shoulder with the hazards on, the cop car cruising behind you, the exit five lanes over that you have about thirty seconds to get to if you can make it past the eighty cars between you and the ramp. In mountainous Western Massachusetts it was a whole different game. There was a road. You were in a car. And you drove that road straight until you got off on your exit.

That night, Peter could do no right. The Saab wasn't fixed because the part that was needed wasn't manufactured any longer. And they couldn't afford a new car because the wedding was so expensive. In addition to the normal expenditures, they needed to pay for a hotel room for the week before the wedding for Mitzy, unless they wanted her staying in their house, which they did not.

When Lexie suggested that Peter sell more guitars to help pay the bills, Peter said he'd sold too many guitars, he couldn't make all the ones he promised, and he was having a hard time collecting the money for the ones he'd made already. This infuriated Lexie. How could he expect to support a family if he couldn't collect the money he was owed? What would he do when she got pregnant?

"Babe, I'll take care of it." Peter said this while looking at Lexie in the bathroom mirror. He was brushing his teeth and Lexie was flossing. Her engagement ring sat on the counter in a small puddle. The past few days Lexie had gone from feeling swoony and soft when she looked at the ring to feeling irritated and huffy when she looked at it. She imagined brushing it into the sink with the water running so it would wash down the drain.

"How exactly will you take care of it?" Lexie asked.

"We'll use the money in the honeymoon account."

"What about the honeymoon?" It was such an antiquated idea, but Lexie wanted one. She'd always wanted one. Her parents had never even married and, therefore, never had a honeymoon. But Mr. and Mrs. Simms had more than once spoken of their honeymoon in Niagara Falls. They stayed in the honeymoon suite of a high-rise hotel on the Canadian side of the water.

"We'll plan something simpler. Something superromantic." They hadn't paid for anything yet, but Lexie had bookmarked on her computer resorts in the Caribbean, Florida, and South Carolina.

Lexie let the floss drop midtooth. The two ends of the string hung down the sides of her chin like skinny tusks. "Simple but superromantic?" The honeymoon savings was what Lexie had put away once she'd moved in with Peter and stopped paying rent. Ultimately, it was up to her to decide how to spend that money. "Like, Niagara Falls?" For all she knew Niagara Falls had turned into a sewage sinkhole since the Simmses had visited. But anything would be better than sitting at home with the sawdust.

Peter spit out his toothpaste. He rinsed his mouth. "If that's what you want, that's what you'll get." He kissed Lexie, poking his tongue in her mouth, floss intact. She tried to gently push him away. He pursued the kiss further. "Stop it. You're being gross!" She shoved him away.

"I was only trying to have fun." It was rare for Peter to get his feelings hurt like this. When he left the room, he deliberately turned out the bathroom light.

Lexie finished flossing in the dark. Would Daniel kiss her with floss in his mouth? She decided that indeed he would. But it would be fun. Lexie would laugh. She'd kiss him back. The urge to text Daniel and tell him that she'd kiss him with floss in her mouth (or floss in his mouth!) propelled Lexie downstairs to the kitchen where her purse and phone were sitting on the counter. There were two texts from Amy.

Text or call ASAP.

Text or call tonight!

Lexie remained standing. She held the phone up high and texted.

What's up? Should I call?

Is Peter home?

Yes. He's upstairs.

Talked to Janet Irwin after dinner tonight. Subject of fund-raising came up. I mentioned D.W. and she went off about him and his WIFE and a recent cocktail party at THEIR house, yadda yadda. From everything she said it is clear they are ABSOLUTELY NOT SEPARATED. Janet knows about apartment in Boston—he's always had it—McClear and others use it for trips to the city, etc. DANIEL WAITE LIED TO YOU!

Lexie dropped into the kitchen chair. It felt like there was steel wool in her lungs. She reread the text, letting her head drop toward her lap.

Are you certain?

YES!

Lexie breathed through the scratching in her chest. She didn't want to think about this, she didn't want to feel the crowd of emotions that were banging at her, trying to get in: heartbreak, hurt, shame, regret . . . humiliation!

Lexie reread Amy's message three more times before deleting it. She wrote: *Can't talk about this tonight. Too intense.*

Love you! Amy texted back.

Lexie went to the freezer. She pulled out the ice cream Peter had bought a few days ago, ice cream she had teased him about because it was so full of junk (brownie chunks, broken peanut butter cups, and veins of caramel) that she didn't consider it ice cream. With a fork, Lexie picked through the ice cream, moving aside layers so she could get to the richest, chewyist bits. She forked at the ice cream for so long that the edges melted and she was able to shift entire, glacial slabs of it, turning it upside down in the container so she could pick out the brownie and peanut butter cup that had settled on the bottom. It was the ice cream version of plucking the cardboard-textured marshmallows from a box of Lucky Charms.

When the ice cream had been picked clean, only tattered puffs of vanilla remaining, Lexie returned it to the freezer. What would Peter think when he opened the denuded carton? He'd think she was half nuts. Lexie retrieved the ice cream from the freezer again. She spooned it down the garbage disposal and then she crushed the carton, which she hid under the pile of junk mail in the recycling bin. Lexie hovered over the bin as if she were about to vomit into it.

"Fuck." The grinding in Lexie's chest had been replaced by a bloating in her stomach. Amazing to think she'd been bitchy to

Peter for days, all because of some asshole who had her thinking she'd met the yin to her yang. "Fuck, fuck, fuck, fuckity, fuck-fuck," Lexie whispered.

An hour later, she went up to the bedroom. Peter was in bed, naked as usual, his arms crossed behind his head. He watched Lexie cautiously, as if he were worried he might say the wrong thing and set her off. Her phone buzzed. Lexie pulled it from her pocket and stared at Mitzy's face—crosshatched like elephant skin—on the screen. Lexie had to answer. She'd been so nutzo all weekend she hadn't made her usual call to Mitzy. Also, talking to Mitzy was better than contemplating how dumb she had been falling for Daniel Waite and how shitty she'd acted toward Peter.

"Hey, Mom." Lexie's voice was singularly toned. Flat and thin.

"You know what the worst thing about your father was?" Mitzy often started phone calls as if they were in the middle of a conversation.

"Mmm . . . his beer and cigarette breath?" The horrible ways of Bert were a topic Mitzy liked to revisit. Usually, Lexie only half-listened. She didn't find Bert any more offensive than Mitzy. If Lexie knew where Bert was, she'd certainly talk to him with the same sense of duty she felt when she spoke to her mother every week.

"Nope. And it wasn't the cheatin' either, but something like that." Mitzy made a short breathy pop and Lexie knew she was exhaling the smoke from her menthol Kool.

"Are you going to tell me, or am I supposed to guess?" Lexie undressed to her panties and bra and got in bed. She shifted in close to Peter and put her cold feet under his legs. She'd barely had physical contact with him since the afternoon with Daniel. Peter's legs felt foreign to Lexie, as if she'd forgotten the way his body worked and would have to learn the map of him all over again.

"Well, you're a psychiatrist, you can guess." The sound of ice cubes in a glass punctuated this last sentence. Lexie wondered if her mother had switched from beer to hard liquor. Although, it was probably a Coke.

"I'm not a psychiatrist, Mom, I've told you that many times."

Peter pulled down the covers, crawled to the end of the bed, picked up Lexie's left foot and started massaging. She shut her eyes in relief.

"Yeah, but if I say counselor it sounds like you work at a summer camp or something. Like you're the canoe instructor!" Mitzy snorted and laughed. Lexie couldn't even smile.

"Why can't you say *therapist*?"

"Isn't that an everyday word for psychiatrist?"

"Fine. Psychiatrist. I don't care." Peter looked at Lexie and mimed a laugh. He put down her left foot and picked up her right.

"Okay, so do your psychiatry work and guess what the worst thing about your father was."

"The hair in his ears?"

"What? He never had no hair in his ears!"

"His truck with the cab that always smelled like French fries and gasoline?"

"No! It's a mental thing. It's like a mental torture."

"A mental thing, huh?" Peter stopped rubbing. Lexie gave him a pleading look and he picked up her foot and went at it again.

"Yeah. Mental games, you know?"

"He never made you feel pretty? Or loved? He never rubbed your feet?" Lexie said, and Peter looked up and winked at her. Lexie wanted to weep at his sweetness.

"Nope. Here's what it was: He had these flings with those women, see?"

"Yeah, at the bar." Mitzy had bitched about this regularly over the years. When she was a little kid, Mitzy often screamed at Bert about "dipping his wick" and "forking his tuna." Those metaphors, and others, made young Lexie wonder about all the strange candle-making and food-eating trouble that could befall a bartender. As soon as she was old enough to realize that her mother was hollering at her father about sex, Lexie would turn on the kitchen radio and do the dishes, or simply leave the apartment. Anything to avoid seeing images in her head of Bert doing things she'd rather not associate with the idea of *father*.

"Right. And those flings weren't the worst part. The worst part was that I knew about it and when I said something to him, he acted like I was all crazy and out of control accusing, you know, and he was all normal. You see what I'm saying?"

"I think so." Lexie watched Peter dote on her feet. How could she have wanted more than this? How could she have been so un-grateful?

"He was, like, brainwashing me into thinking that something was wrong with me, when, meanwhile, he's down at that bar sticking his wanger in anything that'll let him get close enough. Now you tell me who the wrong one was?"

"The wrong one?"

"Who was bad? Me or him?"

"I can see how his making you feel like you were the bad one would be its own sort of torture."

"So you get what I'm saying?"

"Yeah." Lexie pulled her foot from Peter and he slid up and lay by her side. She didn't deserve Peter. "I get what you're saying. It's cruel-hearted to do something shitty to someone and then to act as if they're the one who's wronged you."

"Exactly!" Mitzy said.

"It's like the person who's having the affair is trying to build a case against their partner. Like they're trying to gather evidence to support their case, to support their reprehensible actions."

"Yup!"

"And then the adulterer shifts the entire framework through which they now view the relationship and their partner, and that in turn shifts their reality, while the person who's been cheated on is living in the old reality. It's a total mind fuck." And Lexie herself, she thought, was a total mind fucker.

"Now you get me! Now you see why I was so cranky all those years! I was livin' a mind fuck!" Mitzy sounded elated to be understood. Lexie had never before clarified or reiterated her mother's thoughts. She had always believed it was service enough to simply allow Mitzy to talk about this stuff.

"Yeah, you were living a mind fuck." Lexie looked at Peter and a bolt of terror shot through her. What if Peter found out about what she had done? What if Jen Waite found out? God, why wasn't there a rewind and erase button in life?

"Your father was a royal asshole." More clinking ice.

"You can't define someone by a single action. People are more multifaceted than that." Lexie hated that there was a way in which she and Bert were alike. Lust was lust was lust was lust. And it didn't matter if you were screwing a thirty-year-old divorcée on the sticky, beer-soaked bar after closing, or if you were screwing a lawyer in Frette sheets at the Inn of the Lake. At their essential core, the acts were entirely equal.

"Oh, so Miss Psychiatrist is getting all sympathetic for her dad, huh?" Ice clink. Ice clink. Ice clink.

"Mom, I'm sorry he did that to you. Honestly. I am." Lexie looked at Peter when she said this. She needed to apologize to him without letting him know she'd committed a crime against their relationship. Like her father before her, Lexie was a dumb-ass cheater. Which, in her book, was far worse than a simple dumb-ass. Lexie's actions, like Bert's, bordered on cruel.

When she got off the phone, Lexie felt relieved that she wouldn't have to talk to her mother again for another six days. Mitzy's birthday was on Saturday and Lexie would call her first thing, as she always did on her birthday (a necklace had already been ordered and was due to arrive soon). Lexie rolled onto one side and backed herself into Peter. He threw his arms and legs around her. A human blanket. Lexie shut her eyes and tried to release thoughts of both Mitzy and Daniel. She wanted to focus on being there with only Peter.

"I'm sorry I've been so bitchy about the car and everything else," she said.

"You're not bitchy." Peter kissed the top of her head. "You work hard, you're tired, you're entitled to feel a little fed up with things."

Those words made Lexie feel even worse. To compensate for this bad feeling, or maybe to overcome it, Lexie turned so she was facing Peter. She reached down and shook hands with his dick, up down, up down, *so nice to meet you.* Peter responded appropriately. He tugged off Lexie's panties. Lexie opened the drawer in her nightstand and took out a spermicidal film. It was around the same size and texture as a Listerine Breath Strip and Lexie couldn't help but equate her vagina to her mouth each time she inserted one. Before Peter could take charge, Lexie climbed on top of him. Her stomach was far too bloated for the weight of a body. Even one as reedy as Peter's.

When they were done, Lexie rolled off Peter, sucking in her stomach so tightly it felt as if there were a railroad spike pinned through her belly button. Peter remained on his back and fell sleep—instantly, like a man who'd dropped off a cliff. On her back, Lexie repeatedly jammed her toenail into her ankle until she felt a smeary droplet of blood. She'd fucked up big time and she needed to make amends.

8

LEXIE GOT SEVEN TEXT MESSAGES FROM DANIEL DURING HER drive to work. She read them by holding the phone above the steering wheel so she could see both the (nearly empty) road and the phone. Each time her phone pinged, the Daniel bell rang down her spine. It was amazing that she knew he was an asshole, she hated him for what he'd brought out in her, but at the sight of his texts, she wanted to be with him again.

"The heart wants what the heart wants," Lexie said aloud, quoting Woody Allen who had misquoted Emily Dickinson. Once upon a time Lexie had known the Dickinson poem from which that famous line was taken. But Woody put it more concisely, more simply. She preferred his misquote although she shuddered to think she'd have anything in common with a man who cheated on his partner with her daughter and then misquoted Emily Dickinson to justify it. Yes, Lexie's heart yearned for a liar and cheater, but she was not Woody Allen. Lexie was going to end this thing.

She was going to shut it off and shut it down so she could return to the person she was before she met Daniel Waite.

As if to prove how despicable she was, Lexie forced herself to answer the question of who she would pick if the world were about to blow to smithereens and she *had to have sex with one person* during her last hour on Earth. Daniel, goddammit. She'd be dead in the end anyway, so she might as well enjoy the one who made her feel like she'd live forever.

Lexie turned into the faculty lot at Ruxton. She parked the car, killed the engine, and then picked up her phone. Daniel's last text: *Must see the panties you have on today.* They were yellow, a color Lexie would wear only in panties, and they matched her bra. Everything lace with a tiny pearl at the center of the bra, and another pearl at the top center of the panties. Lexie exclusively wore stuff that she wouldn't mind getting caught in. As soon as there was a hole in the seam, a stain from her period, a wire slipping out, she threw the garment out. A continual attempt to obliterate the bad-underwear years.

Getting dressed that morning, Lexie had been aware of how the yellow looked against her suede-colored skin. She knew it made a striking contrast. But she also knew that Peter would be the only one to appreciate it. She'd even lifted her shirt and dropped her fitted slacks before walking out the door. "What do you think?" she had asked Peter. He laughed and kissed her between the breasts.

Lexie replied to Daniel's text: *We need to talk.*

Daniel replied: *We need to kiss.*

Lexie wrote: *Through various conversations at school it has come out that you are completely and truly married. Also, you've always had your apartment in Boston. Don, Janet, and others use it from time to time. Do not contact me again.* Lexie hit send. She scrunched up her face in agony. Why did she want *him* to be her last fuck on Earth?!

The phone rang. It was Daniel. Lexie stared at his name, her heart flipping like a dolphin against the walls of her rib cage. With a half-conscious impulsivity, she lowered the phone to her crotch and held it there like a vibrator until it went to voice mail. "I've gone completely nutzo," Lexie said aloud.

Despite her shame (Lexie saw the shame as a little fat-filled balloon sitting on the bottom of her stomach) and heartache (which sat, well, in her heart) Lexie deliberately pulled her head up and lengthened her stride as she crossed the campus. In changing her physiognomy she was hoping to change her soul. Yes, her body craved this motherfucker, but she craved marshmallow Peeps, too, and she didn't sit around and eat those all day. (Although maybe she would if they were right in front of her, stacked by the case in her kitchen.)

Lexie paused at the door to her office. She texted Peter: *Turning my phone off for the rest of the day so I can catch up. If you have to call, call the office phone. I LOVE YOU MORE THAN EVERYONE IN THE WORLD! Xxx* And then she added *xxxxx* so that there would be more kisses on her text to Peter than on her earlier texts to Daniel.

Lexie turned off the phone. Completely off, so that it would take a minute (eternity in computer and phone time) to start up again. She placed it inside the zipper pocket of her purse. As she was unlocking the door, Dot Harrison came charging down the brick walkway. For an eighty-year-old who looked like an egg in an orange dress, Dot moved fast.

"We need to talk!" Dot said, as she reached Lexie.

"Good. You're my favorite talker in this school."

"You only like me because I hate that old prude Janet Irwin." Dot barreled into the office ahead of Lexie and sat on the couch. "You got any coffee?"

"Yup." Lexie went to the machine in the corner and made a pot.

"None of that girly stuff. The real deal. With lead in it."

"That's what I'm making." Lexie sat in the wing chair opposite Dot, crossed her legs and looked over at her purse containing the shutdown cell phone. Shit. She truly had a problem if she couldn't relax while the phone was off.

"I need some advice," Dot said.

"Sure." Lexie forced herself to look at Dot, to *be there*.

"My sister-in-law and I are going to the outlet shops at Wrentham Village this coming weekend and I want to buy a dress to wear to your wedding."

"That's so nice," Lexie said.

"So, two things I want to make sure of before I spend all that money."

"Yeah?" Lexie recrossed her legs, left over right this time.

"One: Am I invited to the wedding?"

"God, yes! Amy's a bridesmaid."

"I know, and I figured if Amy was invited I might be invited, too. I am one of the girls, as you know."

"Yes, you are." Lexie wanted to laugh. She and Amy frequently sat with Dot during lunch, the three of them gossiping about everyone from Janet Irwin to the Russian exchange student whose head was nearly the size and exactly the shape of a keg. But Lexie would never put Dot in the same category as Amy. Dot was more of a fabulous grandmother than *one of the girls.*

"You're not inviting the assholes, are you?"

"No, no assholes. You, Amy . . ." Lexie paused as she thought she heard her phone buzz. She remembered it was off and refocused. "You, Amy . . . oh, Don and his wife because, you know, he's my boss."

"Well, yeah, you gotta invite Don. Is that coffee ready?"

"I can pour midbrew." Lexie got up and poured two cups into the blue ceramic mugs Peter had bought her at a craft show at the church near their house. Coffee sizzled and singed on the burner plate as it kept brewing. The smell reminded Lexie of rotted out, derelict buildings, like the one that backed into the apartment complex where she grew up. "So what's the other thing you want to be sure of before you buy a dress? By the way, you don't have to buy a new dress. It's a casual wedding." At a certain point in life, when your body had reformatted into its last incarnation and your skin was so wrinkled that you resembled an apple doll, did it matter what dress you wore? Maybe, Lexie thought. Maybe what we hope for in our imaginary personae can be realized through what we throw on our exteriors. Elegant dresses, silky underwear, and good shoes might be the pathway to the ideal self.

"Oh, I'm dressing up. I'm getting my hair done and everything." Dot's hair was comprised of thin, white dashes across her scalp. It resembled the blond hair on Lexie's forearms.

"Well, don't get your hair done this week. The wedding's not until December." Lexie handed Dot her coffee. She sat in the chair and put her own coffee on the side table with the checkerboard leather inlay. Everything in Lexie's office reminded her of '80s

JESSICA ANYA BLAU

movies about rich people. She had never asked, but she assumed the furniture was castoffs from the redecorated homes of the board of directors.

"I know, I know. So, here's my second item of business. Before I spend money on this new dress I want to make sure you're going to go through with this and marry the guy."

Lexie was taken aback. Instantly, she was visited by her old bunkmate, Anxiety. "Why would you ask that?" Lexie kept her voice calm so as not betray her internal turmoil.

"Because at my age, when you buy a dress, you only have a certain number of years to wear it. See, if you amortize each purchase over the time you have left on the planet, clothes are pretty damn expensive."

"No, I mean, why would you think that I wouldn't go through with the marriage?" Anxiety turned on an electric teakettle in Lexie's stomach. She could feel the water heating up and prayed it wouldn't start to boil.

"Oh, that." Dot waved her hand. "I think you probably will. But you never know. Sometimes the happiest-seeming couples are the most miserable people around."

"But Peter and I are genuinely happy. Can't you tell we're happy?" They'd been deliriously happy until she slept with Daniel Waite. Before then, Peter was Lexie's final lover in the last hour of mankind on Earth.

"Honey, don't get all worked up. This is about nothing more than the dress and me wanting to be abso-fucking-lutely positive I'm going to wear the damn thing before I spend money on it."

"So you think we're well matched?"

"Oh, well . . ." Dot paused.

"Well what?!" No one had ever doubted her pairing with Peter. Most people claimed they were perfect together.

"Let's see here . . ." Dot scrunched up her already contracted face.

"What?!" Lexie kicked out her leg, as if to tap Dot on the shin.

"Well, I see you as someone who is forward-moving, expanding. You won't abide this private school routine long—you're gonna bust out and see the world one day."

"Yeah, I want to travel—"

"I'm not talkin' travel. What I'm saying is that you're not settled. You're not contained. And I'm not sure if you ever will be."

"And Peter is contained?" Lexie knew the answer. That Peter wasn't searching for anything and was content with his life was one of the things that drew her toward him originally. But maybe it was a quality that flipped on you: What you love in the beginning, you hate in the end.

"Hell, yeah, he's contained. One job his whole life."

"Aren't all artists one-jobbers?" The internal teakettle was simmering. Lexie eyed her purse on the desk and considered how to sneak a Klonopin without Dot knowing.

"I suppose. And he's been in Massachusetts since birth, right?"

"What's wrong with Massachusetts? You live here. I live here." She could claim a headache and tell Dot that the Klonopin was a Tylenol.

"It's a fine state. Half the residents are box-brained assholes but the other half are pretty darn great." Dot took another sip of coffee.

"Do you think I shouldn't marry him?" There was always the option of telling Dot about her anxiety and simply taking the damn pill in front of her.

"Hell no. Everyone needs a first husband. That's how you figure out what you don't want!" Dot laughed at her own joke. Lexie faked it.

"So you, who has had *three* marriages, think he's my first of more than one husband?" Lexie hoped this motherfucking anxiety would fade away on its own. She didn't want to be a pill-popper.

"I had three because I'm dumb. It took *two* first husbands to figure out what I don't want."

"Peter is definitely what I want." Lexie eyed her purse. "I love him."

"I'm sure you'll have many wonderful years together. But if you don't, remember that the only life worth living is the one where there's been numerous fuckups."

"Wait. Do you think I'm fucking up?!" What if Lexie punched herself in the stomach and manually killed the teakettle and its boiling bubbles of anxiety?

"For godsakes, I'm an eighty-year-old shriveled hag with a brain like a leaky outhouse. Shit just drips out!" Dot readjusted the string of pearls on her neck and Lexie suddenly saw her as vulnerable, too, like Lexie herself. It must be scary getting old.

"OK, I'm sorry. I was making a big deal out of nothing." If it was nothing, why was Lexie so anxious? She had always believed that Dot possessed a third eye that peered into other dimensions.

"I shoulda kept my damn piehole shut." Dot shot down the rest of her coffee, placed the cup on the table, then stood.

Lexie stood, too, and walked Dot to the door. "I totally love him. This marriage is going to be great." Great, though Dot was right. Lexie *had* always yearned for a bigger life, anything to break apart the tight container of claustrophobic chaos she'd felt living with Mitzy and Bert. Peter, the son of a soft-spoken music teacher (his mother) and an accountant (his father), had come out of warm stability and peaceful routine. He was programmed for and operated optimally within a small, simple life. For the past year and a half, Lexie had been perfectly content not being aware of her and Peter's essential difference. But now that she'd seen it, it was impossible to unsee, like a scar in the middle of her face that could not be avoided or denied.

"Listen, if you change your mind, don't go through with it. I can tell you from experience, it is a fuck of a lot easier and cheaper to cancel a wedding than to get divorced."

"I'm not going to change my mind." Instead, Lexie thought, I'll put all my anxious, chaos-based energy into embracing the small life and making it work.

"Alrighty my dear, I'm buying a dress and keeping my hair appointment." Dot hoisted her pocketbook higher onto her shoulder and then exited with her signature age-belying speed.

Lexie locked the door and rushed to her purse. She took out the pills and her phone, setting both on the desk. Lexie dared herself to *not* open the bottle and *not* turn on the phone.

"Accept," Lexie went to the first therapeutic step for anxiety. She would accept her thoughts, her anxiety, without judgment. "Accept . . . Fuck it." Lexie took out a pill and bit it in half before swallowing both sides. It would take a few minutes to enter her bloodstream, but knowing it was inside her soothed everything immediately, like baby powder on sticky, hot skin.

Next, she turned on the phone. Several new texts from Daniel lit up the screen. Each one made claims Lexie had heard before: He was separated, Lexie was the first woman he'd been with since his wife, Lexie was the only person on his mind. She stared at them for twenty minutes, until the Klonopin had fully, truly, kicked in. Then Lexie called Daniel's number.

"Hey, beautiful." Daniel was whispering. Lexie's body felt electrified from just the sound of him.

"You lied to me." She wanted to sob.

"No, I didn't." He sounded so calm. Confident.

"Every single person who works in the administration at this school knows you and your wife and knows that you are married to her. Not separated. Married." Lexie paced from one end of her office (the desk) to the other (the couch).

"Sweetheart. Listen to me. Every single person at that school knows my son, knows me to some extent, knows who my father was, and knows who my grandfather was. Those people are the last people I let in on any of my personal business." He said each word clearly, as if he didn't want Lexie to misunderstand anything.

"You've always had that apartment in Boston."

"Yeah, and?"

"You told me you got that apartment because you two separated. You lied."

"Lexie. It's impossible that I told you that, because it's not true. I've had the apartment for years. It's near my office in Boston. My wife's house, where I only go when my son is home, is on Loon Lake."

"You led me to believe it was your new bachelor pad."

"No, I didn't. I told you I lived in the apartment. That's the truth. When we separated, I moved into the apartment full-time."

"Well, if you live there, how do Don and others stay there when they go to the city?" Lexie stopped pacing. As if to better hear what he had to say.

Daniel laughed. "Oh, god, they're offering up the apartment for staff retreats again?"

"Um . . ." Lexie didn't know the details of the arrangement. All she knew was what Amy had told her in the text.

"Before we separated, so before last spring, we offered the apartment to Don and others to use during the weekends when we were at the lake house. If you want to ask around, you'll find that not a single Ruxton person has stayed in the apartment since last spring. Not one. Because it's my home, not my pied-à-terre."

There was silence while Lexie took it all in. She sat on her Windsor chair and leaned against one arm. There was an easing in her body. "Okay, I believe you." So, she wasn't a complete dumb-ass fool. She was only a cheat and a liar. "But I can't see you anymore."

"Oh, baby, don't do this to me."

"I don't want to be the kind of person who has an affair." Lexie lowered her voice, even though no one was around. She slid half-way down the chair, as if she were hiding.

"You're not. This is not a normal affair. This is so beyond any-thing else in life that I actually walked out of a meeting with the former prime minister of Canada so I could talk to you."

"Seriously?" She was impressed. Peter didn't even go to meet-ings that could be walked out of.

"Yeah. He's been here since seven this morning. The guy likes to start early."

"Wow." Lexie couldn't wait to tell Amy this tidbit. To let her know she'd completely cut things off with a guy who (a) wasn't a liar, (b) wasn't married, and (c) walked out on a former Canadian prime minister to take her breakup call. "Which prime minister is it?" Not that Lexie could name any other than the two Trudeaus.

"Chrétien," Daniel said. "He's old as fuck, speaks out of one side of his mouth, and is pretty damn hilarious."

"The hilarious former prime minister. Could be a sitcom or something."

"The only problem is I've had about eight cups of coffee and when we took a break he went to the only public john in this wing of the building and I didn't want to go in there, because, you know, it seems wrong to stand at a pissoir next to a former prime minister. So I'm starting to feel a little bladder pain."

Lexie laughed. "But men pee en masse. Surely he pees with other people all the time."

"But what if he has a teeny, tiny cock? I don't want to know that."

"What if it's huge?" What harm was there in having a little fun banter before never speaking to Daniel again?

"If it's huge I'll feel completely insignificant. Not only have I never been the prime minister of anything, but I don't even have a prime minister–worthy dick."

"Hey, I've seen what you've got. That could easily be a prime minister's dick."

"Aren't you sweet. I thought you were banishing me from your life?" Daniel had a teasing lilt in his voice as if he were confident that Lexie couldn't bring herself to break things off.

"Oh, yeah, but . . ." But if there were only one hour left to live, Lexie thought, she would revert to her worst self and spend that hour in bed with him.

"Give me another chance. Please? I haven't lied to you about anything."

"I love Peter and I'm going to get married." Lexie said it quickly. Like swallowing food she didn't want to eat.

"But I'm completely mad about you. I'm out of my mind over you."

"I need to be a good person." Her voice had slowed. Why did it feel like she was reciting lines she hadn't properly memorized?

"Sweetheart. Please." Daniel sounded slightly choked.

"I have to get married," she managed.

"You don't *have* to do anything."

"I am committed to my fiancé and I want to follow through on my promise." Lexie pushed her forehead into her palm and cringed. Life was unfair. She wanted this guy and goddammother-fuckingsonofabitchfuckface she wasn't going to have him.

"You're breaking my heart."

"I'm sorry." Lexie wanted to sob. Or throw up. Or scream. Or expel something from her body.

"Damn." Daniel's voice was croaky. "You were like an incredible dream that abruptly ended."

"I'm so sorry." She was cringing, recoiling.

"I'll give you some space, but—" Daniel lowered his voice to an airy whisper, "shit, I have to go. The secretary is calling me back in. Listen, I refuse to give up on you. But I'll give you a little break to let you sort things out."

"There's nothing to work out," Lexie recited dutifully.

"I've gotta hang up. Don't forget, I'm coming back for you." The phone went silent.

Lexie threw the phone across the room and onto the couch. She pulled her feet up onto the chair, folded over her knees, and let herself cry for the first time since she met Daniel Waite. Hidden deep inside herself—in a place she wanted no one to discover—was the hope that Daniel would indeed swoop in and save her from her decision.

Lexie remained curled up on the chair for fifteen minutes, until the bell tower gonged the hour. She got up, brushed her hair, put on lipstick, and then quickly patted her cheeks and under her eyes to bring some blood to her face and release the puffiness from crying.

Through each of her student sessions that morning, Lexie listened while simultaneously running over the last conversation with Daniel and the conversation with Dot. Certainly she was relieved—the tension, the anxiety, the guilt of cheating had turned to vapor and drifted off. But nothing was the same. Lexie's world had changed into something misshapen and soiled. Life as a soiled dishrag.

At lunchtime, Lexie brought two plates of pasta with red sauce to Amy's office. Amy filled the electric kettle and Lexie was reminded of the kettle of anxiety she'd drugged out of her system first thing this morning.

They sat across from each other on the old-fashioned beds. Amy was wearing a yellow-and-white-striped dress that reminded Lexie of a parasol. She wore a headband that was also striped.

"You look like a Southern belle today," Lexie said. She could tell Amy was waiting for her to bring up the subject of Daniel, but Lexie wasn't ready.

"Sun's going to stop shining soon, so I gotta get my pretty dress wearing in while I can." Amy ate as if it were her first meal in days.

"Yeah . . ." Lexie took a deep breath. She put the plate down. Eating felt impossible.

"Oh no." Amy looked up from her plate. "Did you run over to that hotel and fuck him this morning before class?" Amy took another bite of pasta.

"No. I broke up with him." Lexie pushed the plate away.

"Honestly?" Amy shoved more pasta into her mouth.

Lexie repeated to Amy everything Daniel had told her. She hopped off the bed, went to the cupboard where Amy kept cups and tea bags, and made them each some tea. Amy had yet to respond.

"You don't believe him?" Lexie looked over at Amy. "Honey, right?" She squeezed the small, plastic bear and let a few oozing bits elongate and then drop into each of their teacups.

"I suppose it doesn't matter what I believe since you broke up with him anyway."

"Well, don't think poorly of Daniel," Lexie said. "Even if you don't believe him, you can see there are great things about him. And you have to admit he's accomplished." Lexie put each of the teacups on a saucer. She placed one saucer on each of the sickbeds.

"Assholes can be accomplished. And you don't know for sure that he's great. You only know he's great in bed." Amy started eating again.

"But why did it feel so perfect?" Lexie delicately hoisted herself up onto the sickbed without knocking the tea.

"That's your hormones talking." Amy's words were muffled by the chewing. "I can't have an orgasm with a man without thinking that I want to marry him."

"You want to marry every person who gives you an orgasm?" Lexie sipped at her tea. Her stomach was so empty she could feel the liquid entering her body like a sliding, hot rope.

"Yup. It's come to the point where I deliberately stop myself from orgasming so I won't bond with him."

"So billions of women across the planet are chasing the ever-elusive partnered orgasm and you're trying to stop it?" Not that Lexie had difficulties finding her own orgasms. She had taught herself with her hand sometime in the beginning of sixth grade and hadn't had a problem since.

"I'm like a guy or something," Amy said. "He sticks his *thang* in me, and before the tick can bite the dog, I'm having myself an orgasm as big as a bull on steroids." Amy pushed away her empty plate and pointed at Lexie's untouched plate. Lexie had always thought it was great the way Amy ate: like a man, completely un-conscious of quantity or calories. She put food in her mouth when she was hungry, and didn't when she wasn't.

Lexie picked up her plate and handed it to Amy across the gap between the beds. "So how do you stop yourself from having an orgasm?"

"Right when I'm about to come, I think of garbage." Amy indicated toward the plate with her fork. "You're sure you're not going to eat this?"

"I'm not hungry. You think of garbage?" Lexie looked toward the wire trash can near Amy's desk. It was half-full of balled up paper and the plastic clip-ons for the ear thermometer.

"Not that kind of garbage. I think of the gunk you pull out of the sink after you've done the dishes." Amy dug into her second plate of pasta.

"The stuff from the strainer?"

"Uh-huh." She swallowed. "All that slimy, smelly, food gunk. And then I don't even have those preorgasm-shudders."

"You know, I'm going to detox from Daniel by imagining the putrid slime from a sink strainer every time he enters my mind."

"Great idea." Amy raised her teacup. "Here's to fish skins and oily old chicken bones." Lexie raised her teacup and they motioned toward each other as if making a toast.

"Do you think I ruined everything with Peter?" Lexie hoped her feelings for Daniel were like her past love for the film *Rent*. Lexie had almost cried at the opening scene the first time she saw it at the theater. She went back five times before it came out on DVD. Years later, Lexie dug out and watched the DVD (which had moved with her from apartment to apartment to apartment) and she couldn't even understand or remember what she had liked about the film in the first place.

"No, you haven't ruined anything. After Billy and I kissed I was out of my mind crazy. You coulda told me my mama was dying of cancer in the hospital, waiting to say good-bye, and I still woulda stopped off at Billy's house and fucked him before seeing her. There was no way out but down." Amy hopped off the bed with her teacup. She went to the cupboard, took out the honey, and squeezed several more teardrop-shaped globs into her cup.

"I'm not like that, am I?" This thing with Daniel had presented Lexie with a whole new version of herself.

"Hell, no. No one knows but me, right?" Amy licked the pour-tip and the sticky head of the plastic bear and then shut the lid. Lexie made a mental note to never use Amy's honey again.

"Yeah. You're the only one who knows."

"Then you and I will die with this secret. And once that ring is on your finger you can honestly say you never cheated on your husband." Amy sat at her desk chair and sipped her tea.

"But I did."

"You cheated on your fiancé. Change the word and you've changed the circumstances."

Lexie's phone buzzed with an incoming text. Her heart knocked once, a fist on a door. Lexie hopped off the bed and picked up her purse from the floor. She pulled out her phone. Peter. Lexie was relieved that she didn't have to read a text from Daniel and be forced to face whatever feelings might float up from it.

Peter's text read: *Bought a black Jetta. 5 yrs old. Looks brand-new. Won't deplete the honeymoon account.*

"Peter got me a used Jetta. Nice, right?" Lexie looked up at Amy.

"Well, yeah! How many girls have a guy out there finding a car for them? Do you know what a pain in the ass it is to car shop? Plus, who has the money for a car these days?"

"The parents of every single kid at this school," Lexie said. No point in mentioning Daniel in particular. And no reason to confess that the money was Lexie's savings—Peter had simply gone through the effort of procuring the car.

Amy rolled her eyes. "Stay the course, honey. Stay the course."

"LET'S DO IT IN THE CAR." LEXIE WAS STARING OUT THE KITCHEN window, looking at the Jetta in the driveway. She had done the dinner dishes and swept the wood shavings.

"Won't the bed be more comfortable?" Peter was at the kitchen table, cruising music sites on his iPad.

"Let's go wild. Go crazy! Right?"

"Okay." Peter was craned toward his iPad. Lexie put away the broom, went in the bedroom to insert her birth control, and then went out to the long, sloping driveway. She opened the back door of her new car, lay on the seat and stared at the ceiling, which was the color of eggshells and looked like it was made of felt. There was an ashy gray-brown smudge directly above her head. It reminded Lexie of the brown contrail created by her father's cigarette butt she had found floating in the toilet each day when she got home from school.

Eventually, Peter loped out to the car.

"I didn't know where you were." Peter pulled off his T-shirt.

"Waiting for you, babe." Lexie kicked off her shoes and then slipped off her pants and let them dangle from one ankle. She pushed aside the crotch of her yellow underwear. Peter dropped his pants in the driveway. As was his habit, he wasn't wearing underwear, something Lexie had never quite grown used to. She couldn't help but imagine the inside point-of-view of Peter's jeans against his slightly gluey balls and dick.

Peter climbed on top of Lexie, his forearms on her hair, pinning her to the seat.

"Wait." Lexie worked her hair out from under Peter. "Okay, go ahead." Peter did and Lexie drifted off into her mind and successfully avoided thinking of Daniel. Mostly she focused on the ceiling smudge, wondering how it got there and why the person who was selling the car didn't clean it off.

Peter dismounted. "Let's switch positions."

"Okay." Lexie clumsily worked her way out from beneath Peter. She was a spaz, like her mother had always claimed. As they resettled, Peter's fist knocked into Lexie's breast giving her a painful jolt that ran straight to her gut and made her momentarily breathless. Lexie didn't complain. She deserved all this and more.

They carried on with Lexie on top. She stared down at Peter's closed eyes and carefully watched his clenching and counterpushes so she would know when they were coming to an end. Peter wasn't a noisemaker or a panter; it wasn't always obvious.

At last, Peter was done. "That will bring us good luck in the car," Lexie said. She slid off Peter, readjusted her panties, and put on her pants.

Peter leaned out the open car door and grabbed his jeans from the driveway. "Where'd you hear that?"

"I made it up." Lexie wondered what the distance was between making things up and lying. She'd done a lot of both lately.

"So is this car sexier than the van?" Peter pulled on his jeans.

"Way sexier than the van. Sexier than the Saab even." That he asked, that he cared, filled Lexie with a sudden and untouchable tenderness toward Peter. It was as if he were a glass egg that she had knocked off the counter, but caught seconds before it shattered on the tiled floor.

Back in the house, they settled into their regular seats on the couch: Lexie on the right, Peter on the left. Peter picked up the remote control, turned on the TV, and then, without taking note of what was on, left the room. Lexie picked up the novel she'd been reading and stared at the page she was on. She read the first sentence of the new chapter over again three times before giving up and lowering the book to her lap. Her mind was so knotted up she couldn't unravel it enough to take in much more than her own thoughts.

Peter returned with two cereal bowls filled with butter pecan ice cream. He placed Lexie's bowl on the coffee table and picked up the remote again, which he immediately started clicking, landing finally on a late '70s Woody Allen movie.

Three minutes had barely passed when Peter clinked his empty ice cream bowl down on the coffee table.

"You gonna eat that?" Peter pointed to the bowl he'd brought for Lexie. She hadn't touched it.

"I'm not in the mood for sweets." Since her fling with Daniel, lying to Peter had become second nature. The truth was Lexie was in the mood *only* for sweets and was trying to keep from binging on them. After skipping the pasta with Amy, Lexie had picked up a plate of cookies from the teachers' lounge with the intention of having them in her office for her student patients (as she had loudly stated to the group who was in the lounge at the time). But before her next student patient had shown up, Lexie had eaten every single cookie. She had wanted to hit the gym to burn off at least a fifth of the cookie calories, but never made it there due to an emergency session with Lizzy Aleman who had wanted to see Lexie "right away." With the encouragement of her roommate, Lizzie had confessed to being bulimic. As they talked, Lexie felt like she was right there with Lizzie (even fantasizing about leaning over her delicate office wastebasket and hurling up the cookies). Lexie had never purged, but she fully understood the urge to undo what had been done and to control a body—a life—that felt out of control. If she had continued to carry on with Daniel she might have, eventually, been fingering her own throat.

WEDNESDAY, WHEN ETHAN STROLLED INTO HER OFFICE, LEXIE'S flesh reacted as if Daniel himself had appeared. Biology, Lexie thought. She was smelling something on Ethan that she had smelled on Daniel and damn if that didn't get the blood rushing to central points on her body.

Ethan sat on the couch across from Lexie, kicked off his boat shoes, and lay down with his head on one armrest and his feet on the other. He lifted his feet once before letting them drop again. "Either this couch got shorter, or I got longer."

"I think you got longer," Lexie said. "You're at that age where boys grow like aliens—like time-lapse photography."

"Yeah." Ethan lifted his head and looked at his feet. "My mom thinks I'm too big." He lay back again.

"Too big?"

"Like if me and my dad are watching a game together on the same couch, there's no room for her. She hates that she's stuck in the chair, or on the floor if she wants to sit near us."

"I see." Lexie wondered if watching TV together was a regular activity when they were all home. Did Daniel mind hanging out with Jen for the length of a football game?

"Did you ever notice that if there are no seats left, it's the women who always sit on the floor?" Ethan looked up at the ceiling, like he was thinking this all through.

"Yeah. I have noticed that. And I think it's great that you've noticed that."

"Like at senior meeting this morning there weren't enough seats and Toni and Megan were sitting on the floor." Ethan continued to stare at the ceiling.

"Maybe you can be one of those guys who moves to the floor. You can change the pattern for all of mankind."

"One human at a time, right?" Ethan looked so serious. Lexie was heartened by the idea that he'd try to make a change in this way.

"Exactly. So, you and your dad are always taking up the couch and your mom sits on the floor. Do the three of you watch a lot of games together?" Lexie's internal voice told her to quit prying.

"Hmm, I dunno. I guess when I'm home. But I'm rarely home." Ethan turned his head toward Lexie. She wanted to snap-freeze him so she could unabashedly study him. Lexie could see in Ethan the Daniel of the past. It was clear that the way Daniel was now was the way he'd always been: relaxed, fearless, comfortable in the world.

"And how are you doing with those essays?" Lexie didn't give a shit about college application essays, but it was essential to focus on Ethan alone. Her yearning heart could remain unattended.

THAT NIGHT WHILE LEXIE AND PETER WERE HAVING SEX DANIEL KEPT slipping into her mind like a slideshow that wouldn't rotate to the next photo. There he was: his square face, his hard body pressed against hers, his sweet smell that reminded her of sunlight on fresh-cut grass. It felt impossible to conjure up sink-strainer garbage.

Lexie stared at Peter. She said *Peter* in her mind. Once she put her hand on his chin, turned his face and asked him to open his eyes. *Peter. Peter. Peter.* Lexie was so intent on seeing Peter that she could barely feel the stirrings in her body. She faked an orgasm because she didn't want Peter to worry that he was doing something wrong. And he wasn't doing anything wrong. He just wasn't Daniel Waite.

TWO DAYS LATER, LEXIE WOKE UP WITH THE WORDS *FRITO FRIDAY* IN her head. She said it aloud: "Frito Friday."

"Huh?" Peter wrapped his arms around Lexie and pulled her

into him. There was nothing else in life that gave you that perfect feeling of skin against skin, Lexie thought. And when you shut your eyes, that skin could belong to anyone.

"Nothing."

"You said 'Frito Friday.'"

" 'Cause last Friday I met that Ruxton dad at the Inn on the Lake and we had Frito pie and he called it Frito Friday."

"Maybe we should serve Frito pie at the wedding," Peter said.

Lexie thought how cruel it would be to serve the food that she'd come to associate with the best sex of her life. "Maybe we can use Pringles cans to hold the flowers on each table."

"We could put whoopee cushions on each seat."

"And use beer pull tabs for our rings." Now that Lexie had fully recommitted herself to this relationship and the pending marriage, she planned to also recommit herself to the ring. In her short time with Daniel, the ring had started to represent a factory-discount-outlet life she had never wanted. Lexie knew she needed to reimagine the ring as charming, quaint, understated.

"I'd marry you with whoopee cushion seats and beer pull-tab rings and Frito pie for dinner any day," Peter said. "I'd marry you in a dingy linoleum-floored courthouse in Northampton."

"I'd marry you at an unsanitary, pubic-hair-laden, nudist colony in Florida where no one wears underwear but everyone's carrying a gun." Hell yeah, Lexie could play this game. She could play it full-on. With devotion! It was time to make the best of her days and nights with Peter. The more fun she had with him, the sooner Daniel would fade to a blurry smudge.

"I'd marry you at a nudist colony in Alaska, in the winter, where everyone's stuck inside some ice cave that smells like BO because there's no hot water and no one's showered for thirty-seven days and there are outhouses without even a sink, and everyone is related, except us, and they're all bitching at each other the whole time, nonstop bitch bitch bitch."

"And they all want you to make guitars for them, so you're filling, like, thirty-seven guitar orders while we're there and you're sanding a guitar while we're getting married, naked, in the smelly igloo . . ."

"Yeah." Peter pulled Lexie in closer. "Even like that, it's worth it."

Daniel flashed in Lexie's mind. Was she deliberately, or subconsciously, creating the impulse to see Daniel at every tender interaction with Peter as a way to punish herself? Was this going to turn into something like her (currently waning) door-locking OCD?

"Let's cancel the wedding and—" Lexie dared herself to say something crazy and destructive. Why not blow it all up and get a do-over? She turned her head and looked at Peter. Was she cursed to spend every day of her marriage contemplating a possible end to it? Maybe.

"Cancel the wedding and what?" Peter asked.

"And get married in the igloo." No, she wouldn't blow it all up today. She would try to be better than her parents. She would try to make this relationship work.

"I'd love that." Peter leaned in and held his lips against Lexie's in one long, slow, honest kiss. The wedding had always been for Lexie. If they had done things Peter's way, they would have gone to a linoleum-floored courthouse in Northampton.

"Done." Lexie slipped out of bed and went to the shower. "Go away," she whispered to the image of Daniel as she showered. She had done so well all week, glutting her brain with images of sink-strainer gunk; mostly avoiding the topic of Daniel during her session with Ethan. But today was testing Lexie's resolve. She was sick of sink-strainer gunk. She was sick of smelling imaginary dead shrimp.

"Accept," Lexie said aloud. *Accept this crush, this obsession, without judgment.* She would allow Daniel into her mind with the hope that the act of acceptance would dilute his power, would weaken the allure of the forbidden.

"Accept," Lexie said, again, and she saw an image of Daniel opening a quiet door and slipping into a dark room where Lexie lay waiting. Before she could go to step two, she allowed herself to masturbate while thinking of Daniel Waite.

9

LEXIE LOOKED OUT HER OFFICE WINDOW AND SPOTTED DOT speed-walking straight toward her. She opened the door and waited.

"Honey, come over to my apartment and see the dress I bought," Dot said.

"Sure." Lexie stepped outside and locked the office door. "You didn't have to come over here, you could have called."

"I read that walking fast keeps you alive. And the faster you walk, the longer you live." Dot started down the brick path toward her dorm apartment. Lexie followed.

"Then, it looks like you'll be checked in for a couple more decades." Dot's speed was terrorizing Lexie's feet, which had on four-inch platform heels. She was going mod today in flared white pants and an embroidered blouse that looked like it was from Mexico. On Mondays, when Lexie taught the sexuality part of the Health and Human Sexuality class, she tried to wear clothes that were relaxed and less authoritarian. While the American and European kids were—for the most part—completely comfortable talking about sex, some of the Asian and African kids could barely lift their eyes from their notebooks. Lexie tried to assess the group the first day so she knew how to pace herself, when in the semester to bring out the condoms that they'd practice rolling over bananas.

She and Dot approached the cathedral-looking dorm called Rilke. It was one of Lexie's favorite buildings on campus. Two hundred years ago it had been a Catholic seminary, and so it had a bell tower, stained-glass windows, and a craggy, muggy, European chapel that smelled like incense. Ecumenical services were held here on Sunday, and more students than Lexie would ever have guessed attended. Sometimes, after lunch, Amy liked to go into the chapel and pray. Lexie often went with her, sitting silently on the smooth-indented wooden pew, staring at the thick shafts of dusty light that looked like they could be cut with knives.

Dot scanned her ID to open the heavy front door. Lexie followed her down the dark, dusty hallway to her apartment. Unlike the halls, the apartment was a gorgeous (though beat-up) place with massive windows, ornate crown moldings, and herringbone-patterned hardwood floors.

Lexie looked at Dot's fifty years of accumulated junk (stacks of paper on every surface, books spread across the couch, an ironing board obscured by wrapped gifts with yellow Post-its on them saying what was inside, framed photos crowded over two round tables with dusty, red tablecloths that reached to the ground) and thought there was much to be admired in Dot's focus in life being life itself, rather than the arrangement and care of the things one acquired while living.

At one time the apartment had belonged to a bishop of the seminary. Certainly he hadn't cooked there (and neither did Dot), so the kitchen was a later add-on, upgraded in the '70s with avocado appliances and a chipped linoleum countertop with a pattern of copper maple leaves.

"Did you use the kitchen when Beau was alive?" Lexie asked as they walked past it. Lexie had heard many stories about the brilliant and kind Beau Harrison. He didn't tap dance like his wife, but he was reputed to have been equally fun.

"Nah! He was as cheap as me. There was no way that man would buy food when we could get it for free a five-minute walk from the kitchen."

"Five minutes if you're snorting crack." Lexie paused in the doorway and watched Dot rearrange a closet's worth of clothes on her bed.

"Beau liked to walk fast, too." Dot picked up an embroidered and jeweled burgundy dress. It had a built-in satin slip and a scalloped hemline. "What do you think?" She shook the dress out and laid it back on the bed, on top of the other clothes.

Lexie went to the dress and delicately lifted the hem. It was too shiny and ornate—Dot would look like an overdecorated Christmas tree in it. "It's for my wedding, right?" Lexie's words caught in her throat, but she wasn't hit with anxiety as she'd been the last time she and Dot discussed the marriage.

"Hell, yes! Where else would I wear something like this?"

"It's gorgeous. I love it." Lexie stared at the dress. If they made eye contact Dot would know she was lying.

"Okay, good. 'Cause this thing cost a small fortune."

"I thought you were cheap?" Lexie hated that Dot would

spend *a small fortune* on an event that wasn't as simple, sure, and pure as it had been at its inception.

"I am! That's why I bought the damn thing at an outlet."

Lexie turned the dress over and examined the tiny satin buttons that went down the back. She wondered who would button them. Another reason marriage was good: You always had someone to button you up, to tell you when you looked pretty, to pick you up when the car broke, to make dinner when you worked late.

"It's Escada," Dot said.

"Escada?"

"A real designer. Not like The Gap or one of those other everyday dress shops."

"I'm not sure I'd call Gap a dress shop." Lexie turned the dress back so the front was face out. "I'm sure it looks beautiful on you."

"Guess how much it was."

"A hundred?" Lexie had heard of Escada but didn't know it well enough to know how much it cost.

"More."

"More? If it's more than a hundred you can no longer call yourself cheap."

"Outlet store, goddammit it! Only cheap people go to the outlet stores! Now guess."

"One fifty."

"More."

"Two hundred."

"More."

"More?"

"More. Guess."

"Three hundred?"

"More."

"Come on! This is Western Massachusetts. No one around here pays more than three hundred for a dress."

"Guess."

"Five hundred?"

"More."

"You're kidding me. What about the poor amortization?"

"I know, but why the fuck not? I can look at it as poor amortization or I can remind myself that I can't take it with me, so I might as well spend it."

"Okay. Six hundred."

"Yup."

"No way." Lexie had spent $480 on her wedding dress. She knew that most people spent much more on wedding dresses but even when she had felt entirely confident in the decision to marry, she couldn't bring herself to drop big money on some overly fancy frock she'd only wear one day. So she'd bought a simple, short, satin dress—something she could dress down and wear again and again. She loved it. Peter loved it. Amy, who had gone shopping in Boston with Lexie, loved it. Lexie was embarrassed that Dot had spent more than she.

"It was originally eighteen hundred dollars. Can you believe that? What kind of an asshole would spend eighteen hundred on a dress?"

"So you got it for, like, sixty-six percent off. That's a great deal." In truth, Lexie thought it was absurd to spend that kind of money when a hundred-fifty-dollar dress would surely look equally good (or equally bad!).

"My sister's granddaughter has a wedding coming in the spring and my great-nephew is graduating from medical school a week later. So if I wear it to your wedding, the other wedding, and the graduation, it comes out to two hundred bucks a pop."

Lexie pushed aside some blouses and sat on the bed. "Well, I'm glad you're wearing it to my wedding first. You'll be the star of the show."

"I want to look better than Amy!" Dot hooted big and crackly. She adored Amy but she pretended to compete with her in all things, including for Lexie's attention.

"When you're in that dress, Amy is going to look like your scullery maid."

"That's all I want, dear. Gonna put her to shame."

THAT NIGHT, LEXIE TOLD PETER ABOUT DOT'S DRESS. THEY WERE ON the couch, her legs across his lap, his legs up on the coffee table. Peter was watching a baseball game. Lexie had abandoned her book to the coffee table. Her computer sat on her belly.

"She's going to look like the grandmother of the bride," Peter said.

"Maybe I should ask her if she can act as grandmother of the bride." Lexie loved the idea of having a grandparent. Betsy Simms had grandparents and they were, as the name says, grand. They brought Betsy presents. They thought everything she did was brilliant. They had watched Betsy and Lexie do dances to current songs that they'd choreographed themselves. Usually there was a double somersault in the dance—Lexie holding Betsy's ankles and Betsy holding Lexie's as they rolled together across the lawn. The Simms grandparents also liked to sit and listen to Betsy and Lexie play duets on the piano. Betsy would teach Lexie one part that Lexie plunked out with her pointer fingers while Betsy's hands ran like spiders up and down the keyboard. Betsy's grandparents acted as if there was nothing on earth they would rather do than simply witness Betsy being alive.

Lexie's grandparents, on the other hand, were more of a concept than a reality. Mitzy's parents had disowned her when Lexie was born. They were strict Catholics who had claimed they would rather not have a daughter than have one who had mothered a child out of wedlock. So Lexie never once saw them, even though they lived only a BART train ride away in Hayward. But she knew their faces well from a framed photo of them Mitzy kept in the bathroom. In saturated color, Lexie's grandfather stood on a ladder at an apple tree. He was round-faced, blue-eyed, with blond hair shaved close to his head. Lexie's grandmother stood at the base of the ladder: a brown-haired woman with tight curls, a tighter mouth, and a jacket with a fur collar that coiled around her neck like a ferret.

Lexie's father's parents had lived in Omaha and had refused to enter the state of California because they thought it was full of "freaks and weirdos." Twice Lexie's father had loaded Lexie into his sleigh-back truck and the two of them drove eighteen hours to Omaha. During the night Lexie slept with a pillow propped against the window. On both trips Bert stopped once during the day, at the same rest stop, where he slept on a picnic bench. Lexie sat in the truck, as she'd been told, and read her book until her father woke up.

Her grandparents were formal and distant on those visits. Lexie felt like she was a neighbor girl selling Girl Scout cookies to strangers who had invited her to come in the house and stay for a while. Bert, who vocally occupied every room in the apartment when he was awake, went nearly silent in the presence of his parents. It was a version of her father that Lexie never saw at home, and one that vanished as soon as they were on the road out of Omaha.

Around the time Lexie was fourteen, before she moved into the Simmses' house, Lexie's grandparents died, one week apart from each other. Her father drove alone to Omaha for the funeral. Lexie had always believed no one would have told her about their deaths if she hadn't run into Bert at the 7-Eleven where he had stopped to buy road food before taking off.

"Hey, Dad," Lexie had said, quietly. She didn't want her three school friends to know that the guy with the stained T-shirt and skin hanging under his eyes like old, round tea bags was her dad.

"Oh, hey!" Bert cuffed Lexie's chin lightly, like he wasn't sure how to act in public with his daughter. Unlike her mother, who Lexie often saw when she and her friends went to Heidi Pies, her father was a presence entirely connected to the apartment.

"What're you getting?" Lexie knew the shelves of 7-Eleven as well as she knew the cupboards in her kitchen. Along with the Simmses' home and the public library, it was one of her daily stops. A place to take refuge from the apartment.

"Road food." Bert held up a bag of Fritos and a bag of Bugles.

"Why do you need road food?" For a second Lexie worried her father was running away, abandoning her and Mitzy. Could her mother afford the rent on her own?

"Didn't your mother tell you what happened?"

"No. What happened?"

"My mom died last week. And Dad died yesterday." Bert turned to the case of drinks and perused them as if he were looking for something in particular.

"How'd they die?" This was Lexie's first experience with death. She examined how she felt. So far, nothing. Her father, too, appeared to feel nothing. It was more like two TV characters had died and not her actual grandparents. Where was the sadness? When did the crying start?

"She had a stroke and he just died. Old age, I guess." Bert plucked a Mountain Dew from the case.

"That's sad." Lexie shut her eyes for a second and tried to feel sadness.

"It's not so sad. I got me a house in Omaha now." Bert looked at Lexie and winked.

It wasn't until years later, when Lexie was reading an Agatha Christie novel, that she realized the connection to the death, the house in Omaha, and her father's later disappearance to, possibly, Reno. Once the estate was settled and he'd had money enough that he didn't have to live with Mitzy, he'd freed himself. Lexie was collateral damage.

"What would Dot do as grandmother of the bride?" Peter asked, now.

"I don't know. Sit at the same table as us, my mother, and the Simmses?"

"Do it. She bought an expensive dress. Why not make it a special night for her?"

"Done." Lexie sent an email to Amy telling her the plan. Next she sent an email to Dot asking if she'd do the honor of sitting at the family table and acting as Grandmother of the Bride. Lexie didn't expect Dot to answer until morning. Like many people her age she didn't fear she'd miss something if she put her phone away for the night and stayed off the computer. Amy, like Lexie, usually had her phone on her body somewhere, if not within reach of a darting arm.

Lexie grew impatient waiting for Amy's reply so she went to Facebook to pass the time. She clicked on a few posts of old high school crushes, but nothing was particularly new or intriguing. Someone she knew from graduate school had a baby. Lexie thought the newborn looked like ET or the house elf in *Harry Potter*. She hit *like* under the photo.

A picture of Lexie's mother popped up in her feed, posted by one of the waitresses from Heidi Pies. Lexie clicked in further and discovered that her mother had been thrown a surprise birthday party last Saturday night. Lexie had called her mother and sang her the birthday song first thing that morning, so she'd heard nothing of the party.

"The girls at Heidi Pies threw my mom a party." This made Lexie happier than she would have guessed.

"Cool." Peter stared intently at the TV. He was jiggling his leg, getting nervous for the Red Sox.

Lexie clicked on a picture of her mother holding a glass of champagne. Someone must have brought the bottle in. They didn't sell champagne or hard liquor at Heidi Pies. There was beer and wine, usually ordered by people who were having a potpie or the meat loaf, something savory. Mitzy didn't look trashed in the photo, although she certainly wasn't sober. She looked like someone who *could* have been a good mother.

Lexie continued to click through the party photos. Everyone

loved Mitzy at Heidi Pies—Lexie knew this from experience, and she could see it in the photos, too. The waitresses, line chefs, cashiers, and the hostess were all laughing, arms thrown around one another. In one photo, there was a cigarette burning in Mitzy's hand, ready to ignite the curly, frosted hair hanging on the shoulders of the person she was embracing. There was a picture of the birthday cake; the icing showed a white-aproned waitress with a pie held up in one hand. And then there was the photo of a smiling Mitzy holding up from her chest, like a medal, the necklace Lexie had sent her. It was a gold circle made of her initials in cursive. Viewed abstractly it looked like lace—a monocle-sized doily. Lexie had seen the girls at school wearing necklaces like this so she figured it was the latest trend. When she'd gone online to buy one for her mother, she found that the pure gold ones ranged from $250 to around $500. She'd bought a gold-plated one that was $99, shipping included. At the time she'd considered it a smart move, considering her and Peter's finances. But as Lexie looked at the picture, at her mother's face, which appeared undeniably proud, she felt ashamed for having cheaped out. Yes, she and Mitzy never spoke about anything meaningful. They saw each other once a year at Christmas when Lexie flew out to California and spent a week visiting. Lexie stayed at the Simmses' house on these visits as Mitzy was in a one-bedroom apartment that was usually shared with a boyfriend. But in spite of Mitzy's unmothering, in spite of their lack of common ground, she was the person who had brought Lexie into the world. And by the look on her face in the necklace photo, she was proud of her creation.

"I'm an awful person," Lexie said.

Peter looked over at Lexie and rubbed her knee. "Huh?"

"Look." Lexie turned the computer and showed Peter the picture.

"That the necklace you got her?"

"Yeah. And look how happy she is about it. I should have splurged for the solid gold one."

"You're feeling guilty about *that*?"

"Yeah. She is my mom."

"She didn't send you a birthday present."

"She's a waitress!"

"Last I checked, career waitresses make about the same as school counselors."

"Ha!" Lexie snorted, then she stopped and thought for a second. "You think so?"

"Probably. With tips and everything."

"No. No way she's making what I'm making."

"You're getting a little competitive, aren't you?" Peter squeezed Lexie's knee as he refocused on the game.

"Listen, I truly hope she makes more than me. That would make me happy. But I don't believe it." Besides, Lexie thought, it didn't matter if Mitzy never sent her a thing for her birthday. What mattered was that Lexie did the right thing. "When I was girl—" Lexie bounced her leg on Peter to get his attention. He turned his head. "When I was a girl, my parents never threw me a birthday party."

"You've told me that before."

"Did I tell you that we'd go to Heidi Pies on my birthday?"

"Hmmm, maybe. Tell me again."

"We'd go Heidi Pies and I got to order whatever I wanted. And the waitresses would bring me, like, five desserts, each one with a candle in it. I thought that was great when I was little. I thought it was the coolest thing ever and that I was the luckiest birthday girl in the world. I actually bragged about it at school."

"That's sweet."

"But don't you think it's kind of cruel that I didn't get a party?"

"No. Not if you thought the five desserts at Heidi Pies was the coolest thing ever. Perception is reality. And your perception was that it was great."

"Yeah, I guess you're right." What was her perception, her reality, of Peter since Dot had pointed out their essential difference? Or, more pressingly, since she'd committed the error with Daniel? It had changed, that was for sure—she no longer saw Peter as the single love of her life. And the love that she did have for him—however great or small—had lessened when compared to the passion she'd had for Daniel Waite. But slowly, in a barely noticeable way, Lexie felt herself shifting back to her fiancé. Her body pulsed toward him, expanding, loving him more, even, now that she'd been so horrible and he had blindly, blithely, sailed past it. Each day she didn't text with Daniel, Lexie felt a little less lust for him. It was almost like a fantasy she'd had—something too intense and perfect to be part of reality.

"I love you." Lexie rubbed her foot on Peter's leg.

"Love you, too, babe." Peter trapped the foot and held it in two hands, the way you might hold a guinea pig. He kept his eyes sharp on the game.

10

LEXIE WOKE UP FROM A DREAM IN WHICH DANIEL WAITE WAS A penguin peeing on her. She laughed, relieved it hadn't been a sex dream.

She got up and peed. Peter was in the shower. Lexie didn't flush—no point in scalding Peter. She peeled off the T-shirt and the yoga pants she had slept in and walked into the shower. Normally she liked to shower alone: too much dripping mascara for a couple's shower to be sexy. And who wanted to scrub out every nook and crack in her body when there was a witness to the digging? Also, Lexie was certain she looked like a rat when her hair was wet. But she and Peter were getting married. If she looked like a rat, he better get used to it. This was the advantage of Peter: She could trust that he'd love her more than anyone even if she looked like a rat. Daniel Waite would probably run back to his wife if he caught a glimpse of Lexie with her hair plastered against her head.

"I've got a Skype meeting." Peter stepped out as Lexie stepped in. "That guitarist who plays on all of Wainright's records . . ."

He turned on the sink and started a quick touch up shave while talking to her. Lexie couldn't hear what he was saying.

"Have fun, I love you!" Lexie shouted when he left the bathroom. She had never said *I love you* as much as she had lately.

Lexie didn't think of Daniel when she dressed for school. And she didn't think of him during the drive (she sang along with Taylor Swift on the radio). She also didn't think of him when she parked the car in the faculty lot. However, the moment Janet Irwin caught up with Lexie on one of the brick pathways that crossed the school, Lexie was remembering when Daniel flipped her from her back to her stomach in one swift, acrobatic maneuver.

"You're late for the meeting," Janet said.

"What meeting? And if I'm late, you're late." Lexie could almost feel the pressure of Daniel's hands clamped onto her hips.

"I was already there." Janet spoke in a typewriter staccato. "I ran back to Don's office to get some papers he needed."

It was sunny but chilly out. Though Lexie wore a coat, the students she saw didn't even carry sweaters. In general, students refused the cold until they were closing in on frostbite. Many kids said hello to Lexie as they passed. Only a couple said hello to Janet Irwin.

"Well, I didn't know there was a meeting." In Lexie's mind, naked Daniel continued to perform acts that she assumed—perhaps wrongly, she was willing to admit—Janet Irwin didn't know were possible. Had anyone ever touched Janet's upright-Hoover-vacuum body? Had her skin ever pushed against someone else's with such a delirious intensity that she wished she could merge with the other person and be absorbed into his or her flesh? Doubtful.

"Didn't you get the email?"

"I haven't checked my email yet." Unlike her personal email, which was on Lexie's phone, checking her Ruxton email was like taking out the trash. A necessary chore. There were so many other things Lexie would rather do with her hands.

"How long do you have to be at this school before you learn that you should check your email every morning and every night?"

Lexie walked faster. Dot-speed. It was childish but she actually hoped to lose Janet, to walk so fast that she would soon disappear behind the dining hall or the athletic center. Janet effortlessly hustled alongside her. Lexie shouldn't have expected less. The only personal detail Janet had ever divulged was that she had been a star field hockey player during her boarding school days at The Guilford Academy (Ruxton's sister school from before both schools went co-ed) through her years as an undergraduate at Smith College.

"I only check my work email at work. Like a lot of people on this campus." Actually, most of the faculty and staff were so devoted to the school, they didn't even have a personal email account.

"You need to check your work email before you leave the house."

Lexie was almost jogging. She started to turn down the path that led to her office. Janet reached out a fast, ropy arm and clasped Lexie's shoulder. "Where are you going?"

"My office." Lexie was panting. Goddammit, why couldn't Janet be breathless, too? "I want to drop off my stuff, I'll be there in a minute."

"Lexie, this is urgent. You didn't read the email, so you don't know, but it's urgent. Drop your stuff off after. Come on." Janet clapped her hands together twice, quickly, as if Lexie were a dog.

Lexie wanted to kick Janet. Or bite her, like a dog might, on her calcified, scraggy ankle. "Okay, relax." Lexie stepped ahead of Janet and rushed toward the faculty center. Janet, with her sinewy low-estrogen legs, had no problem keeping up.

Lexie entered the meeting room and looked at the stiff faces. The large black conference table was encircled with about thirty black Windsor chairs, each with the gold Ruxton seal on the back support. All the seats were taken except the one to the right of Don McClear. Janet Irwin dropped into that seat, as expected. Extra chairs were along the three walls facing the head of the table, and many people were standing. With a hundred faculty for the 385 students, meetings were usually held separately for each grade or department.

Amy sat at the back wall; her purse was on an empty chair beside her.

"What's going on?" Lexie picked up Amy's purse, put it under Amy's seat and sat. She shoved her own purse under her seat, and then she reached back down and retrieved her cell phone, a notepad, and a pen. Just then, the cell phone buzzed. It was a text from Daniel.

Frito Friday isn't the same with out you. Can we revisit this topic in person? 3 at Inn at the Lake? My body misses your body.

Lexie could feel blood rushing up and down, to each end of her trunk. She was flooded with desire. Almost sick with it. She held the phone in front of Amy so she could read it.

Amy took the phone, swiped her finger across the text and deleted it. Lexie winced. It felt violent.

"Ignore," Amy said firmly.

"It's hard." Lexie took back her phone.

"Stay tough. Don't think about him."

Don McClear shuffled through and straightened the papers Janet had handed him. He looked up, waiting for the group to look at him. "Everyone here?"

Lexie held her phone low on her lap, under her notepad where Don couldn't see, and started playing Yahtzee. The game would surely stop her monkey mind from playing the tambourine and might even help her forget that Daniel had texted.

"Bill's sick and everyone else is accounted for," Janet finally said.

"Dot's not here," Amy said, and Janet gave her a scolding look as if to tell her that faculty attendance was none of her business.

"Well, Bless Janet's heart," Lexie whispered in a Southern accent. She started a new game, canceling out the last one before the final roll. Even if she hit Yahtzee the score would come in only at 222.

"I'm sorry to say that Dot passed away last night," Don said.

Lexie felt an instant emptiness as if a trapdoor had opened and everything inside her had plummeted to the ground. She gulped at bites of air, searching for something to fill the unfamiliar hollow before she floated off.

Amy took Lexie's hand, grounding her. Lexie noticed a shifting, jostling sound as the people around her readjusted their bodies. The news was being absorbed physically as well as mentally. Lexie released a choking cough before she began silently crying. Her chest heaved up and down as she stuttered for air. This simple and absolute grief was completely new to Lexie. When her grandparents died, she had been only baffled as she waited for a sadness that never came. But the screaming whoosh of Dot being yanked from the living had jolted Lexie with a new sensation. It was utterly foreign, startling, a complete scraping out of her insides. She looked at Amy, whose eyes appeared magnified by tears. Yes, Amy was feeling it, too.

Don went on, his voice sounded like it was coming from inside a fish tank. "She was with her sister Ann and her nieces and nephews—it was Ann's birthday yesterday." Don pulled a white handkerchief from his pocket and blew his nose. "Ann told me that Dot had done one of her signature tap dances—the opening sequence from *Forty-Second Street*. After the dance, she said she felt dizzy and so she lay down on Ann's bed and, well . . . they thought she was sleeping." Don's voice cracked. He blew his nose once more. Then he returned the handkerchief to his pocket and gave a too-long speech about Dot's fifty-plus years of service to Ruxton, her humor, her *potty mouth* (Don's words specifically), her speedy way of walking, and the many generations of Ruxton students who had loved her.

Lexie tried to remember the email she had sent to Dot. Did she sign it *love*? Had Dot even read it? She certainly hoped she had; she wanted her to have had that small, half-joking thrill of knowing that she would be at the bride's table and Amy wouldn't. And the dress! Lexie shouldn't have let her spend all that money on the dress.

"Why did I let her buy that dress?" Lexie whispered in Amy's ear.

"What about the dress?" Amy whispered back.

Both Lexie and Amy's words were garbled with tears.

"Why didn't I tell her I wasn't going to get married after all?" What Lexie meant was, why didn't she tell her she wasn't getting married simply so that Dot wouldn't buy an expensive dress. But after she said those words, they started to take on the more obvious meaning. Lexie thought back to her last couple conversations with Dot. Dot wasn't only pointing out the differences between Lexie and Peter. She was urging her not to get married.

"Lexie." Amy turned Lexie's face toward her own so they were eye to eye, both of them shiny-cheeked. "You *are* getting married. Remember?"

"She spent way too much money." Lexie could feel mascara pooling below her eyes but she didn't care.

"No, it's good she spent the money." Amy used her thumb to wipe Lexie's face. "She had fun shopping with her sister."

Lexie heard her name and looked across the room at Don. "Sorry?" she said, sniffing.

"Can you clear your calendar for the influx of students who might want to talk about the loss?" Don was abrupt. Annoyed maybe that Lexie and Amy were whispering in the back of the room.

"Yes. Not a problem."

"Thank you. Now, we need to discuss housing," Don said. "Dot resided in Rilke, as most of you probably already know, and we have a responsibility to make sure we have a faculty dorm parent there . . ."

Lexie's ears felt like they were filling with warm syrup. Her breathing bumped out like a rutted road. Snot and tears fell on the glass screen of her phone as she started a new game of Yahtzee.

"That's what you want to do at this moment in time?" Amy looked down at the game. Her skin was so thick and smooth that when she lifted her brow her forehead folded, rather than wrinkled, into layers that resembled poured cake batter.

"I'm playing for Dot." Lexie finger-dragged down two 5s.

"What does that even mean?"

"I think Dot knew the marriage was wrong." Lexie's fingers kept working the game.

"She bought the dress. She knew it was right."

"No." Lexie stared at the phone and moved her fingers faster than ever, leaving the decisions in the game to her subconscious. "She told me that if I married him, it'd be my *first* of more than one marriage. If I get over three hundred points—" Lexie stopped speaking as she zoned in on the game.

"If you get over three hundred points?" Amy asked, urgently.

"It means I should leave Peter and stay in Dot's apartment until I figure things out." Lexie used her left thumb as well as her right—both sides paddling like little flippers.

"Listen, it's one thing to let Yahtzee decide if you're eating carbs or not—" Lexie had made many diet decisions based on the outcome of her games, "but you can't end an engagement on the very day that your good friend dies, because of some random rolls on your iPhone." Amy's voice was edging out of a whisper. She almost sounded angry.

"Oh my god!" Lexie stopped playing and looked at Amy—she couldn't see clearly for the flow of tears. "I think Dot knew she was going to die. We are mammals after all, don't we all sense these things inside our bodies?"

"No, we don't."

"But maybe Dot did. Maybe she knew she was going to die and she hurried it up a little so that I'd have a place to live. She created the space for me to leave Peter." Lexie started playing again.

"So Dot died to give you an apartment, and Dot is jumping

into your phone and controlling your Yahtzee game to help you do what *she* thinks you should do?"

Lexie stopped rolling once more. She had 260 points. Only a full house remained and that was worth 25 points. "I can see myself from the outside and I recognize that I am totally and completely not in my right mind. But I can also feel myself from the inside and I know that I have to play this game in order to decide what to do."

"Well, go ahead and roll. It's impossible for you to get over three hundred." Amy tapped a nail on the screen of the phone.

"But if I roll a second Yahtzee, it's worth a hundred points and I'll have well over three hundred." Goose bumps rushed up Lexie's flesh—it felt like a sheet had been yanked off her body.

Amy wiped her eyes. "So do it. Let's see what Dot and Our Father who art in Yahtzee say about your future."

Lexie rolled. Three 3s and two 5s: a full house. She dragged the three 3s down to hold them, then rolled again to let go of the two 5s. She got another 3 and a 6. She held the 3, making it a total of four 3s, and released the 6 to roll again. The fifth 3 showed up.

"Yahtzee." Lexie felt a shock of relief. An incredible lightness. A life sentence pardoned at the last minute. And then what felt like an ocean wave unfurled beneath Lexie's skin, and the empty space inside her was suddenly washed with another thrust of sadness. Lexie was audibly crying. She fully felt it all: the loss of Dot and the loss of Peter. But one was more painful than the other. She wanted Dot back.

"Well, dang." Amy put one arm around Lexie, and took the phone from her. She stared at the screen while Lexie cried into Amy's shoulder.

"Don." Lexie pulled away from Amy, pulled herself together and spoke as loudly as she could. She waved her hand to get his attention. "I'm sorry, I've lost track of the discussion. Did someone volunteer to be the dorm parent in Rilke yet?"

Before Don could answer, Janet clucked out a response like a hen pecking corn: "Jim is staying there tonight and Artie is staying the next night. Beyond that we have no idea."

"I can stay there tonight, and I can stay for at least a few weeks."

"Great. I'm sure the kids will appreciate having you down-stairs." Don nodded at Lexie. She had redeemed herself for whispering with Amy.

"Hold on," Janet said. "Hang fire. We can't have a female dorm parent in a boys' residence."

"Dot—" Lexie choked out. "Dot was a woman, Janet." Lexie heard snickering from the front of the room.

"Dot and Beau lived there together. The only reason Dot was there alone was because Beau had passed and Dot had been there so many years by then."

"Surely the boys are used to having a woman downstairs. They'll be fine." Don turned his face toward Janet and stared at her in a way that froze her out and shut her down. He was one of the most boring men Lexie had ever met, but he exerted an authority that was impossible to dismiss.

"Well, let's make sure they all have Jim or Artie's number so they have access to a male faculty member for emergencies." Janet pulled herself up straight—as if her head had been attached to a string hanging from the ceiling.

Don looked away from Janet and straight toward Lexie. "We'll talk after the meeting." He immediately switched the discussion to the memorial service.

Lexie sniffed hard. She took her phone from Amy and then

tapped out a text to Daniel while Amy looked onto her lap, reading the words as they appeared. *Meet you at Inn on the Lake this afternoon. Can't talk until then. Someone I love died.*

Your fiancé?! Daniel texted.

No. I'll tell you when I see you.

Be strong. You can cry in my arms @3.

Lexie looked over at Amy. "I'm meeting him at three and the Yahtzee was with threes. You don't think that means something?"

"Oh honey, everything means something if you decide it does."

"Are you mad at me?"

"No." Amy leaned in and hugged Lexie. "Peter's going to be heartbroken and there's gonna be a shitstorm of anger coming your way. But no matter how crazy you act, I'm on your side."

DON MCCLEAR WAS CALM AND DISPASSIONATE AS LEXIE TOLD HIM she was breaking off the engagement and leaving Peter. He didn't ask why. Lexie figured if she were having the discussion with a woman, she would have asked why. But like many men she knew, Don didn't dig further than what was laid out before him. It was an admirable quality, Lexie thought. She herself had a ravenous curiosity about most people and sometimes hated her need to keep scratching at the information people were willing to give until she'd dug herself into a tomb-sized crater before their feet.

"We'll need you to move in tonight, if you can," Don said. "I hope that doesn't feel too soon, too—"

"That's fine." Lexie couldn't focus on what Don was saying. Dot was gone and she was leaving Peter: Those two ideas were all her brain could hold.

"And I'm sure you already know this, but I have to say it anyway: It is required that you sleep there every night school is in session. Although you could have another faculty member cover for you if you need to be away a night or two. And overnight guests are forbidden." Don looked down at his desk, he seemed embarrassed to be discussing this.

"I understand. I remember the story about the woman who worked here who had the boyfriend in town—"

"Melanie Birkin. She was too young for . . . well, for everything that came to her while she was here. You're much more together." Don looked at Lexie quickly and then shuffled some papers.

"Thanks." Hopefully Don would never discover that Lexie's decision had been made by the outcome of a Yahtzee game. That alone would likely make her the loser in the Melanie Birkin/Lexie James *shit together* race.

"Oh, Janet sent me an email to remind me that the buffet belongs to the school. I think she wants it in her apartment. But you get first choice since the buffet's already in Dot's place."

"I've never had a buffet. I'm not even sure what a buffet is."

"Neither am I. But keep it if you want it."

"If Janet wants it, I probably wouldn't like it." Lexie blushed. She had never been so bold as to discuss her dislike of Janet with Don.

"I'll shoot her an email and tell her it's hers." Don winked at Lexie in a way that made her actually smile. "I know you had a special relationship with Dot. I'm sure this is terribly hard on you."

The loss of Dot was something Lexie could feel from her feet up. She wanted to plant Dot beneath herself; Lexie's roots would grow into her, connecting them in the way of families and bloodlines. A daisy chain that would never end.

11

IN SEPTEMBER, LEXIE HAD PRACTICALLY PASSED OUT FROM ANXI-ety after flirting with Daniel Waite. And now it was October: Dot was dead, Daniel was waiting for her at the Inn on the Lake, Lexie was hours away from breaking Peter's heart, and she was still standing (or sitting, just then). Handling it all. Answering emails. Filling out paperwork. Amy, with whom she had been on and off the phone all day, said she thought maybe Lexie was in a state of shock. Was this the gentle, quiet building up of something that would soon explode? Was she experiencing a bodily version of earthquake weather? (Mitzy loved to point out earthquake weather. Earthquakes came, she claimed, on glaring sunny days when it was too bright to read a magazine outdoors. The birds would quiet and nothing moved. Not even the air. Once, after a rare shopping trip to Ralph's, Lexie and Mitzy were walking through the parking lot, each holding a bag of groceries in their arms, when Mitzy pointed out the earthquake weather. Seconds later, like magic, the blacktop beneath them shifted back and forth as if it were a giant skateboard on which they both were standing. A booming echoed from the sky and Lexie dropped her bag; a jar of Ragu smashed on the ground. The spaghetti sauce quivered and ran like thick blood toward her feet. Lexie stepped away from it and looked toward her mother. Mitzy was beaming, so proud of herself for having predicted the quake, that she wasn't even mad about the lost sauce.)

Lexie put down her pen, pushed the papers away and shut her eyes. Dot was projecting on the screen in her head. Immediately, her brain slapped on the dress Dot had bought for Lexie's wedding. The image was so incongruent, so off-kilter that Lexie laughed. Lexie decided that Dot would not have looked like an overly decorated Christmas tree in the dress, as she'd originally thought. She'd have resembled a goat in an evening gown.

The more Lexie laughed, the more she felt Dot's presence. Dot would have loved the simile. She would have come up with something equally absurd. *Look at me! I'm a piece of broken crockery glued together and held in place with a fucking wad of satin!*

Was the dress satin? Or was it silk? Lexie would see when she got into the apartment. And it was then, when she thought of Dot in her apartment, the dress laid out on the bed, that the crying started up again. She didn't worry about the noise—the only person who showed up at Lexie's office without an appointment was Dot.

Lexie straightened her desk while she cried. It was a strange impulse, but it felt right at the time. She chugged and slobbered and made odd donkey noises as she sorted papers quickly into the trash, or into *To Do Later* and *To Do Soon* files. Once her desk was clean, while the crying continued to chug out of her like a freight train with endless cars, Lexie went to her office closet and pulled out her small vacuum. She plugged in the appliance; it wailed the way most cheap machines do. Lexie cried louder and harder while the vacuum swept over the old Persian rug, the wood floors, and even the couch. Afterward, Lexie (still crying) dusted with Pledge and a netted dust cloth she'd ordered over the Internet. When even the baseboards had been wiped clean, the crying let up. Lexie stood in the middle of her office and inhaled deeply. The room smelled like chemically created lemons. A line from a Gwendolyn Brooks poem came to her, but she wasn't sure exactly how it went. It was a poem about a dying old woman and there was something in there about perfume, refueling, pulling up the droop. Of all the people Lexie knew, Dot was the only one who would have known the Brooks poem offhand. She probably would have recited it in her scratchy, metallic voice. Lexie cried a little more at the thought.

NOT ONE RUXTON STUDENT CAME TO TALK ABOUT DOT. LEXIE KNEW it was unlikely. Once you hit sixty, teenagers thought you were old enough to die. And eighty? Yeah, they were sad. But it was okay to them. Dot had had a long life.

At ten of three, Lexie put a note on her door: *Gone to a meeting off campus. If this is an emergency, call my cell phone.* Every student she had treated had her phone number. And tonight when she moved into Rilke, every student resident of that dorm would have her number, too.

LEXIE SAT IN THE JETTA AND STARED AT THE DOOR TO THE CAFÉ OF the Inn on the Lake. She knew it was selfish and unreasonable to see Daniel and break up with Peter on the very day that Dot died.

But she felt she could no more stop herself from these two abhorrent acts than she could have stopped Dot from dying. Maybe she'd inherited a genetic inability to properly respond to tragedy and that was why she was sitting in a car, parked at the inn.

Lexie thought of Derek Clifford the newscaster who was on the local news from the time Lexie could talk until the summer after seventh grade. When Derek sat in Mitzy's station at Heidi Pies, Mitzy would later report to Lexie everything he'd said, what he'd been wearing, how much tip he'd left, and how his brown-sugar-colored hair looked that day. It seemed a relationship so intimate that Lexie, at age eight, often bragged at school that her mother was best friends with Derek Clifford. She didn't think it an exaggeration when she told Tammy Lunden, who was brand new to the school, that she called him Uncle Derek.

Then, when she was thirteen, Lexie and Mitzy went into a gas station mini-mart to splurge on Dr Pepper and pink Sno Balls, a combo Mitzy swore gave you enough energy that it was the only meal you'd need all day (and would, therefore, be the only meal Mitzy would provide that day). Derek Clifford came in, picked up a bottle of water, and stood behind them in line. Water was a luxury Lexie wasn't allowed to buy. (*Why pay money for something that comes free from the tap?*)

Lexie had smiled up at Derek. *Uncle Derek.* She waited for Mitzy to say something, to hug and kiss him hello, to at the very least mention the last meal he'd had at Heidi Pies. But not a sound issued from Mitzy's mouth. Lexie wasn't even sure her mother was breathing; she stood so rigid, so flush-faced, that Derek was the first one to speak. "You're up," he said, and he flipped down his sunglasses from where they'd sat on top of his head and then pointed toward the cashier. In the car, as they drove away, Mitzy happily reexamined the encounter. "He said, 'Your turn, Mitzy,' didn't he?" she said. "He knows my name!" As young as she was, Lexie knew better than to disagree.

A few months later, when Derek Clifford's taxi-yellow convertible was hit by a truck, Derek suffered brain damage that wiped him as clean as a wrung-out sponge. He had to learn life all over again. This time, however, he was missing the personality-molding experiences of dodge ball games, first love, underage drinking, and heartbreak. According to Mitzy, his new personality was identical to that of his caretaker: a woman the shape of a soft ice cream swirl who held each of Derek's hands in hers as they dropped their head in prayer before each meal at Heidi Pies. *It's a damn shame,* Mitzy would say. *A tragedy.* And then she'd light a cigarette, smile real big, and say, "Remember, before he lost his marbles, he knew my name!"

Mitzy's blitheness sat in Lexie's mind like a snapshot carried in a wallet. It was filed beside another thought snapshot: her father's behavior following the death of his parents. That had always seemed to be about the importance of a bag of Bugles chips on a road trip to Omaha.

"At least I've been crying," Lexie said aloud. But wait. Did the sobbing in her office count, since she had simultaneously vacuumed and dusted like it was a game-show competition? Lexie needed to escape her own mind. "Onward," she said, and she reached into her purse, pulled out her phone (holding it high to avoid neck wrinkles), and quickly worked her thumbs for a text to Peter.

Dinner duty tonight. Dot passed away at her sister's house last night. I'll be staying in her apt. for a bit. It's so sad. Let's talk when I'm home packing my bag.

She knew it was wrong to tell Peter about Dot's death in a text. But she also knew she couldn't speak to him until she told him she was breaking up. It was too cruel to have any other conversation in light of what was next to come.

A text buzzed in from Peter: *Shocked. Talk when you get home. Yours, like the sun.* Lately Peter had been signing off his emails and texts with a poorly bastardized line from an old Jefferson Starship song he had been teaching Lexie on the guitar. The only kind of music Peter listened to other than classical and jazz was '70s rock. It was the stuff her mother used to sing around the house or in the car, belting it out in a way that made Lexie suspect she was imagining herself on stage in a sold-out arena.

Lexie turned off the phone, dropped it in her purse, and got out of the car. She pushed both her palms into her cheeks to stop herself from smiling. She couldn't help it. The anticipation of seeing Daniel erased all decorum.

Daniel was waiting for her at the same table they'd had the other two times they'd been there. He stood, walked to Lexie, and hugged her so tightly she could feel his body heat through his dress shirt.

"You okay?" Daniel pulled back, held Lexie by the shoulders and stared at her.

"Yeah, I think I am." Lexie willed herself to think of Dot so that her mouth would close and her face would convey the appropriate emotion.

"Who died?"

"Uh . . ." She realized Daniel probably knew Dot. Had likely known her for years. While Lexie and Daniel were intimate enough to have sex, she didn't feel close enough to him, yet, for her to comfort him over a death. She had no idea how he'd react. Or how she should react to his reaction. If he cried, was she supposed to hug him and rub his back? Or was she supposed to patiently and dispassionately wait through it as she did when students cried in her office?

"I have a room tonight. Should we go there and talk?" Daniel lowered his head so it was even with Lexie's. He appeared to be examining her as if to make sure she wasn't going to collapse on the floor wailing.

"Yes." Again, Lexie saw Daniel flipping her, naked, from her back to her front. What was wrong with her that her mind jumped straight to sex when she was minutes from telling Daniel of Dot's death?

"We can get Frito pie delivered." Daniel cupped Lexie's elbow and escorted her out of the restaurant and into the lobby of the inn. While they waited for the elevator, Daniel leaned in and kissed Lexie. Gently. Like a whisper.

They kissed again inside the elevator. This time it was more intense. A real kiss. They kissed in the hallway outside the elevator; the hallway outside the door to the room; inside the room on the other side of the door; next to the bed; on the bed; and, finally, in the bed. Amy had once taken Lexie around the Ruxton chapel and explained the fourteen Stations of the Cross. The kiss parade felt the same: stops on a journey to a divine end.

An hour later, Lexie and Daniel were naked, lying side by side, holding hands like a cutout paper train of people. They turned their heads toward each other at the same time and laughed, although there wasn't anything to laugh at.

"I'm ordering food." Daniel rolled over and picked up the phone on the night table. From the back, undressed, if you didn't look at the pencil scratches of gray in his hair, he didn't look much older than Peter. Lexie propped herself up on her elbows and examined her belly, which the past couple of years had been rounding in spite of her weighing the same she always had. It wasn't fair the way men's bodies barely shifted with age.

"Will you get me ice cream or a milkshake?" Lexie pushed her fist into her belly, sucked it in.

"No Frito pie?" Daniel covered the mouthpiece with his massive hand like he was a pitcher holding a baseball.

"No. I want something cold. And something chocolate." What she truly wanted was something sweet and indulgent. She was at once completely relaxed and high from the sex, and also wound up, contracted, ready to explode. She needed something to balance the two: sugar and fat. Currently, the only two food groups from which she would eat.

Daniel placed the order. He sat back against the headboard. "So . . ."

Lexie pulled the sheet under her armpits and sat upright beside him. "Dot died."

"Dot?" Daniel squinted his eyes into two wide slits. The named didn't appear to trigger any memories.

"She was an English teacher. I thought you might know her from . . . I don't know, from all the fund-raisers and things you do with the school." As she said this, Lexie remembered Dot saying that she'd rather go to a "fucking herpes convention" than sit through any fund-raiser for Ruxton.

"Is that a real name? Dot? Like, does she have a twin brother named Dash?"

Lexie laughed. And then she groaned. "I can't believe I'm

laughing at Dot's name. She was my friend. I loved her!" She gave Daniel a playful slap on the arm.

"How old was she?"

"Eighty."

"Wait. Are you talking about Mrs. Harrison?"

"Yes! Dot Harrison. Her real name was Dorothy. She was born Dorothy May Tavis." Saying the name made Lexie gasp for breath. She looked at Daniel, and all was okay again.

"Yeah, she and her husband were my dorm parents. Mr. and Mrs. Harrison. They were sweet."

"Not sure I'd call her sweet."

"Maybe not." Daniel turned his head toward Lexie. "She used to sing in class. And she had that crazy voice—like someone who'd smoked unfiltered cigarettes since the age of five. Oh! And she'd tap-dance, too."

"She tapped something from *Forty-Second Street* last night. Then she felt dizzy, so she lay on her sister's bed and never got up again."

"Great way to go. . . . Are you sure she was eighty? I mean, I knew her thirty-five years ago and I thought she was eighty then."

"The students probably look at me and think I'm eighty." Lexie was relieved Daniel wasn't crying, or going into some soulful daze like what had overcome Peter the day his former guitar teacher, a man he called Spondee, died.

"You?" Daniel yanked the sheet off Lexie and then repositioned himself so that he could kiss her soft middle. "They probably think Janet Irwin is eighty. But you . . ." With one hand on each of Lexie's shark-fin hip bones, Daniel kissed his way down to her pubic mound. He looked up at her and said, "I bet those boys are wacking off every single night while thinking about you."

Lexie shook her head. "That is totally and completely disgusting to even imagine." She tugged Daniel up. He pressed himself against Lexie and she turned so that he was shelled around her back, his arm dangling across her belly, which she reflexively sucked in. Lexie wondered if the Ruxton boys ever did have a crush on her. You couldn't tell. Most of them were usually a little flustered and nervously attentive. Except Ethan. He was as comfortable with Lexie as if she were his aunt. She doubted he had a crush on her. Lexie put her hand on top of Daniel's and tried to suck in further. She held her belly like that. Barely breathing. Until she fell asleep.

There was a knock on the door. Lexie opened her eyes. It took a second to remember where she was and who was behind her. Daniel unstuck himself from Lexie and rolled off the bed. Lexie pulled the sheet up to her eyes. She was hiding, or mostly hiding, even though there was no chance she knew anyone who worked at the inn (and by the end of the night she would be a single woman). But it was late afternoon and they were naked—to have anyone enter the room was to announce that they'd had sex.

Daniel went into the bathroom. Seconds later, he emerged wearing the hotel's white, waffle-weave robe. He opened the door and let the uniformed, bald man roll in a cart with a thick, white tablecloth and two silver-lidded platters. Lexie's eyes darted from Daniel to the man, who politely looked at the floor as he waited for Daniel to sign the check. Daniel wrote his name so quickly, Lexie imagined his signature couldn't have been much more than a straight line. The uniformed man nodded his head, said thank you, and quickly left. Daniel rolled the cart closer to the bed.

Lexie sat up, pulling the sheet with her. Daniel sat on the edge of the bed, facing her. "While you were sleeping, I remembered something that happened with Mrs. Harrison when I was a student."

"Oh yeah?" Lexie pulled the silver lids off both platters. She picked up the bowl of three perfectly round scoops of chocolate ice cream and slid in the silver spoon. Then she readjusted the sheet again, pulling it tighter under her armpits. Light streamed in through the sheer curtains. Lexie felt too illuminated to sit naked while eating ice cream.

"For some reason I had stopped in at her apartment in Rilke one night before homecoming and she pointed at my chest and said 'Take that shirt off and let me iron it! You're not going out looking like a hobo who stepped off the rails!'" Daniel did a good approximation of Dot's voice. It brought forth the quiverings of a cry in Lexie's throat. She shoved a giant spoonful of ice cream into her mouth and swirled it around without swallowing. As she focused on the cold, velvety ice cream, the urge to cry fizzled out.

"So, I agreed to stay in Dot's place, in Rilke." Lexie dug her spoon into the bowl again.

"And they'll let your fiancé live there with you before you're married?" Daniel took a bite of Frito pie.

"No. I'm leaving him. I'm calling off the wedding." Lexie casually flipped the ice cream balls over with her spoon so she could get to the melty, soft bottoms. She didn't want to look at Daniel for fear she'd be disappointed by his reaction.

"That's fantastic."

Lexie finally looked up. Daniel had paused with a spoonful of Frito pie hovering in the air. The edges of his mouth were creeping into a grin. "That's the best thing I've heard in a long, long time." He shoved the Frito pie into his mouth and chewed with his mouth shut while smiling. The crunching sounded like boots walking on gravel. "How'd your fiancé take the news?" He took another big bite of Frito pie.

"I haven't told him yet." This gave Lexie a jolty feeling that smoothed out when she took an enormous bite of ice cream. If Daniel hadn't been there, she would have leaned over the bowl and sucked in an entire chocolate ball—choked herself with it.

"Are you going to tell him about us?" Daniel looked like a man at an awards ceremony who wasn't quite sure if the emcee had announced his name as the winner or not. Half happy, half anxious.

"I hadn't planned to." Why was he asking this? Wasn't he officially separated? The confidence she'd felt seconds ago was suctioned out of Lexie like dust up a vacuum hose.

"Tell him after Jen and I are out of the closet with this separation." Daniel stirred the Frito pie. "Tell him when Ethan graduates." He was relaxed. And he appeared undeniably happy that Lexie was leaving Peter. Confidence flitted around her—particles that hadn't yet coalesced.

"So, you think we'll be seeing each other eight months from now when Ethan graduates?" Lexie needed more confirmation. She wanted Daniel to answer quickly, before her brain filled in the silence with every crazy, heartbreaking scenario: Daniel no longer wanted to see her now that she was available. Daniel was using her for sex. Daniel liked the challenge of fucking his son's counselor. The bad possibilities were limitless.

"If it were my choice, you'd be my official girlfriend starting right this second." Daniel leaned his head down and looked into Lexie's face. "But maybe you need to figure out how you feel about me."

After weeks of trying to ignore her feelings for Daniel Waite,

Lexie felt free to look openly and directly at her heart. She was in love. Undeniably and completely. And now that she could admit these feelings (if only to herself) she was seeing their first encounter, on the lawn at Ruxton, through a different lens. True love had been there from the start, Lexie decided. Exactly as it had been with the three other men she'd loved in her life. (With each one she'd immediately felt a blood-rushing intoxication. She had never gotten to know someone better and *then* realized that he was the one.)

"Tell me this—" Lexie said. "To whom, other than me, are you actually going to say the word *girlfriend* if you're not out with the separation?" If she was going to be his girlfriend, the breakup with Peter would be permanent. No delicate easing out. No taking it through palatable stages. She'd have to stay in Dot's place until she . . . moved in with Daniel?

"I might tell a couple of my close friends. And I'd definitely tell my brother." Daniel talked about his brother more than he talked about Ethan. He was immensely proud of his younger sib, a Silicon Valley hotshot.

Lexie swirled the remainder of the ice cream into an icy pudding. "Hmmm, I'll agree to be your girlfriend if you pass a three-question test."

"Do I have to get all three right?" Daniel was grinning.

"Yes." Lexie had no idea what the questions were. She'd make them up as she went along.

"Yes? Shit. You're hard."

"Question one." Lexie spoke in the stilted announcement voice Don McClear used when he approached the microphone in the dining hall or the auditorium. "Have you ever named your penis?" She licked a dollop of ice cream off her spoon.

Daniel nodded toward where the named or unnamed object resided. He looked at Lexie and said, firmly, "No."

"Correct!" Amy had advised Lexie long ago to never get involved with a man who referred to himself in the third person and to never, ever, sleep with anyone who had named his dick. (Amy had once ended a date midcoitus when she discovered that the guy had named his dick Carbuncle.)

"Question two." Lexie took another mouthful of ice cream. She swirled it in her mouth while she thought up the question. "Have you ever cheated on a girlfriend or wife?"

"No." This answer came out quickly, with an upswing in tone as if it were an impossibility.

"Correct!" Mitzy once told Lexie a story about a Dear Abby column. A reader wrote in to say that it wasn't true that men never left their wives for their mistresses because her lover had left his wife and had married her. Abby replied something along the lines of *Congratulations! You're married to someone who cheats on his wife!* At the time, Lexie wondered if Mitzy was trying to tell her that she had stolen Bert from another woman, a wife, perhaps. But she didn't ask. No need to learn more than what Lexie already knew.

"Okay, question three." Lexie put the ice cream bowl on the cart and pushed the cart away from the bed. "Do you want to have sex one more time before I run out of here for dinner duty?"

"Yes, but I'm fifty-three. Even a girl as amazing and beautiful as you can't bring this"— Daniel pointed at his crotch with his thick, square hand—"this never, ever, ever been named and never-ever-ever-cheated-on-anyone dick back to life only an hour after orgasm."

Lexie wanted to laugh but she knew, from Amy mostly, that

it was unwise to laugh when a man was discussing his penis. "You pass!" Lexie said. "I fully accept the position of girlfriend!"

"And I am the winner." Daniel leaned back against the headboard and Lexie curled into his chest where the robe was gaping open. "Hey, Peter's not violent, is he?"

"No, not at all." The small, wiry hairs on Daniel's chest tickled Lexie's face. When she pushed into him the hair felt spongy and aerated. This was a new sensation. She'd never been with a man whose chest was filled in with fur.

"He's not going to try to hurt you when you tell him you're leaving?"

"No! He makes guitars." Lexie looked up at Daniel.

"If I were him, I'd want to kill someone. You sure he's not going to El Kabong you?"

"Huh?"

"It was this cartoon when I was kid. This guy, I think he was Spanish or Mexican—wait, he may have been a Mexican dog . . . or no, he was a horse. Anyway, he played guitar and when he got mad he'd lift the guitar and smash it on people's heads and yell *'El Kabong!'*"

"I can't imagine Peter causing harm to any of his guitars." Lexie wanted to burrow into Daniel's chest and hibernate—his hair as a blanket over her body—until the Peter breakup had passed.

"Yeah, but a broken heart can make people a little crazy. You know, make them act out in ways that even they themselves would never have imagined."

"Half the problem with Peter is there's nothing about him that challenges the imagination," Lexie said with certainty. "I'll never be surprised by him."

12

PETER WAS WAITING WITH A COFFEE CUP WHEN LEXIE WALKED IN the house. He hugged her, the drink in his hand hot against her back, and rocked her in his arms as if he were mothering a child.

"I'm okay." Lexie pulled away from the hug. She took the drink, gulped down a mouthful, and then jerked her head back and coughed. It was Irish coffee. And stronger than she would have made it. But probably a good thing considering what she had to accomplish tonight. She took another couple glugs before handing the cup to Peter who slurped from the top as if it were too hot to swallow (it wasn't).

"Yeah?" Peter brushed the hair from Lexie's face. "Are you ready to talk about . . . your shitty day?"

The whiskey in the coffee gave Lexie a cottony feeling in her head. But it wasn't enough to provide the courage needed to break up with Peter. Why hadn't anyone started a business where you could hire a surrogate to do the hard things that should be done face-to-face: breakups, quitting jobs, asking for money owed, telling someone they'd disappointed you? After growing up in a household where conflict was the central interaction, Lexie was so averse to confrontation that she regularly accepted the normally unacceptable (being overcharged in a restaurant, Janet Irwin's petty demands, a student complaining about a grade, etc.). Lexie took the cup from Peter and sipped down as much as she could before he removed it from her hands.

"I'll be ready in a second." She felt the alcohol like an elevator rising into her cottony skull.

"Did she ever answer your grandmother-of-the-bride email?" Peter finished off the coffee. Maybe to keep Lexie from sucking it down so quickly.

"No. I hope she read it, though." Lexie stared at Peter. How awful would it be if she did this by text? Beyond reproach, she knew.

"I bet she did. She probably was going to say yes in person."

"Will you talk to me in the bedroom while I pack?" Lexie walked upstairs ahead of Peter. Maybe she could put off the conversation until after she'd packed her bag.

Peter sat on the bed, watching while Lexie filled her rolling bag. Next, she got the big, ancient suitcase from the hall closet, the one she'd used when she'd moved from California to the East Coast.

"How many nights do you have to stay?" Peter lay back, his arms crossed behind his head.

"Hmmmm, not sure." Lexie felt like vomiting. Was it possible to load everything into the car and then tell Peter seconds before she drove away? It would serve the face-to-face obligation while saving her the agony of discussion. More than anything, Lexie didn't want to see Peter's reaction when she told him it was over. She didn't want to feel his feelings.

"Can I stay there with you?"

"No. Ruxton might buy condoms for the students, but there's no way they'd let two people who aren't married sleep in the dorm together."

"We should move to Amsterdam. You could work at a private school there and we'd sleep together and smoke pot at night and I'd sit out on the quad and play guitar."

Lexie actually laughed. "Yeah, all those quads on the canals in Amsterdam. And I looove pot, don't I?"

"We could live on a houseboat. I'd play guitar on the boat deck."

"And smoke pot on the boat." Lexie surreptitiously wrapped a sweater around her wooden jewelry box, placed it in the big bag, and then zipped everything up. "Okay, this is it." Was she actually going to do it this way? Was she so conflict avoidant that she would break up and then drive off? *Say it,* Lexie thought. *Do the right thing and tell him now. In the bedroom.* Lexie looked at Peter. She opened her mouth to speak but before a word came out, Peter got off the bed, hoisted up the giant bag, and held it against his chest. He walked out of the room and carried it down the stairs. Lexie slipped the engagement ring off her finger and then placed it on the nightstand next to Peter's side of the bed. She grabbed the rolling bag and hurriedly bumped it down the stairs to catch up with Peter.

"I don't understand why you have to take all this stuff. This is crazy."

He hasn't seen crazy yet, Lexie thought. Crazy was minutes away if she didn't sit him down in the living room and explain as well as she could what was going on. Without context, this breakup would feel as random and unexpected as a bomb deployed on Western Massachussetts.

Peter let the big bag drop on the landing by the front door. He stood straight and took a few deep breaths.

"Peter," Lexie said.

"Yeah?" Peter leaned down and picked up the bag again—it looked like he was carrying a coffin. Lexie opened the front door for him and stepped aside. She waited a couple minutes before following him out as she tried to figure out how to start. Nothing sounded right in her head. It would be so much easier if they'd been fighting and miserable for weeks on end. Maybe she'd lie and tell him she was afraid of marriage.

Lexie stepped out of the house pulling the roller bag behind her. Peter stood at the open trunk staring down at the big bag that filled the space.

"Let's put that one in the backseat." Peter shut the trunk. He took the roller bag from Lexie and put it in the middle of the backseat where it sat like a squat child. "I'll follow you down to help you get the big one out of the car."

Lexie felt a bolt of shame run through her. How could she do this to a guy who was nice enough to follow her twenty minutes to school to help her schlep a suitcase out of the trunk? "There are a hundred able-bodied boys there who can get it for me."

"If you prefer the young boys, that's fine by me." Peter pulled Lexie in and hugged her, hard. Lexie was unable to formulate the breakup sentence. Words were backed up in her throat like train cars stuck in a tunnel. "It'll only be a few days, babe. Don't worry." Peter squeezed her tighter. Lexie wished she could burst into flames and burn up instantaneously. Disintegration would be easier than conversation.

"I have to tell you something." Lexie spoke into Peter's chest. Hairless. It felt hard as a piece of plywood.

"Hmm?" Peter didn't loosen his grip.

"I have to say something." Lexie pulled away and looked at Peter. Tears released from her eyes and streamed down her face.

"About Dot?" Peter wiped Lexie's face with his index finger. Lexie shook her head no. Yes. No. She was almost choking from the softball in her throat.

"I—" Again, the words didn't come. Lexie inhaled, sniffed, and then pulled away from Peter and got in the car. She turned the key so she could roll down the electric window. "I'm sorry." She cried in a sniffy, little way—her head rocking against the back of the seat. "I'm sorry." Lexie said again.

"What are you sorry about? I'm sorry your friend died. I'm sorry you have to live in her musty old-lady apartment until they find someone to move in there. I'm sorry I won't get to sleep with you tonight." Peter leaned in through the window and kissed Lexie on the lips.

"I'm sorry." Lexie was making squeaky hamster noises as she tried not to cry. She knew she should get out of the car, go in the house, and talk to Peter, but it felt as if her body was working against her, her hands were working against her. She started up the engine. "I—" Lexie's head shook and the hamster noises increased.

"It's gonna be okay." Peter's forearms were folded on the open window ledge. He was so gentle, so patient. Lexie thought of llamas—their soulful faces, their human eyelashes.

"But . . ." Lexie squeaked out. "I want to cancel the wedding."

"You do?" Peter looked surprised, but not crushed.

"Yes." Lexie's voice was so high, she barely recognized it as belonging to her. The shaky-head, twittering cry continued.

"That's fine, babe. You know we were always doing it for you. I never needed a wedding." Peter reached in and rubbed Lexie's forearm.

"We're going to lose a lot of money. All those deposits!" A choky wail came out.

"It's only money. I want you to be happy." Peter leaned through the window again and kissed Lexie once more.

"I'm breaking up with you." Lexie pushed out the words and instantly felt herself zoom away from her body so that she was floating on the ceiling of the car. It was an art she had practiced all her life—floating on the living room ceiling as her parents threw half-full cans of beer at each other; floating on the locker room ceiling when the girls teased her about her underwear; floating above her bed at night when she realized her father had abandoned her and she might never see him again.

"What?" Peter's face went through a series of emotions that was almost cartoon-like in its rapidity. Lexie focused on how bone-less his flesh was and not on what he was feeling. She looked down at herself and could see that she was crying, but she could no longer *feel* the crying.

"I'm permanently moving into Dot's apartment." Yes, she had used the word *permanently*. Lexie had heard it all as if it had been spoken by a stranger sitting beside her.

"Wait." Peter flashed a smile of confusion. "You're really breaking up with me?"

"Yes." Lexie checked on herself and was glad to see the crying persisted.

"I don't understand. You're leaving me? Why?" Peter's face continued to flip from one expression to the next, like someone flicking through channels with a remote control. Lexie stayed afloat and watched. She knew she wasn't going to turn off the motor. She knew she was about to do the supreme asshole move and simply drive away.

"I'm sorry." Lexie sniffed. There was nothing on which she could wipe her nose and she didn't want to use the sleeve of her blouse or the back of her hand, at this age, at this time. She sniffed again. "I'll come back soon to get the rest of my stuff." She let down the emergency break.

"WAIT!" Peter's voice screeched. "What happened? I don't understand what happened!" He started sobbing, his face a wild-eyed, rubbery mess of emotion.

Lexie watched herself as she put the car in neutral and let it roll back down the driveway. She hoped that of everything she ever did in her life, this would be the cruelest act. In that case her worst self would soon be behind her.

"Turn off the car. Come inside! I don't understand what happened?" Peter walked along with his hands on the window. Lexie checked in on herself again. Was she still crying? No, she wasn't. That was the thing about detachment. When you did it right, you became emotionally novacained.

"I don't love you anymore." Lexie hadn't wanted to say it, and she wasn't even sure it was true (she had no idea how she felt, other than numb), but it was the sharpest knife she could use: a swift, metallic cut, rather than sawing through Peter with a plastic utensil.

"Do you love someone else?"

"No." As promised, she wouldn't tell Peter about Daniel until Ethan knew about his parents' breakup. Lexie put the car in reverse and stepped lightly on the gas. Peter ran along with her, crying in hiccupping gulps. Lexie gunned the car to break free of him. She backed to the bottom of the driveway, shifted into gear, and zoomed away.

Once she had turned the corner, Lexie landed back in her body and a hysterical wailing poured out of her. It felt more like vomiting than crying. She pulled the car over and put her face onto the steering wheel, delirious with guilt, shame, and grief. Sick with it.

Lexie's cell phone rang. She looked at Peter's face on the screen. "I'm sorry," she said aloud. She shut the phone off, shoved it to the bottom of her purse, and then wiped her nose with the back of her hand.

TWO SENIOR GIRLS FROM THE LACROSSE TEAM WERE WALKING across the parking lot when Lexie pulled in.

"Can you two help me get this bag to Rilke?" Though she'd had them in her Health and Human Sexuality class, Lexie didn't know these girls well. One had already been recruited to play lacrosse for Hopkins, the other had been recruited for Dartmouth.

Orange-haired Megan Haliday reached into the trunk and pulled out the big bag with two hands. "Is there a body in here?" she asked.

Lexie laughed and wiped the tears from her eyes.

"You okay, Miss James?" the other girl, Toni Bell, asked. Her black skin was so shiny in the lamplight she looked like she'd been polished.

"Oh you know, it was a hard day today."

"I'm sorry about Mrs. Harrison," Toni said. "She was your friend, right?"

"Yeah, she was a great friend." Lexie held back from crying. It unbalanced students' sense of things when they witnessed their teachers being too human. Crying was as bad as being drunk or half-dressed.

"I had her for English three times. She was hilarious," Toni said. She and Megan held each side of the giant bag and walked with Lexie toward Dot's old apartment. Lexie pulled the roller bag.

"I only had her for English freshman year," Megan said.

"She sang all the time in AP English. She even made us sing once."

"Oh my god, I would have died if I had to sing."

"At least she had a good long life," Toni said.

They were at the door to Rilke. Lexie swiped her faculty ID. At the end of the hallway, she used the key Don had given her to open the apartment. She stepped back so the girls could walk in with the big bag.

"Should we put it in the bedroom?" Megan asked.

"Yes. Please." Lexie stood in the center of the living room and stared at the old, stuffed furniture. The floral couch was so overused it sank in on one end; next to it a side table was stacked with books.

The girls returned from the bedroom and stood near Lexie.

"Doesn't it look like someone's sitting there?" Lexie pointed to where the cushion dipped in the shape of a bottom.

"Totally spooky," Megan said.

"Her bedroom's going to freak you out," Toni said. "The bed's unmade, there are clothes everywhere, and there's a cup of tea on the nightstand."

"It's totally freaky," Megan said.

"Do you want us to help you change the sheets?" Toni asked.

"Mr. McClear said he'd send in housekeeping to change them." Lexie looked from one girl to the other. She wanted someone else to be in charge, someone else to take care of everything.

"Well, obviously they didn't get that message," Megan said.

"Do you have to sleep here tonight?" Toni asked.

"Yeah." Lexie looked down the hall to the bedroom. Dust balls bobbed in the corners like the empty fur sacks of dead mice.

"I have an air mattress from when my friend from home stayed the weekend," Toni said.

"Do you have sheets?" Lexie asked. In her rapid, anxious pack session she had failed to grab any linens. She wasn't ready to enshroud herself with Dot's linens, no matter how clean they were.

"Yeah," Toni said. "I'll give you one of my pillows, too."

"I'd love it if you let me borrow all that." Relief swooshed through Lexie's body. One less thing to think about. "Do you girls know who the proctor is here? Mr. McClear told me but . . ." Lexie tapped on her forehead. This must be what it's like to get old, she thought. Information slip-slides away.

"Cole Hanna," Megan said. She appeared to be blushing.

"He's Megan's boyfriend," Toni said.

"Ah." Lexie nodded. Surely Megan had snuck into his room sometime after seven thirty when boys weren't allowed in the girls' dorms and girls weren't allowed in the boys' dorms. Before then, if you were entertaining the opposite sex the door had to be open and at least three shod feet were required to rest on the ground. Lexie had laughed when she first learned this. Did the person who'd thought up that rule honestly think sex couldn't occur if kids wore shoes and kept three of four feet on the floor?

"Do you mind texting Cole for me and asking him to round up everyone for a meeting in the Kafka room in ten minutes?"

"No problem." Megan was texting before she even finished speaking.

IT WAS AFTER ELEVEN. LEXIE LAY ON THE AIR MATTRESS IN THE center of the living room. Sleep felt so far away it was like a forgotten skill: handstands, biking with no hands, or a backbend started from standing. Lexie got up, went to the kitchen and opened the cupboard where Dot kept her liquor. She unscrewed the gin bottle and took three giant slugs before returning to the air mattress. Immediately she felt like she was spinning. It was anxiety. Motherfucking anxiety. She couldn't take a Klonopin because she'd had the gin, and the Irish coffee earlier in the night.

Using an old trick from college, Lexie placed one foot on the floor and focused on a single spot on the ceiling. The spinning didn't stop. Peter was inside Lexie churning and kicking with hobnailed boots. And where was Dot? Lexie wished she felt Dot inside herself instead.

"Accept . . ." Lexie started. "Ah, fuck that. Change the channel!" Lexie knocked on her head as if that would shift her thoughts. She focused on the residents' meeting in the Kafka room. While the other boys had been rustling around, talking, eating chips from snack bags, or tussling over seats on the couch, Ethan had sat settled as a grown man in the blue-and-gray-chintz chair near the fireplace. His legs were open in a confident V and one cheek rested on the back of his hand, his elbow on the arm of the chair.

Lexie had stared at Ethan, a beat too long, perhaps, so that he pointed at himself and tipped his head forward as if to ask if she wanted something from him. Lexie had nodded no, and then looked around the stately, elegant room (giant wrought-iron chandeliers, two massive stone fireplaces, framed portraits of the long-dead founders of the school), pretending she was in the act of accounting for everyone when she was simply covering up the too-long stare. She remembered exactly what she had been thinking when Ethan caught her eye: *I'm in love with your father; I broke a man's heart for him.*

During the meeting Lexie read off a sheet of rules Don had given her (more for Lexie's sake; the kids had been living with the rules for years): no drinking, no smoking, no drugs, and no sex in the rooms. Each boy had to be in his own room by ten, although because these boys were seniors, there was no lights-out time. No leaving campus unless you had permission from your campus advisor. If you left for the night, you had to give Lexie a copy of your leave form, signed by your advisor. Even if your parents were picking you up. The dorm proctor, Cole Hanna, was to walk each floor every night at ten to check that all eighteen Rilke residents were where they were supposed to be. Afterward, he would fill out a report and slip it under Lexie's door. Lexie had to log this report each night, noting who had been off campus, who had been in the infirmary, who had been tardy for curfew, etc. Every Monday and Friday after breakfast there would be a meeting where the residents worked out any problems or conflicts, as well as make announcements, etc.

When Lexie had finished her dry recitation, the Rilke boys informed her that Dot's meetings included donuts, coffee, and, often, dancing. When Dot put on show tunes, she'd roll back the carpet and tap on the wood floor. Several boys liked to mock-tap with her, although two Rilke residents—Aaron Gotleib and Boston Connors—actually knew how to tap. When she put on rock music, Dot performed her signature move: The Funky Itching Chicken. Most boys danced with her. Asher Sherman often took over the floor to do full flips in the air and break-dance spins on his back.

Lexie pulled up the sheet and rolled to her side. "No donuts," she said aloud. It already took her too long to get ready in the morning (showering, where she shaved her fuzzy bits and sanded down her heels with a pumice stone; blow-drying her hair; putting on makeup including several coats of mascara; picking out the right clothes; making the bed; and drinking half a pot of Green Mountain coffee since the stuff in the dining hall tasted like the warm runoff from a rain gutter). Dancing she could allow, but one of the boys would have to be in charge of music. (Lexie wondered if teenaged boys danced by themselves the way girls did. Doubtful. The prior dance sessions had to have been a unique set of experiences brought out by the presence of Dot.)

Lexie flipped the pillow over to feel the cool cotton against her cheek. She saw faces: Daniel, Peter, Ethan. And then Peter leaning through the car window, his eyes wild with pain. Lexie didn't want to see him; she didn't want to feel the appropriate emotions. How could she take care of these boys, assorted like dolls in drawers in the rooms above her, if she was folding in from guilt and shame? She better keep things together: focus on work, eat well, exercise, be productive. She had to release Peter, let him float off like a flower on a stream. Someone would pluck him up soon enough. In Western Massachusetts, a guy like Peter was as rare and lovely as a wild orchid.

The spinning, the anxiety, dissipated and was replaced with a spaghetti-legged, blunt-edged looseness. Drunkenness, perhaps. Lexie got up, went to the kitchen, and retrieved the phone from her purse. She needed to call Betsy Simms and Betsy's parents to tell them she'd canceled the wedding. Hopefully, Mr. and Mrs. Simms could get their money back on the ticket they'd bought for Mitzy. Lexie needed to call Mitzy, too. Her mother would likely be relieved to hear the news. In regards to most of the forward-moving events in Lexie's life, Mitzy had been disinterested, if not scornful.

Lexie leaned against the counter with one hip, turned on the phone, and waited for the screen to light up. Dot's dishes were in the sink: a teacup, a coffee cup, a glass. No plates. Lexie had already gone through the cupboards and found that the only food in the house was a red holiday tin of cookies and a jar of olives. She knew Dot's meals were taken with many other people in the dining hall. But the three single glasses, not one having a twin to suggest a beating heart had had a drink with Dot, felt so lonely. How could the Buddhists be right about peace and solace in aloneness? Lexie wanted nothing more than to never feel alone. To never find a single teacup in the sink.

The phone made chirping noises as it loaded up everything Lexie had missed. There were texts from both Daniel and Peter. And twenty-two voice mails from Peter.

Instead of listening to Peter's messages, Lexie read Daniel's texts. He was worried about her and wanted her to text as soon as possible. Lexie called his number and it went to voice mail. She texted him: *Extremely difficult breaking it off. He didn't El Kabong me. Feel like such a shit I should go out, buy a guitar, and El Kabong myself. But I'm relieved. It's the right thing.*

Daniel wrote: *Stay strong! I'm with you in spirit.*

Wish you were here in body, Lexie texted.

At a boring, too-long dinner party in body. Am texting under a starched tablecloth. Brandy and dessert on the table.

Wish I had my foot under that tablecloth and was twaddling your zipper.

Is twaddle a word, Miss James?

Is now. Gonna twaddle the hell outta you soon.

Mon raison d' être. More later. Must pull hands above table before host suspects me of jerking off. Xx

Lexie was grinning from Daniel's texts as she clicked over to Peter's texts. He wanted to talk. He didn't understand. He was heartbroken. She stopped reading and ran her thumb over his name, deleting them all. It was kinder to cut him off with an assertive finality.

The phone rang. Peter's face was on Lexie's screen. She dropped to the floor, butt on the ground, her back against the cupboard, knees up. If she answered he might think there was a sliver of an opening into her heart when she knew it was shut and sealed. But he was ringing in her hand. She could do the phone. Phone confrontation was easier than in-person.

"Peter." Lexie started crying. Peter was crying, too, and that was all they did for a couple minutes until Peter coughed and cleared his throat.

"What happened?"

"Something shifted." Her words came out with a wet stuttering.

"But why? Why did things shift?"

"I don't know. I'm so sorry."

"I never even saw this coming."

"I couldn't stay with you if I wasn't feeling it anymore. I didn't want to fake it."

"Were you faking it?"

"No! Never."

"Don't you love me?"

"I . . ." She wasn't going to tell him again that she didn't love him. "I don't want to be together."

"This is fucking brutal!" Peter sounded angry rather than sad. "Brutal!"

"I'm sorry." They were silent. Lexie could hear him breathing. Her body rocked with her own deep breaths.

"Fuck you." Peter hung up. Lexie felt relieved. It was so much easier to process his anger than his grief. Grief made her hate herself. Anger let her off the hook.

Twenty-five minutes later, Lexie was still on Dot's kitchen floor, sniffing, thinking, spacing out, when the phone rang. Peter again.

"I'm putting all your things out on the driveway and changing the locks," he said. "You can get everything tomorrow night after nine." He hung up again.

"Okay," Lexie said, to no one. She remembered he was playing music with friends at nine tomorrow. He wouldn't bear witness to the gathering of her stuff. Lexie was grateful for that.

13

'M LIKE A SCHIZOPHRENIC," LEXIE TOLD AMY. THEY WERE AT THE top of the long driveway of what Lexie now thought of as "Peter's house," organizing and assembling her clothes, cosmetics, shoes, coats, boots, framed artwork, vases, dishes, pots, and pans. The spotlight above the garage door lit up what had been removed from the house. It looked like everything had been dropped by a crane from an eagle's height. "One second I'm happy," Lexie continued, "the next I'm bawling, and now I'm . . . I guess I'm relieved more than angry."

"Well, keep reminding yourself that you're relieved." Amy sat on a folded blanket, her legs spread into a V. She was piecing to-gether broken plates.

Lexie pointed toward the plates. "Forget it."

"But y'all only bought these dishes last year when you moved in together."

"I know, but you can't glue ceramic. It will never survive a dish-washer." Lexie had learned this after gluing together a teacup Peter had accidentally knocked off the counter with the headstock of a guitar (he had been serenading Lexie while she prepared dinner).

"There's a dishwasher in Dot's apartment?"

"It's about twenty years old, but it's there."

Amy tossed the plate pieces toward the pile of things to be thrown away.

"I'm glad silverware can't break. I like this set." Lexie held up a knife, looked at it, and then feigned stabbing herself in the neck with it.

"Oh, that's no joke, honey. The way he smashed up this stuff, he mighta knifed you if you'd been nearby."

"No way. This is probably the worst thing he's ever done in his life."

"*So far.* Worst he's done so far."

"If he were truly a bad guy he'd be here watching me deal with this heap of garbage." Lexie surveyed what amounted to her estate. Twirling in the back of her head like a fuzzy white dandelion was the idea that she didn't need any of it. Once she and Daniel were openly together it all would be replaced.

Lexie opened one of the giant Hefty bags she'd brought and filled it with the garbage. She dragged the garbage bag to the pile of framed pictures and lobbed in every one. The glass was cracked on most of them.

"You don't want those frames, at least?" Amy asked.

"Even with different pictures in them, I'll remember that they once had pictures of Peter, or me and Peter."

"You sure aren't acting like a girl who grew up poor. You would never see a poor girl from Alabama throw away perfectly good frames like that." Amy rescued the frames and plucked out the shards of broken glass. Already, she had amassed a trunkload of things bequeathed to her: snow boots purchased by Peter (Lexie had never liked them), a couple of throw blankets that had been on the couch (used when Lexie and Peter snuggled while watching TV), the red wrap dress Lexie wore the night Peter proposed, a boxy leather storage-ottoman Lexie had bought Peter for Christmas, and a speaker system Peter had purchased for Lexie's iPhone that she'd never learned to use.

"How would you know how a poor girl from Alabama would act? You were a debutante!"

"And Young Miss Huntsville, too, don't forget." Amy curtsied.

"Poor people from California throw everything away." Lexie placed the Crock-Pot into the trash bag.

Amy reached in and pulled it out. "Come on! There's nothing even wrong with this!" She held it aloft like a tennis trophy and examined the sides and bottom.

"It's Peter's. When he cooked dinner, that's how he did it. He even cooked dessert in it awhile back."

"So why's he throwing it out?"

"He probably didn't even *throw* that one. I bet it doesn't have a single nick on it."

"Yup, it's clean." Amy placed the Crock-Pot on her keep pile. "Maybe we should leave it for him."

"Nah. Let him believe it's in my apartment. He definitely put it here so that I would use it and think of him." Lexie put the bags destined for the Salvation Army in the trunk and what little she was taking on the backseat, floor, and the passenger seat of her car. Amy put her take in the back of her old Bronco.

Together they hauled the two big trash bags into the cans at the side of the house. When they'd returned from the trash, Lexie walked the driveway, picking up stray chunks of glass or ceramic, which she dropped in a plastic grocery bag. She surveyed the driveway one last time. "Wait. My wedding dress isn't here."

"I guess he wants to keep it."

"I was going to return it. I never cut off the tags." Although it had cost less than Dot's outlet dress, it was the most expensive piece of clothing Lexie had ever purchased.

"Well, you can ask for it back. Or consider it the price for your freedom."

"What's he going to do with it?"

"Save it for his next fiancée?"

At the sound of a car coming up from the road, they both turned their heads. The headlights from Peter's van blinded Lexie for a second before he passed Amy's car and parked halfway on the lawn, beside Lexie's Jetta.

"Uh-oh." Amy waved and smiled like the Southerner she was. Lexie felt an undulating roll from the bottom of her gut up to her throat.

"How you doin', Peter?" Amy said when Peter got out of the car.

"Terrible." Peter's eyes were pinned on Lexie.

"I'm sorry." Lexie's voice felt like it was made of broken rubber bands.

"There's one thing I forgot to put out for you. Wait here a second." Peter went into the house.

Amy and Lexie huddled together. "I'm sure he's bringing you the dress," Amy said.

"I feel sick," Lexie said.

"Say thank you, put the dress in the car, and then we'll drive outta here."

"I hate this feeling." Lexie's head was swirly. She was edging into a panic attack. "I'm gonna pass out."

"Do you still have that old bottle of Klonopin?"

"Mm, maybe. I'll look." Yes. Of course she had the Klonopin. But Lexie's need to have the bottle with her at all times was something she had a hard time admitting. Even to herself.

Lexie opened the back door of her car, dropped the little bag of broken bits onto the floor, and then took her purse from the seat. She found the battered old pill bottle, but her hands were shaking so hard she could hardly get past the child safety lid. Once it was open, she fingered out a pill and swallowed it dry.

Peter walked out of the house with an unvarnished, unstrung, raw guitar. Lexie shook out another pill and bit it in half. She shoved the bottle back into her purse before flinging the purse past the open car door onto the floor next to the bag of trash.

"I was making this for you for a wedding present." Peter held up the guitar like he was presenting a child.

"It's beautiful." Lexie's voice squeaked out.

"Do you see this inlaid wood?" Peter pointed to the swirling pattern of brown and green leaves that surrounded the hole. "Do you know how long it took me to do those leaves? Do you have any idea how many hours I've spent on this?"

"It's an amazing guitar," Lexie said honestly. "You should finish it and sell it."

"That's real beautiful," Amy said.

Peter jerked his head toward Amy for one instant, and then turned back to Lexie.

"Fuck you both." Peter lifted the guitar over his head. Lexie screamed and ran to Amy.

"Fuck you!" Peter brought the guitar down onto the hood of Lexie's car.

Lexie huddled into Amy. They watched as Peter pummeled the car until he was only holding the guitar's skinny neck, which had broken into the shape of a pistol. He hurled the neck, Frisbee style, in the direction of Amy and Lexie. They both ducked, but it didn't come near them, instead landing quietly on the lawn.

Peter turned and walked back into the house. Amy pushed Lexie toward her car.

"Go! Get outta here quick!"

LEXIE PARKED AT RUXTON. SHE FELT LIKE SHE HADN'T BREATHED since Peter's driveway. She snatched up her purse from the floor of the backseat and then pulled out her cell phone to send a text to Daniel. With shaky hands, Lexie typed *El Kabong*.

Lexie got out of the car and staggered to the hood. Using the flashlight on her phone, she examined the paint. There were faint gray lines, like Daniel's stray gray hairs, etched into the hood. The minor damage didn't match the enormity of the act. How sad, for Peter, that the wedding-present-guitar had been destroyed while her car barely felt the hit.

By the time she unlocked her door, the Klonopin had kicked in and Lexie was feeling a juicy liquidness. The El Kabong incident receded like smog on the distant horizon.

Lexie inhaled the sharp, rubbery smell of new paint. Five painters had come in that morning. They had done the walls and the kitchen cupboards, which were miraculously, beautifully, new-looking. The trim and ceiling hadn't been painted yet, but Lexie figured that would happen tomorrow.

Lexie thought about Dot living between these walls. Her furniture was there, somewhere, but mostly invisible as everything had been pushed together and covered with tarps. Lexie didn't know when Dot's family was picking up her things, but she didn't care. Even though she couldn't sleep in Dot's bed, she liked being surrounded by her things: the physical evidence of Dot.

There was a knock at the door and Lexie's phone rang simultaneously. A picture of Amy giving the finger was on her screen. Lexie answered the phone and walked toward the door.

"Hey," she said into the phone. "Hey!" she said to Ethan Waite standing in her doorway. "Come in."

"What?" Amy said. "Are you talking to me?"

"No, I have a student here, I'll call you back," Lexie said, into the phone. She motioned for Ethan to come in.

"Who? I've been trying to get you since we left the house."

"Ethan Waite. I couldn't reach my phone while I was driving. I'll call you later, okay?" Ethan sat on the floor and started to lean back against a wall. Lexie waved her free hand back and forth to stop him. He turned, looked at the wall, then dove forward and lay back on the floor, his arms folded behind his head as he examined the plastic-covered mountain in the center of the room.

"Should I pick up a bottle of wine and come calm you down?" Amy asked.

"I think it's all okay. My aunt was with me, remember?"

"Your aunt? You got your period?"

"No, the other aunt, the one who's a nurse practitioner, like you—you know, she can write prescriptions and all that . . ."

"Oh, that's right, you took the Klonopin!"

"Yes. I'll call you tomorrow, okay?"

"Okay, you sleep well. And call me at any hour if you need me."

"I will. Promise." Lexie ended the call and put the phone on silent.

She sat on the floor next to Ethan. He sat up.

"You okay?" She was glad he'd stopped in. An imperative to focus on someone other than herself was exactly what she needed.

"I dunno." Ethan shrugged and looked around the room as if he didn't want to look Lexie in the eye. "I've been in this apartment so many times but I can't remember what color the walls used to be."

"Did you ever know anyone who chewed tobacco?" The couple years Bert chewed tobacco, his lower lip bulged like he'd been punched in the face. Every few minutes, he'd turn his head and spit into a Slurpee cup. In the morning, while she was gathering the empty beer cans, Lexie also picked up the Slurpee cup and threw it in the trash. Often Bert would stir awake, reach into his pocket, and pull out a one- or a five-dollar bill that he'd hold in the air. Lexie would take the money and mumble something about buying a Slurpee and bringing home a new cup for him. Bert would smile, but he never opened his eyes. She always thought it was dumb luck when she landed a five.

"I've seen people chew, but I can't think of anyone I know who does it."

"Well, the walls were the color of tobacco spit. Or maybe more the color of a chewer's teeth. Sort of a gooey stain that you know was once off-white."

"Gross."

"Yeah. Don't ever start chewing. Unless you're interested in the kind of woman who likes guys with brown teeth."

Ethan smiled in the shape of a rectangle on its side. Like his dad. "What are you gonna do with all of Mrs. Harrison's stuff?" He bobbed his chin in the direction of the heap.

"Her family's taking it and I have to buy new stuff. Or, actually, Ruxton is buying new stuff for me to use. Want to help me pick out furniture?" With many students, and boys especially, Lexie had found that it was often easier for them to talk if you got to the problem indirectly. Ask them a question straight on and they felt under attack. In her office she kept both a crossword and a sudoku book and she occasionally handed one or the other to a student claiming she needed help on a half-filled puzzle. While working one of the puzzles, most students would slyly but precisely let Lexie know why they were there. Maybe furniture shopping would bring forth whatever problem had compelled Ethan Waite to stop in.

Lexie brought her computer out from the bedroom and placed it on the floor in front of herself and Ethan. She went online to the Crate and Barrel catalogue. "I was thinking of doing everything in yellow and gray." A lie. Until she said those words, Lexie hadn't given her furniture palette more than a glancing thought. But yellow and gray were the colors Mrs. Simms used for Betsy Simms's room when Betsy turned sixteen. "These are colors that can take you through adulthood," Mrs. Simms had said at the time. Adulthood was so far away then. Yet here it was, and Lexie barely felt any more adult than she had that day.

"I like that one." Ethan pointed at a rug on the computer screen.

Lexie clicked on it. "I like that one, too." She took this as a sign that she and Daniel would have the same taste. "Where are your pals tonight?"

"I didn't feel like hanging out with everyone. My head felt all speedy."

"Did someone give you their Ritalin?" Lexie made sure she came off as cool and casual. That was the way to get to the Ritalin source.

"Nah," Ethan said. "There are, like, five guys in Rilke who have prescriptions and none of them will give up any."

"Are you doing straight speed?" Again, casual. Nonchalant. When Ethan didn't answer right away, Lexie looked around the room. "How big do you think this room is?"

"Maybe . . ." Ethan stood and walked along the wall. "Fifteen—" He walked the other direction. "By eighteen. And I'm not doing speed."

"Okay." Lexie clicked on the twelve-by-fifteen rug and dragged it into her cart. "So you're not doing speed but you're feeling a little speedy."

"Yeah. My head was rushing." Ethan sat again. "And it suddenly hit me that Mrs. Harrison, who has been sleeping two floors below me for four years—"

"You've always been in Rilke? Only seniors are allowed here."

"My dad loved Rilke so much senior year, he made sure I lived here every year."

"Interesting." The life of an über-privileged kid. Thank god Ethan was a kind person. "Okay. Your head was speeding and you

190

were thinking about Dot." She should have said Mrs. Harrison. Too late for that. And who cared at this hour?

"Yeah, I was thinking that this is the fourth year she's slept below me and suddenly it seemed so strange to me that she isn't here."

"Do you feel sad?"

"Well . . ." Ethan pointed at Lexie's computer screen. "I like that couch." Lexie zoomed in on it.

"You were saying you felt sad." He hadn't said that, Lexie knew. But she wanted him to clarify if he could.

"Yeah, I'm totally sad. And it . . . it feels so incomprehensible. The idea of someone being there and then, poof, she's gone. She doesn't exist. It's like she disappeared off the planet. I like the other one better." Ethan pointed at a couch on the screen.

"This one?" Lexie clicked back.

"Yeah. It's sleeker."

"It's seventy-two inches. You think that'll fit?"

Ethan stood and walked along the wall again. "The couch would go from here"—he walked in the other direction—"to here."

"Perfect." Lexie put the couch in the cart. "So you were pondering nothingness . . ."

Ethan sat cross-legged beside Lexie. "I was thinking about life and death and what's the point in anything if in the end you disappear?"

"I guess it's a matter of how you're going to spend the time between today and the disappearance." Lexie looked at the plastic-covered furniture. Would she remember Dot any less once her belongings were hauled away? Had Peter felt that Lexie would be forgotten once he dumped out all her stuff? The wedding dress was probably making a hell of a clang knocking around the closet next to Peter's flannel shirts.

"But in the face of death, isn't everything pointless? Like, should I actually spend four years of my life at some school my parents want me to attend?"

"No. You should spend four years at the school that you want to attend. Did you download the Berkeley and UCLA applications?" Lexie lowered the top of the computer so Ethan wouldn't be distracted by the images.

"Yes."

"So stop worrying about it. If you get in, you'll think about how to deal with your parents."

Ethan shrugged. "But if we're only spanning time between now and nothingness then nothing's important."

"Well, you're right in some ways. I mean, most things that we think are important aren't important."

"Like which school I go to?"

"Yeah, sort of. I mean, being at a school will connect you to people and people are important. The exact school you go to probably isn't as important as your parents—all the Ruxton parents—think. What's important is that you feel like you're part of something bigger, that you feel a connection to humans and feel your life as part of their lives."

"I guess I feel that here."

"Yeah, you do. That's why you're sad about Dot not sleeping two floors below you anymore. That's why you and J.T. are cracking up every time you're together. You have a connection. You matter to each other."

"I'm not sure how much J.T. matters to me." Ethan cracked

a smile. Lexie could tell he was about to go off on some guy-put-down humor but then thought better of it.

"And something like this couch we picked—" Lexie flicked a nail at the half-shut computer. "This couch definitely isn't important. The truth is, it's shallow, vain, and self-centered for me to spend the school's money on a couch that I think reflects my taste or some idealized version of myself."

"Okay, so connecting to people is the only thing that matters?"

"Mmm, yeah, I guess. How you love, who you love, and that you love are the only things that matter." Lexie was glad she loved Daniel. She was glad she wasn't going to stay with Peter when he wasn't the great love she had thought he was. She was sad Dot wasn't around to see how it all turned out.

"That's so John Lennon of you."

"You like the Beatles?"

"My dad loves the Beatles, so I know all the songs by heart from listening to him play them."

"On the guitar?"

"On the piano. He likes to play piano and sing Beatles songs."

"Neat." Daniel had never mentioned that he played the piano. Lexie liked that about him. Loads of guys played the guitar. Every guy in college who wanted to get laid learned how to play the guitar (it usually worked). But piano? Not that many guys played the piano beyond "Chopsticks."

"If love is all that matters, was Mrs. Harrison's life well-spent? I mean, she lived in this crowded apartment by herself and barely left the campus except to pick up donuts for us."

"Did she seriously do that?"

"What, the donuts?"

"Yeah. Did she go out two mornings a week to buy you all donuts?"

"Yeah, she did that. She also ironed our clothes if there was some important event and we needed to look nice. She was more of a mother than a teacher." Ethan laughed. "Except she cursed in front of us all the time! Never in class, and never at morning meetings. But if we were in her apartment, she'd say *fuck* or *shit* and she even said *motherfucker* once and, I swear, it was totally hilarious."

"I'm sure it was." It made Lexie happy to think of Dot swearing.

"And sometimes after she swore, she covered her mouth, like she'd burped or something and she'd say, *Pardon my fucking French*."

Lexie laughed. She wished she'd videotaped Dot, if only to hear that old vinyl record voice say *What the fuck, Lexie? What the fuck is that fucking whore-faced Janet Irwin even thinking?!* "So are you worried that Dot didn't live a great life?"

"Yeah. I mean, what kind of life is that, ironing clothes for some spoiled shit like me?"

"Well, a well-lived life is all about human connections. And living here, ironing your shirts, buying you donuts, that gave Mrs. Harrison a whole lot of connection to a whole lot of people. Do you have any idea how much she talked about you guys? Especially the senior class. She would predict which colleges each senior would go to and, I'm not kidding, nine times out of ten she was right."

"Where did she say I was going?"

"I don't think she'd made her list yet. Or, at least, I haven't seen it."

"Bummer. I thought all my problems would be solved." Ethan

looked at Lexie with a half-sly grin. Lexie wondered if he was as sad as he had pretended when he first walked in.

"You're alive, so things are great for you."

"And you think things were great for Mrs. Harrison, too, right?"

"Absolutely. There is a passel of boys sleeping above us this very second who all knew her and loved her, and will never forget her. No one forgets the woman in high school who buys you donuts."

"You're having a hard time getting over that donut thing, aren't you?"

"Yes! I don't want to get up early and drive off campus to Stop and Shop for donuts two days a week!"

"You could buy cases of them ahead of time."

"They're bad for you anyway. Anyway. There are a bunch of people up there"—Lexie pointed at the ceiling—"and they all carry her memory. I mean, you probably knew about her from your dad before you even met her here."

"How did you know my dad knew Mrs. Harrison?"

Lexie's heart thrummed for a second until she remembered. "You said he lived in Rilke. Mrs. Harrison always lived in Rilke."

"Oh, yeah." Ethan looked at the plastic-covered mountain again. "My dad never mentioned Mrs. Harrison. But when I have kids and I tell them about this school, I'll totally tell them about her."

"That's nice. And maybe your kids will tell their kids about her—about the wacky old lady who tap-danced and sang when their grandpa and great-grandpa went to Ruxton."

"But eventually the chain will burn out and no one will remember her."

"That will happen to everyone. Except a few, like Shakespeare. I mean, do you know who Tonya Harding is?" Lexie flipped up the lid of the computer and typed Tonya Harding into Google images.

"No. Who's Tonya Harding?"

"She was an ice-skater who hired someone to slice open her competition with a skate, or hit her on the head with a brick, or break her leg or something. I don't remember. It was a pretty big scandal at the time, and my mom—who was obsessed with her—said over and over that Tonya Harding would forever be a part of history. Well, guess what, she's already not a part of history. Few of us are. We do disappear, but not for a while." Lexie clicked on a picture of Tonya Harding and turned it toward Ethan. He pulled his head back and looked at the computer with his eyes flattened into horizontal slits.

"Okay, I'm not sure you're making me feel any better. You've confirmed that even someone who spent a year or two in the spotlight is totally forgotten a couple decades later."

Lexie had to smile. "Let's look at it another way. Why is it important to you that you're remembered forever? Isn't it enough to simply be here now?"

"Are we back to *love is the point*?" Ethan was starting to loosen up. Whatever sadness he'd felt appeared to be lifting. He was resuming the role of a lanky, broad-shouldered boy with giant feet, sitting on Lexie's living room floor.

"But love *is* the point!" Lexie said.

"Did you find a chair yet?" Ethan pointed to Lexie's laptop. She clicked over to Crate and Barrel.

"What about this?" Lexie showed Ethan a streamlined, yellow upholstered chair.

"You're not very girly, are you?"

"Not when it comes to furniture."

"I like it. Get two."

"Two it is." Lexie put the chairs in the cart.

"So we all disappear and nothing matters except love." Ethan's face glowed blue and yellow in the light of the computer screen.

"Yes. Love the people you love, be open to love, be good and do good."

"Is that what you're doing?"

"I'm trying. It's hard to be good and do good sometimes, but I'm always trying." Lexie thought she needed to try harder. She hoped she could be a better person—the person she advised her students to be—from here on out.

AFTER THEY'D PICKED OUT THE NECESSARY FURNITURE AND EATEN most of the stale holiday cookies from the tin in the cupboard, Ethan left. It was almost midnight. Lexie went to her email, found Mitzy's hotel confirmation for the wedding week and canceled the room. It was on Peter's credit card and who knew if he'd remember to cancel it. She wrote a long email to Betsy Simms and a shorter email to Mr. and Mrs. Simms. She told everyone about the canceled wedding but no one about Daniel and only Betsy (and not her parents) about the El Kabong incident. Lexie reassured everyone she was fine, relieved, and that no one should worry. This was a step in the right direction. She also mentioned that Mr. and Mrs. Simms should get their money back for Mitzy's ticket. And if it was too late for a refund, Lexie would pay them back.

Once she'd finished emailing, Lexie picked up her cell phone. It had been sitting facedown on the floor with the sound off. Lexie expected there to be a text or phone message from Daniel. Wasn't he worried after reading the El Kabong text?

Lexie texted: *Did you get my message? He didn't hit me w/guitar, he hit my car w/it. Car fine. Guitar totaled.* She considered getting his attention by mentioning Ethan's visit but she knew it was wrong. Even in her apartment, they were ensconced in the bubble of confidentiality. She'd mention it to Amy because it was part of their professional relationship—they treated students together (with medication from Amy and counseling from Lexie) in many instances. But short of Ethan being suicidal or homicidal, there was no reason for her to tell Daniel.

Lexie's text burp sat there. Gray. Unanswered. Daniel must not have his phone with him, she thought. It was odd to think of him as someone in the same category as Dot (and Janet Irwin!), but he was: the over-fifty crowd, the people who didn't see their cell phone as an extension of their hand. Lexie went to bed confident that she'd wake up to a text from Daniel.

14

IT WAS A LUXURIOUS SLEEP EVEN THOUGH LEXIE HAD BEEN SLUIC-
ing across the air mattress like a Slip 'n Slide. If there were no such
thing as addiction or side effects, Lexie would take a Klonopin
every night to put herself into that dreamy-cushioned sleep.

Lexie reached beneath her pillow and pulled out her phone,
plugged into the wall beside her. A text from Daniel read: *Occupied (faking it) with extended fam all wkend. Will leave and drive to
Ruxton if you need me. V. v. v. concerned about the El Kabonging.*

In the clear morning light Lexie remembered that Daniel had
mentioned earlier his in-laws coming to town. Catholics. Jen hadn't
told them they were separated so Daniel had to stay home and play
house. Lexie typed, *All fine. Ordered furniture, getting ready for a
new life!* She took a picture of her lips making a kiss. She hit send.

Five seconds later, a text from Daniel: *Love that photo! I'll call
Mon. morning. Now impossible. Xxx*

Lexie swiped over to the next text. It was Amy making sure
she was okay, urging her to call when she woke up. Lexie didn't

want to call; she didn't want to rehash the El Kabong incident. She'd rather it floated away so that her memories of Peter would be everything before the breakup: the singing, the smell of fresh-cut wood, slipping her cold feet under his calves on cold winter nights, her icy hands warming in his armpits.

As Lexie was texting Amy, telling her that all was fine, the phone rang. A picture of Mitzy in her Heidi Pies uniform, smoking a cigarette, appeared on the screen. Lexie's stomach lurched. She hadn't yet told Mitzy about the canceled wedding.

Lexie touched the green answer button. "Hey, Mom." She wriggled off the air mattress, leaned over the open coffin-sized suitcase and pulled out jeans, underwear, and a soft sweater.

"Bonnie Simms said you canceled the wedding. Did he hit you?"

"No, he didn't hit me. I fell out of love." Lexie held the phone against her ear with her shoulder as she pulled on the panties and then the jeans. The painters would be arriving within minutes.

"Well, everyone falls out of love. That's why they invented marriage. To lock you in!"

"Ah, funny." Lexie wasn't smiling.

"Why didn't you tell me you canceled?"

"I was about to call you. I emailed the Simmses first because I was worried about them getting their money back for that ticket." Lexie threw back the first bra she'd pulled out and exchanged it for a black one that matched her panties.

"They gave it to me."

"What?" Lexie paused with her bra hanging off one arm. Her body was cocked with tension, a gun ready to fire.

"The ticket. They gave me the ticket. They said they didn't pay so much because they used credit card air miles for one half the trip or something and that I should keep it and go visit you."

"You want to visit me?" Mitzy had never visited Lexie. Anywhere.

"Well, it'll be nice to see where you live and everything. We can have fun! You can take me to bars and we'll meet guys and tell them we're sisters!"

"That would be great, Mom." Lexie quickly hooked her bra and pulled the sweater on. She was a razor's slice from tears. To put her mother on an air mattress in this apartment—or the bed, while Lexie herself slept on the air mattress—would be like being stuck in an elevator between floors. You know you'll get out eventually, but still you want to bang on the doors screaming. The only option was a hotel and Lexie could barely afford that. Yes, Daniel would pay for a hotel. But Lexie had no interest in launching their relationship with a request for him to pick up her mother's tab.

"Too bad your dad's not around to see me getting on an airplane. He once said he'd bet his life I'd never step foot on one of those things."

"Because you're scared of flying?" Maybe Lexie would get lucky and Mitzy would chicken out. Her mother was so San Leandro–based she rarely even went to San Francisco and that was only forty minutes away.

"I'm not scared, I just don't wanna go nowhere. Why should I leave San Leandro when everything I need is here?"

"You've got a point there." As soon as she discovered there was a world beyond San Leandro, all Lexie had wanted was to leave.

"He's probably rolling around in his grave, jealous as hell that he's not the first one of us to get on a plane."

"Why would he be rolling around in his grave, Mom? That's something you say for someone who's dead." Lexie dug through her bag, searching for boots. She found one each of two different pairs. Hopefully the mates weren't at Peter's house.

There was a startling silence on the other end of the line. Lexie dropped the boots to the floor and stood straight in the center of the room.

"Mom?" Lexie said. "Dad's not dead, is he?"

"I thought I told you."

"You thought you told me that my dad was dead?" Here it was: evidence that Lexie was the genetic offspring of two people incapable of properly responding to death. Why was she surprised that she'd decided to leave Peter the day she found out about Dot's death? Look who she'd come from!

"Well, maybe I told you and you forgot."

"Are you kidding me?! We're talking about my father!" Lexie put the phone on speaker and placed it on the floor. She pulled all her clothes out of the bag and flung them onto the air mattress. The mate to each boot was at the bottom of the bag. Lexie sat on the pile of clothes and put on her socks and boots.

"Well excuse me if I didn't know that you two had some sort of relationship!"

"We don't! Or, we didn't." Lexie swept the clothes off the air mattress and lay down. "I don't even know where he lives. Lived!"

"So why are you giving me all this crap about not telling you that he's dead?!"

Lexie breathed deeply, focusing on using her diaphragm. She wanted to take a Klonopin but she wouldn't. This wasn't a panic attack. This was . . . she couldn't even name what this was—it was something brackish and foul—not grief, not regret, simply a general unsettled discomfort. Lexie often felt like this when she thought of her parents, although now she felt it more acutely than ever. "When exactly did he die?" Lexie's voice had calmed. She was easing into the narrative: Her father had died. Her mother had forgotten to tell her.

"About two or three months ago. Let's see, we were doing the plum pie special, so it must have been summer."

"So during all these conversations we've had about him the past couple months, you were thinking of, and talking about, *dead Bert*?" Lexie tried to remember the last time they discussed him. Was it when her mother had last brought up the affairs? Had Mitzy used the past tense in referring to him?

"You're too damn busy with all them rich kids to remember that I already told you."

No point in getting into that. "Where did he live?"

"In Omaha."

"So he never went to Reno?"

"Fuck if I know. He didn't keep in touch with me."

"Well how did he die?" Lexie stared at the spiderweb cracks in the ceiling. She wondered if Dot had ever noticed how crinkled the ceiling was. Did she care?

"I dunno. They just found him in a chair in his apartment. Dead."

"Who found him?" Lexie always associated her father with the couch. It was hard to place him in her mind in a chair.

"The supe."

"What kind of chair was it?"

"I dunno! How would I know what kind of chairs he had?"

"He was just sitting there? Was he doing drugs or something? How old was he anyway?" Bert had been gone so long, Lexie had never kept track of his age.

"I guess he was fifty-three."

"Ugh." The word came out without her realizing it. Bert was, or had been, the same age as Daniel. It was an idea that made Lexie a little queasy; an idea she didn't want to explore further. Especially now.

"Ugh what? Whatchu uggin?"

"Nothing. Death. What was he doing when he died?"

"He was watching TV."

"How do you know that?"

"His cousin Gordy told me that the supe found him in his chair watching TV."

"I never met Gordy."

"No, you never met no one except his parents a couple times."

"What was he watching?"

"How the fuck would I know?"

"Well, do you know what station the TV was on?" Lexie imagined Bert watching an old movie on TNT. It would have been nice for him to have departed from the living while Audrey Hepburn was on screen. Or the Nicholas brothers were tap dancing.

"Lexie, what's your problem? No one else in the whole dang world gives a shit what station the TV was on when your dad died!"

"Mom, I'm trying to process this, okay? It's a lot to take in." In truth, Lexie felt far less immediate grief over this loss than she did about Dot. She had mourned her father years ago, when he had left. After that his only appearances had been in the form of a birthday card her mother dropped off at the Simmses each year until Lexie went to college. By the time Lexie got the card (there was never a return address), the envelope had already been opened by Mitzy, and whatever cash he'd put in—usually mentioned in the note, *Buy yourself something sweet with this!*—had been removed.

"How did his cousin Gordy find you?" Lexie slid off the mattress. She threw the scattered loose clothing back into the suitcase.

"He called me at Heidi Pies."

"Was there an estate?" Lexie knew there'd be nothing coming her way. But she wanted to know what was left since her father had, in the words of Ethan Waite, disappeared off the planet. Who took the television? Where was the chair he'd been sitting on? Who was driving his truck, assuming he owned one? Was there someone who would be remembering him through the things he'd left behind?

Mitzy laughed. "If he ever had anything, you can be sure he pissed it away. That was a man who'd spend ten bucks if he had five in his pocket, and forty bucks if he had twenty. Always in debt."

"Do you know if he had a girlfriend?" Lexie hoped he wasn't lonely. She liked to imagine Bert ended his life in a relationship better than the one he'd had with Mitzy.

"Honey, he always had a girlfriend. Even when he already had a girlfriend he had another girlfriend."

Lexie found it difficult to imagine that women were drawn to Bert the way Mitzy claimed they were. The sacks of loose flesh he'd prematurely had under each eye years ago could have only gotten worse. And he smelled like a litter-strewn back alley: cigarettes and booze. Though they were the same age, he and Daniel Waite were as similar as a warthog and a panther. But her mother had loved him once. So maybe, as Mitzy imagined, others could love him, too.

There was a knock at the door. Lexie went to the living room and opened the door. Five Korean men nodded their heads and walked in with their painting supplies. They immediately started setting up.

"Mom, I've gotta go. The painters are here and I have to show them where to paint." That was a lie, but Lexie needed to get off the phone.

"Whatchu getting painted? Bonnie Simms told me you were moving into the dormitory on campus."

"It's an apartment in a dorm building on campus. The school is repainting the whole thing. They're buying me new furniture, too."

"Well, aren't you fancy." Mitzy's voice was sharp as razor wire.

"Let's talk later, Mom. We'll plan your trip." Lexie rolled her eyes. She'd rather plan her own funeral.

"Bonnie Simms said I could change the dates. Go after the snow melts since I don't have any of them moon boots or whatever you people wear out there."

"Don't know what you're talking about with the moon boots. But it'll be a lot warmer in spring, so maybe you should come then. But I've gotta go. I'll talk to you soon."

Lexie hung up and stared at the phone. She shut her eyes and repeated the word *compassion* over and over again. It was the only sane approach when dealing with her mother. They were two grown women and Lexie had all the advantages. To resent or blame Mitzy for Lexie's childhood would be a pointless act of adolescent whining. Lexie was in charge of her own life, and the past—how her parents had parented her—was no longer relevant.

Lexie tapped out a text to Amy: *Found out my dad died a few months ago. Feels like a splinter compared to the axe in my heart from Dot.* Lexie copied the text and sent it to Daniel, too. How strange that she already felt as close to him as to Amy.

Lexie clicked back to the last text Daniel had sent her. Simply seeing words he had written gave her a feathery feeling in her chest. Impulsively, Lexie leaned in and kissed the phone right where the text lit up the screen.

Spring
SEMESTER

15

IT WAS MARCH 31 AND THE WEAK MASSACHUSETTS SUN FELL through Lexie's office window like a drunk who had tripped on the curb. Lexie turned her head, caught the light on her face, and shut her eyes for a few seconds. She looked back at the computer and read over the email she'd written to Betsy Simms. Treacle. Bathos. Mawkish drivel. It was impossible to write about love without sounding like her brain was soaking in store-brand pancake syrup.

Lexie erased it all. She started again: *Hey! Things are great with Daniel. Please come visit with my mom in June. No way I can deal with her on my own. Love, Lexie P.S. The students are finding out about colleges in emails sent tonight after midnight. Reminds me of when you and I sat by the mailbox waiting, waiting, waiting.* She hit send.

Lexie picked up her cell phone and clicked through pictures of Daniel and herself. She had wanted to download them to her computer but the computer belonged to the school and Daniel implored her not to put anything personal on it. He'd seen too many cases in business and in life where personal information on company computers led to more trouble than one could imagine. Daniel was going to buy her a new computer soon enough—she could store all her photos on it and they'd be able to email freely. There were rumors about the next generation Apple, and Daniel was waiting for it to come out. In the meantime, everything was on Lexie's phone—thousands of texts, hundreds of photos—the documentation of a courtship that had been so wonderful it made everything that came before it (the bad and the worse) worth it. Even Amy had given up doubting Daniel. Her initial distrust dissipated the day Daniel gave Lexie the log-in names and passwords to all his email accounts. It was his idea, something he insisted on, when Lexie mentioned in passing Amy's skepticism. Lexie and Amy logged into Daniel's email the next day. Amy clicked on and read the emails from Jen. Lexie refused to read them, her stomach clenched as she waited for Amy to complete the reconnaissance mission. "It doesn't look like they're married," Amy had finally said. "It's all about *did you call the stone guy for the wall out front, did you know Ethan got an A on his apartheid paper,* and *Bob so-and-so called in regards to updating the wills.*"

The next day, when they were having lunch at the Inn on the Lake, Lexie handed Daniel an index card with the log-in names and passwords for her computer, her phone, and her email accounts. "What am I going to do with this?" Daniel had asked, and Lexie had insisted he file it away. If she had his passwords, he should have hers. Fair was fair. She knew then that he'd never open even one of her accounts and read anything. But after the breakdown of the relationship with Peter, total electronic transparency made Lexie feel secure. Neither of them had anything to hide.

Lexie zoomed in on a picture of Daniel sitting up naked in bed. At the sight of his face, Lexie could feel her flesh light up. She was a chameleon. Or a glowing jellyfish. Or a firefly. Her skin went through a chemical reaction that changed her cellular structure. Finally, gratefully, at thirty-three, Lexie understood true love. Everything made sense now: Hollywood movies, crimes of passion, suicide even. Lexie felt bad for anyone who had to live without this feeling. She hoped Peter had it with his new girlfriend, Celeste. She was a guitar player they'd socialized with from time to time. Peter no longer talked to Lexie, but she and Celeste were Facebook friends and so Lexie had tracked the relationship, without a tinge of jealousy, through Celeste's various postings.

The schedule with Daniel worked like this: Wednesday nights, Lexie went to Boston and stayed with Daniel in his apartment. Amy, who had her own key, stayed in Lexie's place at Rilke. On Friday nights, Daniel and Lexie checked into the Inn on the Lake, where Lexie stayed as late as she could, sometimes returning to Rilke around two or three in the morning. On Saturday Lexie was in charge of study hall and had student appointments so there was no time to meet, though sometimes they'd have a quick coffee or lunch at the Inn before Daniel returned to Boston. Often Daniel drove all the way into Ruxton on Monday morning so they could have breakfast at the Inn on the Lake after Lexie's first period class. Lexie thought Daniel's willingness to endure the traffic between Boston and Ruxton and back again showed his true devotion to her more than any words or gift ever could. Between their visits Lexie and Daniel texted innumerable times each day. Phone calls were less frequent, because Lexie was busy with students and Daniel was busy with work. At winter break, Lexie stayed for four days in the Boston apartment with Daniel before flying home alone to California for Christmas.

How Daniel worked out his schedule with Jen, his in-laws, and Ethan, happened softly and quietly outside of his and Lexie's time together. They had decided early on that Lexie wouldn't get involved in the spindled intricacies of Daniel's slow-motion divorce.

Lexie's phone buzzed with a text from Daniel. *Let's stay at the lake house while Jen and Ethan are in Ireland for spring break. We can swim! Have sex! Swim! Sex! Swim! Sex! Did I mention sex?*

Lexie replied, *Jen okay with you in her house for the week?*

Not a problem.

But what about ME in her house? I don't want to sneak around.

I told her about you. She's okay with it. Not okay with Ethan knowing yet.

Lexie paused. She reread the note. She read it once more. This, above all else—Daniel's daily declarations of love, Daniel's dreams for their future together, Daniel claiming he could barely breathe without her—made what they had feel real. Serious. Permanent.

Spring break at the lake house! Woot woot! Xxxxx!

Lexie went to the infirmary to talk to Amy. Abioye Balewa was there. He blushed when Lexie walked in.

"Oh, excuse me," Lexie said, and she stepped out and sat on the small front porch waiting for The Prince to leave. She tried to remember where The Prince would be going to school next year. She knew he'd gotten in somewhere early decision. Columbia or Penn. Or maybe it was Cornell.

When The Prince came out he paused in front of Lexie. "How are you today, Miss James?"

"I'm great. You excited about . . . Columbia?" Lexie hoped she was guessing right.

"Yes, I'm looking forward to Columbia. But right now I'm suffering from the common heartbreak."

"Oh, I'm sorry to hear that. Do you want to come to my office one day this week to talk about it before everyone clears out for spring break?"

"That might be good for me. I'll think about it."

"Well, call me when you're ready and we'll make an appointment. Okay?"

"Yes. Thank you very much, Miss James." The Prince nodded and walked off.

Lexie went into the infirmary and shut the door behind herself. "He okay?"

"Broken heart. And I don't want to give up any confidences but it looks like chlamydia's going around the school. I've got six cases of it already." Amy was unbothered by this. For Lexie, chlamydia was only a few symptoms away from leukemia.

"Six!"

"Well, it's a teeny, tiny pool they're all swimming in here. I suspect if six have come in, at least three times that many have it. I'm going to send out an email today."

"We should throw condoms at them as they walk down the halls."

"Hell yeah, Janet Irwin wouldn't mind that, would she?" Janet Irwin was opposed to the school's providing condoms for students.

"So guess what?" Lexie sat on one of the beds and swung her legs so that her boot heels clanged against the iron bed frame.

"Your mama's staying two weeks instead of one?"

"Ha, yeah, funny. We changed her ticket *again* so at least she's coming once the students have all moved out."

"Well, bless her heart," Amy said.

"But listen. You know how I was going to stay with Daniel in Boston during spring break?"

"Uh-huh." Amy looked down at her computer and started clicking. Her fingers moved rapidly, fluidly, while the rest of her body remained perfectly poised. Lexie figured she was writing the email suggesting that anyone who was sexually active be tested for chlamydia.

"Well, we're actually spending the week at the lake house where Jen lives."

Amy stopped typing and looked up from the computer. She swiveled on the seat so that she was fully facing Lexie. "Where's Jen going to be?"

"She's taking Ethan to Ireland, remember?"

"I can't keep track of where these kids go. It's like a world invasion by Ruxton students. When I was in high school in Alabama, you know where we went for *Easter vacation*?"

"Georgia?"

"No. Church! We went to church on Easter Sunday and other than that we roller-skated around the neighborhood, watched *The Price Is Right* on TV, did each other's hair, painted our nails. These kids are knocking off a new continent each time they jump on an airplane."

"Yup. So, anyway, Ethan and Jen will be gone and Daniel and I will be in the lake house."

"And that's okay with Jen?"

"He told her about us." Lexie waited for Amy's reaction.

"Huh." Amy paused. She was calculating something in her head. "Did he tell Ethan?"

"No. They'll tell Ethan everything once he graduates."

"Did he ever tell his brother?" The calculations continued. Lexie knew there was a wrong or right answer to this question.

"He did but I haven't met him yet. He's been so busy and Daniel himself hasn't seen him since we started dating."

"He hasn't been to California in all this time?"

"Do you want to go into his email again and make sure everything's on the up and up?" Lexie wished Amy would fully let go of her hesitations and relax. Lexie didn't need an overseer.

"You're right." Amy threw up her hands. "I'm sorry."

"If you give me some chocolate I'll forgive you." Lexie pointed to the drawer where Amy kept the Hershey's Kisses. Amy pulled out a handful and dumped them on the desk. She threw one to Lexie.

"So where's Ethan going to school, anyway?" Amy's voice was back to what Lexie thought of as *blond*: light, airy.

"Umm." Lexie unwrapped the chocolate. "I guess he'll find out tonight. He didn't get into UCLA and that was his first choice."

"Poor little boy, he'll probably end up having to slum it at Harvard like his daddy."

"Terrible, isn't it?" Lexie told Amy the story of when she got into UCLA with a full ride. She called every friend she had, and she even phoned Mr. Simms at work, but she neglected to tell her mother. That night, when Lexie, Betsy, and Mr. and Mrs. Simms sat in a booth at Heidi Pies ordering blizzard sundaes, Mitzy asked what they were celebrating. Lexie didn't realize how cruel her omission was until Betsy blurted Lexie's good news and Mitzy's face flushed candy-pink from her chin to her forehead.

"It's not like she was Mother of the Year," Amy said, chomping into a Kiss.

"It's not like she was Mother of the Minute," Lexie said. "She was more like a babysitter I had for a really, really long time."

"Kids like Ethan got it made," Amy said.

"Yup," Lexie said. "Must be hard being the son of Daniel Waite." Lexie popped the kiss into her mouth. It tasted so good that she shut her eyes for a couple seconds while she let it melt down her throat.

THE FOLLOWING MORNING THERE WAS LOTS OF DRAMA: KIDS HUG-ging one another, cheering, a few crying. Many students got into their first choice school and the ones who didn't were trying to put a good spin on the places where they did get in. As expected, the intense overachievers would be at the Ivies and other top East Coast schools; the more courageous overachievers were hitting up Berkeley, Stanford, and the University of Chicago. The artists and writers planned to colonize the schools in New York City, or Bowdoin, Bates, and Bennington. The party crowd was headed for the University of Vermont and the University of New Hampshire. And the rest were filling in the spots at small private colleges that often their parents had attended or maybe their grandparents. Lexie imagined Dot's list would have been a hundred percent right. What a shame that no one veered off course and surprised them all.

Ethan Waite was the only student who didn't share his news. Lexie wanted to call Daniel (surely Ethan would have told his parents what was up) but he was at meetings in Toronto and had told Lexie beforehand that he would be away from the phone all day.

The speculation among students was that Ethan Waite had aimed too high and hadn't gotten in anywhere. Lexie worried over it until she approached Ethan on the way to dinner and he mumbled, his head hanging low, that he would be going to Harvard. She figured he hadn't told anyone because he wanted to act cool and not brag on a day when bragging was the norm.

When she left the dining hall, Lexie saw she'd received a text from Daniel. *Miss you, beautiful. At cocktails now, will call later.* Lexie replied: *Miss you! Great news about Ethan—woot woot!* She looked up. Janet Irwin was walking toward her. Janet stopped in front of Lexie on the brick pathway. Lexie dropped the phone into her purse. It buzzed with an incoming text and Lexie felt a current run down her right arm.

"You shouldn't use your phone like that on campus." Janet's long, flat-shod feet created the number eleven on the ground.

"Are you talking about texting?" Did Janet honestly not know the verb *text*?

"Yes. It's bad enough that the students do it, we shouldn't have faculty doing it as well. It's terrible. A technological advancement that has created a serious regression in human development."

"So you think we're all worse off now that we're in more frequent contact?" Lexie stuck her hand in her purse and fingered the phone. Janet had the distinct ability to make Lexie feel like a teenager, and in being that teenager she wanted to rebel.

"People are losing IQ points, losing social skills, losing the very thing that makes them human because they are focusing their energy onto an apparatus rather than onto another human." Janet's feet remained even, as if she might never take another step. She was upright as a flagpole.

"Well, I'll put some serious thought into that." Lexie pulled her cell phone from her purse as she walked away. She could sense Janet watching her but didn't look back to confirm.

Daniel had texted, *Yes, I'm very proud. Will you pick up a bottle of champagne and drop it off at my boy's room?*

Lexie glanced back over her shoulder at Janet, who had entrapped three senior girls. They were probably getting the text lecture, too. Lexie typed, *Happy to drop off champagne! Please note that would be my last official act at Ruxton since surely I'll be fired!*

Daniel replied, *Who cares! You'll be out of there soon enough when you're my wife. The Boston apartment is too far for the commute.*

Lexie sucked in an estatic little breath. She swiped her ID at the door to Rilke. Once she was in the apartment, with the door firmly shut, Lexie unbuttoned her blouse, lowered the camera, and took a picture of her breasts in the black bra she'd put on that morning. She didn't want to reply in words, as words could appear either desperate and excessively anxious, or overly happy and needy. A photo would convey her message more concisely: *Buy the ring. I'm yours!*

More, Daniel texted, and Lexie obliged.

Her slacks were around her ankles and her panties were flossed to one side as Lexie was trying to figure out the best photo angle when there was a knock on the door. Lexie dropped the phone to the floor and very quietly reassembled her clothes. Her thoughts zoomed out to the imagined overhead camera shot of herself, half-dressed, acting porny on one side of the door while some upstanding Ruxton citizen, be it faculty or a student, waited on the other side of the door.

Lexie picked up the phone and opened the door. Cole Hanna stood there, his blue tie knotted like a fist. He held out one of Lexie's notebooks.

"I found this on the walkway," Cole said. He was so conventionally good-looking, nice, and conscientious that Lexie worried he'd live a life as dull as a wooden spoon.

"Ah! Thanks." Lexie took the notebook. She must have dropped it while texting Daniel. Good thing Janet Irwin hadn't found it. Another reason not to text! "So, is there a lot of celebrating planned for tonight?"

"Some celebrating and some mourning." Cole, Lexie knew, would be attending Dartmouth.

"Text me if you think I need to make a surprise visit to keep things under control tonight. I'd hate for anyone to get suspended and have his or her acceptance standing in jeopardy."

"Do they do that?" Cole asked.

"Yeah, they do. There was a kid headed to Duke a couple years before I arrived who got into big trouble at the end of the year and lost his invitation to attend."

"That's terrible."

"It is. So, keep me in the loop and I'll try to derail anyone intent on getting suspended." Lexie couldn't quite remember the story of the Duke-accepted kid. It was something with drugs and alcohol and defacing school property. Had he gone into the chapel, carved a giant penis into a pew, and vomited on the penis before passing out? Someone had done that, although maybe it was a different boy, a different year.

The kids at San Leandro High had done much worse on many more occasions. But it was public school, no one kept track of what happened off campus, and even if there was a transgression, there were so many on such a regular basis that it was rare for a detention to be handed out.

Since she'd been living at Rilke, Lexie had confiscated alcohol three times—two of the three from the same boy. She assumed it was like mice: If you see one, it means there's a hundred.

AT MIDNIGHT THERE WAS A RHYTHMIC RAPPING ON LEXIE'S DOOR; IT sounded like the William Tell Overture. She pulled on yoga pants and a T-shirt then went to the door and found a wet-cheeked Ethan Waite.

"You okay?" Lexie tried to step back as Ethan stumbled in past her, his solid body brushing against hers.

"Not really." Ethan collapsed onto the gray chair that he and Lexie had picked out in September.

"Were you rapping the William Tell Overture on the door?"

"Yeah! No way! You could tell?!" Ethan was obviously drunk. His gestures were big and sweeping, like he was directing a symphony.

"I've got a good ear for that stuff." Lexie sat on the matching chair beside Ethan. She remembered one night with Peter in which she had lain naked across his lap and he had patted out songs on her butt. She had to guess what song he was patting. They were both amazed that she could get a good number of them, and when she'd correctly guessed Madonna's "Like a Virgin," they were hysterical with laughter.

At the time, Lexie believed that it was a meeting of the minds between herself and Peter that gave her the songs. Tonight, she credited her skills to a simple gift for rhythm.

"Amazing ear." Ethan rolled his head back and forth against the chair like he was trying to shake something out.

"So, what's up? Is this urgent?"

"I can't believe I didn't get into UCLA."

"Well, Harvard's not as dummy-school slummy as its reputation would have you believe." Lexie wanted to laugh but she didn't.

"We both know I got in because of my dad."

"Maybe you did, but I'd never say you were a slacker. What's your GPA again?"

"Three point seven nine."

"See."

"Everyone else who got in has, like, four point seven."

"Ethan, you're not some idiot fool eating cut-up steak with a spoon. You'll do fine there."

"I wanted to be in California."

"Okay, it's midnight and you're . . . a little out of sorts, so I'm going to lay some truth on you." If he weren't Daniel's kid, if she weren't certain that this conversation wouldn't get back to the Spoken Word Police Officer, Janet Irwin, Lexie wouldn't say what she was about to say. But through her relationship with Daniel, and the simple intimacy she had with Ethan from living in the same dorm as he, Lexie felt her professional relationship with Ethan had become a flimsy pretense. He was her future stepson. And after seven months of dating Daniel, the transition to family status had already begun, if only in her mind.

Ethan leaned forward and clapped his hands once, like a football coach talking to the team. "Lay it on me!"

"You are a spoiled rotten brat."

"Are you kidding or serious?" He sat back again.

"Serious."

"Why would you say that?" Ethan rubbed one eye with the back of his floppy hand.

"Because you're complaining about going to a school that kids all over the world are knocking themselves out to go to. And because you get to go college without even taking out a student loan or going through the seventy-million impossible-to-understand pages of applying for financial aid or scholarships, and because the whole world is available to you, waiting for you to conquer it. And you're sitting here crying because you don't get to go to school in California? Fly to California on spring break! Go there for the summer! Go for a long weekend!"

"I totally get what you're saying." His head dropped a little, as if he were ashamed. "And I'm not saying I disagree with you. But this doesn't take into account that for me, Harvard is a given, UCLA is what I was reaching for and I didn't get the goal I was reaching for." Ethan lifted his head and looked at Lexie, as if he were imploring her to agree with him on this one point.

"Yes, that's a bummer." Lexie softened her voice. She didn't want him to feel bad. "But you need to step back and take a global perspective. You can go to UCLA for grad school, or summer school. We'll take you to San Leandro to visit my mom and we'll drive . . ." Lexie stopped talking as she realized she had veered into a reality of which Ethan was unaware: herself, Daniel, and Ethan as a family.

"We?" Ethan cocked his chin up as a question mark. Lexie was relieved he was drunk. In his current state, she could probably convince him of anything.

"I meant me. I. I could take you to visit my mom." It would never happen if she weren't with Daniel, Lexie thought. She would never be a single "I" who would engage in such an intimacy as travel with a former student.

"I'd love to go visit your mom, Mrs. James!"

"She's never gone by Missus in her life. Her name's Mitzy." How odd it would be if Lexie actually showed up at Mitzy's apartment with Daniel and Ethan. Would her mother want to make a group run to 7-Eleven for Sno Balls and Dr Pepper?

"Mitzy? We had a dog named Mitzy once."

"Most people have had a dog named Mitzy once. You're the second person in the last couple months who's told me that."

"Who was the other person?"

"I can't remember." Lexie looked off to the right as she rummaged through her brain to come up with who had been telling her a story about Mitzy the dog. She blushed when she remembered it was Daniel. "I have no idea," she finally said.

"Well, our Mitzy was a pretty crazy dog. She tried to commit suicide."

"Gun? Poison? Knife?" Lexie said, and Ethan laughed. He may have been drunker than she had originally thought. She was certainly more half-asleep than she had originally thought.

"Jumping. She jumped off the balcony onto the stone patio."

"Did she break any bones?" Daniel hadn't mentioned the jump.

"One of her legs. But no death. She was catatonically depressed for a couple weeks. My mother sent her to a therapist and she was fine after that."

"They have dog therapists in Western Massachusetts? I thought that was only in California."

"No, my mom took her all the way to Northampton to see the dog therapist. My dad went nuts. He hated that she was giving money to a huckster."

"Did you agree that the dog therapist was a huckster?" Lexie sure as hell did.

"Yeah, I guess." Ethan patted out a tune on his thighs. "What song is that?"

"'No Scrubs'?" Lexie hadn't been listening. It was the first song that popped in her head.

"No! Listen." Ethan tapped out the rhythm again.

"What time period of music are we in?"

"Seventies funk. I figured you wouldn't know current stuff."

"Hey, I wasn't alive in the seventies! But I do know the music and I know current stuff, too." Even as Lexie was saying it she knew it wasn't true. She barely knew current music. She listened to the radio but she had never downloaded or bought music. Lexie's musical inclinations were dictated by whomever she was with most often: Betsy Simms, her mother, her college roommate, her grad school roommate, the two boyfriends she'd had, her former fiancé (Peter!), and lastly, Daniel, who rarely listened to music at all.

"Okay, this is seventies. Listen." Ethan patted it out again. As he did so, he stared at Lexie straight in the eye, his mouth hanging open in concentration.

"'Ooh Child'?"

"Huh? I don't know what that is."

Lexie was worried she was losing her touch. She'd have to try the bare-butt bongo with Daniel later to see if it worked with him. "Do it again. With deliberation, okay? No extra beats."

Ethan stuck his neck out a little and patted hard and slow. He rocked his head to the beat.

"'Brick House'?"

"YES!" Ethan threw his fists up and pumped his arms into the air. Lexie laughed.

"Okay, let's quit while we're ahead." Lexie stood.

"Are you kicking me out?"

"Yes. Go to bed. Forget about UCLA. Be grateful. Don't be a whiney dumb-ass."

"Don't be a whiney dumb-ass. Good advice." Ethan stood and slowly walked toward the door.

"It's life advice. Think about it the rest of your life. Or do it the rest of your life. For the rest of your life don't be a whiney dumb-ass."

"I'm going to miss you when I graduate."

"Ah, you're sweet. But I bet we'll see each other again after you graduate." To be safe, Lexie added, "I see a lot students after they graduate." She held the door open for Ethan.

"Never again in my life will I be a whiney dumb-ass." Ethan walked slowly out the door.

"Sleep well."

"Night, Miss James." Ethan lifted his long arm and waved it behind him as he went down the hall. From the back, silhouetted by the hall light, it could have been Daniel.

16

LEXIE'S BAG WAS PACKED. SHE STOOD IN THE DOORWAY OF THE guest suite of the Waite lake house and watched Daniel pull the linens off the bed and shake them out. "What are you doing?"

"She was nice enough to let us stay here. I don't want to rub it in her face by leaving a pair of my underwear behind."

"Well, check for my underwear, too." Lexie wondered what kind of underwear Jen wore. How would it look lined up next to Lexie's collection of lacy, stringy ribbons of fabric? From their one meeting, Lexie imagined Jen as someone with well-made, silky but sensible underwear. No prints. No lace. Nothing that would cut into her flesh, dissecting her body into graspable parts: cheek, cheek, crotch.

Lexie had wanted to explore the house, to poke around Jen's bedroom (and her underwear drawer) the way she'd poked around bedrooms as a babysitter in San Leandro (the way all babysitters since the beginning of babysitting have done). But she refrained in an effort to give Jen Waite the privacy she deserved after the generous gift of her home.

The week had been unimaginably dreamy, holed up together like they were on a luxurious island. In the mornings Lexie had read on the dock while Daniel worked on the computer or took calls. By late afternoon, Daniel put away his work and they putted around the lake in the boat, pausing to drift, kiss, have sex, eat. Each night before Lexie fell asleep, Daniel kissed her and said, "Good night future Mrs. Daniel Waite." The old-fashioned use of *Mrs. Daniel Waite* was the kind of thing Lexie and Amy liked to knock and mock. But Daniel had been so earnest and Lexie was so in love that she never clicked on her critical apparatus. She had been drenched in perfect happiness: wanting nothing, needing nothing, only wishing for time to stand still.

"I forgot about your delicate panties." Daniel dropped to his knees, lifted the bed skirt and peeked under the bed.

"Doesn't a cleaning lady come?"

"Twice a week." He got up and arranged the bedding into a heap in the center of the mattress.

"Where was she this week?"

"Actually it's two guys, a couple. Jen canceled them because she wasn't sure how she'd explain us."

"If anyone would understand it would be two gay guys, don't you think?"

"No, why?" Daniel visually checked the room from corner to corner.

"I don't know. They tend to be more open about nontraditional relationships."

"Other than the fact that they're gay, these guys are pretty straight." Daniel flung open the closet doors and looked around. "And conservative. They're friends from her church."

"Gay, Catholic, conservative house cleaners?"

"There's every type of human out here on the lakes." Daniel pushed the closet doors shut, came to Lexie and pulled her toward himself. He kissed her in a way that felt like flower petals in her face.

"Yeah, you're here," Lexie said.

DANIEL LOCKED THE FRONT DOOR USING A KEY THAT WAS HIDDEN under a fake rock in the front garden.

"You don't have your own key?" Lexie asked. They had never left the house as there had been enough food and wine for them to have stayed a month without replenishing the supplies.

"Nah. I gave her my keys when I moved out." Daniel put Lexie's suitcase in her trunk and clicked it shut.

"Why? Doesn't she trust you?"

"She trusts me. I didn't want them anymore. It's her house." Daniel opened the door to Lexie's car and stood there like a valet, waiting for her to get in.

He kissed Lexie one last time before she slipped into the car. She was parked at the center of the circular stone drive, directly in front of the house. Daniel's car was parked in front of hers. Lexie started the engine and pulled away, around Daniel's car. Before leaving the property, she looked in the rearview mirror. Daniel hadn't gone to his car. He was standing by the front door, looking down at the rock that hid the key. Lexie waved, but he didn't see.

LEXIE WAS IN A DREAM STATE AS SHE DROVE THE NEARLY EMPTY highway back to Ruxton. She anticipated a difficult start to the week—her brain felt resistant to work, focus, productivity. Love, Lexie decided, was an ambition eraser. Or maybe contentedness erased ambition. You had to passionately desire more than you already had in order to endure a struggle toward lofty goals.

A Ben Folds song was on the radio. Lexie turned it up and sang along. Betsy Simms had loved Ben Folds in high school. When the song ended, the froggy-voiced woman deejay said, "It's ten minutes before twelve and the sun is shining down on Northampton—" Lexie slapped off the radio. She was supposed to be on campus by noon for the early post–spring break arrivals. Even at seventy miles an hour, she'd be twenty minutes late. Hopefully no one would notice.

At twelve thirty, Lexie dropped off her bag in the apartment and headed over to the dining hall. She scanned the room—it was half-empty as many students weren't returning until later in the day or early evening. There were two tables with faculty. One was full and the other had a single empty seat next to Janet Irwin (the last empty seat was always next to Janet Irwin). Lexie shored up her strength, crossed the room, and sat.

"You're late," Janet said.

"I was in my office." Lexie hated that Janet brought out the worst in her. Not only was Lexie lying, but she was snippy, too.

"I walked by your office on the way here and you weren't there."

"We must have missed each other."

231

"We've been discussing the MILF," Lenny Bilkin said. He was a history teacher, a child-sized man with an old, hangdog face.

"What's the MILF?" Lexie looked at Janet and wondered if she knew what this acronym usually meant.

"Don't engage. They're being rude and unprofessional," Janet said. Everyone around the table laughed.

Jim Reiger said, "It stands for Most Irritating Little Fucker."

"Oh!" Lexie laughed. "So most irritating student?"

"Entirely unprofessional." Janet's fork clanked against her plate as she stabbed up bites of salad. The sound reminded Lexie that she should eat, but she didn't want anything that was being served: meat lasagna, salad, vegetarian-looking pasta. There was a basket of French bread in the center of the table. Lexie grabbed a hunk, ripped off the crust and bit into the soft center.

"We're only having a little fun," Lois Wallace whispered. Lexie was surprised she was playing this game. She was usually so docile and well behaved.

"So what'd'ya say, Lexie? Who would you name as the Ruxton MILF?" Jim Reiger was smiling widely. Lexie could see food in his mouth. She looked away from him, around the table.

"Who did everyone else say so far?"

Georgio Profant had picked Robbie Colton, who had once lobbed an orange from his lacrosse stick out the half-open window, shattering a pane of glass. Lois Wallace also picked Robbie because when she'd asked him to stop rocking back on his chair, he'd turned his tie and pretended to hang himself. Janet Irwin, predictably, refused to name the MILF, and the remaining four teachers at the table hadn't yet come up with one.

"So I can only name one?" Lexie asked.

"Yes," Jim said. "Most. It has to be the Most—"

"Irritating Little Fucker," Lois said, and she laughed. Lexie suspected she was laughing at herself for having been brave enough to say *fucker* aloud.

"Dot would love this game," Lexie said, and everyone grew silent.

"Oh, I have mine!" Nancy Crantz said, breaking the moment of remembrance. "Kennedy Colson."

"You people are horrible," Janet said. "You need to stop this." Nancy blushed and dropped her head.

"You know, I think Kennedy Colson would be mine, too." Lexie was happy to save Nancy from her embarrassment. Kennedy was the only girl at Ruxton whom Lexie disliked. She had even tried to force herself into loving Kennedy. *Give love, give love, give love,* Lexie would think while waiting for Kennedy to finish whatever perfectly relevent thoughts she happened to be conveying in class.

"Seriously? Why?"

"You go first." Lexie wanted to give Nancy permission to rip apart Kennedy Colson.

"No, you go. I want to hear your reason." Nancy was the worst people-pleasing version of Lexie, a version that she had been trying to train out of herself since graduate school.

"If Dot were here," Lois said, "she'd say something like *will one of you fuckers just go!*" Lois was on a roll. Lexie wondered if she were popping Klonopin or maybe was on beta blockers. She'd never been so outspoken before.

"I'm not sure why I don't like her." Lexie was stalling. What she wasn't sure of was whether or not she should confess the reason she didn't like Kennedy. The girl was full of herself. At seventeen! When there was no completely-formed self to be full of yet.

"She's a gorgeous girl," Jim Reiger said. Everyone, including dog-faced Lenny Bilkin, shot him a look.

"They're all gorgeous at that age," Lexie said.

Janet said, "This is disgusting."

"Wait, why do you hate her?" Nancy asked.

"I don't hate her," Lexie said. "But I do think she's the Most Irritating Little Fucker. She sits in my class and I have some cellular reaction to her." That was all she'd say.

"Maybe it's because she's sleeping with Ethan Waite," Jim Reiger said, "and he's your pet."

"She's sleeping with Ethan?" Lexie was surprised by her internal revulsion. Why would Ethan sleep with a girl like that? Did he not want someone more human? Someone who had never dated Skyler Bowden (whom Amy had dubbed Patient Zero in the Ruxton Chlamydia Crisis)?

"I guess they're not getting their condoms from you," Lois said, and everyone laughed.

"No, they're not," Lexie said, not laughing. "And why do you think Ethan's my pet?"

"I see you joking with him," Jim said. "You don't treat him like the other kids. You chat with him like he's one of the teachers."

"He's more mature than the other kids," Nancy said.

"Yeah, he is." Lexie's face burned. She worried someone might intuit that the reason Lexie treated Ethan differently was because she was going to marry his father. She needed to push the conversation away from Ethan before someone sensed her discomfort. "Nancy, why do you think Kennedy's the MILF?"

"She acts like she's better than everyone and she kinda is, you know?" Nancy was looking directly at Lexie, who nodded in agreement. She knew exactly what Nancy meant. Kennedy's abundant confidence—which was backed by her abundant intellectual and physical gifts—could be too much for anyone with a self-critical voice in his or her head to bear. Kennedy Colson made Lexie feel irrelevant. For the insecure Nancy, the experience was probably worse.

"Something is terribly amiss with you people," Janet said.

"How is she better than everyone?" Lois asked.

"She's prettier," Nancy said. "She's smarter."

"She's my favorite student," Ben Whiteford said, shrugging. Ben was a schlubby, cardigan-sweater-wearing man. Lexie figured his favorites were arranged by grades: the better you did in his class, the more he liked you.

"She corrected my pronunciation of vestigial," Nancy said.

"She's certainly going to be more successful than all of us," Lexie said.

"As her goals and your goals are different, your successes and failures can't be compared," Janet said. "And as far as her behavior on campus goes, she should be admired."

Lexie couldn't help but note that in this particular instance Janet might be right.

The conversation switched to speculation about which kids might be sociopaths. The faculty were giddy with gossip and conjecture. It was a mood that hit every year when the end of the term—freedom—was in sight. As Lois rattled off the characteristics of the typical male sociopath (*they never confess so, like, if you find your sociopath boyfriend in bed with another woman he'll say he's getting a massage . . .*) Lexie felt an almost-embarrassing flush of gratitude for the differences between herself and the group: (1) She had never, and would never, be with anyone like the deranged men Lois had dated. (2) She wasn't sentenced to decades of the repetitive academic cycle. Once Daniel's divorce was final, Lexie would have a brand-new life. One that wouldn't end in a dormitory apartment with a 1980s dishwasher and a Crate and Barrel rug owned by the school.

THAT AFTERNOON, LEXIE AND AMY MET UP IN THE INFIRMARY. LEXIE had wanted to report everything: how beautiful the lake house was; how great the sex at the lake house was; how in love she and Daniel were, at the lake house and now. But before she could get started, Amy launched into her own story. She was in love. And it appeared to be mutual.

"So, did you *not* do the sink-strainer gunk when you had an orgasm?" Lexie opened the top drawer of Amy's desk and looked for the Hershey's Kisses.

"They're here." Amy opened a side drawer and handed a palmful to Lexie, who dumped them on the sickbed before hopping up to sit beside them.

"How did it all go down?" Lexie sucked a chocolate. Amy chewed one.

"I actually waited to have sex with him." Amy picked through her hair as if she were fluffing it up.

"No!"

"Yup."

"How long?"

"Second date."

"Hey, for you that's an eternity."

"And he's every bit as into this thing as I am. I think this one's gonna stick." Amy unwrapped another chocolate and stuck it whole into her mouth.

"Details, y'all! Give me the details!" Lexie unwrapped another chocolate. She swore to herself this would be the last one. Although she did nothing to move away the handful that sat on the bed beside her.

"Oh, you are so bad with your y'alls. It's supposed to refer to more than one person, so you could say it to me and Cal—"

"His name's Cal? I love that name. Like California." Okay, *this* is the last one, Lexie thought. She unwrapped one more.

Cal was short for Calvin, but he had lived in California for many years. He owned a charming bookstore the next town over. On Friday and Saturday nights he kept the place open until nine, unless there were customers, in which case he'd stay open until the store was empty. (Cal never kicked out anyone who wanted to buy a book.) He'd been married once, had no kids, wore glasses that always looked clean, and he smelled like spicy lime. He was five years younger than Amy, which didn't bother her, or Cal, one bit.

Lexie thought there was a nice balance in her and Amy being in love and having boyfriends at the same time. It reminded her of a happy summer in Hermosa Beach when Lexie's best friend from college was dating Lexie's boyfriend's brother. She never had to abandon one person to be with another as they all wanted to be in the same place at the same time. A blissfull synchronicity.

"I can't wait for the four us to hang out," Lexie said. And she popped the last of the handful of Kisses into her mouth.

17

IT WAS FRIDAY EVENING AND LEXIE WAS SLOWLY MAKING HER WAY to the dining hall. The topic for tonight was the First Amendment. Normally when she walked to dinner, Lexie gathered her thoughts, came up with questions for the students, and asked herself how she felt about that night's subject. But there was only one week of school left and Lexie was as unable to focus as the students themselves. An unsettled itchiness had spread through campus and every single human around wanted simply to be free of it.

Lexie planned to spend most of the summer in Daniel's Boston apartment. She figured she'd come to Ruxton on occasion—all her stuff was here, she'd have to pick up a change of clothes every once in a while. Don McClear had even mentioned that if Lexie were dating, and if she were particularly discreet, the person she was seeing could sleep in her apartment once the students had evacuated. Surely he had no idea she was seeing Daniel Waite, but he must have guessed she was in love. He'd probably guessed it of

Amy, too. The two of them together were, Lexie thought, almost unbearable in their cheerfulness.

For the fourth time on her walk to the dining hall, Lexie checked her phone for a text from Daniel. He had been in Asia for nearly two weeks and was so heavily escorted that he was able to eke out only a single text each day. Lexie felt pangs of loneliness with him gone but he'd be home in three days, Monday. Out of simple laziness, Lexie had stopped shaving her body while he was gone and had a Fred Flintstone shadow running down her thighs and a goaty tuft of hair on her pubic mound and in each armpit. Sunday afternoon, she was getting her hair highlighted and her body waxed. She'd be as sleek as a wet seal.

At the dining hall, Lexie took her seat and looked around the table. That week, the kids had rotated groups.

"This is your final dining group for the year," Lexie said.

"Oh my god, I'm going to cry!" Garrison Tauber said. She lived in Arizona and never saw any of the Ruxton kids over the summer.

"I'll visit you in Arizona," The Prince said. "I've never been there." During each of The Prince's Ruxton summers, he visited kids in states he'd never before seen.

Leighton Gaines and Piper Riley were getting the food. Lexie wished they'd hurry as she didn't have the patience or disposition for aimless chatter. She molded her face into a simple half smile, crossed one leg over the other, and floated off in her mind. As Leighton and Piper poured water or milk into the glasses, Lexie thought about the way her naked body and Daniel's naked body sometimes suctioned together as if they were a single entity.

A giant squid that was being rejoined after a temporary split in two.

"Miss James," The Prince said. "Can we please start with a general discussion about the separation of church and state and whether or not that idea is being fully practiced in the United States?"

"Certainly." Lexie blinked. Did her face look different when she was thinking about sex? "Why don't we have Kaeli start?"

Kaeli Tripp was from Nashville, Tennessee. Her parents were famous country singers who fell in love after recording a duet together. Most of the kids at Ruxton didn't listen to country music so Kaeli wasn't as sought after as a friend as, say, Cooper McBride, the boy whose mother was the president of one of the major movie studios, or Cece Neale, whose father was a sportscaster who had been a star pitcher for the Red Sox. But Kaeli, as a practicing and faithful Christian and as president of the speech club, would be the perfect person to articulate one side of the argument.

"I'd love to start," Kaeli said.

"Great. Why don't we have Dewey speak next and we'll all fall in from there." Dewey Summers came from a long line of Boston Democrats. Kaeli and Dewey could lead the table into an energetic verbal hacky-sack volley that would relieve Lexie from the burden of engaging.

The kids talked and Lexie drifted off. In the midst of remembering a moonlit night when she and Daniel had sex on the dock at the lake house, Lexie sensed eyes on her. She turned and caught Ethan Waite staring. Ethan's eyes so resembled Daniel's that Lexie startled. It was as if her fantasy had materialized. Lexie smiled. Ethan smiled. They both turned back to their own tables.

That evening, Amy lay on Lexie's bed and watched Lexie pick

out an outfit. They were going to a local bar for drinks before Amy met up with Cal.

"This?" Lexie held up a short red dress that she could never wear on campus.

"That looks like something a reality TV star would put on for a girls' night out."

"Is that good or bad?"

"I s'pose if you were meeting Daniel it'd be good. But since you're not going out with him, it could bring you lotsa trouble."

"Are you kidding? I don't even flirt with other people." Lexie took off her blouse and skirt and shimmied into the dress. "Also, I haven't shaved since Daniel left." She lifted the dress and flashed her inner thigh at Amy.

"I guarantee no one at this bar will care about that hair you're sprouting."

"Yeah, the townies are probably used to furry women."

"Don't get snobby on me just 'cause your boyfriend's rich. You're a townie girl yourself."

"I know. You're right." Lexie opened the closet and took out the strappy silver sandals she'd bought for the canceled wedding. She stepped into them and stared at herself in the mirror. As long as her legs were closed, you couldn't see the hair.

"You're really gonna wear that dress tonight?" Amy clucked her tongue.

Lexie turned from side to side. She checked out her backside. "You're in a dress."

"Mine is to my *knees*." Amy was wearing a blue shirtdress with panty hose and flesh-colored pumps. Sometimes when Lexie looked at Amy's stockinged legs she thought of her mother. Mitzy wore thick suntan support hose every day to work. She swore by them. Whenever she walked from the shower to the bedroom (a thin, burgundy towel wrapped around her frame) she would stop for an audience, if anyone happened to be sitting in the living room. "These legs," Mitzy would say, holding out one solid, muscled limb like she was posing for a pinup picture, "look years younger than my face thanks to Sheer Energy!" Or she'd say, "Have you ever seen legs like this before? Have you? Seriously?" Once she even did the cancan in her towel. Lexie, eight at the time, had hidden her eyes behind her splayed fingers so she wouldn't have to see what was going on below the towel flapping open in front of her. Bert had been beside Lexie on the couch, a beer in one hand, a cigarette in the other. He'd laughed so hard that he dropped the cigarette off the back of the couch and Lexie had run to fetch it before the house burned down.

"Take off your stockings and put this on." Lexie pulled a short black dress from the closet and tossed it to Amy.

"My hips are way too big for that." Amy stood and held the dress in front of herself with two pinched fingers like it was a dirty handkerchief.

"It stretches." There was a knock at the apartment door. Lexie and Amy looked out the bedroom door toward the living room.

"Oh gawd, if the students see us in these getups they'll know what sluts we are." Amy threw the dress on the bed and then brushed out her shirtdress.

Lexie yanked down her dress and then went to the door. Ethan Waite was there. "Can I come in?" he asked.

"Is it urgent? Miss Hagen's here." Lexie looked in Ethan's eyes to assess the situation. Did she need to be the school counselor or could she tell the kid to come back at a more convenient time?

"Wild Friday night in Rilke?" Ethan grinned all big and dopey. Lexie was relieved he wasn't in crisis.

"We're going to get a drink off campus. So why don't you come back tomorrow and we'll talk."

"You drink?" Ethan was as solid as a pillar in Lexie's doorway.

"A little. Why would you think I wouldn't?" Soon enough, he'd see her drink at dinner with Daniel, or when the three of them went to Rome or Paris or any of the other cities Daniel had promised they'd visit.

"I don't know. The two weeks you spend on alcohol abuse and alcohol brain damage and all that in your class." Ethan sauntered in like he lived there. Lexie stepped back and let it happen.

"Well, I certainly don't abuse alcohol."

Amy emerged from the bedroom looking like she was planning to attend a church potluck.

"How you doin', Ethan?"

"Okay, I guess. How are you, Miss Hagen?"

"Fair to middlin'."

"Can I sit?" Without waiting for an answer, Ethan dropped into one of the gray chairs.

"Do you want me to leave so y'all can talk alone?" Amy asked.

"I don't think this is a crisis. Is it, Ethan?" What could he possibly need to talk about on a Friday night when Lexie had maybe one hour to hang out with Amy before she went off to be with Cal?

"It's not a crisis, you can stay, Miss Hagen. I just wanted to talk to grown-ups, you know?"

Lexie and Amy both sat and looked at him, waiting.

"It's my eighteenth birthday today." Ethan sounded unenthused.

"Happy birthday! You're an adult," Amy said.

"Free to vote, buy cigarettes, and go to prison," Lexie said.

"Yeah, so . . . I know I'm being ridiculous but, like, my parents are away celebrating their wedding anniversary, which was last Monday, and they, like, didn't even call or send me a card or anything. And I dunno, I feel so . . . I don't know, I'm embarrassed but I feel totally bad that they didn't send anything."

The room went silent. Lexie felt a roaring fire in her ears. She consciously composed her face: settled her eyes into their sockets, relaxed her mouth with her lips slightly parted, smoothed her forehead, straightened in her seat. She looked at Amy, who stared at Ethan with a half-concerned smile.

"Oh, no." Lexie spoke as if her concern was entirely for Ethan and not at all for herself. "Let's start at the beginning."

"Yes," Amy said. "When did your parents leave town? Was there any acknowledgment of the upcoming birthday?"

Lexie felt like she couldn't breathe. Thank god for Amy. Amy could figure this out. Amy could be the adult in the room.

"They left almost two weeks ago; they went on a cruise around Italy and Greece. They always do something big for their anniversary."

"So, if they always do something big, do they always miss your birthday?" Amy asked.

"No, they usually call. But I know it's hard to get phone service from the ship. And they usually mail something, so that I get a present on the day, you know? But this year, there was no phone call and no packages came. And I feel like an idiot for even caring, you know, I mean, I'm eighteen, you'd think I'd be over this, but shit—excuse me—damn, I mean, my whole life I've always had this strange feeling that my parents loved each other more than they loved me and when stuff like this happens it just confirms that." Ethan dropped his head and picked at a hole in his jeans.

"You've always had this feeling?" Lexie asked. The words came out too forcefully, too quickly. Better not speak again, she thought.

"I don't think about it much. Only on my birthday. I swear, I think the whole reason they sent me to Ruxton is so they could have the house to themselves."

There was quiet again. In her head, Lexie said the word *breathe*.

Amy said, "Honey, there's not a parent on earth who loves their spouse more than their kids. It's a whole different kind of love. And if there was no present or phone call this year, maybe it was 'cause they were way out at sea and couldn't get a connection, you know."

"Isn't every corner of the world connected?" Ethan asked.

Lexie couldn't speak. She couldn't open her mouth. She could barely keep her face intact. Thankfully, Ethan continued to stare at the hole in his jeans.

"Well, some places are spotty. Have they contacted you at all since they've been on this trip?" Amy asked.

"My mom sent photos. Of the two of them. I mean, give me a freaking break! Who wants photos of their parents kissing?"

There was a whirling in Lexie's head. She wanted to rush out of the room, go to her purse, and take a Klonopin. Instead, she forced herself to remain in the chair. "She really sent a kissing photo?" she managed, her voice hoarse and barking.

"Yeah, can you believe it!" Ethan took his phone from his pocket, pulled up a picture, and held it out for Lexie and Amy to see. Lexie stayed in her chair, afraid she'd collapse if she moved.

Amy leaned forward, took the phone, and examined the photo. "They look like real nice people, Ethan." Amy handed the phone back. "And I'd bet my life they love you more than anything. I'm sure it's a problem of Internet connection, slow mail, delivery all the way from some far off Greek island to little ol' Ruxton."

Ethan shrugged. He looked up at Amy. "You're probably right. Maybe I'm more upset with myself for actually feeling this way than I am by what's happened. Like, I can't believe I'm eighteen and I actually care about this shit. Excuse me, this crap."

"You know, we're all like that," Amy said. "I'm in my thirties and sometimes I can't believe how much I care about things that I thought I'd outgrow by the time I was eighteen."

"Me, too," Lexie blurted. She wanted to run into the bathroom and retch out the mosaic of thoughts that filled her head: Daniel, Jen, Peter, the canceled wedding, the wedding dress hanging in Peter's house, the pending weeklong visit from her mother, the idea that she owned nothing of value except a five-year-old German car with a smudge on the ceiling, and the fact that in her lowest emotional state she was sporting a pubescent boy's beard up her thighs and into the crack of her ass.

"Ethan, I would bet my bottom dollar that there will be a package and a phone call coming your way tomorrow," Amy said. "I think you have to give your parents a little break since they're so far away. You need to trust that something's coming."

"Exactly," Lexie said, and she breathed out as if she were blowing a gnat out of her lungs.

"You okay, Miss James?" Ethan jerked his head toward Lexie.

"I might be a little fluey." Lexie couldn't lift her head. She was unable to fend off the grief and humiliation that was roaring through her.

"I was about to take her temperature when you showed up." Amy clapped her hands. Lexie wondered if she wanted to distract Ethan with the clap the way you might distract a dog lunging at a piece of cheese on a platter.

"I thought you two were going out to get a drink?"

"We were, but I was insisting on taking her temperature before she walked out this door!" Amy looked at Lexie. Lexie, dumbly, remained mute.

"Okay, well, I'm sorry I'm such a dumb-ass." Ethan stood and stretched; his body towered over Lexie and Amy like he was a full-grown man.

"Oh honey, you have nothing to apologize for." Amy stood, too. Lexie stayed seated. She wished she could anesthetize herself into oblivion, darkness, silence. A Michael Jackson sleep.

"I hope you feel better, Miss James." Ethan stared at Lexie. Tiny lines of worry radiated above each of his eyebrows.

"Thanks, Ethan." Lexie pushed her mouth into a smile and lifted her right hand. A flap instead of a wave.

Amy stood at the door and had a few final words with Ethan while Lexie pushed herself out of the chair and wobbled into the bedroom. She popped a Klonopin and then hid the pill bottle under her pillow. She wanted to hit that townie bar and hit it hard. And there was no way Amy would let Lexie drink if she knew she'd taken the Klonopin.

Amy returned to the bedroom. She sat beside Lexie on the bed. "You okay?"

"I feel sick."

"Do you want to cry?"

"I want to get drunk."

"Don't get drunk. We each need to take our own car tonight." Cal's house was in the opposite direction from Ruxton and the bar. It would add forty minutes of driving if Amy had to take Lexie home before meeting Cal.

"Fine, no big deal."

"Are we going to talk about this?"

"I can't talk about it. It's sitting in my stomach like a giant lump of clay and I . . . I can't talk." Lexie fell back onto the bed. She stared at the spiderweb-cracked ceiling.

"Are you sure?"

"Were they actually kissing in that picture?" Lexie hoped there was something she didn't understand. Maybe it was an old picture. Maybe they were cheek-to-cheek and this was the send-off holiday before the divorce. The last hurrah.

"Yes. They were kissing." Amy said it firmly, as if she knew Lexie was searching for an alternate reality.

"Let's talk about this tomorrow." Lexie rolled over, stuck her face into her pillow and started sobbing. She pushed her head in deeper, muffled her mouth and screamed.

"I think we better talk." Amy rubbed Lexie's shoulder.

Lexie came up for air, sniffed and gulped. "I don't want to sit around and analyze anything. I want to not feel it."

"Well, you gotta feel it at some point."

"I'll feel it tomorrow." The truth was, Lexie felt the pain so intensely she could almost see it as a physical thing: a vibrating sheet of silvery magenta that clanged against her like cold aluminum. "Let's get a drink."

"YOU'RE DRUNK AS COOTER BROWN," AMY SAID. THEY WERE SITTING on greasy wooden stools. Lexie's cheek was on the bar, her face turned toward Amy. Five empty shot glasses encircled Lexie's head. Amy held on to the neck of a light beer.

The place was as dark as a closet and smelled like a hamster cage into which beer had been spilled. There were three TVs on, a pool table with a crowd around it, and a vintage Donkey Kong game in the corner. Lexie and Amy were the only women in dresses.

"I can't believe I did that to Peter." The aluminum sheet of pain had been rattling forth a ruckus of emotions. Mostly shame, guilt, regret, and humiliation.

"You didn't know."

"You knew." It was hard to enunciate with half her mouth smashed into the bar.

"No I didn't."

"You warmed me."

"I warmed you?"

"WARMed me."

"Warmed you?!"

"WORN."

"Warn?"

"Shit, I'm drunk. I need another shot." Lexie sat up.

"I'm puttin' you in a cab." Amy pulled out her phone.

"What time is it?"

"Nine. Cal texted, no one's there so he's closing shop."

"Go meet him. He loves you. I'm a fuckup. I fucked a fucker and I fucked off a guy who wasn't a fucker because I'm a fucker like my dad."

"You're nothing like your daddy." Amy cupped her hand over the mouthpiece and turned her back to Lexie so she could hear the phone.

"I have better legs than my dad." Lexie turned so her legs weren't under the bar. "He was all bloated in the belly and he had these chicken legs sticking out." She kicked up her right foot and her silver sandal flew across the room. It skimmed a guy's shoulder before landing on the ground. The guy picked up the shoe. He turned around, trying to see where it had come from. Lexie attempted invisibility by blowing on her nails as if she'd just had a manicure. When she looked up, the guy was engaged in conversation, her shoe sitting casually on the bar next to his beer.

"Cab will be here in five minutes." Amy consulted her phone again. "Shit."

"What?"

"Cal wants to make a nine thirty movie."

"Go!"

"I'm not gonna leave you like this." Amy pointed at Lexie's bare foot. "Where's your shoe?"

"O'er there with that beer." Lexie waved toward the guy. She started laughing.

"How did it get over there?"

"Hell if I know."

"Honey, you're so drunk, you ain't got the good sense God gave a goose."

"Thought I was as drunk as Hooter Brown."

"Cooter Brown. And drunk as a goose."

"I am a goose. A stupidy dumb-dumb goose. I deserved this."

"You do not deserve this."

Lexie held her wobbling pointer finger up toward Amy's mouth. "Yes, I do. I broke Peter's heart. I chose to be with the motherfucker. His wife! His wife, Amy! There's a wife! I fucked someone with a wife! Not at the same time, like, that's gross, she's fifty—"

"Stop right there." Amy held her palm up. "First of all, we're both gonna be fifty one day if we're lucky, so don't start bitchin' on older women. Secondly, you're in no frame of mind to look at any of this clearly. So let it go for now and we'll pick through it all over breakfast tomorrow." Amy checked her phone. Lexie knew she'd rather be with Cal than babysitting drunk Lexie. Who could blame her?

"No breakfast. I've caught a bout of anorexia."

"Oh, don't kid about that. Let's get your shoe; we gotta get you to the cab." Amy tried to help Lexie off the bar stool.

"I don't want my shoe."

"You don't want your shoe?" Amy gave a little tug and pulled Lexie off the stool. She steadied her on her rubbery legs.

"It's one of my wedding shoes. They both shoulda stayed with the dress."

"Fine, leave the shoe." Amy put a few bills on the bar while holding Lexie with one hand. She hoisted Lexie's purse onto her own shoulder, and helped her walk, limping, outside.

"Go to the mooovies," Lexie slurred.

"I'll leave when your cab shows." Right then, the only cab in town pulled in. Amy opened the back door and almost fell in her-

251

self as she tried to keep Lexie from face-planting on the seat. She sat Lexie up and put her purse on her lap.

"Can you take her to Ruxton?" she asked the cabbie.

"Sure thing." The cabbie tilted the rearview mirror and watched as Lexie slumped toward the door.

"I'll wake you up with croissants and coffee tomorrow." Amy molded Lexie into a straighter sitting position.

"No, I have anorexia now. Remember?"

"Hush! I'll see you tomorrow." Amy shut the door and rushed off.

Lexie looked at the cabbie who was now turned in his seat looking at her. There was no bulletproof glass partition, no credit card slot, nothing that made the cab feel like a cab from the inside. Out the front window she saw Peter and his girlfriend, Celeste, walking toward the bar.

"Oh, lookee lookee." Lexie groaned as she watched them. Celeste was wearing a denim jacket, a white satin skirt, and cowboy boots. Lexie wished she were wearing that outfit. There was far more confidence in cowboy boots than a pair—or a single, right now—of strappy sandals.

"You going to the town or the school?" the cabbie asked.

"I'm stayin' here." Lexie slid across the seat and opened the door.

"You sure?" The cabbie looked like Bert, Lexie thought. Or maybe it actually was Bert. Was he driving cabs in Western Massachusetts? But wait. Bert was dead. Right?

"You're the same age as Daniel," Lexie said, to imaginary Bert. "Tha's kinda gross, huh?"

"You okay?" The cabbie asked.

"Yup." Lexie put her shod foot on the gravel and half hopped and half limped back to the bar. She opened the door and peered in. Celeste and Peter were sitting where Lexie and Amy had sat. She was holding a martini glass to his mouth and he was taking a sip.

Celeste lowered the glass and wiped Peter's lips with her fingertips. The gesture was intimate, tender. Peter leaned in and kissed Celeste. Lexie gasped.

The door opened behind Lexie and a large man with a large head and a beard that grew out into a trapezoid appeared at her back. "In or out?"

"Huh?" Lexie's couldn't stop watching Peter and Celeste.

"You coming or going?" The man's head nodded up and down as he examined Lexie from stem to stern.

"Goin' where?"

"Are you leaving the bar or entering it?" He unabashedly stared at Lexie's breasts. As if he were about to bite her there.

"I hafta watch my ex-fiancé with the very beautiful, beautiful, beautiful Celeste."

"Why?"

"To see how I blew it."

"You didn't blow it with him. I'll fucking marry you." Again the man's eyes roved Lexie's body, as if assessing a purchase.

"ZZ Top," Lexie mumbled. The mind/mouth passageway was too drenched to create sentences for what she was thinking. If she had been better able to speak, Lexie would have said she was worried that guys like the one speaking to her now, whom she thought resembled someone in the band ZZ Top, would be all she'd have to choose from in the future. Compounding this fear was a belief that her social life, henceforth, would be spent in sweaty bars playing Donkey Kong.

"Yeah, I like ZZ Top, too, so let's fucking get married."

"I cheat." She looked back at Peter and saw that he was staring at her, a pained look on his face. Celeste pivoted to see what he was looking at and her jacket swung open. She wasn't wearing a satin skirt; she was in Lexie's wedding dress.

Lexie turned and rushed out the door. "I don't care if you cheat as long as I get you in the sack every day!" the guy shouted after her.

Lexie stagger-hopped around the parking lot, looking for her car. She talked to Peter, though she knew he couldn't hear. "Didn't leave you for ZZ Top . . . that dress looks cute with boots . . ." The gravel hurt her bare foot more than when she'd left the bar the first time. She needed a shoulder to hold her up; she needed a human crutch.

The Jetta was hidden between two giant SUVs and so it took Lexie much longer to find it than it should have in a parking lot of only fifteen cars. Upon discovering it, Lexie clicked the lock, got in, and started the engine.

18

LEXIE LIFTED THE FAKE ROCK IN THE FRONT GARDEN AND TOOK out the key to the Waites' lake house. She let herself in the front door, dropped the key into her purse, and started wandering, flicking on lights as she went. First stop: living room. There had been a few framed pictures on the grand piano when she and Daniel had spent the week there. Tonight there were three or four times as many. Half of them were pictures of Daniel and Jen.

Lexie slipped her purse off her shoulder and swept her arm across the piano top, sending the pictures to the ground. She pushed the heel of her single sandal into one of the frames. The glass refused to crack. She pushed harder and toppled to the ground. Lexie lay still and looked up at the ceiling. It was coffered, pristine white, with not a single visible crack. In all her life, Lexie had never lived in a room that didn't have at least one crack in the ceiling.

She rolled up to sitting, picked up the picture closest to her and stared at it. Jen and Daniel on the boat, the wind blowing Jen's hair into a long blond mustache across Daniel's face. Both of them laughing. Lexie threw the picture across the room. It landed on the carpet, intact.

Lexie crawled across the floor and gathered the photos into one pile. Then she held on to the leg of the piano and pulled herself up to standing. One by one, Lexie lifted the photos off the carpet and tried to arrange them the way they had been.

Once that was done, Lexie picked up her purse and hobbled toward Jen's bedroom. Or, she amended in her head, the bedroom she had been told where Jen slept alone. She pushed open the door and turned on the light. The bed was perfectly made. It looked like a showroom bed—everything white and pale blue, pillows just so. Lexie imagined it smelled like lavender, or lilacs, or something else pure and fresh.

"I hate you, Daniel Waite." Lexie wobbled to the bed, dropped her purse onto the floor and stared at the pillows. "Fuck you!" She threw the pillows, one by one, onto the floor. Then she fell to her knees, crawled across the floor, and tossed each pillow back to the bed. Most of them made the target. When they didn't, she kept trying until they did.

Lexie stood and surveyed her work. It was difficult to remember how the pillows had been arranged when she had walked in. For a good five minutes Lexie adjusted and readjusted the pillows. How did people know how to do bed pillows? When did you get that lesson?

The master bathroom felt overly opulent and impossibly clean. There were two separate toilet rooms off the white marble room. It was like a mausoleum. Lexie pulled out her phone and took a picture. Without thinking, she texted the picture to Betsy Simms and wrote, *like a mooosalini.*

Lexie walked into the closest toilet room. It contained a toilet and a shiny silver toilet paper roll. She walked into the second one. That one contained a toilet, a shiny silver toilet paper roll, and a silver magazine rack that had *Forbes,* the *Wall Street Journal, Harvard Law Review,* and several copies of a slim little magazine called *Bottom Line.*

"LIAR!" Lexie kicked the magazine rack with her bare foot. It felt like a hammer had been swung into her toe. Lexie screamed and held the throbbing toe. "I hate you!"

Lexie returned to the first toilet room where she sat and peed. She may have fallen asleep because suddenly she had the sensation of waking up. She grabbed a wad of toilet paper to wipe and realized she'd failed to pull down her underwear. Lifting her hips, she awkwardly worked off the wet panties, then wiped, flushed, and left the panties like a washed-up red rodent at the base of the toilet.

There were two sinks and seven mirrored doors across the vanity in the main part of the bathroom. Lexie washed her hands, then opened each door in order. In the first cabinet was Daniel's stuff: deodorant, saline nasal spray, L'Occitane aftershave, Prada cologne. She picked up the bottle of cologne and tossed it onto the marble floor. It made a chinking sound but miraculously didn't break.

Lexie went to the cabinet that held Jen's makeup. She considered putting it on, and then thought better of it. She'd already applied makeup before leaving Rilke. She didn't need more.

The last medicine cabinet held prescription pill bottles, cortisone creams, eyedrops. Lexie rotated each bottle until she could read the label. There was nothing familiar or interesting. Until she found the Klonopin. The dosage was the same as Lexie's prescription, .05. She opened the bottle and dry-swallowed a pill. She poured the rest into her hand, looked around the bathroom for her purse, and then stuffed them down her bra. The pills tickled her skin. She put the lid back on. Inexplicably, she licked the outside of the bottle before returning it to the medicine cabinet, exactly where she'd found it.

Lexie left the bathroom and surveyed the bedroom. She was looking for something, but she couldn't remember what. Her purse! It was on the floor by the side of the bed. She had every intention of removing the Klonopin from her bra and sticking them in the internal pocket of her purse, but instead she dove onto the bed face-first.

With her head resting on one cheek, Lexie stared at the bedside table. The wood was so shiny she could almost see her reflection. Who polished it? The gay housekeepers? Were there really gay housekeepers or had that been a lie, too?

Lexie reached out and opened the drawer in the bedside table. She leaned over and peered inside. A large rubber vibrator shaped like an exclamation point rested beside a glass jar of earplugs.

"But why?" Daniel had told Lexie that when Jen went through menopause two years ago, she'd lost interest in sex. That was one of the reasons, he claimed, their marriage fell apart. Lexie picked up the vibrator, rolled onto her back, lifted her dress, pushed the on button, and pressed the rubbery wand against herself. She could barely feel it. She imagined her body as a lump of molded lard.

Lexie gave up, lifted the vibrator to her face and sniffed at it. She rolled to her stomach and rubbed her nose back and forth into the pillow, as if to rub off whatever bodily juices may have infected her. The vibrator felt like a small hand weight as she dropped it toward the gaping bedside drawer. It missed and landed in her sack purse instead.

Lexie rolled to her back and kicked her arms and legs out in a letter *X*. "I'm *cavorting* on your bed." She looked to the side of the bed that belonged to Daniel and started crying. The sadness inside Lexie ran like a wash cycle: circling, swirling, rotating, swishing. It came straight out of her mouth, eyes, and nose, everything wet and running. Lexie wanted to flip a switch and shut it all down.

And somehow she did. Lexie flipped the switch. And the light in her head didn't turn on again until the moment she was awakened by Jen Waite.

19

I'M SO, SO SORRY," LEXIE SAID TO JEN. IN HER HEART SHE WAS sorry for much more than having fallen asleep on the bed.

They were at the open front door. Daniel was halfway across the stone, circular driveway, headed toward Lexie's car.

"Excuse my husband," Jen said. "We landed in Boston from Athens and drove two hours to get here because he wanted to wake up on the lake and . . . I think he's a little jet-lagged and cranky." Jen formed a pouty face, like she was talking about her child.

"Did you have a good trip?" Lexie hoisted the purse higher on her shoulder.

"It was our anniversary so, you know, we went for the romantic thing, a European cruise."

"That's so nice." Lexie forced herself to smile.

"If we find your shoe, I'll drive it to campus for you." Jen pointed at Lexie's bare foot.

"I'm almost certain I left the apartment without it." Lexie

stepped off the porch and onto the driveway. "Ambien! That stuff's supercrazy, right?!"

Jen smiled and waved, and Lexie hobbled to her car. Daniel opened the door. The keys were sitting in the ignition. He shut the car door once Lexie was seated, but stood there as solid and firm as a steel column. She turned on the car and rolled down the window. Daniel leaned his head in. He pointed toward the road. Lexie figured he was making it look like he was giving her directions home. *"The fuck are you doing here?"* Daniel whisper-yelled.

"I'm sorry. It was a mistake."

"It was a mistake that you took an Ambien, drove to my house, and went to sleep on the bed I share with my wife?" Daniel was actually gritting his teeth. Lexie felt disoriented, as if maybe this wasn't Daniel. Her Daniel didn't share a bed with his wife. Her Daniel loved her and wanted to marry her. Her Daniel had that very morning sent her a text from Asia saying he missed her so much his gums hurt!

"You said you were in China and wouldn't be home until Monday."

"I said I'd call you on Monday. I didn't say when I'd be home."

"I thought you were separated. I thought you had told her about me. I thought you loved me."

"We'll talk about this later." Daniel stepped back from the car, pointed toward the road once more, then turned and walked away.

Lexie rolled up the window. She watched Daniel shoulder his way past Jen Waite, who remained in the doorway, staring at Lexie.

Lexie lifted her left hand to wave and knocked her knuckles

against the glass. She gasped and nervously laughed. Once she'd put the car in drive it took immense concentration to stay within the borders of the driveway.

Lexie edged the car slowly forward until she was closer to the house. Right in front of Jen Waite, who was watching her the way you might watch a bobcat prance across your lawn. Lexie waved again—with deliberate control so she wouldn't knock the window. Then she putted past Jen and out onto the road.

A couple minutes later, Lexie pulled over. She rolled down the window and hung out her hair. Then she rolled up the window, keeping as much hair trapped against the frame as possible. It was a trick she'd seen a friend do in college, a way to be jerked awake if you accidentally nodded off while driving. Naturally, for the system to work, your head would have to fall forward or toward the passenger seat. A tilt to the left and you'd have to hope that the bonk against the glass would wake you.

Lexie talked while she drove. "That's a stop sign, so stop . . . Daniel doesn't love me . . . yellow line to the left . . . he's been lying to me all along . . . yellow line to the left . . ." Pangs of breath went in and out in short, uneven spanks. The idea of crying flashed in Lexie's head, but the whooshing fogginess of the last Klonopin tablet blotted out her ability to cry. It was like Lexie's heartbreak, shame, and shock were in a bottle floating out in the ocean, a couple yards ahead of her. Every time Lexie swam toward the bottle, trying to reach it, a giant wave slapped her down and washed her clean of even the idea of it. She could no longer get close enough to her feelings to experience them.

Back on campus, the walk from the parking lot to Rilke proved difficult. Lexie tripped and plummeted to the ground on the brick pathway. Her purse fell off her shoulder and the vibrator tumbled out. Lexie put the vibrator back in her bag and then rolled to her back and looked at the starry sky. It was well past midnight, past curfew; any student who was out of his or her dorm room would be hiding so as not to be seen by faculty.

Lexie kicked off the remaining sandal and watched it sail into the hedge beside her. She noticed a thin line of blood running down her knee. With her knee bent, Lexie lifted her head and licked the wound. When she pulled away, blood appeared again, like a Magic Marker that couldn't be erased. Lexie licked her knee once more before rolling over and hoisting herself upright.

When she reached the front door of the building, Lexie spotted Ethan Waite sprinting across the lawn. He didn't see her until he scrambled to a stop.

"Shit." Ethan bent over his knees to catch his breath.

"I have no idea what time it is, but I know it's past curfew." Lexie tried to adjust her face into that of a stern disciplinarian.

Ethan straightened and stared at her. He appeared more like a hologram than an actual person: his face shifting back and forth between himself and Daniel. "Can we talk about this before you write me up?"

"Sure." So much for the disciplinarian. The tip of the vibrator jutted out of Lexie's purse again. She shook it down. "Do you have your key card?"

"Yeah." Ethan pulled his ID from his pocket and scanned open the door. He followed Lexie down the hall to her apartment. Lexie blindly rummaged through her purse, searching for her keys. When she found them, she unlocked the door.

"You okay?" Ethan followed Lexie into the apartment.

"It's only a little blood."

"What blood?"

"Oh, my temperature?" Lexie turned around so she was facing Ethan. He had been closer behind her than she had realized. Their chests almost touched.

"No, you were sort of wobbling."

"Was I?" She had thought she had her body fairly under control. Lexie looked toward the chair. She didn't want to cross the room to it, or the couch, lest she wobble even more.

"Yeah. Are you drunk?" Ethan started laughing.

"I think you're drunk," Lexie said, trying to distract him.

"Not as drunk as you." Ethan stuck his finger out as if to point and gently poked Lexie right at her collarbone, directly above her heart.

"Oh, shit, I think you're right." Lexie wobbled to her sleek gray couch and sat. "Don't tell anyone that you were with me and I was drunk." She leaned forward and licked her bleeding knee again. This time, the blood didn't reappear.

"I'd never tell." Ethan dropped down beside her. They were silent for a few seconds. Then Ethan said, "I'm glad we picked this couch."

"Yeah, you decorated the whole apartment with me." They lifted their heads and simultaneously looked from side to side, like a pair of birds.

"Where are your shoes?"

"Ha!" Lexie lifted one leg and pointed her toe. Ethan dropped to his knees on the floor and captured the moving foot as if it were a jumping fish. The tickling sensation felt so bubbly and good that Lexie forgot she was miserable.

"Your foot is filthy." Ethan held Lexie's leg aloft.

"I'm filthy."

"I'm serious! You have to see the bottom of your foot. It's completely black!"

Lexie tried to bend her leg to see her foot, but Ethan had a firm grip. She went for another tactic and bent her body to see the foot in Ethan's hand but tumbled off the couch, landing on the floor beside Ethan. They broke apart laughing, each of them lying on their back, side by side.

"Oh my god," Lexie said. "I had such a shitty night. I can't tell you how good it feels to laugh."

"Me, too."

"Oh yeah, your birthday." Lexie turned to one side and looked at Ethan. In profile he was less Daniel and more Ethan, although there was a soluble wavering happening.

"I'm eighteen now."

"Yup. Prison. Cigarettes."

"And I can buy porn."

"Because no one under eighteen ever watched it online before, right?" Lexie started laughing again.

Ethan rolled to his side and put his face a couple inches from Lexie's. "Can I kiss you?"

"Why would you kiss me?" The question was sincere. Lexie knew there was a reason they shouldn't kiss, but like a lost memory, that reason was currently inaccessible, hidden in the folds of her wet, doughy brain.

"Because you're beautiful."

"Okay." Lexie stopped searching for the reason not to kiss Ethan and pleasantly fell into the moment. A kiss sounded like a good thing. Something to erase Lexie from Lexie. Something to wipe out the night like a wet sponge on a chalkboard.

They kissed. Ethan's leg pushed in between Lexie's legs and she closed her eyes and responded by rote reaction. It all felt familiar. And it smelled familiar, too, the scent of Ethan's neck boyish and grassy. Lexie's head was awash in drugs and alcohol; the sloshing was so intense she could barely hear her internal voice. One thought floated up however: *I am barely human, just a skin-bundled mess of sensation.*

Ethan tried to pull Lexie's dress off over her head but instead trapped her in it as her arms were crossed in front of her face. Lexie thought she probably looked ridiculous and this made her laugh. Ethan laughed, too. He tugged hard and the dress came flying off. Ethan fell back on the rug with it. Without missing a beat, he pulled himself up and they continued to kiss.

Before she had realized what he was doing, Ethan had unhooked Lexie's bra, skillfully, and removed it. A small shower of Klonopin tabs fell from Lexie's breasts. Several were stuck to her skin like pale yellow moles. "What's this?" Ethan plucked a Klonopin off Lexie's breast.

"Oh, don't touch that." Lexie took the pill from Ethan's hand and swallowed it.

Ethan leaned forward, kissed Lexie's nipple and licked off a Klonopin.

"Did you eat one?" Lexie asked.

"Yeah." Ethan brushed off the remaining pills.

"Don't eat any more. And don't tell anyone."

"But what is it?"

"Baby aspirin." Lexie lifted his chin so they were face-to-face and started up the kissing again. She felt like she was moving in and out of consciousness, seeing herself in a series of jump cuts, like a movie that needed to push the action forward without much explanation. One second she was kissing Ethan and the next his face was between her legs. Without any transition, he was on top of her and then she blinked and she was on top of him.

"It's more like marble or granite than flesh," Lexie said.

"What?"

"Was I talking out loud?"

"Yes." Ethan's hands were on Lexie's hips and he was moving her slowly across himself, as if she were a block of cheese he was grating. "You said it's more like marble or granite than flesh."

"Your dick. It's not like that when you're older."

"I'm not older." Ethan put his hand on the center of Lexie's back and pulled her toward him so they could kiss more.

LEXIE OPENED HER EYES AND SAW THAT SHE WAS IN BED. SHE strained to read the clock on the nightstand. Was that a five or an eight? There was a warm body behind her making the soft ocean sounds of sleeping; an arm was wrapped around her waist. Lexie looked down at the hand on her belly. She had a vague idea that it might be Ethan's hand but she wasn't sober enough to think about what that meant. Ethan was a student. He was in her apartment. That was normal enough. Lexie closed her eyes and went back to sleep.

20

THE NEXT TIME LEXIE OPENED HER EYES AMY WAS STANDING beside her bed holding a cardboard box with two cups of coffee and two croissants. She was wearing a blue floral dress and had a blue headband woven through her thick blond (seeming) hair.

Lexie looked from Amy to the clock. She remained too numb, drugged, and drunk to read it. She looked behind herself and saw Ethan but couldn't quite get why he was there.

"Get dressed!" Amy whispered. She put the cardboard box atop the books stacked on the night table and pulled Lexie out from under Ethan's arm. "Quick, before he wakes up."

Lexie stumbled naked around the room. She instantly forgot that she was looking for her clothes.

"Here!" Amy handed Lexie a pair of jeans, a bra, and a T-shirt.

"I need a bra."

"I gave you one!"

Lexie looked down at the bundle in her hands. "I mean I need panties."

"Go in the bathroom." Amy gently pushed Lexie out of the room.

In the bathroom, Lexie turned toward the mirror. She couldn't see herself, couldn't see anything. Everything that had happened in the past fifteen hours felt blank, too. Lexie pushed her eyes shut for several seconds and then opened them again. She saw her face: eyes red and puffy, black crumbs of mascara on her cheekbones, lips dry, and slightly swollen. As she leaned closer to examine her face, the image of herself in the Waites' bed, Jen hovering beside her, came charging into her head like a full-speed train. Lexie blinked. She saw herself naked, sitting atop Ethan Waite.

The train crashed.

Lexie gasped. She put one hand on the vanity to steady herself. She looked at the toilet, flipped up the lid, held her hair away from her face, and vomited.

Lexie washed her face. She cupped her hand under the faucet and fed herself a palm-full of water and then rinsed her mouth. Amy knocked once on the door before letting herself in. She had a pair of Lexie's underwear in her hand. She shook her head, her eyes big and rigid.

Lexie turned to the toilet and vomited again.

"Stop that and get dressed!" Amy said.

Lexie washed her face once more, this time with icy cold water. Amy handed her the bra. Lexie put it on. Amy handed her a T-shirt. Lexie put it on. Amy handed her the panties. Lexie put them on. Amy handed her the jeans. As Lexie was putting them on, there was a knock at the door to her apartment.

"Make sure Ethan doesn't come out of that room." Amy rushed from the bathroom.

Lexie pulled on the jeans. They felt enormous, and were dragging on the ground. Had Lexie herself shrunk in the night?

Outside, Lexie could hear the voice of Cole Hanna, the dorm proctor. She opened the bathroom door, stepped out into the hall, and looked at the closed bedroom door. She opened it carefully, hoping no one would be there. Maybe she had hallucinated having sex with Ethan Waite last night. Maybe Amy was hallucinating, too.

Lexie stuck in her head. There Ethan was, naked and sound asleep on his belly with the sheet kicked down to his ankles. She wanted to vomit again, but breathed it away. Lexie quietly shut the door and went to the living room, joining Cole and Amy.

"Hey, Miss James. I'm so sorry to hear you've got the flu, too." Cole's cheeks looked like he'd been slapped. Lexie figured that for the ultraupstanding Cole, a barefooted Lexie, dressed casually as she was, might as well have been naked.

"Thanks. I'm sure I'll be fine." Lexie bent down and rolled up the bottom of the extralarge jeans.

"Cole was worried about Ethan Waite, who went missing from his room last night. I was explaining to him that he spent the night in the infirmary." Amy scanned Lexie's jeans from the hem to the waist. She and Lexie locked eyes and Lexie read her mind. She was wearing Ethan's jeans.

"He was there at nightly check-in," Cole said. "But then Kennedy texted this morning and said she was with him later on and," Cole blushed again and dropped his head. He was ratting out both Ethan and Kennedy who clearly had slipped out together after curfew.

"Honey, make sure Kennedy stays away from the infirmary.

Tell everyone to stay away. This is a mighty awful illness and I don't want it spreading through the whole school on the last week y'all have to hang out together and have fun."

"Okay." Cole looked up from his phone. "Sorry to bother you when you're sick, Miss James."

"Not a problem. Thanks for doing your job." Lexie pushed her face into a smile and waved as Amy walked Cole to the door.

After the door closed, a silence vibrated in the air. Lexie didn't know what to say. Finally, Amy spoke.

"Is there any chance he was too drunk to remember what happened?" All that Southern sweetness was gone. Amy might as well have been a New Yorker.

"I'm not entirely sure what happened."

"You woke up naked in bed with the boy and now you're wearing his pants." Amy forcefully jabbed her finger down, as if she was indicating toward the rolled hems.

"I know." Tears flowed down Lexie's face. She had never felt so stuck, so failed, so bottomlessly horrible.

"There is no time for crying." Amy spoke with an unsympathetic staccato. "We've got to convince this kid that he took off his own clothes, put himself in your bed, and that you slept on the couch."

"Okay." Lexie sniffed. "Whatever you say." Lexie didn't trust that she herself had a right thought in her head.

Amy rushed to the bedroom. Lexie followed. Amy opened the door carefully, pulled Lexie's jeans out of the wicker hamper and handed them to her. Lexie changed quickly, right there. Once she was dressed, Amy threw on the bedroom light.

"Ethan, honey," Amy said, fully Southern-smooth again. Ethan opened his eyes and looked from Amy to Lexie. His eyes were blinking and soft. "I know you weren't feeling well last night and that you chose to crash here, but that isn't proper. So for the record let's say that you had the flu and you slept in the infirmary last night. Okay?"

"Okay." Ethan rolled to his back and then sat up, fully exposed. "Can I have one of those coffees?" Was it possible that he didn't remember what happened last night? Lexie wondered.

"Sheet," Amy said, pointing to where it bunched at his feet. Ethan reached down and pulled it up, covering himself. Amy handed him a cup of coffee. "Ethan, it is real important that you never tell anyone that you slept in Miss James's bed." Lexie stood silently beside Amy like her witless child.

"Yeah, I get it. Can I have a croissant?" Ethan took a long, slurping pull off the coffee.

Amy handed him a croissant. "So what are you going to tell your friends when they asked where you slept last night?"

Ethan lopped off half the croissant in one bite. "I slept in the infirmary." He caught Lexie's eye and winked at her with a sly, crooked smile. Lexie's stomach tumbled.

"When you came here and said you were sick, I wasn't thinking right. I should have put you to bed in the infirmary instead of in my bed. And boy, I'll tell you, that couch was not comfortable." Lexie's voice rushed out off-kilter, but at least she was able to speak.

Amy and Ethan both stared at Lexie. Ethan had a disbelieving smile. He knew exactly where Lexie had slept last night.

"Do you promise me that you'll never tell a soul?" Amy said sternly. "You have to promise me on Miss James's life."

"I promise." Ethan shoved the rest of the croissant in his mouth, smiling at Lexie.

"I'm sorry this happened," Lexie said. "I'm sorry we're asking you to lie."

"It's not much of a lie," Amy said, sharply. "Stick with the story, okay? You were sick. You slept in the infirmary."

"I totally get it." Ethan took another slurping sip of coffee. "This is good coffee."

"You're gonna have to get dressed and leave real soon. Do you have activities today?"

"Intramural."

"You feeling fit enough to play?"

"Hell, yeah." Ethan's smile was so big it was cartoonish. "I feel great! What about you, Miss James, do you feel okay?"

"I'm a little fluey." Lexie put her hand on her stomach. "We'll be in the living room. Why don't you get dressed and meet us there." Better start acting like a grown-up.

"Tell people it was a quick recovery," Amy said, to Ethan. She picked up the cardboard box with the other coffee and croissant and went with Lexie into the living room. They sat on the couch side by side and shared the coffee. Neither one touched the croissant. Neither one spoke.

Finally, Amy said: "You have to thank the good lord that that boy turned eighteen seconds before you fucked him."

Ethan walked into the living room holding his flip-flops and wearing boxers and a T-shirt. "I can't find my jeans."

"Maybe I put them in my hamper." Lexie rushed into her room and came out with Ethan's jeans. He put them on right there, as if there were nothing unusual about this scene.

Amy stood and walked Ethan to the door. "Not a word, okay?" she said.

"Promise." Ethan looked back at Lexie with adoring eyes. Lexie tried not to respond, but she couldn't stop herself. He was so unaffected, so genuine; as if what had gone down between them had been an act of love rather than flailingly blind insobriety. Lexie winked at him. Hopefully, Amy didn't notice.

Amy locked the door behind Ethan. She turned to Lexie. "Put on some shoes. You can tell me everything in the chapel."

THEY WERE ALL ALONE IN THE MUSTY, INCENSED CHAPEL. AMY pushed down the padded kneeler in the third pew and lowered herself. Lexie knelt beside her. They both put their hands in prayer. Normally when they went to chapel together, Amy prayed and Lexie sat by and spaced out. She liked the peace and quiet of the chapel. She liked the smell of it. She liked the shots of color from the long panels of stained glass that lined the upper half of the stone walls. And she liked the warm wooden benches that undulated from two hundred years of bodies in them.

"We're both going to ask for forgiveness," Amy said sternly.

"You start." Lexie was willing to seek help from any channel at this point, but she had no idea how to formulate a proper prayer. Her beliefs had always centered around hope, karma, and, over the past three years, the Yahtzee God.

"Please God, forgive me for having an affair behind my husband's back. Forgive me for sleeping with his best friend, betraying my friend—his wife, humiliating my family, humiliating my husband's family, humiliating myself, and for laying down so much unkindness on so many good human beings."

"Amen," Lexie whispered.

"Your turn."

"Okay." Lexie inhaled and exhaled like she was in a yoga class. "Forgive me for having sex with Ethan Waite, even though I don't remember it. Forgive me for having sex with Daniel Waite. I sure as hell remember that. Forgive me for betraying Peter, leaving him suddenly, canceling the wedding, and screwing him over . . ." Lexie could no longer speak. Had she really done all those things? And yet there was more. She took a breath. "Forgive me for breaking into the Waites' house last night—"

Amy dropped her hands and turned toward Lexie. "Are you kidding?" She moved up to the bench. "What happened to that cab I put you in?"

Lexie scooched in beside Amy and put her feet on the knee rest. "I saw Peter and Celeste go into the bar and I had to follow them."

"Did you talk to Peter?"

"No. Celeste was wearing my wedding dress."

"Seriously?"

"Yeah. But she made it all funky and cute with cowboy boots and a denim jacket. I mean, why couldn't I ever think of wearing a dress like that with cowboy boots and a denim jacket?"

"Honey, you must still be wasted. No sane person would obsess about a pair of cowboy boots and a denim jacket after fucking a student."

Now Lexie had another thing to add to her list of shames: irrelevant thoughts about cowboy boots and a denim jacket. "Peter had this look on his face . . . it was like I had gutted him with one of those medieval spiky balls."

"So you took the cab to the Waites'?"

"No, I drove there."

Amy rolled her eyes. "Thank god you didn't kill anyone on the road—yourself included."

"Yeah." Lexie's body sizzled with panic as she tried to remember the drive there and home. She hoped that if she had hit someone it would have been jarring enough to lodge into her muggy brain. For the time being, she was going to assume no one was killed.

"Did you climb in a window or something?" Amy was sounding less angry and more sad. She felt sorry for Lexie and this made Lexie feel only worse about herself.

"I used the hidden key Daniel had used the week we stayed there. I don't remember it too clearly, but I do know that I took some of Jen's Klonopin that I found in the medicine cabinet. And I fell asleep on their bed."

"Well, good thing they won't be home until Monday. I hope you cleaned up after yourself."

"They came home last night while I was there."

"No!" Amy's hands went up in the air as if a gun was being pointed at her.

"Yeah. They found me in their bed." Lexie felt bile rise in her throat and swallowed it down. She blinked back tears.

"Were you dressed?"

"I was in that red dress I was wearing last night—" Lexie paused as she remembered the wet underwear left behind on the bathroom floor. Maybe she could keep one detail to herself. "Anyway, I haven't shaved for two weeks and there's bristly hair—"

"Hair? Cowboy boots? Why are you even thinking about these things? So does Jen know everything now?"

"No."

"Did she know who you were?"

"She recognized me from Parents' Day. I told them I took Ambien and somehow ended up there—sleep-driving, I guess."

"And they believed you?" Amy's voice held a snarl of incredulousness.

"She did. He didn't. He was pissed. He walked me to the car and was saying all sorts of things to me before I drove off."

"Like what?"

Lexie shook her head. Her heartbreak, which had been tamped down due to the intense panic this morning, pulsed through her body in full force at the memory of Daniel speaking to her in that foreign voice. "I don't remember what he said as much as I remember that he seemed to hate me."

"So you came here, woke up Ethan, and revenge-fucked him?"

"No. That was totally unplanned. I think I ran into him when I was going into the building. Or maybe I ran into him in the hall. Wait. I ran into him outside the building. And I was messed up on the Klonopin—"

"How many did you take?"

"One before we went to the bar—"

"And you did all those shots?! Are you trying to kill yourself?"

"Maybe a couple more at the Waites' house? And—" Lexie suddenly remembered taking the Klonopin off her breasts with Ethan. She cringed. "I took one with Ethan."

"He took one, too?!"

"Yeah." Lexie wanted to bang her head against the pew in front of her and knock herself out cold.

"So you drugged him *and* fucked him?"

"Uh-huh. And it gets worse."

"Honey, I don't know how much worse this could get. Did you

and Ethan run out and rob a convenience store, pick up a hitch-hiker on the way home, and then blow him together in the car?"

"I accidentally stole Jen Waite's vibrator."

Amy looked at Lexie and then she burst out laughing. Within seconds Lexie was crying and laughing at the same time.

"All right," Amy said, once she had pulled herself together. "This is supremely fucked up, but I think you'll be able to get out of it. I don't think Ethan will tell anyone."

"Yeah. He's way more mature than most boys his age."

"Apparently." Amy gave a sly smile. "And if Jen Waite was dumb enough to buy your story, there'll be no problem there. Daniel's not going to tell her the truth."

"I have to get my shit together." Lexie pushed the meat of her palms into her eyes to stop herself from crying. "I need to forget about what happened last night and forget about the eight months I wasted being in love with someone who wasn't who he said he was." She dropped her hands.

"Have you heard from Daniel since they found you in their bed?"

"No." Lexie pulled her cell from her jeans pocket and clicked over to her texts. Betsy had written *huh?* in response to Lexie having sent her a picture of the Waite bathroom. Lexie clicked on Daniel's name. "Oh shit." Her stomach lurched. "I have no memory of this."

"Did he text?" Amy took the phone from Lexie's hand. She looked down at the screen. There was an outgoing text from Lexie. It said: *I just fucked Ethan. He's a way better lover than you.*

21

SHE MIGHT AS WELL HAVE HAD THE FLU, FOR LEXIE COULD BARELY get herself out of bed. Daniel hadn't contacted her all day and Amy would not allow Lexie to call or text him, though she was desperate to do so.

"What time is it?" Lexie had slept for what may have been ten minutes and may have been ten hours. The curtains were shut but the bedside lamp was on, giving the small room a glow like the inside of a train car.

"Six." Amy was sitting beside Lexie, reading one of the books that had been on Lexie's nightstand.

"Go meet Cal for dinner. I promise I'll be fine."

Amy closed the book and stared at Lexie. "You're not going to call him, right?"

"I swear. Well, maybe. Okay, yes, I'm going to contact him. I can't let that last text sit there undiscussed."

Amy sighed. "Fine. Get it over with while I'm here. And remember, tell him that as far as that text is concerned you made it up to be mean."

"I know, I know." Lexie sat up. She wore a Ruxton T-shirt and a pair of Daniel's boxer shorts she had taken from his Boston place. When she had put them on, she told Amy they were Peter's. Peter, who didn't own underwear. Amy would have thrown them away had she known the truth.

Lexie reached under the pillow and pulled out her phone.

"Welcome?" Lexie turned the phone to Amy. "Why does it say *Welcome?*" The word *welcome* in several different languages scrolled across the screen.

"Let me see." Amy took the phone from Lexie's hand and touched the word in English. "This is ridiculous!" Amy jerked her head from Lexie to the phone and back again.

"What? Did I send another unconscious text?" Amy's panic woke up Lexie. It felt like her blood had finally thawed and her brain was only now getting enough oxygen to think clearly.

"Your phone's been erased!" Amy swiped off the WELCOME screen and then handed the phone to Lexie. "Put in your password."

Lexie typed slowly with her first finger. "Why is it erased?" The password didn't work. She typed it again. It still didn't work.

"Gimme that." Amy took the phone. "What's your password?"

"Three two six four three five. It spells *Daniel.*"

Amy rolled her eyes. She punched in the numbers slowly, with deliberation. "What a fucking asshole!"

"What?"

"Your password's been changed. Did you back up everything onto your computer?"

"No. Daniel told me not to because it's the school's computer."

"Well, what about the cloud? Doesn't the cloud back it up automatically?"

"Well, yeah, normally, but Daniel fixed my phone so it doesn't back up to the cloud. He was worried about someone at Ruxton taking my computer and—" Lexie stopped as she realized what was gone: every photo of herself and Daniel. Every text between the two of them. Besides a couple pairs of earrings and a watch, the texts and photos were the only artifacts she had from her eight months of believing she was with her one great love.

"He is such a Yankee asshole." Amy appeared to be more furious at Daniel than she'd been at Lexie for sleeping with Ethan.

"Did *he* erase my phone?" Lexie couldn't align the Daniel she thought she knew with the Daniel who was currently presenting himself.

"Yes! You traded passwords, IDs . . . everything!" Amy gave Lexie a slap on the shoulder with the back of her hand.

"I can't believe he thinks I'd send that stuff to Jen . . . that'd I'd out him." Lexie was genuinely hurt. Yes, he was a lying asshole. But she wasn't! She wouldn't betray him!

"Do you remember his password?" Amy got off the bed and fetched Lexie's laptop from the dresser. She brought it to the bed and handed it to Lexie who immediately started typing.

"It doesn't work." Lexie looked up at Amy.

"I bet it only worked the week he gave it to you, the week you and I went through his email. And you know what else?"

"What?" Lexie didn't want to know. Hadn't she bottomed out already?

"I guarantee he had cleaned out, deleted, and erased any emails that would indicate he was married and had left those few to throw us off."

"To throw *me* off. He probably didn't imagine you were checking with me."

"Oh, no. He imagined that. Someone as sinister and underhanded as Daniel Waite knew perfectly well I would get on that computer with you and check. This is bullshit!" Lexie had never seen Amy so angry. It was nice to know that there was someone in the world who was fully on Lexie's side.

Lexie closed the computer and pushed it aside. She leaned over the edge of the bed and let her cell phone drop to the floor. "I'm done."

"What do you mean you're done?"

Lexie pulled up the covers and wormed down deep into the bed. "I mean, this is over. It's probably better that he erased my phone. It will prevent me from sitting around looking at photos, reading old texts, and wallowing about what I thought we had."

"What you had was not real."

"I know." Lexie closed her eyes. "It'll be easier for me to move on if there's no evidence."

"You probably sent me a picture or two." Amy scrolled through her texts with Lexie.

"No, I didn't." Lexie shook her head. She'd never thought of herself as someone so easily duped. But evidence to the contrary was right before her. Daniel had asked her to never download or send out a photo of the two of them together until Ethan knew about the relationship. He claimed he didn't trust the Internet and Lexie had honored his wishes. And they had never emailed because Daniel had told her the desktop computer at the lake house had all his accounts on it, password free. Ethan used that computer when he was home and Daniel didn't want him finding out about them—their pending marriage (*ha!*)—until he had told his son the full story.

"You're right." Amy kept searching as if she didn't quite believe it. "I don't have any photos of you two."

"I'm going back to sleep." Lexie shut her eyes. She'd had enough of reality. Unconsciousness in any form—sleep or death—was all she wanted.

SOMEONE WAS POUNDING ON THE DOOR. LEXIE OPENED HER EYES. There was no knowing how long she'd been out. The bedside lamp was on and the curtains were closed but Lexie could tell it was night. Amy was gone. There was a note on the bedside table: *I'm at Cal's. I stuck a notice on your door that says you're sick and to call Artie if there's an emergency. —A*

The pounding continued. Lexie got out of bed, pulled off the boxer shorts, and pulled on her jeans. She stood firm as a pointing dog, listening to the persistent thumps. Her heart beat along with the rhythm. If Amy's note was on the door, it couldn't be a student banging. They were, for the most part, too obedient to disregard the note. And it couldn't be Amy. She had a key. None of the faculty would be so rude as to bang like that . . . it had to be Daniel.

Lexie couldn't stop herself from running into the bathroom, putting on mascara and brushing her teeth. What she wanted more than anything was for Daniel to tell her that he'd made a mistake, he was leaving Jen and he wanted to be forgiven. All the deception . . . well, it was a mix-up! He wasn't that horrible guy after all!

Lexie smeared Vaseline on her lips and went to the door. Ethan was on the other side. His face was red; his eyes were redder. He pushed in past Lexie and stood in the middle of the living room.

Lexie locked the door behind him in case someone else decided to pop in. "What's going on?" She tried to remain calm but her heart pummeled against her like a trapped animal.

"You tell me what's going on!"

"Shhh." Lexie put her finger to her lips. Her hand shook. "Sit down."

"I don't want to sit down."

"I'll sit." Lexie sat on a chair and looked up at Ethan. She felt the physical imbalance in power as he hovered over her. But standing with her wobbly legs offered a worse option than cowering below Ethan. Soon enough, Ethan sat on the couch opposite her. He leaned over his knees and dropped his head into his hands.

"Please tell me what's going on," Lexie said.

"You fucked my dad." Ethan looked up at Lexie.

"Watch your language." It was all Lexie could think to say.

"You and I fucked, so I can say fuck. You. Fucked. My dad." Ethan used his long, thick finger to point out each word.

"Why do you think that?" Lexie asked carefully.

"Because he and my mother took me out to the Inn on the Lake to warn me about you."

Lexie's stomach was like a falling elevator. "Warn you?"

"You fucked my dad. You fucked me. You told my dad you fucked me. You broke into my house and you stole personal items from my mother."

"What did I steal from your mother?" Would they actually tell Ethan about the vibrator?

"Personal stuff from her bedside drawer and her prescription antianxiety meds, which I ate off your tits, by the way." Ethan stared at Lexie's chest in a way that made her feel like she had no control over her own body. She focused on her breathing. It was entirely possible that she might pass out and so she put all her energy into staying conscious.

"I'm sorry," Lexie whispered. There wasn't energy enough to speak louder.

"You're a low-life, poor girl from some shit-hole town in California and you became obsessed with me, my dad, my family—"

He wasn't particularly wrong. She was a poor girl from a shit-hole town. And if loving Daniel so much that she would leave her fiancé for him wasn't an obsession, what was it?

"Is this who you want to be?" Lexie asked Ethan. "Someone who sees people not as fortunate as himself as lowlifes?" *Breathe,* Lexie said to herself.

"Who should I be? Someone like you?" Ethan's nostrils flared like a bull's.

"No." At least not the person she'd been the past couple days.

"I thought we had something cool going on!"

"What we had was—" Lexie had no idea how to finish that sentence. She was glad when Ethan interrupted.

"Don't sit here and lie to me. My dad told us everything."

"What is everything? What exactly did he tell you?" Lexie asked carefully.

"You met my dad in a bar, got him wasted, and fucked him. Then you stalked him like a crazy lunatic, you broke into our house, and when you couldn't have him again, you seduced me instead. Well, guess what? You are fucked. My dad's meeting with

Mr. McClear and maybe even the police tomorrow afternoon. You're going to be out of a job, out of a home . . . you're probably out of the whole state because there is no one in all of New England who will hire you now. My parents will be sure of that."

"I see." Without photos, without texts, it was her word against theirs. There was the option of finding someone at the Inn at the Lake to confirm her and Daniel's weekly night there . . . or speaking to the doormen at Daniel's building in Boston . . . but this was Daniel Waite. The doormen, the room service guy, the clerk at the Inn at the Lake, likely they would side with the guy who regularly slipped them folded bills. When your job depends on discretion, why vouch for the low-life girl from a shit-hole town in California?

"Everyone in this school's gonna know that you fucked a student." Ethan stared at Lexie as if daring her to hold his gaze. Or maybe daring her to deny the charges.

"I suppose they will." She didn't believe that. Don McClear and Janet Irwin and even Daniel Waite were committed to the idea that The Ruxton Academy was a place where nothing sordid, dark, or slippery went down. Lexie couldn't imagine they would risk the press finding out that the school counselor at one of New England's most elite boarding schools had slept with a student. Other than charges of racism in the '60s (all of it justified, Lexie assumed), no bad press had come out of Ruxton. It was as locked down as the Vatican.

"My mother's scared out of her mind! Do you know my dad is hiring a bodyguard for her? Seriously. My mom is going to have a fucking bodyguard! And we know that you probably drugged my dad to fuck him because you sure as hell drugged me. He says he doesn't even remember what happened! That's how good a fuck you were; my dad has *no memory* of ever even fucking you!

The only reason he knows it happened is because of the relentless stalking you did."

Lexie was half-tempted to tell Ethan the truth. Although he probably wouldn't believe her. Also, she didn't want to change his world that way; she'd already altered things enough. This was her gift to Ethan Waite: She'd allow him to carry on thinking that he had grown up in the most fortunate circumstances with the most wonderful people. She'd let him walk through life certain that the genetic matter that had created him was all good and he, therefore, could have faith in his own goodness. "So why are you here?" she asked gently.

"I don't know. I was told to avoid you and to not say a word to you about anything. Ever. They're going to ambush you at some point, like when all the students are at their first period class on Monday. They'll have security and everything and you'll have to leave right then. They're even going to confiscate your computer."

Maybe Daniel was worried that Lexie had downloaded photos in spite of what he'd asked. Lexie supposed when you were always lying yourself, it was hard to imagine that everyone else was being true. Daniel probably planned to have the computer handed over to him so he could destroy it. Don McClear wouldn't second-guess anything Daniel suggested. With annual donations that could build entire schools in needy neighborhoods, Daniel Waite could ask for and get whatever he wanted at Ruxton.

Lexie swallowed away the urge to cry. "Why aren't they coming tonight? Why not right now?"

"My mother is so terrified of you getting out on bail and seeking revenge that she insisted that my father not do anything until everything is in place. A bodyguard for her, the locks changed on every door on the house, all the cell phone numbers changed . . . She wants my dad to buy new cars so you won't recognize them on the street!" Ethan shook his head like he couldn't believe it. He was blinking rapidly. Lexie thought he might also be on the verge of crying.

"I need you to know something." Lexie looked Ethan straight in the eyes. "I need you to know that you honestly were my favorite student, and we did have a special relationship. I shouldn't have had sex with you, that was completely wrong. But everything that came before then was real. And true."

"Whatever," Ethan mumbled. He broke eye contact and dropped his head.

"Ethan, you're a great kid and a great student. You didn't do anything to be ashamed of. It was all me. I messed up. And I'm so, so very sorry." Lexie's voice cracked. It felt as though her bones were splitting open and breaking apart. She was quaking.

"Yeah?" Ethan looked up. His face was red again. "Well, fuck you." He stood and went out the door.

Lexie returned to her bedroom, opened her computer, and sent Amy an email telling her what had happened.

Then, Lexie deleted everything on her computer—wiped it clean, cleaner than her phone even. She would leave it behind along with her grade book, files, keys to her office, and anything else that Ruxton might possibly say belonged to them. She may have been a fool, but she wasn't a thief.

IT TOOK UNTIL TWO A.M. FOR LEXIE TO SORT THROUGH HER STUFF and load her belongings into the car. She had put the coffin-sized suitcase in the trunk empty and made several stealthy trips back and forth to fill it. Jen's vibrator was in that suitcase only because Lexie didn't want it to be discovered in a trash can somewhere and then connected to her.

Lexie drove slowly off campus, with the idea that slow meant quiet. The quaking in her bones had calmed and she was feeling a heavy, sated sadness. But she was no longer scared. Like Melanie Birken, the teacher with the townie boyfriend, they would let her disappear into the night, eventually forgotten. And when Lexie was old and dried-out—shriveled into something predators like Daniel don't even notice in a room—the past few months would be a mere blip on her lifeline. She could pretend it had never happened.

Lexie turned onto the highway. She was going in the direction of Amy's apartment. Hopefully she and Cal were there and not at Cal's place, as Lexie had no idea where he lived. She needed to make sure Amy would move into Rilke for the final week of school. Lexie didn't want to leave Don McClear with the same problem he'd had the day Dot died.

Lexie wondered if Dot would have foreseen the series of pitiable events, which ended with Lexie naked in bed with a student. After all, Dot had been entirely correct in pointing out that Lexie could never abide the beautiful small life of Peter. She knew better than Lexie herself that Lexie had been borne out of too much chaos to ever sit still. Dot probably had written on a piece of paper how many years until Lexie and Peter's marriage ended. Or maybe— even after she bought the dress—she knew it wouldn't happen; knew the engagement was one of many mistakes Lexie was bound to make as she emotionally worked herself away from San Leandro.

Lexie looked in the rearview mirror. She was alone on the

stretch of highway. She saw Dot in her mind, heard her barking rasp as clearly as if she were sitting on the seat beside her . . . *remember, the only life worth living is one where there's been numerous fuckups.*

Lexie smiled at her internal Dot. And it was during this smile, these simple few breaths of peaceful relief, that she noticed a red light rotating and flashing behind her.

Lexie was being pulled over.

22

THERE WAS A PAY PHONE IN THE JAIL CELL. A PHONE BOOK DAN-gled below it, attached with a braided wire. Half the pages had been ripped out. You needed more than a quarter to use the phone and Lexie had nothing as all her belongings—her purse, her erased phone, her earrings, and watch—had been taken away from her when she "checked in," as the cop had said.

She'd been arrested for breaking and entering the Waite house. She had also been charged with the petty theft of "one personal appliance," which had quickly been discovered in the suitcase in her trunk. The theft of the Klonopin hadn't been mentioned. Maybe Jen didn't want the local police to know she had a prescription. Although once she'd reported the vibrator, what difference did a handful of antianxiety meds make?

The cement-floored cell had two room-length benches on either side. Lexie and four other women sat on one bench. An enormous woman slept along the other bench. In the back of the cell, behind a wooden plank—like what you might see in an outdoor shower—was a toilet that was currently unflushed and full. On the floor around the toilet, spilling out into the room, were wet clumps of toilet paper sitting in foul water. Amazingly, one or two of the woman in the cell (Lexie wasn't quite sure who) smelled as bad as what emanated from the toilet. Lexie thought of the Middle Ages—congested cities with dirt roads and horseshit, life before deodorant and plumbing—and figured this is what it smelled like. Humans had likely lived entire lives surrounded by this stink. Lexie only had to endure it for . . . well, she wasn't sure how long she'd be there. She hadn't asked any questions when she'd been charged, fingerprinted, and photographed. She'd barely said a word.

Since she'd been pulled over, Lexie had been waiting for panic to hit. Surprisingly, it never did. Maybe anxiety showed up only when your body needed to tell you something you hadn't yet faced. Currently, there was nothing left to uncover.

Lexie studied the large, sleeping woman across from her. Her white belly fell out of her shirt, the skin shimmery and striped like a fish. A string of drool, like a spider thread, connected the edge of her mouth to the bench. It broke and disappeared.

Beside the toilet, outside the privacy plank, was a small drinking fountain. Lexie stood and went to the fountain, gingerly stepping around the wet areas of the floor. The four women on the bench watched intently. One of them smiled as Lexie held her hair in one hand and started to bend over the fountain. It was a sly smile, an anticipatory smile.

"Should I not drink this?" Lexie asked. She backed away and let her hair fall.

"It's fine, drink it." The woman smiled. Her eyebrows were plucked into a graph line chevron; half her teeth were gone. Her face was dotted as if she had acne, but it wasn't acne: flat, purple, bruisy-looking circles on her pale, pinkish skin.

"Don't drink it," a blond frizzy-haired woman said. She, too, had sketch-thin brows. Her long, white, spaghetti-strand arms dangled between her open legs like a macaque monkey. Her eyes were lizard-wide, pale blue, and her nose was so stunted it didn't seem to be a nose. Lexie figured she had been a fetal alcohol baby. Poor thing, she didn't have the wits not to end up here. This made Lexie feel only worse. She had a whole working brain, and she and this woman were now equals.

"Why can't I drink it?" Lexie nodded toward the fountain.

"Girls have been smearing things all over it. It's gross."

"Huh." Lexie wondered why and what they'd smeared over it. An act of rebellion, she supposed. Cage someone like an animal and they'll behave like one. "I guess it's a biohazard."

"Biohazard!" The woman said, and she smiled revealing teeth that looked like canned corn (in size and color). "This whole place is a biohazard." She stood and her baggy jeans fell to her hips. With one hand she pulled up the jeans, with the other she reached in her pocket and pulled out a handful of quarters. She held them in her open palm in front of Lexie.

"That for me?" Lexie asked.

"If you need them. There's five bucks here."

"Where'd you get it?"

"Sometimes the cops will give you change if you ask nice enough."

"Thanks so much." Lexie plucked up two quarters.

"Take it all." The woman encircled Lexie's wrist with her free hand and let the quarters fall into her palm. They were sticky and warm, like hard candy that had already been sucked on. Lexie wondered what kind of biohazard she was now holding.

"I'll pay you back." Lexie was touched by the generosity, while also repulsed by the intimacy. She closed her fist and went to the phone. Lexie picked up the receiver (another biohazard, she assumed) and stood there. A terrible, weighty aloneness fell over her like a thick, wool cloak. She remembered her conversation with Ethan about Dot's death. Lexie had pointed out that a life worth living was one where you gave love and felt loved. If she had been right about this, Lexie thought, her own life was currently of no value.

One by one, Lexie dropped in the quarters. Each falling coin made a beautiful, hollow clinking that Lexie hadn't heard since she was a kid. She dialed the only number she knew by heart. The one person who likely loved her no matter how badly she'd fucked up.

Mitzy picked up on the first ring.

"Mom," Lexie croaked.

"Honey, can you call me later? Russ and I are tryin' to figure out where to put his canoe."

"Who's Russ?"

"Russ! Russ!" Mitzy said. Lexie heard a roaring man's voice in the background shout, *Russ is the man! The man of the house!* Mitzy laughed. "He cracks me up!"

"Well, thanks for telling me his name, but I still don't know who he is." Lexie looked behind her to see if anyone was listening to this conversation. The frizzy-haired girl who had given her the quarters watched. One girl was braiding another's hair, her fingers working the thick strands like someone playing a stringed instrument. And a giant of a woman with brown hair in a tight bun on top of her head had one bare foot on the bench and was bent over, picking at her toes. The fish-bellied woman across from them remained sleeping.

"My boyfriend!" Mitzy said. "He moved in tonight."

"But it's after midnight. How many hours have you been moving him in?" Lexie wasn't surprised Mitzy didn't notice that Lexie was calling after three in the morning Lexie's time. Mitzy never could keep track of the time differences and had more than once called at an odd hour because she thought the East Coast was three hours earlier than the west.

"He didn't get off work until eleven."

"How long you have you been seeing Russ?" Lexie wasn't sure why she cared. Men came and went—each one a variation on the same model: an alcoholic (from what Lexie could guess), always with a bursting, pregnant belly, waspy-looking in essence, pale eyes, paler skin, ruddy cheeks, and loose jowls.

"We've been together a week. But this is it, honey! This is the real thing. My true love. Russ is the last one!" It sounded like Russ and Mitzy were kissing.

"Mazel tov," Lexie groaned. One of the best things you could say about Mitzy was that she was an optimist: always believing in her next great love.

"What did ya say?" Mitzy asked.

"I said mazel tov. It was kind of a joke. Jewish people say it when you want to congratulate someone."

"Don't tell me that boyfriend of yours is Jewish! You wouldn't do something stupid like that, would you?" There was a giant bang in the background. The falling canoe? Mitzy didn't audibly react.

"There are so many levels on which what you just said is wrong, but I don't want to go into it now." The smear of half affection toward her mother that had been brought out by Lexie's desperate aloneness was evaporating. Mitzy was not her people. Her mother's love, or her love for her mother, did not make Lexie feel like she had a reason to be alive.

"Lexie, you gotta be careful what kinda men you date! Those Jewish men will take all your money! There was a girl at Heidi Pies who—"

"Mom! He's not Jewish and I don't have any money for anyone to take. Anyway, I've gotta go, I was only calling to say hello." Lexie glanced behind herself again to see if Frizz-head was listening. She was, it appeared.

"Well, you've been warned. Stay away—"

"He's *not* Jewish!" Lexie whisper-yelled, trying to keep her mouth far from the receiver (biohazard!).

"No! That corner!" Mitzy was clearly talking to Russ. "Honey, I got too much to deal with here. Call me tomorrow or something." The phone clanked a couple times as if it had been dropped to the floor and then Mitzy, or maybe it was Russ, picked up the receiver and hung up.

Lexie replaced the receiver and waited for her change. Very little came out; it was like playing penny slots. If Lexie hadn't borrowed the money from Frizz, she would have left it there so as to avoid sticking her fingers in the slot.

"You dating a Jewish guy?" Frizz asked.

"I'm not dating anyone." Lexie fingered out the coins before there was time to overthink it. "Thanks again for the money." She handed the coins off to Frizz, then sat opposite her, at the feet of the woman who was lying on the bench alone.

"Were you dating a Jewish guy?"

Lexie leaned her head back against the wall and shut her eyes. She pretended she had instantly fallen asleep.

"I dated a Jewish guy once," someone said. Lexie wasn't sure who, as she didn't open her eyes. It wasn't Frizz's voice. "He had a huge dick." The other women laughed and then the four voices on the bench across from Lexie discussed the various sizes of penises they'd encountered over the years. One woman, in a series of sentences that jolted Lexie's stomach, described her uncle's large penis. She qualified it by saying maybe it only looked large because she was twelve at the time.

"I'm sorry you went through that," Lexie whispered, a form of a prayer for whomever had been speaking.

LEXIE WASN'T SURE WHAT TIME IT WAS, AND SHE WASN'T EVEN SURE if she'd actually slept, but it appeared to be morning when a cop stood at the cell door, unlocked it, and motioned to Lexie.

"Me?" she asked. He nodded.

Lexie stood and followed him out. She looked back once and waved to the women on the bench. Only Frizz waved back.

In the small room where the cops had taken all her personal belongings, Lexie was handed a plastic basket with her purse, cell phone, watch, and earrings. She was also handed a clipboard with a paper on it that she was asked to sign. Lexie signed without reading it. She turned to the cop who stood with her and said, "Am I free?"

"Charges were dropped."

"Will you give this to that blond, skinny, frizzy-haired woman in there?" Lexie opened her wallet and pulled out a twenty.

"Tammy," he said, and he shoved the bill in his pocket.

Lexie followed the officer down a cement-floored corridor. "Please don't forget to give her that money," she said. The officer nodded and then opened a door and let Lexie exit into the blinding sunlight.

There were two cars, about ten feet apart, facing the entrance of the elementary school–sized police station. One of the cars was Lexie's. The sun hammered the windshields making it impossible to see if anyone was inside either vehicle. Don McClear stepped out of Lexie's car and walked toward her. As he approached, Lexie lifted her hands to her face and started crying. Don put a stiff arm on Lexie's back and patted her. She thought he was saying *there there,* although she was crying so hard she couldn't hear him well, so maybe he was saying, *dear dear.*

"Let's sit in my car for a minute," Don said. Lexie stopped crying and took one long juddering breath.

Don's car was a four-door, burgundy-colored thing. He opened the back door and Lexie got in. Janet Irwin was in the front passenger seat.

"Oh god," Lexie gasped.

"How many people know?" Janet asked.

"Know what?" Lexie asked. Don got in the driver's seat and shut the door. Lexie had never been traditionally parented, but right now, in this position (two adults turned to her from the front seat, a concerned and scolding look on their faces) Lexie understood what it would have been like to have had "normal" parents. That she had disappointed Don and Janet gave her shame a sharper, more pointed form.

"Know about your affair with Daniel Waite and your . . ." Janet shook her head. She wasn't going to say whatever it was aloud. The break-in? The vibrator? Sex with Ethan?

"The encounter with Ethan Waite," Don said.

"Amy knows everything. But she won't tell anyone." Lexie felt a surge of tears, but forced them to recede. She didn't need to humiliate herself further.

"I'm furious that he would do this to us again!" Janet said. It was an uncharacteristic outburst and she quickly righted herself—pinning her mouth shut and tugging on the hem of her skirt as if her slip was showing.

"Has Ethan slept with other teachers?" Lexie was stunned.

Janet took a breath, shored herself up, and said nothing.

"Of course not," Don said, and Lexie instantly understood that it was Daniel she had been speaking of. Daniel who had done this before.

"Wait . . . did Melanie Birkin also have an affair with Daniel?"

Don jerked his chin toward Janet who barely flinched. And there was the answer. Lexie leaned back and thumped her head against the seat. How many had there been? Maybe it was like mice—if you saw one, it meant there were a hundred.

"This Ethan business," Janet said. "That should never have happened. It's reprehensible."

"I'm sorry." Lexie shut her eyes. "I was on drugs, antianxiety medication and alcohol, and I didn't know what I was doing."

"Well, I should hope not. Anyone who would do that in their right mind is very sick indeed." Lexie felt Janet staring at her waiting for Lexie to open her eyes. She did, and then Janet looked away.

"We have something for you." Don pointed to the glove compartment. Janet opened it and pulled out a thick manila envelope that she handed to Don. He held his hand over the seat and Lexie took the envelope. "Your summer sabbatical money."

"But aren't I fired?" Lexie opened the envelope and looked in. It was more money than she'd ever seen. When Lexie was a kid she always wished she'd find an envelope of cash. She'd take it straight to 7-Eleven and buy whatever she wanted for herself, Betsy, and anyone else who walked in. As she got older, she still wished for envelopes of cash—enough to start a nonprofit, and maybe buy a couple pairs of soft, leather boots, too.

"Count it later," Janet said.

"You have been dismissed," Don said.

"If I'm fired, why are you giving me summer sabbatical money?" Maybe if she had slept more, or if she hadn't done any drugs the past two days, things would make sense. Everything felt backward.

"Lexie," Don spoke in his formal meeting voice. "Ruxton has an international reputation that we'd like to uphold. And we believe that if no one catches wind of your indiscretions, things would be better for the school as a whole."

"So you're paying me off to keep quiet?"

"As we said," Janet said firmly, "it's summer sabbatical money." She stared at Lexie as if to drill information into her. A bubble of meaning popped into Lexie's brain. The Waites funded the faculty sabbaticals. This was hush money from Daniel Waite. That's why the charges had been dropped. Don and Janet were Daniel Waite's lackeys. Stoolies. Henchmen. Lexie felt worse for them than she did for herself. How terrible to be continually squirming at the well-shod feet of Daniel Waite.

"Are you going to tell the students I was fired?"

"We'll tell them you fell ill," Don said.

"Well, feel free to kill off someone in my family if that makes the story any better." Lexie opened the envelope again and peered in. The bills in front of each bundle were hundreds. She shifted the money around to see if there was a letter, a note, a single word on an index card.

"We're going to ask Amy to stay in Rilke for the last week," Janet said. "I'm sure she'll be happy to send you anything you've left behind."

"Can you give me her number? I don't have any numbers because Daniel erased my phone and changed the password." Lexie waved her phone in the air as if to show them.

"Son of a gun!" Don said, and he slapped the center of his steering wheel. Lexie had never seen him angry like that. He turned to Janet, whose face was as tight as a childproof pill bottle.

"I'll tell Amy to email you as soon as we get in touch with her," Janet spoke as if Don hadn't had his little outburst. Then she turned and pressed her back flat against the seat as she stared out the front window. Was that her good-bye?

"Let me see you to your car," Don said, even though the Jetta was parked beside them. Just as he stepped out, Don's cell phone rang. He answered the call and then hustled out of hearing distance.

Lexie lingered in the backseat, waiting for Janet's final words, something she could report to Amy that they might later laugh at.

"Okeydokey," Lexie finally said. She got out of the car and stood at the open door for a last look at the envelope she'd left on Don's backseat. Even a poor girl from a shit-hole town in California could walk away from a pile of Daniel Waite's cash. Even a poor girl could value the truth more than money.

Lexie threw the door shut and went to the Jetta. She started the engine. Don paced as he talked on the phone; his eyes alit on Lexie every couple beats. There was no doubt Daniel Waite was on the other end of that call. After a minute, Don tucked the cell phone in his breast pocket and approached Lexie's window. She rolled it down.

"Be safe." Don gave Lexie an awkward pat on the shoulder. When he shuffled back to his car, Lexie knew it was the last time she'd see him. Or Janet. They'd soon become memory, fictionalized. No more real to Lexie than characters in a book.

one year later

Epilogue

LEXIE STOOD ON THE STEPS OF THE BOSTON PUBLIC LIBRARY. THE baby was bound to her chest, face-out, in a contraption that reminded her of a parachute pack each time she put it on. She had one hand on the baby's belly and one hand under his warm rump.

"Hey." Lexie smiled down at the baby, who grinned up at her, all gummy and fat-cheeked. At this age he was smiling a lot and even silently laughing. It seemed he was always happy to see her.

It was noon, bright and sunny out. Lexie descended the steps and quickly fell into the crowd at Copley Square. It was busy in a way that made Lexie feel not claustrophobic, but connected. She, like all these people around her, was a part of the city. At the lawn, Lexie turned in a circle so the baby could see the fountain, the old stone church, and The Hancock, a massive glass skyscraper that hovered above it all. Her walk from her apartment to work at The Charles Center—where Lexie counseled women who had recently been released from prison—led her through Copley Square. It was a beautiful walk, which she was happy to repeat each week or so during her maternity leave in order to check on her patients' progress.

Today the blue sky was reflected on The Hancock so that it was camouflaged within the clouds around it, almost invisible. Like Lexie herself, she thought. Ever since her stomach had bulged out, and then once she'd had the baby strapped to her body, or nested in a stroller, men didn't look at her the way they used to. Women, sure. They caught her eye and then leaned over the stroller or peered at the package against her chest and asked how old, or was it a boy or a girl, or what was its name. But men didn't see her the way they once had. Lexie had been recategorized. That was fine by her. Currently, she had all the love she could handle; Lexie was overflowing with it.

The baby kicked his legs out and back, *keep going*, so Lexie walked past the church and toward the tower. It was the highest building in Boston, something that demanded to be seen, and yet Lexie had never crossed the road to go near it.

She paused on the sidewalk in front of the building. People poured out of the revolving doors: men in suits, women in suits, everyone looking like they were a busy working part of an elegant machine. And then she saw him. Daniel Waite. That giant rectangle smile opened up like a window; his eyes were glinting. Lexie planted herself on the pavement where she stood. Everything went silent, save the sound of blood rushing in her ears. Was she returning his smile? No. But her mouth was open in what she imagined looked like a perfect letter *O*. Lexie forced herself to close her mouth, bite her lip.

Lexie followed Daniel's gaze and realized he wasn't looking at her. He hadn't even seen her. He was beaming at the bone-legged fawn of a woman on Lexie's right. Her slacks were so tight she couldn't have worn underwear with them. And her white blouse ballooned behind her so that her breasts were outlined in the front. She looked like she hadn't yet hit thirty.

Daniel reached the woman and kissed her on the cheek. He cupped her elbow in his palm and led her in Lexie's direction. Daniel was whispering in the woman's ear. Lexie knew what he was likely saying: *I've been thinking about you all day . . . you smell so good I want to eat you up . . .*

The woman was smiling, looking straight ahead as Daniel leaned into her. As they closed in on Lexie, the woman stopped. "How old's your baby?" she asked. Her face was as smooth as poured cream. She looked like she'd never smoked a cigarette or had a whiskey or even had a bad thought in her life.

"He's three months old today." Lexie looked up at Daniel whose complexion had turned the mealy white of cigarette ash. His face tensed and there was a pulsating rhythmic popping on either side of his jaw. The woman stepped closer and put her pointer finger on the baby's cheek. He beamed up at her with that big, gooey grin. "Oh my god, he's so cute. Daniel, look! Look how cute he is."

"His name's Harrison." Lexie watched Daniel as he took one stiff step closer to Lexie and peered at the baby.

"Like Harrison Ford?" The woman stroked the baby's nearly bald head and he gurgled.

"Yeah," Lexie said. Her ultrasound had failed to show any protuberances, leading Lexie and the doctor to believe she was having a girl. She'd name it Dot, she'd decided. So when a boy slid out, Lexie and Amy (who was in the delivery room with her) were stunned. Harrison had been Amy's idea. A way to still name the baby after Dot.

"Harrison! You're so sweet." She looked up at Lexie and said, "What's his full name?"

"Harrison Waite James." Lexie spoke deliberately. Precisely. She stared at ash-faced Daniel who refused to meet her eyes.

"Oh my god, Waite?!" The woman straightened and then whacked Daniel on the upper arm. "W-A-I-T-E, is that how you spell it?"

"Yes." Lexie smiled at the woman, then she smiled at Daniel. He reminded her of a prisoner stubbornly standing before a firing squad. Choosing death over giving up state secrets.

"Oh my god, that's *his* last name!" She pointed at Daniel. "Maybe you're related!"

"Doubtful," Daniel said, and then he took the woman's hand and pulled her toward himself. "Let's go. I'm hungry."

A flash of irritation scratched across the woman's smooth face. And then she said, "Bye Harrison Waite James! You be a good boy for your mommy!" Daniel held the woman's wrist like a rope as he walked ahead, tugging her past Lexie, onward down the sidewalk.

Lexie realized her body was trembling, an internal earthquake of sorts. She put her hand to her mouth and pushed in on her lips to still them. Harrison made a chirping sound. Lexie leaned over him and inhaled his cottony, sweet baby smell. He was her Klonopin. Simply feeling him against her, breathing him in, stabilized Lexie in a way that nothing else could. When she looked up again, Lexie caught a glimpse of Daniel and his girlfriend—his height and her white blouse flashing like two beams of light. She lifted Harrison's tiny dumpling hand and shook it as if he were waving good-bye.

"Bye pretty lady," Lexie said, in what she imaged Harrison's voice would sound like if he were to speak. "Bye Grandpa, you lying motherfucker."

With rubbery legs, Lexie continued on, closer to the tower. Was it wrong not to run after the woman and set her straight? Lexie wondered. No, it would do no good. Lexie would come off as crazy. Love creates its own balloon of reality, Lexie now knew, and anything that defies that reality is efficiently bounced away. Until the balloon pops.

She paused at the base of the tower where the suits and skirts flowed past her like water around a rock. Once she felt solid again, Lexie extracted Harrison from the carrier. She held him up by his doughy middle and raised him to face the towering glass obelisk.

"Look at that!" Lexie swept the sky with Harrison, flew him from side to side as he happily paddled his arms and legs. She lowered him to face her and said, "One day, when you and your daddy, Ethan, are both a little more grown up . . ." Harrison opened his mouth and blinked his eyes like he was trying to focus on Lexie's words. She laughed and continued: "You might want to meet each other. And then . . . well, who knows where that could take you."

Lexie kissed each of the baby's eyes and his fat, juicy cheeks. In a flash, she saw everything she had gone through to arrive here: a ruptured engagement, hurricane-force heartbreak, humiliation at a depth to which she had previously imagined herself too sophisticated to reach, jail time (!), and even a bacterial infection that had started with seventeen-year-old Skyler Bowden (aka Patient Zero).

"I'd do it all over again." Lexie dappled the baby's face with kisses.

And Harrison, Lexie's one true great love, happily cooed.

ACKNOWLEDGMENTS

I FEEL INCREDIBLY LUCKY TO BE BACKED UP BY TWO TRULY AMAZING and brilliant women: Katherine Nintzel and Gail Hochman. Thank you both. Enormous and heartfelt thanks to early and multiple draft readers and to those who frequently sat across from me and worked on their own stuff while I wrote this book: Geoffrey Becker, Bonnie Blau, Fran Brennan, Jane Delury, Michael Downs, Larry Doyle, Lindsay Fleming, Elizabeth Hazen, Elizabeth Lunt, Marisol Murano, Claire Stancer, Ron Tanner, Madeline Tavis, Tracy Wallace, and Marion Winik. Thank you to the experts consulted: Dr. Kathy Boling, Jessica Keener, and Don Lee. I am infinitely grateful to the kind, smart, and talented people of HarperCollins: Amy Baker, Gabriel Barillas, Cal Morgan, Jo O'Neil, Mary Sasso, Sherry Wasserman, Margaux Weisman, and Martin Wilson. Thank you to meticulous copyeditor Jane Herman and thoughtful proofreader Marcell Rosenblatt. I must thank my yoga teachers who have kept me moving through the work: Melody, Michele, and Rivka. And I am always thankful for my wonderful family: Mom, Dad, Cheryl, Becca, Josh, Alex, Satchel, Shiloh, Sonia, and all the fabulous Grossbachs of New York, especially the one named David who lives in Baltimore with me.

About the author

2 Meet Jessica Anya Blau

About the book

4 Reading Group Guide

6 Playlist

Insights,
Interviews
& More . . .

Read on

9 Excerpt from *The Summer of Naked Swim Parties*

Meet Jessica Anya Blau

JESSICA ANYA BLAU's third novel, *The Wonder Bread Summer*, was picked for CNN's summer reading list, NPR's summer reading list, *Vanity Fair*'s summer reads, and Oprah.com's "Six Sizzling Beach Reads." Her second novel, *Drinking Closer to Home*, was featured in Target stores as a Breakout Book and made many "best books of the year" lists. Jessica's first novel, *The Summer of Naked Swim Parties*, was a national bestseller and was picked as a Best Summer Book by the *Today* show, *New York Post*, and *New York* magazine. The *San Francisco Chronicle* and other newspapers chose it as one of the best books of the year. All three novels have been optioned for film and television. Jessica cowrote the screenplay for the film *Love on the Run*, which is currently in postproduction. Her short stories have

© David Grossbach

appeared in numerous magazines and have won or been nominated for many awards, including the Pushcart Prize. Several of Jessica's stories and essays have been anthologized in books such as *CRUSH: Writers Reflect on Love, Longing, and the Power of Their First Celebrity Crush*; *The Prose Reader: Essays for Thinking, Reading, and Writing*; *Dirty Words: A Literary Encyclopedia of Sex*; and *The Moment: Wild, Poignant, Life-Changing Stories from 125 Writers and Artists Famous and Obscure*. Recently, Jessica ghostwrote a memoir that is coming out with HarperCollins in the fall of 2016.

Jessica grew up in southern California and lives in Baltimore, Maryland. ∾

Reading Group Guide

1. "The problem wasn't so much that Lexie had taken the Klonopin. And it wasn't even that she had stolen them." These are some memorable and attention-grabbing opening lines. How do they help us enter the world of the novel and introduce us to the character of Lexie?

2. What are the small moments the author uses to illuminate the nature of Peter and Lexie's relationship? How does the author frame the idea of a relationship with Daniel in contrast?

3. Why do you think Lexie is able to cheat on Peter so easily? Considering how happy she and Peter are, and how carefully she plans all other aspects of her life, what about this situation causes her to betray her own morals?

4. How do money and privilege play into Lexie's sense of herself? How do they affect her relationships?

5. Do you think Lexie's upbringing influences her ideas about intimacy and commitment? How so?

6. In what ways do you think Lexie relates to some of the students she counsels?

7. Were you surprised to find that Daniel had lied? Why or why not?

8. Did you have trouble justifying Lexie's actions toward the end or did you sympathize with her? Did you find yourself wondering what you would have done in her shoes? ∽

Playlist

HERE ARE THE SONGS mentioned in *The Trouble with Lexie*. It's a strange, seemingly disjointed list, running from classical to ZZ Top. Then again, a lot of strange, seemingly disjointed things happen to Lexie during her troublesome year.

1. When the Saab is towed, Lexie and Peter listen to a classical station and pretend to sing opera. They're probably listening to **Mozart's "Eine Kleine Nachtmusik"** as it has an easy, recognizable melody that would make faking an opera simple.

2. At Jamboree Ribs, **Patsy Cline's "Crazy"** is playing out of cheap, fuzzy speakers. Lexie thinks she's seen crazy enough for a lifetime with her parents.

3. Peter signs his texts with a line from the **Jefferson Starship** song **"Runaway."** It's also a song he's been teaching Lexie on the guitar.

4. Lexie sings along with **Taylor Swift** on the radio. I didn't write out the song because it didn't work with the flow of the sentence, but I imagined she was singing **"I Knew You Were Trouble."** Of course at this point, Lexie has no idea how much trouble is coming her way.

5. Dear old, craggy-voiced, foul-mouthed Dot likes to tap-dance to the title song from the musical *42nd Street*.

6. Ethan pats out a tune on his thighs. Lexie incorrectly guesses he's aiming for **"No Scrubs"** by **TLC**. She remembers the time when . . .

7. . . . Peter slapped out the song **"Like a Virgin"** by **Madonna** on Lexie's bare bottom.

8. Ethan really wants Lexie to guess what song he's patting out, and, finally, she correctly guesses the **Commodores' "Brick House."**

9. Lexie tells Ethan that love is the only thing that matters. He says, "That's so John Lennon of you." So, let's put **"All You Need Is Love"** by the **Beatles** on this list.

10. When they were younger, Lexie and her best friend, Betsy Simms, liked to listen to the **Ben Folds Five**. Neither one ever had a real boyfriend in high school so they hadn't been dumped by anyone (yet). Still, I imagine their favorite song was **"Song for the Dumped."**

11. Standing near the entrance of the townie bar, a man with a trapezoid-shaped beard tells Lexie he'd marry her. She thinks of **ZZ Top** when she looks at him and she doesn't think of any song in particular, but let's just say that if she did think of a song, she'd think of **"La Grange"** since it's a pretty great song and fun to have on a playlist.

12. When she's driving to Daniel's house Lexie sees a street sign that says Scarborough Road and hears ▶

the **Simon and Garfunkel** song
"Scarborough Fair" in her head.

13. And because no playlist should
end with the slow and elegiac
"Scarborough Fair," let's finish
up with **"Ooh Child"** by the **Five
Stairsteps.** It's another song that
Lexie incorrectly guesses Ethan is
patting out on his thighs. It's also
a hopeful song and just the kind
of thing Lexie would need to hear
near the end of the book. ◜◞

Excerpt from
The Summer of Naked Swim Parties

AFTER ALL, IT WAS THE SEVENTIES, so Allen and Betty thought nothing of leaving their younger daughter, Jamie, home alone for three nights while they went camping in Death Valley. And although most girls who had just turned fourteen would love a rambling Spanish-style house (with a rock formation pool, of course) to themselves for four days, Jamie, who erupted with bouts of fear with the here-now/gone-now pattern of a recurring nightmare, found the idea of her parents spending three nights in Death Valley terrifying. Jamie was not afraid for Allen and Betty—she did not fear their death by heatstroke, or scorpion sting, or dehydration (although each of these occurred to her in the days preceding their departure). She feared her own death—being murdered by one of the homeless men who slept between the roots of the giant fig tree near the train station or being trapped on the first floor of the house, the second floor sitting on her like a fat giant, after having fallen in an earthquake.

Jamie's older sister, Renee, was also away that weekend, at a lake with the family of her best and only friend. But even if she had been home, Renee would have provided little comfort for Jamie, as her tolerance for the whims of her younger sister seemed to have ▸

vanished around the time Jamie began menstruating while Renee still hadn't grown hips.

"I invited Debbie and Tammy to stay with me while you're gone," Jamie told her mother.

They were in the kitchen. Betty wore only cutoff shorts and an apron (no shoes, no shirt, no bra); it was her standard uniform while cooking. Betty's large, buoyant breasts sat on either side of the bib—her long, gummy nipples matched the polka dots on the apron.

"I know," Betty said. "Their mothers called."

Jamie's stomach thumped. Of course their mothers called. They each had a mother who considered her daughter the central showpiece of her life. "So what'd you say?" Jamie prayed that her mother had said nothing that would cause Tammy's and Debbie's mothers to keep them home.

"I told them that I had left about a hundred dollars' worth of TV dinners in the freezer, that there was spending money in the cookie jar, and that there was
nothing to worry about."

"What'd they say?"

"Tammy's mother wanted to know what the house rules were."

"What'd you say?"

"I told her there were no rules. We trust you."

Jamie knew her parents trusted her, and she knew they were right to do so—she couldn't imagine herself doing something they would disapprove of. The problem, as she saw it, was that she didn't trust them not to do something that she disapproved of. She had already prepared herself for the possibility that her parents would not return at the time they had promised, for anything—an artichoke festival, a nudists' rights parade—could detain them for hours or even days. There was nothing internal in either of her parents, no alarms or bells or buzzing, that alerted them to the panic their younger daughter felt periodically, like she was an astronaut untethered from the mother ship—floating without any boundaries against which she could bounce back to home.

Allen walked into the kitchen. He'd been going in and out of the house, loading the Volvo with sleeping bags, a tent, lanterns, flashlights, food.

"You know Debbie and Tammy are staying here with Jamie," Betty said, and she flipped an omelet over—it was a perfect half-moon, and she, for a second, was like a perfect mother.

"Why do all your friend's names end in y?" Allen asked.

"Tammy," Jamie recited, "Debbie . . . Debbie's *i e*."

"But it sounds like a *y*."

"So does my name."

"You're *i e*," Betty said, "You've been *i e* since you were born."

"Yeah, but Jamie sounds like Jamey with a *y*."

"There's no such thing as Jamie with a *y*," Allen said. "But there is Debby with a *y*."

"Well Mom's a *y*—Betty!"

"I'm a different generation," Betty said, "I don't count."

"And she's not your friend, she's your mother," Allen said.

"Oh, there's also Kathy and Suzy and Pammy," Betty said.

"No one calls her Pammy except you," Jamie said. "Too many *y*'s," Allen said. "You need friends with more solid names. Carol or Ann."

"No way I'm hanging out with Carol or Ann."

"They've got good names." Allen sat on a stool at the counter, picked up his fork and knife, and held each in a fist on either side of his plate.

"They're dorks," Jamie said.

Betty slid the omelet off the pan and onto Allen's plate just as their neighbor, Leon, walked in.

"Betty," he said, and he kissed Jamie's mother on the cheek. His right hand grazed one breast as they pulled away from the kiss.

"Allen," Leon stuck out the hand that had just touched Betty's breast toward Allen, who was hovered over his omelet, oblivious.

"Did you find some?" Allen asked.

"I stuck it in your trunk," Leon said.

"What?" Jamie asked.

"Nothing," Allen said, although he must have known that Jamie knew they were talking about marijuana. They rolled it in front of their daughters, they smoked it in front of them, they left abalone ashtrays full of Chiclet-sized butts all over the house. Yet the actual purchasing of it was treated like a secret—as if the girls were supposed to think that although their parents would ▶

smoke an illegal substance, they'd never be so profligate as to buy one.

"So what are you going to do in Death Valley?" Leon asked.

Allen lifted his left hand and made an O. He stuck the extended middle finger of his right hand in and out of the O. The three of them laughed. Jamie turned her head so she could pretend to not have seen. Unlike her sister, Jamie was successfully able to block herself from her parents' overwhelming sexuality, which often filled the room they were in, in the same way that air fills whatever space contains it.

"And what are you doing home alone?" Leon winked at Jamie.

"Debbie and Tammy are staying with me," she said. "I guess we'll watch TV and eat TV dinners."

"You want an omelet?" Betty asked Leon, and her voice was so cheerful, her cheeks so rouged and smooth, that it just didn't seem right that she should walk around halfnaked all the time.

"Sure," Leon said, and he slid onto the stool next to Allen as Betty prepared another omelet.

Jamie looked back at the three of them as she left the kitchen. Allen and Leon were dressed in jeans and T-shirts, being served food by chatty, cheerful Betty. Wide bands of light shafted into the room and highlighted them as if they were on a stage. It was a scene from a sitcom gone wrong. There was the friendly neighbor guy, the slightly grumpy father, the mother with perfectly coiffed short brown hair that sat on her head like a wig. But when the mother bent down to pick up an eggshell that had dropped, the friendly neighbor leaned forward on his stool so he could catch a glimpse of the smooth orbs of his friend's wife's ass peeking out from the fringe of her too-short shorts.

Jamie wished her life were as simple as playing Colorforms; she would love to stick a plastic dress over her shiny cardboard mother. If it didn't stick, she'd lick the dress and hold it down with her thumb until it stayed.

Debbie and Tammy were dropped off together by Tammy's father, who got out of the car and walked into the house with them.

"Did your parents leave already?" he asked.

"Yes, Mr. Hopkins," Jamie said.

Mr. Hopkins looked around the kitchen, toward the dining room, then out the French doors toward the pool, which had an open-air thatched bar in the shape of a squat British telephone booth, and boulders like stone club chairs embedded in the surrounding tile.

"What are the pool rules?" he asked, his belly pointing in the direction of his gaze as if it, too, were scrutinizing the situation.

"No one is allowed to swim alone." Jamie recited the rules from Debbie's house: "No glass or other breakable items by the pool, no food by the pool, no running by the pool, no skinny-dipping, no friends over unless my parents are informed ahead of time . . . Uh . . ."

"No swimming after dark," Debbie said.

"Right. No swimming after dark."

"What are the house rules?" Mr. Hopkins asked.

Jamie was stumped. She had heard house rules at other people's houses during sleepovers but couldn't recall a single one.

"Um." She yawned once, and then yawned again. "We have to behave like ladies." She had little faith that that would go over, but it did. Mr. Hopkins nodded and smiled, the corners of his mouth folding into his cheeks like cake batter.

"Well then," he said, "you girls have fun. And call us if you need anything."

When his car had pulled out of the driveway, the girls tumbled into one another, laughing.

"House rules?!" Debbie said. "He's got the wrong house!"

Tammy burrowed into her pressed-leather purse and pulled out a pack of Marlboro Light 100's. "He's got the wrong century," she said, lighting her cigarette, and then Debbie's, with a yellow Bic.

Tammy was wiry and small with bony knees and elbows, big floppy feet, knobby breasts, and shiny dangerous-looking braces on her upper teeth. Somehow, the cigarette made her look more pointed than she already was. Even her hair appeared sharp, hanging down her back in white clumpy daggers.

Debbie was round and smooth. She had black, shiny hair, thick black eyebrows, and lashes that made it look as if her eyes had been painted with liquid velvet. Her skin was white in the winter, golden in the summer, and always a contrast to her deep eyes ▸

Excerpt from *The Summer of Naked Swim Parties* (continued)

and red mouth, which at that moment was smacking against a Marlboro.

Tammy offered Jamie a cigarette because Jamie had smoked one with her once and Tammy couldn't believe that she didn't plan on smoking another in her lifetime. The problem with smoking, Jamie had decided, was that it didn't look right on her. She had straight, matter-of-fact brown hair that hung to just past her shoulders. There were freckles running across her nose and cheeks. Her eyes were round, brown dots. Her nose was a third dot on her face. If you were to draw a caricature of her, she would be mostly mouth: soft pink lips, straight wide teeth; she smiled when she talked, a broad smile that glinted on her face. In her most self-flattering moments she thought of herself as Mary Ann on Gilligan's Island; she knew she could never be Ginger. ᔐ